FIGHTING INSTINCT

KRISTAL STITTLE

For David Moody and his Survivors,

I don't know what or where these books would be without you.

I
Before

Elizabeth didn't know what was going on up at surface level. She didn't know that a woman bearing the same name as her was pregnant and providing hope to a group of strangers. She didn't know about the people being rounded up and taken to a prison, or of the rebellion that was rising among them. She didn't know about a cruise ship floating off the coast of Nova Scotia that was about to become a haven for survivors. She didn't know that her ex-husband—whom she had sent to find her notes—was dead, and because he had become infected and kept walking around, had his face blown off by a sixteen-year-old with a shotgun.

Elizabeth didn't know that she herself was dead.

Having disobeyed the rules, Elizabeth had become part of the new experiments. These experiments were meant to make the zombies docile, to make them manageable. If they could be controlled, then Marble Keystone, creator and releaser of the virus, would have access to a work force that never tired, never had to be taken care of, and most importantly, never had to be paid. Things did not go as planned, and they did not succeed.

Being a zombie, Elizabeth didn't know anything. There wasn't really an Elizabeth left. There was just a body that looked like her, shuffling back and forth in a small, metal cell, which had one Plexiglas side, down in the laboratories known as the White Box. Her new strain of the infection—which was really a cross between a virus and prion—didn't make her any more controllable than the others. When something living was introduced into her environment, she would hunt it down, infect it by biting it, and then kill it so that the infection could take over the body.

The scientists would walk by her cell, and usually, she would react by smashing herself into the transparent wall, but sometimes, she was just smart enough not to do that. Sometimes, a few fragments of her former intelligence would bleed through, reminding her that she couldn't get out that way, that there was a wall there she couldn't really see. Those times weren't often, however, and so she had thrown herself against the Plexiglas, her teeth gnashing, her fingers clawing, and a snarl issuing from her throat when a small boy had made the mistake of following his father into the room. She had no idea what her actions had set off.

Since becoming a zombie, Elizabeth had no sense of time. There was no difference between when she woke up dead and when she was set free. When memories were no longer being formed, time was not an issue.

When the Plexiglas rose into the ceiling and alarm bells began ringing, Elizabeth wasn't afraid, surprised, or happy. The thing controlling her body sent her out into the hallway, where she was joined by other experiments. For the most part, they ignored one another, interested only when one of them acted as if he had found something to infect. The hallway had been empty at the time, but a few remembered that doors led to places, and the doors at both ends were unlocked.

All the doors in this white-walled place were unlocked, but the zombies wouldn't notice such a thing. Elizabeth wandered about with the other infected, finding new corners, stairwells, and hallways. They entered living rooms, bathrooms, and laboratories, where they found a lot of humans to infect.

If Elizabeth could form memories, she would remember the time she came across a group of her fellow infected trying to push through a barricaded door. She helped them out, and even managed to infect an old man who had been on the other side of it. She might also remember a certain public washroom she had somehow stumbled into, and could no longer find her way back out of. No other infected were in there to help her, and all the stall doors were the same. She had spent days in there until another zombie had pushed its way in at just the right moment for her to escape. Another time, inside an animal lab, she had watched a zombie unlock and lock the same cage door, over and over again.

After watching it many times, Elizabeth found that she could do the same. The skill never came in handy, however, and it was forgotten less than twenty-four hours after leaving the lab.

Eventually, she found herself near a massive industrial elevator. Hundreds of the dead had gathered there. She didn't know it, but the last living human in the White Box had died in that elevator. What was important was the hatch that was open at the top of the elevator's cage. A large pile of the dead had gathered beneath and they were climbing out. This had been where they last saw something living, and the zombies wanted to chase after it, even though none of them knew how long it had been since the woman they saw had left. Elizabeth stood around the pile, watching the others, until she figured out how to climb it. The pile was an ever shifting, writhing mass, and getting to the top was difficult, but after a significant amount of time, Elizabeth succeeded.

There was a second pile on top of the elevator. Her fellow infected were attempting to climb a ladder that led up the shaft. Elizabeth joined them in this pursuit. It took far longer than getting on top of the elevator, although the pile at the base of the ladder moved less. This pile was mostly made up of those who had climbed and fallen, their skulls bashing against the top of the elevator and ceasing their movements forever.

From the elevator shaft, the group of zombies who managed to climb up entered a parking lot. None of the doors here would open, but a large ramp led up, and up, in a giant spiral. The horde of White Box zombies followed this spiral to the very top, where a massive door opened into the middle of a forest.

If anyone alive were to see the human zombies entering the forest, they might have mistaken their movements for wonder and surprise. For Elizabeth and all the others, this was not the case. The only thing they felt was a kind of sensory overload due to all the organic, shifting matter around them, and they didn't know what to attack first. It took only a moment for the zombies to understand wind and bushes, which couldn't be infected—although a few still attempted to attack the plants anyway—and soon, they continued moving, searching for things they could infect.

Elizabeth may have been freed of the White Box, but she was still dead.

Section 1:
Loss

1
Alec's On Patrol

It had been six years, six months, and three days since the zombies had come. That August second was now simply known as the Day. Alec slowly pushed his wheelchair across the balconies of the cruise ship, wondering how so much time could have passed. He could still clearly remember the Day as if it had happened just last week. So much had changed since then.

Alec sighed. It was not a good day. Although the weather was beautiful on this February fifth, as it so often was in the Caribbean, it was a sad day. Alec had a funeral to attend when his shift ended at four p.m. He hated funerals, this one especially. To distract himself, he focused on his task.

Rolling slowly across the seventh deck balconies, on the port side of the ship, he kept an eye out for bodies in the water, ships in the distance, and trouble in the rooms. When the survivors had first boarded the boat, the balconies had been private, with clouded glass barriers between them. They had since discovered it was easy to remove these barriers, and had done just that. It allowed them to have patrols on all five of the decks that had balconies, in addition to the open public decks on four and twelve.

Passing a room that belonged to a child, Alec checked the door's handle. By now, just about everyone had found ways to secure the handle from the inside so that it couldn't be opened from the outside without permission, since the locks built into the doors could be opened from both sides. Alec liked to check these makeshift locks from time to time, especially when the room belonged to a kid.

Rifle sniffed at the handle after Alec checked it, so Alec patted his head reassuringly. The German Shepherd was a great dog, and a wonderful companion, but the nervous energy emanating from everyone was in turn making him nervous.

Looking back out over the sea, Alec focused on the other cruise ship out there. It had been spotted last night, before sunset, and was constantly getting closer. Although not on a collision course with them, it was of immense interest because it was moving under its own power. Attempts to hail it had been made, but there was no response. A boarding team of off-shippers was already on its way to this other ship. They would find out what was going on over there and report back. There could be other survivors on board, or it could be another ghost ship. They had never come across an abandoned cruise ship before, but there was always a first time for everything. Part of Alec hoped it was abandoned. If its engines were running, then there was fuel in the tanks, and there could very well be other supplies on board. Not to mention the fact that more people caused more problems.

On the other side of the Diana—the ship that was home to Alec and roughly two thousand five hundred other people—floated a German nuclear submarine. It had been a good day when the sub, accompanied by a similar one from Russia, had joined them. The submarines and the people on board were very helpful, and most of them were willing to join the Diana. Not everyone they had met upon the ocean was like them, however. Three times, they had dealt with large bands of pirates, and once there was a container ship full of survivors who disagreed with everything the Diana did. In the end, the container ship decided to sail across the ocean, taking those from the Diana who wanted to go with it, and leaving behind their own members who did not. A lot of the Diana's original service crew had gone with that ship. They were from various countries across the ocean, and wanted to know what had happened, maybe even have a chance to find their families, despite how extremely unlikely that was. Small boats had been picked up here and there, many of them joining the Diana, but not all. They used to have a fairly large flotilla until a massive storm came and wiped out all of the smaller ships, the people on them having been safely evacuated to the Diana before it hit. It was shortly after that storm that they lost the Russian submarine. It was believed that debris from a smaller ship had managed to strike it in just such a way that it destabilized the reactor. Although no one really knew if that was true or not, it's what the Russian sailors said had happened when they abandoned the sub and allowed it to sink into the depths of the ocean.

Alec wondered if they had completed the exchange with the German submarine yet. Every day, two of the Diana's lifeboats would go over to the submarine to exchange crewmembers, batteries, and to resupply it. The reactor on the submarine was extremely useful for recharging their batteries, as well as a few small electric generators, and various other personal items. They had once considered hooking the reactor up to the ship itself, but that idea was quickly rejected, as no one wanted to risk having the Diana and the sub sitting so closely together, and so, the two were always kept a safe distance apart. Alec had a portable DVD player that had been sent over for charging yesterday, and he was hoping to get it back today. After the funeral, he was going to need some mindless entertainment before attempting sleep, even if it was a movie that he had seen a hundred times before.

The crack of a door seal separating caused Alec and Rifle to turn around. A young woman stepped out of her room and up to the railing, taking a deep breath of fresh air. Rifle walked up to the woman, allowed her to stroke his head, and then returned to Alec's side. Alec was used to seeing her, as she took care of the plants growing in boxes hanging on the outside of the railings. Every deck had plants and solar panels hanging off the sides, soaking up the sun. The woman was quiet, usually ignoring the patrols, and she often gazed across the sea. Alec noticed that her attention was on the second cruise ship this time. It's what most people had been focused on since it had been spotted less than twenty-four hours ago.

"What do you think?" Alec asked her.

"I think it's a bad sign," she answered without turning to him.

Alec hoped she was wrong as he turned back around and continued to roll himself toward the nose of the ship.

Most of the curtains were closed, allowing the occupants privacy. Many rooms had plants growing in pots in the spaces between the curtains and the doors. It wasn't mandatory to grow something in their room, but most people did, grateful for the added food and trading opportunities. Many of the plants that Alec saw were tomato plants, but a few were carrots, beets, or plants that Alec couldn't identify. At least one plant was marijuana, but as long as it wasn't causing harm, no one cared.

Whenever Alec came across a set of curtains that were open, he would peer inside. Most of the rooms were empty, but sometimes someone would be home. A lot of the time he or she would be reading or sleeping, or it would be one of the cleaners asked to tidy up the place. Several of those people had the balcony door open, allowing the air to circulate, and those who saw Alec waved.

The presence of the other ship did have one advantage: people weren't bickering today. Being on the ship's defence crew wasn't just about spotting swimming zombies, drifting ships, and warding off pirates, but Alec also had to enforce the rules on the ship, and deal with disputes between people. He was essentially a police officer. People didn't always get along, and not all of them were happy with the rules that had been established, but when a possible threat showed up, most people turned their discomfort and fear toward it, forgetting all about the problems they had with those on board.

Reaching over to stroke Rifle's back, Alec almost wished it were a trouble filled day, so that he had something to take his mind off the coming funeral. Almost.

***

"You ready to go down, Alec?" Misha appeared from the room that he shared with Alec. The two of them found each other easy company, and didn't mind sharing so that fewer people had to sleep in rooms without balconies. Most people found they preferred having two exits.

Rifle trotted up to the skinny man, his tail swishing back and forth. Misha and Rifle had survived the Day together, and were bonded as tightly as brothers. In fact, the young Russian often referred to the dog as his brother in his native tongue. Although

Rifle would assist Alec with his patrols, he would often spend the rest of the day with Misha. Rifle was technically Alec's dog, but Alec thought the shepherd would go to Misha if forced to choose.

"Not really," Alec sighed, "you?"

Misha didn't answer. His eyes, which normally looked too white due to the incredibly pale blue of his irises, were red. He had been crying earlier, or had at least been close to it.

"Well, my replacement is now on duty," Alec looked down the length of balconies to where the man who patrolled after him had started, "so I guess we should go down."

Misha helped him wheel his chair over the bump into their room, and then headed for the door to wait in the hall. The rooms were small, but Alec didn't mind. He had a twin sized bed to himself near the balcony, with Misha's about two feet away. A long, narrow couch extended along the wall next to the beds, and a desk, complete with large drawers, a safe, a mini-fridge, and a large mirror was against the opposite wall. Flanking the door leading out into the ship's interior hall, was a fair-sized closet, and a tiny bathroom, creating a sort of mini-hallway between them. Alec's wheelchair couldn't fit in the bathroom, but luckily for him, he wasn't completely disabled.

Stopping his chair next to the couch, Alec set the brakes. He then reached over to the couch and picked up the pair of leg braces that had been sitting upon it. With the braces, Alec could walk for a fair length of time, but for the long hours of patrol, he continued to need the chair. Ever since he had been strafed by helicopter fire back when he had been a sniper in the military, he had needed the chair and braces. Back when the Day happened, he could only stand for a few seconds at a time, but his legs had gotten stronger since then. Temporarily stripping out of his pants, Alec buckled on the devices from his hips to his feet. He was still self-conscious about all the scars, and never wore shorts, despite the heat.

Making his way to the door, he noticed that the creak in the right knee of his brace was back. He'd have to oil that again once the funeral was over. Misha met up with him in the dark and narrow hallway outside, and together, the two of them made for the stairs.

Power on the boat was limited. There were six diesel generators on board, but only one was run while at anchor. Everything in the bathrooms always had power, but in the rest of the living quarters, there was only one light bulb allowed, and the occupants had to decide in which lighting fixture to use it. In the hallways, only enough light bulbs remained to guide the residents to where they were going. The elevators had been shut down, as well as the rooms' temperature controls, and all the TVs and touch screen maps. Most of the ship's power was dedicated to desalinating ocean water, recycling their used water, and powering the UV lights in the green rooms, although the laundry machines were also run fairly regularly.

After reaching the stairwell, Alec took a brief break while a group of off-duty men jogged up the steps; he didn't like tackling the stairs when there was a lot of foot traffic. As he rested, Alec looked over the edge of the nearby railing at the promenade two decks below. There was a hive of activity down there. What used to be the gift shop was now equipment storage for off-shippers, and the liquor store carried only bottles of water and juice. The clothing shop still had clothing, although it wasn't nearly as fancy as before, and the workers there also performed on-site patch-up jobs. The jewellery store had been converted into a weapons locker due to its inherent security, although everyone who had proven capable and responsible enough to carry a weapon, did. Those people generally weren't the same ones who frequented the pub. The pub was the only place on the promenade that remained the same, but it had been upgraded to include its own distillery equipment. Alec had visited it a few times, but found the drinks there too vile for his taste and the company unpleasant.

Once Alec was ready, Misha helped him tackle the stairs. Alec dearly missed the elevators, but with Misha's help, he could manage. The boy still had a thin frame, but years of swimming with the underwater inspection crew had put some solid muscle on it. The soft rubber of Misha's wetsuit also made him easy to hold onto; Alec wasn't the only one who had just come off the job.

"Alec!" a voice called from above them.

Turning around, Alec spotted Hanna bounding down the steps toward them. She gave Misha a quick smile, and then turned to Alec.

"I hear you are going to a... a, ah... *beerdigung*. What is the word?" Her voice was heavy with her German accent. She had come over with the submarine and had known only rudimentary English when she first arrived. Unlike some of the others who preferred to speak their native tongue whenever possible, Hanna had dived right into her English lessons, speaking German only when she had to. She had mentioned once that speaking too much German made her sad.

"A funeral?" Alec offered.

"Yes. A funeral." She suddenly hugged Alec. Hanna was like that, very bubbly and open with people. She was a sharp contrast to Misha's withdrawn and closed off personality, yet, Alec got along perfectly well with both of them.

"It's okay. We all knew it was coming." Alec had been telling himself that since yesterday, maybe even longer, but it wasn't soothing the pain in his heart.

"I want to ask you, do you want me to clean your room while you are out? I have not cleaned it in awhile," Hanna abruptly changed topics.

"No. It's okay."

"Okay, and you, Misha, do you need your side of the room cleaned?"

Misha shook his head. He never got his share of the room cleaned by the cleaning staff, and always opted to do it himself.

"Very well." She turned back to Alec. "Please, if you need to talk after, come find me."

"I will."

Hanna gave him a quick peck on the cheek and then disappeared back up the stairs.

"Are you ever going to ask her out?" Misha wondered as they resumed going down the stairs.

Alec felt his ears turn red and refused to answer. Prior to his injury, he used to be a ladies man, but now, he mostly just got embarrassed, especially when it came to Hanna. She was at least ten years younger than he was, and she was such a sweet girl that he couldn't imagine her wanting to be with him in that way. No, Alec didn't think he'd ever ask her out.

Upon reaching the bottom of the stairs, the two men, plus Rifle, headed for the door that would lead them back outside. Alec shuddered, feeling suddenly cold. Misha pretended not to notice and went to the door.

Carefully crossing a small gangway, they stepped onto the upper level of a tender boat. The Diana had two tender boats, which could be raised and lowered in and out of the water like its lifeboats. The other one was currently making its way to the mystery cruise ship, if it wasn't there already.

Going to the lower deck of the small boat, Alec saw that everyone was indeed already there. His eyes were instantly drawn to the shrouded body on the small table set up at the end of the row of bench seats. It appeared even smaller than usual.

Shoes.

Poor old Shoes, the Basset Hound had finally passed away. Alec had known Shoes since the Day, when he had met up with the dog's owner, five-year-old Alice. Alice hadn't made it, and Shoes nearly slipped away after that due to depression, but the love of a two-year-old they had met weeks later had saved him. That two-year-old was now eight, and sitting in the front row with her brothers and foster parents. Becky had owned Shoes for at least as long as Alice had, and Alec couldn't help comparing the two. The fact that they were both blondes didn't help, but Becky's hair was as straight as straw, whereas, Alice had had curls.

Alec took a seat at the back of the group. He didn't want to be near Becky; it would make his heart hurt. It didn't matter how much time had passed, the death of Alice would forever weigh on Alec's shoulders. He blamed himself, even if no one else did. He was the one who had shown her how to open the door after all, and he was the one who was supposed to be watching her.

Misha let Alec sit back there without saying a word, while he went up to the front to stand near the preacher, a good man who presided over all funerals, no matter what religion, or how many legs the deceased had. He gave a lovely sermon.

Once it was over, those who wanted to say their last goodbyes to Shoes did. Even Alec walked to the front of the group, on his own, his unsteady legs fighting against the swaying of the boat beneath him. He patted the sheet where he knew the dog's head was and told him he was a good boy. Alec would miss watching him tag along behind Becky.

The preacher gently picked up the body and walked to a small door at the side of the boat. Misha was already sitting in the doorway with flippers on his feet. Normally, a body was just weighed down with rocks or other debris that couldn't be recycled, and dropped into the water. Misha had a special attachment to Shoes, however, and he knew exactly what lingered under the ship. Not wanting to send Shoes down there, Misha had said he'd like to swim the body out, and Becky had agreed. After Misha slipped into the water, he floated on his back and was handed the dog's body, and then he began to swim.

Alec looked at the group that had assembled. It was probably the largest funeral they had held for any animal to date. Alec knew the names of all the mourners: Misha, Danny, Josh, and Tobias, with his girlfriend, Anne; Becky, Bryce, and Larson, with their adoptive parents, Amanda and Bobby; Abby and Lauren, with their adopted kids, Claire and Peter; Danny's older brother Mathias, with his wife Riley, and daughter, Hope; and lastly, there was Riley's twin sister, Cameron. Most of these people had survived the Day with Alec, but some, such as Becky's family, had just grown close to them due to other circumstances. It had been a long time since they had all gotten together like this. Although everyone spoke regularly, they all had their different jobs and different schedules to keep, and couldn't all gather at once.

Among the mourners were a few outsiders. The preacher, for one, as well as a few guards who were watching out for any zombies that might surface from the depths below. There was a grief councillor too, who came to every funeral and stayed politely at the back in case anyone needed her. With her was her little dachshund. The dog she had rescued joined Rifle and two other dogs, Milly and Maggie, who belonged to members of the group, to nose quietly about the mourners' legs. The animals could sense the people's sadness, but didn't understand what was going on.

Misha swam so far out that Alec could barely tell when he had finally released Shoes. Once he began to swim back, the funeral goers picked up a little and started a few, scattered conversations.

"Jon couldn't make it?" Alec asked of Abby when she took a seat beside him. Technically, Alec hadn't met her until twenty-four hours after the actual day of the outbreak, but he considered those first forty-eight hours to be one awful Day. Most of them did.

"His team is one of those going to the other ship." She tried to sound unconcerned, but her eyes betrayed her. She and Lauren were Jon's guardians. Even though he was twenty-one now, and old enough to take care of himself, she still worried when he was off ship. "We're all planning on having dinner together. Can you join us?"

"I'd love to. When and where?"

"About half an hour from now. It should give everyone time to change and clean up if they need to. We're not going anywhere special, just to our usual spot in the dining room."

"Sounds good to me."

Abby smiled at him and got up to rejoin her family.

Once Misha returned and was hauled up onto the boat, everyone began to head back into the big ship, while the guards prepared to return the tender boat to its place hanging behind the lifeboats. They usually kept the tender boats floating alongside the ship during the day, but they always hauled them up at night if the off-shippers didn't have them.

After drying off and scrubbing his jet black hair with a towel, Misha helped Alec onto the ship.

"Can you get to the room on your own? I think Rifle really needs to relieve himself," Misha asked.

"Yeah, sure." Going up stairs took more strength, but Alec actually found it easier than going downstairs. He found his footing better and was less likely to slip.

"Come on, *bratishka.*" Misha patted his leg and bounded up the stairs, two at a time. Rifle quickly dashed up after him, leaving Alec to wonder which crop would be fertilized with his poop this time, or if they were going to the dreaded shit room.

Alec waited for everyone else to head up the stairs, rebuffing offers of assistance from Mathias, before going up himself. He knew Mathias had no problem helping him out, the man could probably carry Alec's dead weight up at least one flight—and they weighed roughly the same—but sometimes, Alec had to do these things on his own.

Seven flights of stairs turned out to be more of a challenge than Alec had thought. He was used to tackling between two and four, sometimes as many as five, but didn't realize how much added strain those two extra floors would be. Still, he fought through it, turning down assistance from a few strangers who passed him going in either direction. By the time he reached deck seven, his legs felt like jelly, and the braces were holding him up more than his own muscles were. He'd have to get his wheelchair out into the hall and roll himself to the other side of the ship where the dining room was, or he'd be late to dinner after a much-needed rest.

Once back inside his room, Alec turned to the bathroom. He needed to take a quick shower to rinse off the sweat he had worked up. Putting his braces back on after stripping out of his clothes, Alec hauled himself into the shower. Showering was awkward for him, but he managed, helped by the tiny size of the stall which allowed him to jam his feet against one side, while leaning his back against the other. Once he felt refreshed, Alec wrapped a towel around his waist and made his way out of the bathroom to grab a set of clean clothes. Upon opening the closet, Alec frowned. On the floor were two orange life vests. Every room had two life vests in the closet, but Alec was confused as to why they were on the floor when they had their own shelf in there. It was possible that Misha had moved them, but there was no reason for that. All of Misha's stuff was in the drawers, while Alec kept things in the closet.

Sliding a hanging pair of pants out of the way, Alec uncovered the slot in which the life vests were normally stored. There was something else there instead. Concerned, Alec quickly lowered himself for a better view.

His last thought was to register the numbers counting down to zero, and then his whole world became fire.

2
Jon's On A Mission

Jon watched as the Diana slowly got farther away. His family would be going to Shoes' funeral soon. Part of him was glad he wasn't going, and that it was his team that was on-call when the foreign cruise ship finally got close enough for them to board it. He didn't handle grief well. Claire, his non-biological younger sister, had asked him to go to the funeral anyway, to ask for a reassignment, but Jon had said no. Six years ago he wouldn't have been able to say no to Claire, but she was stronger now. She could handle a funeral.

"What'cha thinkin' about?" Rose plopped down beside him.

"Shoes' funeral."

Rose pursed her lips, suddenly unsure about what to say. Rose was a bit of a firecracker. You could tell she was a troublemaker just by looking at her short red bob, and devilish features. However, like most people, she was affected by funerals.

Jon swung around to face the new ship. It was closer than the Diana was now, and they would be boarding it soon.

"What do you think we'll find on board?" he asked, changing the subject.

"Don't know. Nothin' good. Bound to be fuel, but we haven't seen any life on the decks yet. I'm jus' hopin' it's not full of the dead, ya know?"

"Yeah, I know. There's probably at least one on board, but it looks like several of the lifeboats have been deployed, so I don't think we have to worry about being swarmed."

"All hands prepare for boarding!" a voice bellowed from the front of their tender boat.

Jon and Rose hopped up from their seats and gathered with the others on the upper deck. Six off-shipper teams had been merged together for this mission, and Jon stood with his on the left side.

"In case any of you don't know me, I'm James Brenner," their leader spoke from the front of the boat. James mostly organized teams and supplies on board the Diana, but he occasionally joined special missions like this one. "You can consider me the ranking officer on this mission. I'd like to go over the plan and make sure everyone knows what they're doing."

The off-shippers were quiet as they listened. Team A, which consisted of Jon, Rose, and the three others from his group, were to go straight to the ship's bridge and either confront whoever might be there, or shut down the engines. Team B was to stay on the lowest level, near the tender boat on which James and the boat's pilot would remain. Their job was to keep the lowest level secure. The other groups, team C, were to follow Jon's team up the stairs, leaving two guards on each deck. Everyone had walkie-talkies hooked up with headsets, so that they could all communicate with one another.

"Once we know what's happening on the bridge, we'll proceed from there. Everyone check their gear."

Jon reviewed his small pack. He had his bolt cutters, extra ammo for the pistol he wore on his belt, and a few small items of food, along with a couple of water bottles in case he got separated and trapped. If they had been going out on a shore mission, he'd have a lot more with him, but this excursion didn't require much. Jon then helped Rose tidy up the ropes she always carried in her bag.

"You should have done this before we left," he commented while untangling a pair of them.

"I was in a rush."

"Because you were spending time with that guy."

"If you had been with Robin still, you would have been spendin' time with her, so shut your face."

Jon grinned, pleased that he had been able to irritate her a little. She was right though. If Robin and he weren't currently on a break, and she hadn't gone into work early to cover the end of Riley's shift for her, he might have run a bit late as well. Robin and he had a complicated relationship, and had broken up a few times over the past six years. They were currently apart, but he could feel their orbits coming together again. Jon didn't know why they kept returning to one another when they knew they weren't really compatible. Maybe it was love, but then that would mean that their love wasn't enough. Maybe they just kept getting drawn to each other out of comfort. It certainly seemed easier than the bed hopping that Rose did.

"You two ready?" Brunt asked as he hunkered down next to them. Brunt was their team leader and would be in charge once inside.

"Well, I am," Jon responded, "but I'm not so sure about this one."

Rose pushed him over and sprang to her feet, her bag packed and ready. Brunt helped Jon up, who was laughing, and they all turned to face the on-coming ship. As they got close enough to pass into its shadow, Jon's cheery mien died off. Most of the off-shippers, who were usually a rowdy bunch, fell quiet. Despite their variety of eye and mouth covers, it was easy to tell everyone was nervous.

The strange ship wasn't moving very fast. It was easy to pull alongside it and lash themselves next to the bow-port-side door. The ship was a different model than the Diana, but the tender boat was a good height for it anyway.

"Boarding team!" James bellowed.

Team B gathered near the door. Four of them flanked a metal bridge that was partly extended from their boat, while the fifth stood on the part hanging over the water, just within reach of the ship's door. Leaning forward, he grabbed the latch and pulled it up, while pushing in on the door. The seal cracked as the door swung slightly inward. The man who had opened it quickly backed up, while the other four pointed various guns at the partial opening. Nothing yanked the door farther inward, and no sounds could be heard above the waves.

Lowering their weapons, the four members of team B grabbed their metal bridge and pushed it the rest of the way across the gap, forcing the door completely open in the process. In was dark beyond the hatchway.

The man who had opened the door snapped on a flashlight attached to the end of his rifle and hurried across the bridge, his four team-mates quickly following after him. Jon found himself holding his breath. He knew the five people who had just entered unknown territory well, and he did not envy their task in the slightest.

No gunshots rang out.

Eventually, one of them popped his head back out of the hatch and waved them forward. Jon and his team entered the ship next. A massive man named Brewster, and a lithe, cat-like woman named Shaidi, led the way toward the stairwell. Rose and Jon followed after them, with Brunt bringing up their rear, and then all of team C behind him. With Shaidi's and Brewster's lights guiding the way, Jon just clicked on the small light that hung from his neck to help with his footing.

It was dead quiet in the strange ship. So much was similar to their home, yet so different at the same time. They passed by the still elevators, Rose tapping a button as she walked by. It lit up. Surprisingly, the elevators here were still running, but the off-shippers were going to stick with their original plan and didn't take them. The stairs were covered in a plush carpet like their own ship's stairs, but they felt reversed. On the Diana, a single set of steps went from the deck to a landing between decks, and then branched into two sets of steps that travelled up from the landing to the next deck. This boat was backwards, with the double steps leading up to the landing, and the single steps going up to the next deck. It was a subtle difference, but it made Jon uneasy.

Each time they reached a new deck, the two members of team C at the back would stop to guard the area. It got significantly brighter once they got past the lowest decks to where windows let in light. It also appeared the promenade still had lights running, but none of the hallways or staircases did. It would have been brighter still if they were on the side with the sun, but it was too dangerous to switch over now. They had to stick to their present course.

As they reached the sixth deck, a howl echoed down the halls. Everyone stopped, searching around for the source of the noise.

"It might have been the wind," Brunt finally whispered, "continue on."

The guards on the lowest levels were already chatting in whispers over the radios. It was too quiet on the ship, and standing silently would make them overly jumpy. Jon didn't listen much, picking up only a few things, like the fact that one of them thought this ship had better artwork on the landings than the Diana did.

"Contact," a voice spoke above a whisper over the radio.

Everyone stood perfectly still.

"Taken care of," the same voice then said. "It was a slow bitch."

Jon didn't need the man's words to know it was a slow one. If it had been alive, there would have been spoken words, and if it had been a fast one, there would have been a gunshot. Slow zombies could be taken out with knives, machetes, and even blunt objects, as long as one was careful, but when it came to the faster, smarter ones, it was always preferable to shoot first.

At least now, they knew what they were dealing with: zombies on board. It was what the people on the Diana feared most happening to them.

Brunt urged them onward, and upward.

Once they reached the tenth deck, they left the final two members of team C, and headed down the hallways. The ship's hallways were nerve-wrackingly narrow, and completely dark outside of what their flashlights revealed. With Brewster's huge frame leading the way, they fell into single file. Jon's eyes flicked from door to door, expecting one of them to be ripped open at any moment, and hundreds of moving corpses to spill out. It didn't happen.

Upon reaching the door to the bridge, Brewster and Shaidi shifted to one side and allowed Rose to step forward. Rose had the best hearing of the group; she placed a glass against the door, and then pressed her ear against its bottom. With her eyes squeezed shut, she listened for any sounds originating from the other side for several tense seconds. When she opened her eyes again, she shook her head back and forth. She hadn't heard anything.

Brewster tried the handle, only to find that the door was locked. Brunt took over then, pulling out a pair of thin tools with which to pick the lock. They had more brutal ways of getting in, like the mini battering ram Brewster carried, or the small amount of explosives Shaidi had hidden about her person, but those would only draw the attention of the zombies.

The presence of people from the Diana wasn't going unnoticed. Jon had heard a few more voices over the coms that spoke of contacts. None of the contacts had been survivors so far.

Brunt got the door open and went in first, keeping low and checking the nearby corners. He soon waved for the others to follow him in. Brewster and Brunt went to the controls to stop the ship, while Shaidi and Rose went to check the far corners and the break room. There was no one on the bridge.

Then how was the door locked? Jon thought. A scuffling sound came from a small closet, quickly drawing everyone's attention.

Jon was the closest to the closet. Holstering his pistol, he drew the katana from the sheath he wore under his backpack. Robin had given him the blade, which had belonged to a friend of hers, hoping it would keep him safer than it had her friend.

His brow was sweaty as he gripped the handle, but his hands were bone dry. Raising the blade in one hand, he yanked open the door with the other.

"Not bit!"

Despite the man's words, Jon still nearly decapitated him, surprised by his explosive exit from the closet.

"Not bit! Not bit! Not bit, not bit, not bit!" the strange man kept screaming over and over.

"I get it, you're not bit," Jon said as he quickly sheathed the blade. He kept his distance from the man, while everyone else held their guns pointed toward him.

A loud roll of thunder reached them from outside, lightly vibrating the bridge's windows. It had been a clear day, and they weren't expecting any storms any time soon.

"Oh, my God," Shaidi gasped, looking out the wall of windows.

Jon turned and saw what she was looking at.

Black smoke was pouring out of a hole in their ship. The Diana was on fire.

***

"Not bit. Not bit," the man continued to repeat, although he had calmed down somewhat.

Jon stood over him where he had been tied up in the corner. The man was barely more than a skeleton, with large, bulging eyes, and extremely thin hair. He smelled rank, and was clearly crazy, saying only those two words, over and over again.

"What's going on?" Jon asked Brunt, trying to keep the fear out of his voice.

"Give me a second!" Brunt snapped. "Everyone on this damn radio won't shut up."

Their organized boarding was falling apart. The fire on the Diana had panicked everyone, but worse, the thunder they had heard beforehand—which Jon was beginning to realize was an explosion—had woken all the zombies on board. The dead were crawling out of all the cracks and alcoves they had been lingering in, and were now wandering about, seeking the living. The guards on the fifth deck saw too many coming at them, which caused them to flee their posts. The guards on the fourth and sixth decks followed suit, not wanting to draw that large a group their way. It was now impossible to make out any of the chatter over the radio.

"Hail the Diana," Rose suddenly suggested out of the blue.

"Our radios aren't powerful enough for that. Only the one on the tender boat is," Brunt frowned at her.

"I'm not talking about our radios. This ship has one, doesn't it?" Rose waved an arm at the control console.

"Of course!" Brunt quickly slid back into the seat he had vacated upon seeing the Diana belching smoke.

As he was calling across the water, a loud banging started up on the cabin door.

"Identify yourself!" Brewster bellowed, striding toward the door.

The response he got was a loud, hollow groan. It wasn't one of their own men.

"Get back to the tender boat!" James's voice cut through the chatter. "Get back to the tender boat in any way you know how! If you cannot reach us, stay put! We will get you when we can!"

Jon looked to Brunt.

Brunt shook his head. "The Diana is still figuring out exactly what happened, but it was definitely an explosion of some kind. The fire fighting brigade is already dealing with the flames."

"Let's get back to the boat. There's another door out of the bridge on this side." Rose moved toward it.

"No," Brunt said, stopping her in her tracks.

"But James said to get back to the tender boat. It sounds like they're going to bug out until things calm down a bit." Jon was worried. The smoke was coming out close to where he and his family lived.

Brunt shook his head. "We still haven't stopped this ship completely. We're going to stay and finish our assignment. If we don't, and someone ends up trapped on board overnight, it'll pass by the Diana and be even harder to get to in the morning. Besides, by staying on the bridge, we can relay information between those trapped aboard, and those on the Diana."

"Not bit, not bit," the man's voice was increasing in volume as tensions on the bridge elevated.

"Shut up!" Rose screamed at him.

"Rose." Shaidi placed a gentle hand on her shoulder, trying to calm her. Rose shrugged Shaidi's hand off and stalked toward the windows, crossing her arms tightly across her chest.

Everyone's nerves were snapped. They were used to being in danger, they were even used to being trapped with no immediate way home, but this was different. On a normal off-ship trip, they didn't have to worry about those left behind. They went out and focused on their mission, knowing that their loved ones still on the Diana were safe. But now, the Diana had suffered a blow, and no one knew anything about what was happening over there. Anyone could have been hurt, or killed. They weren't used to this.

Brunt and Brewster returned to their original job of putting the brakes on the cruise ship. Stopping a boat this large wasn't an easy task. If all they did was shut down the engines, they could coast for a mile, and that wasn't including any winds or currents that could catch them. They actually had to put the ship into reverse until it came to a rough standstill, and then drop the anchors.

"Rose, why don't you and Shaidi see if there are any supplies in the break room?" Brunt suggested. "And Jon, despite what he says, could you check that man over for bites?"

"Sure thing."

Jon told the strange man what he was going to do, but he was ignored. The man just stared off into space, his lips still forming the words, with barely a whisper escaping from them. He was indifferent as Jon lifted his T-shirt, inspecting his belly and shoulders, then turned him around to look at his back. Jon rolled up the man's shorts, and pulled off the worn shoes, but didn't find any injuries there either. Despite the man's thin hair, Jon also inspected his scalp, which was an unpleasant affair even with Jon's gloves protecting his hands from the greasiness. This survivor appeared free of bites, or any other major injuries. Although it was possible he had been bitten around the hips, groin, and buttock areas, Jon wasn't about to check those. He felt he would have seen evidence of blood or bandages had the man been bitten there. Even though he had cleared him for bites, Jon didn't untie the man. There were other ways he could have become infected, and he could also turn out to be more dangerous than the dead while alive.

"Dropping anchors," Brunt announced over the coms in case someone was in their area. Six other people had been left behind and were hiding out in various locations around the ship.

"What do we do now?" Rose asked. Apparently, there hadn't been anything useful in the break room.

"Now, we wait for orders," Brunt told her, leaning back in the control seat.

Rose huffed and sat on the floor, leaning against one of the floor-to-ceiling windows. A zombie battering itself against the door, a seemingly insane man, their home on fire without any information as to why or who was hurt, and no sleeping supplies: it was going to be a long night.

"You know, it doesn't sound like there's any zombies at the starboard side door. Why don't Rose and I go out for a little bit of recon? We can see how many zombies are against the other door, and maybe dispatch them if there aren't many," Jon suggested.

"I agree with this plan." Rose bounced back up onto her feet.

Jon had been working with her ever since he became an off-shipper three years ago. She was like the big sister he never had growing up in foster homes, and he understood her. He knew that the best thing for her now was to keep busy, and he wouldn't mind doing the same.

Brunt looked from Jon to Rose and then back to Jon. He clearly didn't like the idea, but he could see the benefits of it.

"What if you bring some zombies back here and we end up having both doors blocked by them?" he asked.

"We can always break out through a window." Jon knocked on the glass for emphasis.

Brunt sighed. It was the sigh of a middle-aged man dealing with two young adults. Jon had heard that sigh a lot over the course of his twenty-one years, and he was betting that Rose had heard it even more over her twenty-six. Brunt waved his hands at them, indicating that they could go.

Jon drew his katana while Rose pulled the hammer off her belt. They would want to stick with the silent weapons as much as possible for now. Opening the door, Jon headed out into the hallway first. He kept his flashlight off, allowing the sunlight from the bridge to reveal the area ahead of him. The hallway was empty, so both he and Rose clicked on their lights once the door was closed. They listened as someone, most likely Shaidi, locked it behind them. Shaidi would probably stay by that door until they returned.

Following the break room's outer wall, they eventually came to a hallway that crossed from their side of the ship to the other. Looking across the way, they didn't see any zombies, and so headed in that direction. The sounds of the zombie smacking itself against the other door were easy to hear. Upon reaching the corner, Jon poked his head around it for a second, taking in the scene at a glance. They had gotten very lucky; there was only one zombie there.

Turning around to face Rose, he used hand gestures to tell her what he saw. They had a brief kind of conversation in a butchered version of sign language, which resulted in Rose telling Jon why she wanted to be the one to kill it. Jon thought it would be safer and quicker with his sword, but she refused to listen. Eventually, he stepped aside and let her sneak up on the corpse with her hammer.

Jon didn't watch, choosing instead to face the other way and guard Rose's back. He heard the sick crack from the hammer's first strike, followed by the crunches of repeated blows. Rose was taking her anger out on this one dead person, each impact sounding wetter, and squishier than the last. When it was over, she poked Jon's left shoulder. He turned around and inspected her for wounds. There was a lot of blackened blood on her shirt, but her goggles and the bandanna she had tied over her lower face had protected her from getting any of it in her eyes or mouth. If that happened, there would be nothing that Jon could do for her.

With both of the entrances and exits to the bridge cleared, the two of them moved deeper into the ship. Passing by room after room, Jon realized that most of the doors were propped open by their deadbolts. Maybe the people on this ship didn't have a card reprogrammer like the Diana had, and couldn't program key cards to unlock the doors. A handful of times, Rose or Jon would push open one of the doors and take a look inside, but there was never anything of immediate use. There were mostly a lot of empty drawers and a few abandoned items. Later, they would systematically scavenge the ship for everything, but for now, they looked only for things like food, ammunition, and medical supplies.

As they neared a stairwell, they heard the sounds of more zombies. The explosion on the other ship had stirred them all up, so they were all groaning, and moaning, and making whatever other vocal wheezes they could. Jon remembered there had been a lot more screamers back when it all began. Those first few days, it seemed like smart and fast ones were everywhere. As time went on, those disappeared, and the slow, dumb, shambling hordes took their place. Thomas, a supplies keeper who was friends with Brunt, Brewster, and Shaidi, had a theory. He thought that the fast ones died quicker because they ran into the living more frequently. Survivors were more likely to put down a fast one, whereas, they would just out run or avoid a slow one. The fast ones were also more likely to damage their bodies from colliding with things, essentially crippling themselves until they were slow. Jon didn't care what the reasons were, he was just glad for them. Granted, large swarms of shamblers were like a terrifying flood, he still preferred them to the lightning strikes that were the quick bastards.

Reaching the stairs and elevator banks, Jon suggested they take a look out over the promenade, where the lights were still on. The tenth deck was too high to look down upon it, but by silently moving down two decks, they got a clear view of the whole thing.

There were a lot more of the dead here than Jon, or anyone else, had realized.

The zombies weren't packed in shoulder to shoulder, but there was at least one for every five square feet of space. The stench was bad, suggesting these people hadn't been dead for very long. The ones that had died a long time ago, tended to lose their stink after awhile, becoming dried out and withered. These were maybe a few weeks old, give or take a week. If some people *had* escaped in the lifeboats, then how many had been on board in the first place?

Rose gestured that they should return to the bridge. Jon was inclined to agree, especially since the sun was already sinking into the sea. It would get a lot darker soon. They tiptoed their way back to the stairs, but the deck above them wasn't as empty as it had been before. Jon grabbed Rose's shoulder and pulled her back toward the elevators.

Whereas Jon wanted to either wait for the dead thing to leave, or go up the other staircase, Rose clearly wanted to bash its skull in. This time Rose gave in, agreeing they should try the other staircase.

Between the two staircases was some sort of café. It had a large statue of Neptune, or maybe it was Poseidon, standing imposingly before it. As they passed by the statue, a rustle of clothing was the only warning they had before a zombie lunged out at them.

Jon didn't have time to bring his sword to bear. The zombie grabbed his wrist, while Jon used his other hand to grab its throat. Jon's gloved fingers sank slightly into the dead flesh, making him queasy, but he kept the thing's teeth away from him as they snapped at the air. The zombie's other hand clawed impotently at the long sleeve of Jon's shirt. Rose didn't dare risk using her hammer, because Jon's bandanna had slipped down when his back had been pressed into the railing. Instead, she grabbed the zombie by its shoulders and pried him off Jon. Her momentum swung her and the zombie around so that when she let go, it was thrown into the railing. The zombie's hips struck the bar, while its torso continued over it. The dead thing folded in half for a moment, and just when it looked like it was going to stand back up, it over balanced, its feet leaving the carpet as the whole body went over.

Jon and Rose listened to the crunch as it hit the promenade below. They then heard a single moan rise up from the crowd. Looking down at the promenade, they could see that every single zombie was looking back. As one, the horde began to move forward.

The pair made for the staircase to which they had been heading, but a zombie rounded the corner. There was no telling how many could be behind it. Back the way they had come, the zombie on the upper deck was already stumbling its way down the stairs. Jon and Rose ran into the café.

The place was a mess. It was clear that someone had made some sort of last stand here. Tables and chairs were piled up at the back of the room. It looked as though even a few heavy appliances had been shifted around to become part of the barricade. Rose and Jon ran to it.

Rose reached the barricade first, quickly scrambling up the pile and leaping over the top. A single zombie shuffled around behind it. Rose threw her whole body at the zombie, planting both her feet into its chest and knocking it flying backward into another section of the barricade, and landing flat on her back in the process. Jon was following right behind her, landing on his feet and taking the few steps needed to drive his katana into the skull of the dead thing.

As a result of their climbing and leaping, as well as the zombie knocking into it, the barricade shuddered. A few chairs and tables shifted and settled lower, while some cracked under the weight of heavier objects. Rose gasped, but the barricade continued to stand. It was high enough that they could hide inside it, unseen, until they knew what the horde was doing.

Jon turned to help Rose up, the grin on his face not covered by his bandanna. He really needed to tie that thing tighter. His grin disappeared when he looked at Rose. Her face had gone completely pale. Behind her goggles, her eyes were wide as could be. Jon followed her gaze along her own outstretched arm. The arm disappeared unexpectedly under what Jon thought might be a fridge.

Rose started to tug her arm. It didn't move. She yanked harder, and harder, practically thrashing now as she realized she was trapped. Jon dropped on top of her, stilling her movements, as he heard a dead thing enter the café. Rose looked at him with terrified eyes. Jon attempted to reassure her. He slid over to where she was stuck and investigated the situation.

It was bad.

Rose's hand and wrist were completely pinned beneath the large object. The space between it and the floor wasn't much. Rose's hand must be a pancake. Jon tried to wedge his fingers under the object, which upon closer inspection, was indeed a fridge, but he could only get the tips of them under before the gap was too narrow. Still, he tried to lift the fridge. It didn't budge. Rose was breathing fast and heavy. Jon gave her a look, and she clamped her hand over her mouth, trying to keep silent. She was terrified.

Jon let her know he was going to peek over the barricade to see what was going on in the rest of the café. Rose nodded. Going to an area that looked more stable, and was nowhere near the spot Rose was pinned, Jon climbed up just high enough to see over the barricade. There weren't many zombies in the café; the horde probably couldn't find the stairs or didn't know what deck they were on. Five zombies shuffled around, but a sixth did not. Jon watched the way the sixth one moved. It was more sure of its movements, more deliberate. With a creeping dread, Jon realized that the sixth zombie was a smarter one. He climbed back down and sat on the floor.

Rose looked at Jon, her eyes still wide and wanting to know what was going on. Jon didn't tell her. He had to think. Looking around inside the barricade, he saw that there was a door at the back. He pointed it out to Rose and motioned that he was going to check it out. Rose shook her head. She didn't want Jon to leave her. Jon didn't give her a choice.

The back door led into a kitchen that had been stripped of just about everything. It must have been from here that the fridge and other large appliances had been dragged. In the back corner there was a small elevator, maybe twice the size of a dumbwaiter. It probably led down into some storeroom below, and was used to stock the kitchen. Testing the light switch, Jon found that the kitchen was getting power. If the elevator was too, then they had a way out. If only Rose wasn't trapped.

Jon returned to the barricade. Rose was trying to pull her arm free again. She had twisted herself around and managed to plant one of her feet against the fridge and was pushing against it. As Jon watched its complete lack of movement, he knew he wouldn't be able to get it off her on his own. Maybe if he had time and the right tools, he could free her, but he had neither. It was only a matter of time before the smarter zombie checked out the barricade, and it looked like it could climb. Jon didn't want to have to deal with the smart one. There was a much higher chance of it infecting him, and it would most certainly alert the horde to their exact location. If the horde came, the barricade wouldn't be able to hold them off.

There was only one option. Jon got Rose to stop struggling again and went through her bag. She still had some rope in it. As he began to tie off her arm, she placed her free hand against his shoulder. Jon showed her his katana and she understood. They had to amputate. Rose's eyes filled with tears, but she nodded. Once the tourniquet was tied off, Jon prepared to cut. Before he could start, Rose placed her hand against him again. When Jon turned to face her, she handed him her hammer. Jon was confused.

Rose pulled down her bandanna and very deliberately mouthed, *in case the bones need breaking.*

Jon nodded. His sword was incredibly sharp, but he'd be cutting at a weird angle in which he couldn't get his full power behind it. It was possible the sword wouldn't cut through the bone.

It didn't.

Rose was biting her bandanna, her eyes rolling, her ribcage expanded, and her neck tight as she used everything she had to resist making a sound, while Jon hacked at her flesh. Eventually, Jon switched to the hammer and whacked the uncovered bones. His sword had made nicks and gouges in the radius and ulna, which allowed them to break cleanly. Once that was done, another quick flick of his sword freed her. Rose looked like she was about to pass out. Jon didn't let her.

Stripping off his shirt, Jon wrapped it around her new stump, tying it on with what was left of the rope. He half-carried, half-dragged Rose toward the kitchen. He could hear the smart zombie moving toward the barricade to investigate the noises they had made.

Once in the kitchen, Jon hauled Rose up and stuffed her into the elevator, quickly cramming in after her. Rose held her butchered arm to her chest, and refused to look at it. She was very pale again. Jon pressed the button on the exterior that would send them down, and quickly pulled his hand inside. It was a very tight fit with the two of them, and the smell of blood filled the entire space.

"Brunt!" Jon thought they were safe enough to use the radio as they descended. "Brunt, come in!"

"Jon? What's wrong?" Brunt's voice replied immediately.

"We got into some trouble. I had to cut Rose's hand off."

There was a silent pause that lasted about five seconds. "Okay. Where are you now?"

"In a kitchen service elevator, heading downward," Jon told him.

"What end of the ship are you?" a voice Jon didn't recognize came on.

"The bow. Why?"

"Can you make it aft? The lowest level should be clear of the dead. Three of us have secured the medical centre and have holed up here. It's aft on the first deck. One of us is a field medic and should be able to assist," the voice told him.

"Okay. We're going to head to you."

"I'm going out to meet them," another strange voice added. Jon assumed it was one of the three in the medical centre. "They might need some help."

The elevator reached the bottom and opened up. Jon climbed out and pulled Rose out after him. She was more responsive than she had been up above, but still needed to lean heavily on Jon. Jon sheathed his sword and pulled out his pistol, not caring if he had to make noise. Moving as fast as they could, Jon helped Rose through the massive kitchens in which they found themselves.

"We've reached the bottom deck and are moving aft now," Jon reported.

Everything was dark. Jon's and Rose's flashlights bobbled unsteadily around their necks, making it difficult to see where they were going. There were no lights on, and no windows down here. It must have taken only minutes, but the journey was timeless for Jon. Disoriented, scared, in the dark, with his friend dying, all added to the surreal quality of it.

"Here!" a voice finally called ahead of them, a light quickly filling the darkness. The man who said he was going to meet them had found them, his white face mask an odd relief to see. "Let me take her."

"No!" Jon snapped. He didn't know why, but he felt it was his duty to carry Rose to the medical centre. He was tired, and sweat poured off him, but he didn't slow down. "Just lead the way."

The man nodded and led them quickly back to the medical centre.

"Put her on the table."

Jon hadn't realized they had reached the medical centre until he heard the command. The lights in there were on. Jon did as he was told, but he refused to sit down and take a rest. While the others gave Rose antibiotics, painkillers, and who knows what other drugs, he stood by her side and held her remaining hand.

"You're going to be okay. You're going to be okay," Jon repeated over and over. He didn't realize just how much he sounded like the man they had found on the bridge.

3
Mathias Is Having Dinner

After Shoes' funeral, Mathias walked with his friends and family to the large dining hall in the ship's aft. Now that the funeral had ended, everyone's spirits had picked back up.

"You sure you don't want me to at least accompany you?" Mathias asked before heading up the stairs to cross the ship on deck five.

"No, you go ahead," Alec waved him off, "I'll meet you there."

"If you insist."

"Daddy! Come on!" Hope grabbed his hands and tugged on them, putting all of her small weight behind the effort.

"All right, I'm coming. I'm coming." Mathias allowed himself to be dragged off.

They climbed the stairs, then walked onto the promenade and started to traverse the busy space. Hope bounced on up ahead, where she kept pace with her best friend, Peter.

"Do you think she understands what happened to Shoes?" Riley, Mathias's wife and Hope's mother, drifted up beside him.

"She's fine." Mathias hadn't expected Riley to be such a worrywart of a mom.

"No one this close to her has ever died before," Riley continued. "She hasn't asked any questions about it or anything."

"That's because she hasn't really had a chance to. The funeral was right after school, her friends have been around her the whole time," Mathias did his best to make her feel better. "Watch, she'll ask you a bunch of questions when we put her to bed tonight."

Riley sighed and threaded her fingers through his.

"How are *you* feeling?" Mathias could tell that Hope wasn't the only thing on her mind.

"I don't know," she shrugged. "I feel like I'm not sad enough. Does that make sense?"

"Well, we have seen a lot of death. And we know Shoes was very old. He may not have been in constant pain before he went, but he clearly struggled to get around. He went peacefully, which is what we all hope for in the end, isn't it?" Mathias didn't really know what he was saying, he was just plucking a random string of thought in his head.

Riley sighed again. Without looking directly at her, Mathias couldn't tell if she was falling for his bullshit or not.

They reached the dining hall and entered the upper floor of the large space. The dining room was three decks high, going from the fifth deck down to the third, with large kitchens on all three levels. A broad staircase took them down one flight to the level where most of the group usually ate. They gathered together a number of tables and chairs, while a waiter wrote down the names of who was there. The place used to be for fine dining, and was adorned with large chandeliers and beautiful artwork, but now everyone got the same rations depending on their size, and how physically demanding their job was. Mathias got a fair amount being as tall and broad as he was, and having a job as the head of a ship defence squad. He worked from midnight until 8 a.m., organizing all members of ship defence who patrolled decks one through five. It was usually a quiet assignment, as most jobs were either an 8 a.m. to 4 p.m. shift, or a 4 p.m. to midnight shift, meaning a lot of people were sleeping while Mathias was on duty, but a few times things had gotten hairy.

Conversations were struck up all around the table as the adults took their seats. The kids had their own shorter table nearby, where they could be watched without them being too bothersome. Not that Mathias ever found his daughter bothersome.

Their food was promptly brought to them. Without having to go through the hassle of ordering, it never took very long. Mathias started to wonder how long Alec would take, though.

"DAAAaaaadd," Hope cried. "Milly is trying to eat my food!"

Mathias turned in his seat to see their small, white, three-legged husky sniffing toward Hope's plate, which she held above her head.

"Milly! *Psst*, no. Come here." Mathias pointed to his side and Milly slunk over, understanding that she was in trouble. "You have your own food." He pointed out the bowl on the floor next to him, which Rifle had been eyeing. Milly ate her food obediently.

A great rumble shook the entire ship. Mathias was on his feet in an instant, taking the few steps needed to reach Hope. Some people screamed.

"What was that, Daddy, what was that?" Hope leapt up from her chair and grabbed his leg. Riley was already bending over to pick her up, and Hope quickly switched her grip from him to Riley's neck. "Was it a s'nammi, Daddy? Was it a big wave?" Abby had recently taught a few of the older kids about tsunamis and somehow Hope had found out about them. They scared her.

"No, it wasn't a tsunami. Stay here." Mathias started for the exit.

"I'm coming with you." Riley took a few steps to follow him, putting Hope back down.

"No, you're not. You're staying here."

"Someone could be hurt." Riley got that look on her face that meant Mathias couldn't change her mind.

"You have to stay here with Hope," Mathias insisted anyway.

"Abby and Lauren can look after her."

"Mommy!" Hope tugged on the pockets of Riley's pants, crying and frightened.

While Mathias wasn't able to change Riley's mind, their daughter was more than capable. As Riley turned to pick her back up, Mathias ran for the door. He knew he should have said something before taking off, but he had already delayed enough. Dashing into the former casino under the promenade, he made for the stairs on the right, nearly knocking over a few plants along the way. Taking them two at a time, he popped up in the middle of the promenade. Nothing was amiss there, but everyone was looking forward, waiting for word on what had happened and what they should do. Mathias looked up and saw smoke billowing out of the seventh deck hallway. He lived in that area. So did Alec.

Making for the stairs, Mathias had to push his way through a few people heading in the opposite direction. He noticed that some of them were coughing, and covered in soot. Upon reaching the hall, he had to crouch down in order to breathe, while rolling black smoke filled the upper half of the hallway.

"Step back, sir!" a man with a muffled voice brushed Mathias aside. The man was decked out in firefighter gear, and was closely followed by similarly attired men.

"What happened?" Mathias shouted as one of them ran past.

The firefighter shook his head. They didn't know either. All they knew was that there was a fire and it needed to be put out.

Mathias backed away to the stairwell. He went up to the next deck where there was more smoke, although it wasn't as bad because the staircase was drawing it all upward. Pulling his walkie-talkie off his belt, Mathias began relaying orders and information. Other ship defencemen were already gathering and handing out the rest of the firefighter gear. All Mathias could do was to help organize the effort, and help people clear the hallways.

Throughout the chaos, two thoughts kept ringing in Mathias's head: *did this have something to do with the other ship?* and *where was Alec?*

* * *

By the time the fire was completely doused and the smoke mostly dissipated, it was late into the night. Several people, Mathias's family and friends included, had to rely on the generosity of others. Many people were sleeping on couches in the rooms of acquaintances, co-workers, and even strangers. Mathias had seen Riley and Hope only once since the explosion had occurred, and that was when they had come over to tell him where they were staying. A doctor who Riley worked with had offered the two of them and Cameron, Mathias's sister-in-law, the use of his room while he helped with the injured. The doctor normally worked the day shift, but insisted that he wouldn't be able to sleep and had to help. He wasn't the only one either. Lots of people volunteered, Misha included, and they formed a massive bucket brigade to soak the areas around the fire to keep it from spreading. Only the firefighters, with their hoses and protective gear, had been able to get near the actual flames.

As Mathias walked down the blackened hallway, he didn't recognize it. The flooring was burned away to reveal the metal plating underneath. All the art had disappeared, leaving charred remains of metal frames, and broken glass lay in little piles under the places they had once hung. As he moved closer to the source, holes appeared in the walls. The rooms beyond were devastated. Finally, Mathias came across a section where the floor and ceiling were warped and buckled. A few panels were peeled and twisted back to reveal the other decks. Heavy struts continued to hold everything together, but the walls between them were mostly gone.

"Was this Alec's room?" James asked. After returning from the foreign ship, he had immediately joined the effort to get everything under control. Now he, Mathias, Commander Crichton, Lieutenant Boyle, and captains Sigvard, Karsten, and Bronislav, were to be the first to take a look at the source of the damage.

Mathias nodded. Not much was left of the room to tell about its occupant, but he knew this was it. The crumpled and tortured remains of Alec's wheelchair wrapped around a support strut only reaffirmed this. His own room, the one he lived in with his family, had been next door. It was gone now. Everything they had was burnt to a crisp. Everything he and Riley still had from their old life and all of Hope's toys, were gone. A rage burned deep within Mathias's belly, but he had nowhere to direct it.

"And you said he was going back to his room and would meet you for dinner later? Why did he go back to his room?" James continued. He was acting as the mouthpiece for the ship's leaders, willing to take the brunt of Mathias's anger if he lost control.

"He said he wanted to wash up before dinner. I think he was just upset about Shoes and needed a moment to himself." Mathias turned to the five leaders, his hands in tight fists and his teeth clenched. "Don't you dare think he had anything to do with this. Alec was a good man."

"We're aware," Commander Crichton nodded curtly. "Why don't you go spend the rest of the night with your family?"

Mathias shook his head. "It's my watch."

James placed his hand on Mathias's shoulder. "Well, there's nothing else you can do here. We should let the professionals take a look."

"I know about bombs," Mathias told him.

"And I know that you do. I remember you fire bombing the tower at the prison." James carefully directed Mathias back down the hall, away from the destruction. "I know probably as much about bombs as you do, but there are people on this ship who know even more than us. People without as high an emotional stake in it and won't get distracted."

Mathias pushed James away from him. "I understand why you don't want me investigating this, you don't need to explain it. Just promise me that you'll tell me everything you find out. And I mean everything."

"Yeah. Sure." James nodded, although whether he was being honest or not was debatable.

Mathias never completely trusted James. When they first met, James had run Mathias and his group off the road, stuck them into the back of a large truck, and driven them to a prison full of other survivors who had been rounded up. Marble Keystone was planning to use the people there as some sort of labour force. However, Mathias was to be executed, having worked for Keystone and turned his back on them. James had wound up telling him all of this to give him and his group a chance to escape. He had a two-faced quality that made him hard to read.

Understanding that he couldn't keep hanging around, Mathias left the area and headed down to the lower decks. He would continue to perform his duties throughout his shift.

The lowest decks were usually quiet this late, but not tonight. More people than usual were travelling from room to room. Mathias spotted Cameron and flagged her down.

"What's going on down here? What are you still doing up?"

"The explosion disturbed all the animals," Cameron sighed, sweeping her hands through her very short hair, which was the complete opposite of Riley's long braid. The difference in haircuts was the way most people told the twins apart, although Mathias had known them both long enough to pick out several other different features. "Most of them are delicate as it is, with the minimal amount of space we have for them. We're starting to get things under control now, but we lost a few."

There were roughly two hundred rooms down on the second deck, and all of them were occupied by animals. They had sheep, cows, pigs, chickens, rabbits, goats, some geese, a few ducks, and two horses. At any time during the daylight hours, people could be found down there taking the larger animals on walks through the hallways. Most of these animals were grazers, not built to be cooped up in small staterooms, but it was the best place they could find for them. They even converted the larger conference rooms into a kind of veterinarian clinic, so that they wouldn't have to move the animals up or down the stairs if they got sick. All of deck two had been given the name, Noah's Ark.

"We didn't lose one of the horses, did we?" Mathias asked. The horses were the most prone to becoming agitated by the constant confinement, but they really came in handy the few times the Diana was within a few hours journey by tender boat to shore so that the off-shippers could bring them. Any tender boat trip longer than a couple hours became too dangerous for the horses.

"No, they're both okay."

"Is there anything I can do to help?" If anything could take Mathias's mind off what happened, it would be caring for large animals.

"Yes, you can keep Billy company while Nedry helps me with some pigs."

"Who's Billy?" Mathias wondered while Cameron led him down the hall. The top halves of all the doors had been cut off so that all the animals could be viewed as they walked by. The rooms were similar to those upstairs, with portal windows instead of balconies, no furniture, and the carpeting removed and replaced with dirt and hay in most cases. The closets were used to store feed and tools, while the bathrooms were usually used to assist in waste removal. Animal poop was never allowed to sit around for too long. Most of it was bagged and turned into fertilizer, while the rest was mixed with human waste that ran through the purification process. The human survivors hated the idea of drinking water that had been filtered from their own piss, despite being repeatedly told it was completely clean, but giving it to the animals and plants was acceptable. The humans stuck to desalinated ocean water.

As Mathias thought about waste and fertilizer, he began to wonder if maybe the explosive had somehow been derived from it. He didn't think on it long before Cameron opened one of the doors and led him inside a room. A large, black and white cow stood in the middle of the space, while a man gently stroked her face.

"This is Billy." Cameron walked up to the cow and patted it gently. "She's pregnant."

"Billy is a girl cow." Mathias slowly approached the cow, not wanting to startle her.

"We don't always bother with gender correct names," Cameron shrugged. "Now, she's rather nervous, but is quite fond of human contact. We're afraid of her losing her calf, so we need someone to stand with her. Keep her calm, and monitor her, while we finish checking on the rest."

"I guess I can do that."

"If she starts bleeding, or bellowing, call for someone right away," the man who Mathias assumed was Nedry told him. "Feel free to give her some hay or water if she looks like she wants some."

"Okay." Mathias didn't know how he would know if the cow wanted some hay or water, but considering that the bale and bucket weren't far from her, he figured she could take care of herself on that front.

"Come on, Nedry." Cameron left the room without so much as a thanks, or an encouraging remark. She was very focused on what she was doing. Her room had also been destroyed by the fire, and she was clearly trying not to think about it.

Mathias was alone in a room with a cow, and he had no idea what he was doing.

"Hi, Billy," he said, taking a slow step toward her, "I'm Mathias. I'm good friends with your keeper there, Cameron. Don't bite me, okay?"

Moving very slowly, he placed his hand on Billy's nose. She didn't seem to care, so Mathias began to stroke her.

"There. That's not so bad." Although Mathias saw the animals all the time during his nightly patrols, he never paid too much attention to them. Usually, the lights in their rooms would be turned off and they'd be sleeping. He found he rather liked this dim-witted-looking creature.

The next several hours were spent in the peaceful company of Billy. The cow was never bothered when Mathias's walkie-talkie went off, so he could give orders and direct people when he had to, but most of the night was quiet. It seemed that even though a lot of people weren't sleeping this night, none of them were making trouble. They were probably too frightened, and Mathias couldn't blame them. He found himself telling Billy about Alec, and how the man had saved his little brother's life. Danny most likely wouldn't have survived the Day without him, and he and Mathias never would have been reunited.

Mathias wept for his dead friend.

***

By the time Cameron returned, Mathias was drained. All his rage and grief had been poured out of him into the attentive ears of Billy the cow. His physical exhaustion had also managed to catch up with him.

"Your shift is over soon. Why don't you leave now and get some sleep?" Cameron told him. She then covered her mouth, hiding a yawn behind it.

"You look like you could use some rest, too." Mathias said goodbye to Billy, giving her a mouthful of hay.

"Maybe I'll squeeze in a nap if someone can cover for me, but my shift is actually starting soon." Cameron shooed him out of the room. "Now go see my sister and niece. I'm sure they're worried about you."

Mathias nodded slowly and made his way toward the stairs. Climbing them was more tiring than usual, and he almost went to the wrong deck before realizing that Riley and Hope were now on the eighth. He could barely remember the room number, but got lucky and picked the right door on which to knock.

Riley answered the door and upon seeing him, wrapped her arms around Mathias and gave him a huge bear hug. Her eyes were swollen from lack of sleep. She must have had a rough night.

"How's Hope?" Mathias asked, glancing into the room behind Riley. Hope was asleep on the bed.

"She's doing okay. I don't think she knows what happened." Neither of them asked about the other, already understanding how they felt.

"Is she still going to school today?"

"Yeah, Abby and Lauren don't want to change the kids' routines, and a lot of parents can't take the day off to look after them. I think Lauren is going to try to explain things to them in a way that they'll understand but won't terrify them."

"I'm terrified," Mathias admitted.

"Me too," Riley sighed. "Do you mind waking her up and getting her ready? I don't know if you heard, but some of the off-shippers were left behind. James is already out there bringing them in. One of them is apparently hurt pretty badly, and I'd like to make sure everything is in order before they arrive."

"Of course. It's not Jon that's hurt, is it?" Mathias hadn't seen him last night, and so assumed he was one of the off-shippers left behind. Jon would have been in the middle of the relief effort had he been there for it, because that was just the kind of guy he was.

"I don't know. I don't think so. Everything has been so crazy that we're not getting all the information we should, but I think the injured person is female."

"You go to work. I'll take care of things here." Mathias kissed Riley on the forehead. She kissed his cheek in return. After looking around and realizing she had nothing to bring to work with her, she departed.

Mathias walked over to the bed and kneeled down beside it. He didn't often get to wake up Hope. Every morning, when he came off his shift, he'd come home to find Riley getting ready for work and Hope getting ready for school. After they left was when he slept. In the afternoons, Mathias would pick up Hope from school and they'd spend an hour together before Riley came home. Both Riley and Mathias would put Hope to bed, and then they'd have a few hours together before Mathias headed back to work. He liked this routine, and was hoping it wouldn't be long before they got into its rhythm again.

"Hope. Hope, wake up, sweet-pea."

Hope mumbled and rolled over.

"Come on, it's time to get up and go to school."

Eventually Hope got moving. It was a rough time getting her ready. They didn't have a toothbrush, so Hope had to use her finger. Although she liked using her finger, she didn't like the toothpaste here, and complained about wanting the regular kind. There was no hairbrush, as the doctor who gave up his room was basically bald. Mathias had to brush Hope's long, wavy, auburn hair with his fingers. She was displeased about this, saying it looked messy.

"Sorry, pumpkin, there's nothing I can do about that right now."

"Mommy would know what to do."

Mathias sighed. Riley probably *would* know what to do. "Maybe one of your teachers will have a brush you can use."

Hope huffed, not liking the idea. "Why do I have to wear the same clothes as yesterday? I want to wear my pink shirt today."

"We don't have any other clothes for you to wear."

"Where's my pink shirt?"

"Can we talk about it after school?"

"I want to wear my pink shirt."

"Not today."

Hope was getting very grumpy, and Mathias worried she'd start crying and screaming about it soon.

"Come on, let's go get you some breakfast."

With Milly trotting along behind them, Mathias walked through the ship holding Hope's small hand. After getting their breakfast, they ate quickly, and then Mathias walked her to school. The Diana had already had a kids' centre at the back of the ship on deck twelve, which had been very easy to turn into a school. Lauren and Abby worked there as teachers, along with the one remaining crewmember who had worked there previously.

"She's very grumpy this morning. Do not mention what she's wearing," Mathias told Abby once Hope had run into the room to see Peter. "If you have a hairbrush here, you might be able to recover the day."

"We've got a lot of supplies here," Abby reassured him. "I found out which kids weren't able to return to their rooms last night while Lauren found some clothes and supplies to give them. Although she won't have as many things to wear as she used to, we should be able to supply her with a few new outfits."

"Thank you so much."

"You look exhausted, Mathias. You should really get some sleep." Abby sounded quite concerned.

"Yeah. Yeah, I'll do that."

On the way back to the room, however, Mathias spotted the doctor who lived there. He looked bone weary, even more tired than Mathias felt. Mathias didn't much feel like crashing on the man's couch while he was likely to be asleep in the bed. He decided he would head to the library and sleep on one of the couches there, or if they were taken, he'd go out on deck four and snooze in a lounge chair. But first, he should probably tell Riley where he'd be in case of an emergency.

With Milly in tow, Mathias made his way all the way back down to deck one. Whereas the spa and wellness centre were used for regular check-ups and minor injuries, the actual medical centre was used for returning off-shippers and surgeries. Riley would be down there today.

Mathias arrived at the same time the tender boat returned from picking up the off-shippers. He stood out of the way as masked Brewster and Brunt rushed past, carrying a girl on a stretcher between them. Mathias recognized the girl as Rose, and saw that she was deathly pale and not conscious. She might be dead. All the other off-shippers followed behind them. They would all be tested for infection before being allowed back into the general population. Mathias followed the group into the medical centre, but stood off to one side with Milly. Riley was nowhere to be seen; likely she was in the back room to where Rose had been rushed.

Observing the off-shippers being processed, Mathias spotted a man who didn't belong. He looked wasted, and was far thinner than anyone else aboard the Diana. He must be a survivor from the other ship. Seeing Jon, Mathias headed over to him to ask about the strange man.

"Yeah, he's from the other ship," Jon confirmed.

"What's he saying?" Mathias couldn't hear the man over the din of the busy medical centre, but could see his lips moving.

" 'Not bit.' It's the only thing he'll say."

"Jon!" Robin, a girl who worked in the medical centre as Riley's apprentice, made her way over. She and Jon had an off-and-on thing for the last six years or so. When she reached Jon, she held his hands in her own, which were covered in latex gloves. Any contact closer than that was forbidden until Jon got tested.

"You're all right," Jon smiled.

"*I'm* all right?" Robin turned to Mathias. "He just got back from the death ship, his wounded partner in tow, and he's relieved to see that *I'm* all right?"

Mathias shrugged. "We're men. It's what we do."

Robin shook her head and rolled her eyes.

"Is Rose okay?" Jon asked.

"She's in good hands. I'm not even sitting in on this one because they want only the best in there looking after her. She'll be fine."

"What happened?" Mathias wondered.

Jon just shook his head, not quite ready to talk about it.

"Well, let's get your blood tested so you can get out of here." Robin turned to a nearby table and pulled a needle out of a jar of alcohol. They often had to reuse their needles for blood testing and sterilized them constantly. After drying the needle off, Robin expertly tied off Jon's arm and began to take a small sample of his blood. Looking at the blood under a microscope was the quickest and most effective way to tell if someone was infected.

"You look worse than I feel," Mathias commented on how exhausted Jon seemed.

"Yeah, I didn't sleep last night. What's happened here? We didn't get a lot of updates."

"I'll fill you in later," Mathias promised him, "after you get some rest."

"You both look like you could use some rest," Robin told them. "Once we're done here, Jon, I'll let you into my room so you can get some sleep."

"I can't sleep in my room? Is it because of the explosion?"

"They're still determining which rooms are safe enough to use."

Jon's room was near enough to the area to have been affected, but might still be okay. Robin's room was on the other side of the ship, where it had been safe from the fire.

"You should take a shower, too. I recently got a new bar of soap that's much better than the last batch they made. Smells better, too," Robin chatted as she prepared the blood slide. "It'll be nice when they finally get that soap making process down, and we won't have to rely so much on scaven-" Robin cut off mid-sentence, gasping and backing away from the microscope. She suddenly ran out of the room.

Mathias and Jon looked at each other, having no idea what had just happened. Mathias walked over to the microscope and looked through the eyepiece. All the blood drained from his face.

"Jon," he said, his voice half-strangled, "you're infected."

4
Freya Makes Plans

Hearing the footsteps approaching, Freya hurried to bury her makeshift knife beneath the sand. If they found her with it, they would certainly beat her, and perhaps finally just kill her in anger. Not that death could be much worse than what she was living through now.

Unfolding her bedroll back over the spot, she turned to face the tent flap just as it opened. The heavily scarred face of Bob entered the bright blue tent, which was really a propped up tarp, his eyes locking on Freya's. Freya quickly looked away, not wanting to antagonize him. Bob stared at her for an uncomfortable moment, his gaze piercing. He then looked around the tent, searching for anything amiss. He must not have seen anything because he settled into a slightly more comfortable crouch.

"Sher wants to see you," Bob grumbled.

Freya nodded, still not looking directly at him. Bob continued to sit in the tent entrance, watching her. Finally, he stood up again and exited the tent. This allowed Freya to crawl out. As soon as Freya was out from under her tarp, Bob was grabbing her arm and dragging her up onto her feet. Freya didn't fight against him or cry out. She hadn't been able to cry out for a few years now. She hadn't been able to make a single sound for a very long time.

Bob marched Freya through the camp, holding her arm hard enough to leave bruises. This wasn't going to be a good visit. Visits to Sher never were. Other women and children watched as Freya was brought past them. They all knew what happened around the camp, especially to women like Freya, but none of them ever said anything. They never stood up to the men. Freya thought they could all just go to hell.

At the end of the beach, they reached the site where the Dunns River Falls met the ocean. The falls had been a popular tourist attraction prior to the zombies, but now it was their best source of fresh water, and the buildings provided protection for Sher and his cronies. Everyone else was in tents on the sand, protected only by the guards that Sher paid. Nowadays, they rarely had to worry about zombies anymore. Over half of Jamaica had been pretty much cleared of them, and it was only those travelling under the sea and a few that made it over the mountains that were a concern. Still, Sher had the guards continue to patrol the borders of the camp at all times: he didn't want anyone leaving. Sher had ruled the group for two years now, ever since he murdered the last leader. In Freya's opinion, their last leader hadn't been any better.

"Freya, there you are," Sher grinned as she was thrown into the room, barely managing to keep to her feet.

Freya was quiet as always, choosing to look down at her bare toes. She was partly disgusted with herself for not acting out, for not fighting every chance she got, but that hadn't gotten her anywhere in the past. Her only hope was for them to let their guard down long enough for her to spring into action. Soon. She would act soon, but not now. Now she had to continue to endure this humiliation.

"Is Freya not the most beautiful woman you've ever seen?" Sher asked the boy next to him. He couldn't be more than fourteen.

"I don't know," the boy shrugged.

"Do you know what makes her the most beautiful?" Sher continued. "Her silence. Never makes a sound. She can't, even if she wanted to."

"Why not?" the boy asked. Freya had seen the kid around the camp. He was clearly being inducted into Sher's group of warriors, and would most likely get to stay at this camp based on the way Sher was treating him. Only the best got to stay at the large camp, while the others were moved about the various camps and outposts around the rest of the island. There was no way to know for sure how many men Sher actually commanded, but Freya knew it was a lot.

"She got sick. Nothing you or I need to worry about, but it left her without a voice. Good fucking luck on our part, eh?" Sher laughed loudly.

The boy looked at him and grinned, not entirely sure why he was there or what he was supposed to be doing.

"Get to it, woman." Sher waved his hand at her.

Freya's mind drifted off to her place without memory, as she performed her assigned duty.

***

Everything was sore, but she had felt worse before. Sitting on the sand, looking across the sea, Freya thought of escape for the thousandth time. She had it all worked out, save for one thing: she didn't know where to go. She couldn't stay on the island, because there was nowhere to hide from Sher and his men if she did that. Going to the portion of the island they didn't control wasn't an option either. There were still large groups of zombies over there, not to mention all the pirate bands. No, pirates wouldn't be any better. Freya would have to cross the ocean if she wanted to escape, but she didn't know where to go. Travelling alone, with no destination, was a sure way to get killed. Most days, Freya wished she had gone with Captain Martin, but she couldn't leave her brother behind, and her brother wouldn't go. Things weren't as bad then. Now her brother was dead and she was alone. No one cared for her.

That's when she saw it. Way off in the distance, sitting on the horizon, was a pillar of dark smoke. It was hard to make out against the darkening sky, but the sunset was backlighting it just enough.

Freya wondered if anyone else saw the smoke. She didn't react to seeing it, not knowing if someone was watching her. If no one else saw it, then that was her chance. Smoke like that could only be caused by people. She didn't know why there was a fire and didn't care. There hadn't been any lightning storms in over a week, so it couldn't be a naturally occurring fire. It was possible everyone at the base of that smoke would be either gone or dead by the time Freya reached it. She didn't care. Noting the direction, she knew it was toward the Cayman Islands. That had been a possible destination for her before, but she suspected the Islands were too far. This smoke had to be closer, it had to be a boat of some kind. She could go to it, and stop there before continuing on to somewhere like Grand Cayman.

But what if the smoke was coming from pirates? Sailing headlong into a band of pirates wouldn't be any good.

A screaming drew Freya's attention behind her. A mother was trying to protect her daughter from being beaten. Apparently, the young girl had taken something, it sounded like food. The mother was draped over her daughter, completely covering her and taking strikes from a switch to her back.

Fuck pirates, Freya thought. She didn't care who the people under the smoke were; she was going to go to them. Even if it turned out to be a burning ship that had sunk by the time she could reach it, she would keep going. She would sail alone to the Cayman Islands all by herself. Damn everyone else.

Having decided this, she got up from the sand to prepare.

Freya's plan didn't take much preparation, as she had been planning it for so long. She took a walk as close to the camp's border as she dared, noting what guards were on duty and where. They all had their various weaknesses, and she picked out the one she could get by the easiest.

Maybe it was because she couldn't talk anymore—not like she had anyone to talk to—but she found she learned a lot about people just by observing them. This man had a small bladder and always took a piss where no one could see him, that one was deaf in one ear, another was always hoping that Sher would look favourably upon him and allow him a woman. Even the other people in the camp had their observable behaviours, like the woman who always aligned herself with whoever was physically largest, hoping that he would protect her. There was also a young boy who was more at home amongst the goats than with his own mother. Freya was jealous of this one girl who seemed capable of blending into any setting, and could always go unnoticed by those around her. Freya could always find her though. Ever since she stopped speaking, she found she looked and listened a lot more.

After her border patrol, Freya walked along the beach. The water's edge had been combed over many times, but the sea was always revealing new and sometimes useful things, like the small, smooth, round stone she found this time. Although she didn't let on as she pulled it up out of the wet sand, the stone was a great find for Freya. She hoped it was a good sign as well, and would bring her luck. Pocketing the stone in the knee-length, jean skirt she wore over her tight cycling shorts, she continued to look for anything else useful. Sadly, there was only the stone that evening, although it was better than the nothing she usually found.

Once darkness had fallen and the campfires were burning, Freya headed back into her tent. She slipped the stone into her pillowcase and lay down on her mat, waiting for Skunk. Skunk wasn't his real name of course, just Freya's name for him. She called him that because he showed up at her tent just about every night, drunk as a skunk. He always tried to get between Freya's legs, but in his condition, he always failed.

Sure enough, while Freya was lying on her back, looking up at the tarp, he crawled in. He fought with her skirt a bit, but eventually, the liquor caught up with him, and he fell asleep on top of her. Freya gently rolled his bony body over to his own mattress and lay back down. She could handle drunk Skunk, but he had a tendency to wake up in the middle of the night, so she had to appear normal while she worked. Slowly, with only one hand, she began to dig in the sand next to her bed.

The clothes that Freya wore were the best she could get with which to protect herself. Sher demanded that all women wear dresses or skirts, so Freya had picked a knee length, heavy jean skirt because the fabric wasn't easy to roll or push up. She wore tight bike shorts underneath, so that even if Skunk could get the skirt off on his better nights, he fought with the form fitting shorts. She also dressed similarly up top, with a tight, long-sleeved shirt underneath a baggy T-shirt that hid her curves. Even on the hottest days, Freya would rather deal with the heat than the looks.

After a short while, she could reach the knife under her bed. Gently, she pulled out the blade. She had made it herself out of stone, twine, and seashells. The blade was oddly shaped and somewhat fragile, but deadly sharp. In the dark, Freya turned her head toward Skunk. He was lying on his back, head turned toward Freya, mouth open with a rattling snore issuing from it. God, did Freya ever hate that snore.

She didn't have to think twice about it. Reaching over, she quickly drew her blade across Skunk's throat. It sliced open like butter. He woke up, still drunk and very alarmed. If he hadn't been either of those things, maybe he would have sat up and crawled out of the tent, but he didn't. His hands flew up to his neck, finding the separated flesh and trying to hold it back together. He gagged and choked, but was strangely quiet about it. Freya had expected a little more noise from him, perhaps enough noise that she'd have to worry, but he was close to silent. It was a little disturbing in that the noises he made weren't that different from what Freya sounded like when she tried to speak.

He died fast. It seemed like more than a minute, but it was certainly less than five. His blood drained out of him, spilling across his mattress and absorbed by the sand. As soon as he stopped moving, Freya got to work.

Rolling back her sleeping mat, she dug deeper to reach her stash. It wasn't much: a small rucksack filled with what little food and water supplies she had managed to save. Upending her pillow, she dumped out all the stuffing along with the many smooth stones she had managed to collect. Skunk had never noticed she barely ever put her head on that pillow, and now, he never would. Freya carefully repacked the pillow so that the stones would be easy to access, but the stuffing would keep them from clinking together. Near the top of the back pole holding up her tarp, was a rope she unwound and tied around her waist like a belt, securing the pillowcase to it in the process. She then unwound a smaller, leather strap from the front pole, being careful not to move the flap. This, she wrapped around her right hand.

It wasn't the right time yet. Some of the men, those who didn't drink all day like Skunk, would still be sharing a bottle of moonshine around the fire. Freya could wait them out. It was the only reason she put up with Skunk: the men had a code about not disturbing a man when he was with a woman.

By lying down on her stomach, Freya could peer out through the slit between the tarp and the sand. She could see five fires from where she lay, four of which were already burned down to the embers that would be kept glowing all night by the guards. The last still had a group sitting around it.

Shifting slowly around her tent, Freya looked out of all the sides and found only two other fires were burning high. One had a rowdy group around it, but they were at the far end of the beach and wouldn't be a problem. The closer fire had a single woman attending it. She was cooking something over it, possibly fish, and probably for the men. Crawling back to her original position, Freya spied on the men closest to her.

She lay on her belly, watching and waiting like a huntress. One by one, the men began to get up and head to their own tents. When there was only one left, poking at the fire with a look of contemplation on his face, she continued to wait. If she wanted, she could have easily snuck up behind the man and killed him like she had Skunk, but she wouldn't do that. Killing this man would only increase the risk of being caught. She could wait. She had waited for years, she could wait a few hours more if need be.

It wasn't hours, but eventually the man ceased his thinking long enough to stand up and go back to his tent. Freya thought he probably had a woman in his tent, one who was lying in the dark, hoping he wouldn't come back. Freya didn't have any sympathy. Rescuing everyone else was not her problem.

Once ten more minutes had passed, and the fires were as low as they would get all night, Freya slid out of her tent on her belly like a snake. With a wider field of vision, she checked out the surrounding area again. She was in the clear. Moving on her hands and the balls of her feet—a method that was both exhausting and difficult, but that she had trained herself to do—she made for the border. Any time there was a flicker of movement, she would drop to the sand and wait to see what would happen. So far, it was only the wind flapping the canvases.

Upon reaching the scrub at the edge of the beach, she moved slower. She was nearing the guards now. After a slow, methodical search, she located the guard she was looking for. He was standing with his back to her, looking toward some trees. Unwinding the leather thong from her hand, Freya pulled out a rock from her pillow-bag and slipped it into the sling. She had chosen this guard for his slow reaction time, and the fact that the nearest guard to him was the one deaf in one ear. Swinging her sling around in a tight arc, she took careful aim. It hadn't been easy to find the time and location to practice, but Freya had, and was deadly accurate.

The rock bounced off the back of the man's head with a crack. Drawing in a sharp breath, he turned to find out what had happened. Freya had already moved closer and loaded another rock into her sling. This one struck him between the eyes, knocking him flat on his back. Whether he was dead, unconscious, or only stunned, Freya didn't wait to find out. She moved in with her knife and dispatched him as quickly as she had Skunk.

Stepping past the bleeding body, she was outside the ring of guards. She made for the trees, but then moved through them parallel to the shore. Because of her muteness, the men often mistook her for being stupid as well. They talked about things in her presence that they probably shouldn't have. Things like where the boats were kept.

When she spotted them down at the water's edge, she stopped and scanned the area. There weren't as many guards around the boats as there were around the tents. Pretty much everyone living in the area was under Sher's control, and the few free people weren't stupid enough to try stealing from him. Two men were in a tiny shack, half-asleep, while a third sat on the deck of the largest vessel in this particular fleet. That was okay, the boat that Freya wanted was farthest from it.

Circling around wide, she crossed the beach on her belly to reach the water. Once in the surf, she let the sea float her body, while she pulled herself through the shallow water using only her arms, her sack of rocks dragging along the bottom.

The boat was small. It was an aluminium fishing boat with an outboard motor that wasn't really meant for the sea. Freya didn't care. She didn't plan to be driving long, and the sea didn't seem overly rough that night. Very slowly, so as not to make a sound, she lifted both her pack and bag of rocks and placed them gently into the boat. Pausing, she noted that the men had not noticed anything amiss yet.

"Take me with you," a voice hissed behind her.

Raising her blade, Freya turned. Behind her was the girl who could slip by anyone unnoticed. Apparently, she could go unnoticed by Freya as well, when she wanted to.

"Please." Her moonlit eyes were begging.

Freya looked back at the guards who still hadn't moved. She had three options: try to leave the girl behind, take her with her, or kill her. Out of those options, taking the girl with her seemed like the option least likely to get her caught. Freya nodded and gestured at the boat.

The girl had her own pack with her and was even more careful about getting it into the boat than Freya had been. Once it was placed, the girl slithered up on the sand and untied the rope from the large log that anchored it.

Before they could shove off, however, there was something else that Freya needed to do. Moving slowly through the ocean, she crept up behind the little boat next to the one she was taking. Rising carefully over its side, she unhooked the gas tank from within, and then lifted it up and out. She placed the tank in her own boat, and then repeated the stealthy manoeuvre with all the other little fishing boats along the row.

As she was unhooking the last tank, bent awkwardly over the side as she stood in the shallow water, the door to the shed suddenly flew open. Freya froze.

"Oi! Do you want something to eat?" the man in the shed's doorway called to the one guarding the large boat.

"Nah! I'm all right!" the boat guard called back.

"Well, we got some extra if you want any!" The man then disappeared back into the shed, having completely missed seeing Freya.

Although she might have been able to sneak aboard one of the larger boats and steal its gas tank as well, she decided not to press her luck. Once the final tank was gently loaded into her boat, she was ready to go, now with an extra passenger.

Together, the two women eased the boat off the sand and into the ocean. They didn't dare try to climb into it right away. Instead, they each took a side and swam out with the boat. Freya was exhausted, but she didn't quit. She swam and swam until she decided that they were far enough away from shore.

Swimming around the front of the boat, she found the girl was floundering. She hadn't said anything, but she looked half drowned, constantly getting salt water in her mouth which she promptly spit out again. Freya gestured to her that it was okay to climb aboard. The girl barely had any strength left to get up, but Freya couldn't help her; she had to swim back to the other side and hold onto the edge to counterbalance the weight. Once the girl was in, managing to keep remarkably quiet as she rolled to the floor, Freya hauled herself up. When she had made her plans, she hadn't counted on how much her bony body would tilt the boat, and if it hadn't been for the girl balancing the other side, she might have flipped the thing.

Once they were in, Freya still didn't stop. She loaded the oars into their oarlocks and began rowing. She rowed on her own, watching the shore slowly get farther away, while the girl sat in the bow, resting and looking out to sea. Eventually, the girl slid in next to Freya and took over one of the oars.

"I'm Teal," the girl whispered, even though the beach was a distant, glowing speck, and Jamaica was a dark hump on the horizon.

Freya just gave her a side-glance and kept rowing.

"I heard one of the women once say that your name is Freya?"

Freya nodded.

The girl, Teal, didn't say anything else after that.

After a long while, when Freya's arms were about to give up on her and Teal's already had, Freya shifted to the back of the boat to start the motor. She checked the gas can, which was nearly full, pulled the choke out, and yanked on the rip cord. It took a handful of pulls, but the small motor eventually sputtered to life.

As Freya sat back with her hand on the throttle, she was unconcerned about getting lost. Many sleepless nights had taught her to recognize stars, and the direction of the smoke lay burned in her memory. As long as the sea remained calm and she had stolen enough gas, they would get there.

***

Teal was asleep in the front of the boat while Freya drove. She was half-asleep herself, but couldn't rest just yet. Not until she got to where she wanted to go.

If only her brother were with her. She missed him. He had been so carefree, and was always quick with a joke. He had a bright smile.

A foreign noise disturbed Freya. She sat up straighter and began looking around. It was a buzzing, and it wasn't the little boat's engine. Scanning the dark waters, her eyes searched for the source of the sound. Teal woke up as she released the throttle and shut down the engine.

"What is it?" the girl mumbled as she rubbed sleep out of her eyes.

Freya pressed a finger to her lips, urging Teal to be quiet. Teal saw the look in her eyes, her own growing large in the darkness. She began to search the waters as well. Freya couldn't find where the buzzing was coming from, but she thought she spotted light toward the horizon, in the direction the smoke had been. It wasn't sunlight either, which was still a couple of hours off.

"There," Teal whispered, pointing across the water in the opposite direction.

A dark shape was speeding along the waves. It was a boat that was much faster and more powerful than the one that Freya had stolen. It was a boat that Freya knew: Sher's boat.

There was nowhere to hide on the sea. Freya wanted to scream, but wouldn't even if she could. How did they know which way she had gone? Had someone else seen the smoke too, and knew she would head toward it?

The boat had turned and was now coming straight toward them. There was nothing to do but fight. Freya prepared her sling.

"I don't have a weapon," Teal said to her, her voice full of fear.

Freya tossed her the makeshift knife. It was all they had.

As the boat came closer, Freya stood tall, no longer worrying about being seen. It was obvious they had already been spotted, and she wasn't going to let them take her easily. She did hide the loaded sling behind her, however.

As the powerboat drew close, it slowed down. It was being driven by Bob, and Sher stood tall next to him, his white teeth shining in the darkness.

"Here you are!" he called chipperly, as if he wasn't planning on wringing her neck.

Managing to avoid telegraphing her intent, Freya suddenly brought the sling around and let loose the stone within it. The rock whipped across the gap between the two boats, striking Sher above the eye. He went down with a startled squawk.

The larger boat turned and drifted, broadside, into them, nearly knocking Freya over. She grabbed another rock as a third man from the back of the other boat leapt aboard the tiny aluminium. There was no time to load the sling, so Freya simply threw the stone instead. The man ducked, thereby being struck only on a raised arm. Ducking was what killed him. He hadn't seen Teal in the front of the boat, and she viciously slashed him with the knife. She cut deep, his guts nearly spilling out. The pain caused him to jolt back, tipping him overboard and into the ocean.

Bob grabbed Teal by her hair, lifting the girl, screaming, into the air. He tossed her into the back of the powerboat as if she were nothing more than a kitten. There was a sick thump, and Freya lost sight of her. When Bob moved into the front of her boat, it rocked dangerously back and forth. The large man didn't bother with words, he just growled. She had managed to load the sling again, but the projectile just bounced harmlessly off him. With two quick and surprisingly balanced strides, he reached Freya. There was nothing she could do as his meaty hands wrapped around her throat.

Freya couldn't breathe. Her air was cut off as Bob, his face full of rage, squeezed the life out of her. She refused to go out like this and kept fighting. She kicked and scratched at him, but Bob took less notice than he would of a fly.

"Stop her!" the croaking voice of Sher came from the other boat.

Bob suddenly dropped Freya into a gasping, weak heap, as he headed back to the other boat. Through spotty vision, Freya could see that Teal was at the boat's engines, tearing them apart and throwing the pieces into the water, including the extra gas tanks they had loaded up for the long journey. Her face and hands were bloody, and she looked like a demonic creature. She was frenzied as she grabbed the last gas can and threw it overboard. Sher, still dazed, could only watch.

Bob stopped her with ease. Coming up behind her, he grabbed her shoulder with one hand, and her head with the other. There was a very audible snap as her neck broke, and then her limp body was tossed into the sea.

Distracted by what was going on with Bob and Teal, Freya didn't notice that Sher had boarded her boat. Not until he punched her in the side of the face that was. Having knocked her over onto her belly, Sher grabbed her arms and pulled them painfully behind her back. She felt her own sling being used to bind her wrists together.

Sher collapsed backward onto the seat behind him. His eyebrow was bleeding where Freya had struck him with the stone.

"What's the damage?" he asked Bob.

"Mortal. This thing ain't going nowhere." Bob kicked the side of the boat.

Sher looked at the gas tanks in the boat Freya had stolen, checking to see how much was left. "I don't think we can get back in this thing." He then looked up at Freya. "Where were you going, huh?"

Sher looked out across the water, while Bob climbed back into the smaller boat. He checked on their third companion who was floating alongside. "He's dead, boss. Sharks will come soon if they're not already here."

"Leave him to them. Is that where you were going?" Sher turned to face Freya, pointing toward the faint light on the horizon. "Is there something there? I bet there is."

"What's the plan, boss?"

"We're going to find out what pretty little Freya thought was so important she'd kill for it." Sher grabbed her and dragged her away from the motor, then threw her down near the front bench. "We can decide her punishment afterward, when my head doesn't hurt so much. You're driving."

"Sure thing." Bob started the engine with one powerful pull on the cord.

Freya lay curled up, trying to slip her hands free, while Sher loomed nearby.

"Do you think someone there can help you?" he leaned in close and hissed. "Trust me on this one, no one can help you. You're mine. I will kill anyone who tries to take you from me. Do you understand that? If we find people over there, I swear I will murder every last one of them for tempting you away."

5
Misha's In Mourning

Misha wiped at his face, trying to clear the tears from his eyes. He hated crying. Having tears running down his face made him angry, and he already had a lot to be angry about.

His best friend was dead. Again. And he was essentially homeless. Again.

Back when the Day happened, Misha had been forced to drive a broken hockey stick through the zombified eye of his best friend and roommate, then had to flee the house to which he never returned. Last night, his best friend and roommate for the past six years, Alec, had been disintegrated by a bomb, which took out their room in the process. Then, as now, the only things Misha had left in the world were the clothes he wore—a wetsuit in this case—and Rifle.

Although that wasn't completely true. He had friends now. All his friends from before the Day were gone, but those he considered as part of his group were still there.

Rifle grunted in his sleep and twitched his paws. Misha shifted forward and patted his side, calming his dreams. It was uncomfortably hot sitting in one of the lifeboats hanging off the side of the Diana, but it was the only place where Misha knew he could get some privacy. He couldn't stay there for long, but right now, he needed to.

"What do you think, *bratishka*?" Misha asked the sleeping dog. "Who do you think would want to bomb the Diana? To hurt so many people?"

Rifle's only response was to awaken partially, sleepily opening his eyes.

Alec hadn't been the only one killed. The fire had claimed a few more, mostly due to smoke inhalation, and others were injured. Still, the bomb had been in Misha's room. Was it just bad luck, or had he or Alec been targeted? Misha couldn't think of anyone who disliked either of them enough to want to kill them. And to use a bomb no less. If Misha had decided to change out of his wetsuit before dinner, he would have been killed, too.

"Who would want us dead?"

Rifle flattened his ears, sensing either Misha's distress or frustration. Maybe both.

"Do you think I should go to work today, Rifle? They said I can take the day off, but I don't know. Of course, I don't know what to do with you all day if I'm in the water."

Fresh tears sprang to Misha's eyes. Rifle scooted closer to him and began licking his face.

"Ugh!" Misha playfully pushed the big dog's head away. He then wrapped his arms around his neck and affectionately rubbed his ears. "We should find something to do other than just sit around. I'm sure you'll have to poop soon enough."

Scrambling over the seats, Misha made his way to the lifeboat's hatch. With its hard shell on top, each lifeboat formed a kind of elongated pod that could apparently hold a hundred and fifty people. Misha could only imagine how uncomfortable cramming that many people in there would be. Luckily, if they ever needed to evacuate, the twenty-six lifeboats and two tender boats, could hold more than enough. Not to mention the hundreds of quick-deploy life rafts that were also stashed on board.

Once out of the boat, Misha made sure Rifle didn't stumble or hurt himself as he exited, then gave the dog's shoulders a good rubbing. The first thing Misha decided to do was to take Rifle to the fertilizer storage. It was the grossest, smelliest part of the ship, but it was the best place for pets, like dogs, to do their business. Weaving through the throng of people along the promenade, Misha made his way toward the back of the ship. Heading down a fancy spiral staircase to the third deck, he entered what used to be the ship's ice rink. Already the smell reached him, and there was still another set of doors to pass through. Rifle became fidgety as always. He didn't like the smell either, but he knew this was the only place he was allowed to relieve himself.

Just past the first doors was a hallway leading port and starboard. Straight-ahead was what used to be a sort of glassed-in media room. The media folks had long since abandoned it for the much smaller room out by the stairs, and it was only used for storage now. Still, Misha could see through the glass walls, past the dead control panels, and into the ice rink area itself. The rink was now a large pile of dirt and dung.

Once it had been decided that the Diana was going to become a long term home for a lot of survivors, a few large helicopters had begun ferrying supplies to the ship, including a lot of fresh dirt. Over time they had collected enough dirt to fill the pools, and all the pots and planters, but they were always worried about rainwater washing away more than they could replace. To prevent this, they brought on even more dirt and filled the ice rink with it. The pile was a hill, rising higher than the seats surrounding it, and even flooding over the lowest row. The ship's ballast had to be carefully calibrated with its addition, which was one of the reasons the rink, with its low, central location, was chosen for the job.

Walking through the second set of doors, Misha shuddered and gagged from the rank odour that washed over him. The dirt pile was full of worms, which broke down the animal faeces, and dead, useless plant matter that was added to it. Misha usually wore a mask, or at least had a shirt to pull up over his nose, but his wet suit was too form fitting to do that. All he could do was clamp his whole hand over the lower half of his face. It didn't help much. The smell of rot was so strong, his eyes watered.

"Hi, Misha!" a man standing next to the pile waved. He was easy to spot in his bright yellow, rubber suit, and filter mask. The man had been born lacking both a sense of smell and taste, making him the perfect candidate to take care of what was commonly referred to as shit mountain. His job was to turn the dirt regularly, and distribute the poop and plant matter evenly.

Misha only waved back in response, not wanting to move his mouth. He was trying to hold his breath as much as possible. Waving Rifle forward, he waited at the top of the seats, and watched as the large German Shepherd made his way down. Once Rifle reached the edge of the pile, he shifted to one side so that the seats hid him. Alec had once told Misha that Rifle could be oddly shy about pooping, and even as a puppy, he would go in the bushes or behind trees. Most of the time, if he was being watched, Rifle would refuse to look at the person, and his expression was similar to shame. The moment he finished, Rifle dashed backed up the steps, his ears flat against his skull. Misha took no time in getting back out to the spiral staircase, where he took a deep breath of the drastically fresher air.

Since he was already there, Misha went to one side where the small media room was buzzing with activity. There weren't many people who worked on the media team, but Tobias was one of them. On the other side of the glass wall, the crew of three was busy, carefully writing the news on sheets of paper that would be posted around the Diana in public areas. The fourth media worker was probably off hanging up the flyers that had been completed. With what had happened last night, a lot of people were waiting for those updates.

Taking a break to stretch, Tobias saw Misha standing outside. He waved, quickly saying something to the other two, and then stepped out of the room.

"Hey, man, what's up?"

"Nothing," Misha shrugged. "I was just in the area and thought I'd stop to see what you were doing. I don't want to bother you."

"No bother at all."

"I don't suppose you know much about what happened last night, do you?"

Tobias shook his head, his shaggy hair flopping across his brow. "Sorry. We know who's died and who's been injured, but outside of them, the only thing we have to report is that it was a bomb, and the best people are looking into it."

"Okay." Misha looked down at his feet. He hadn't expected any more information than that, and he wasn't sure what he would have done with it if there had been more.

"Come with me." Tobias stepped around him and crossed the space containing the spiral stairs. On the other side was an open shop that had sold professionally taken photos of the vacationers on the cruise. It hadn't changed much. Now, instead of selling photos, it merely displayed them. It was full of pictures that people like Tobias had taken after the Day, as well as a few that people had donated from before then. Anne, Tobias's girlfriend, stood behind a desk where she made sure no one stole the pictures. She smiled as the two entered, but kept quiet. Tobias led them toward one of the alcoves along the back wall.

Misha scanned the photos there, not sure what he was looking for. Just as he started to realize that groups of the pictures contained the same people, he spotted Alec. There were a dozen, maybe more, pictures of him. Most were from around the cruise ship over the years, but two were from Riley's family cabin. In the center of them was a battered picture of a woman holding a German Shepherd puppy.

"He didn't tell me he had donated this picture," Misha commented, pointing out the battered one. It was a picture of Alec's long dead sister on the day she brought Rifle home.

Tobias cleared his throat and shuffled awkwardly. "I was wondering if you maybe wanted to keep it. You were closer to him than any of us, seeing as you shared a room. I thought that since everything is gone..."

"No," Misha shook his head, "keep it here."

"If you see any other photos you like, just tell me and you can have them."

"I'm not much of a picture keeper, but thanks." Misha looked over all the other photos again. "Are these all the people who died?"

"Yeah. Anne thought it would be nice to have a sort of memorial wall, since we haven't lost a group this large in a long time."

They were arranged nicely, in circle patterns, with an older photo in the middle whenever possible. Misha focused on one where the center photo was a family shot. The mother was the one in all the surrounding pictures, but no one else from the family photo showed up. They must have all died before reaching the Diana. So many people were dead.

Living on the Diana was sometimes numbing. There were times when Misha forgot about the outside world. He forgot about the people trying to survive back on land, most likely struggling for basic necessities. His world was the boat, and the waters around her. Sometimes an island was in sight, but he never went there, and the only zombies were those under the sea. Then something small would happen, something like these photos, and it would all come rushing back to him. Things weren't well with the world.

"Are you okay?" Tobias asked, maybe noticing some expression on Misha's face, or maybe he was just asking as a matter of course.

"Yeah. I'm fine. I should be going though."

"Well, if you ever need to talk, you know we're all here, right?"

"Of course," Misha frowned at him, slightly annoyed by the question.

"Okay. Will you be joining us for dinner tonight?"

"Probably."

"Cool. I'll see you then." With that, Tobias crossed the space to chat with Anne before going back to work.

Instead of walking away from the pictures right away, Misha pulled one down from the wall and knelt before Rifle.

"Do you know who this is, *bratishka*? Can you recognize photos?"

Rifle sniffed at the photo, and then looked at Misha, unsure of what he was supposed to do with the object.

"It's okay, boy." He patted Rifle's head and returned the picture. "I wonder though if you realize what's happened. I'm sure you'll figure it out soon enough."

Now that Rifle had relieved himself, Misha figured he should probably go and check with his maintenance crew, to make sure they truly didn't need him underwater. Although the explosion and fire had been contained to the decks higher up, all the maintenance teams were very concerned about what the shockwave might have done to the structural integrity in other places, especially those below the waterline.

While crossing the ship again, Misha passed by a group of sailors from the Russian submarine, including Captain Bronislav. They were having a heated discussion about something in Russian, but the moment they spotted Misha, they fell silent. As far as Misha knew, he was the only person outside the former submarine's crew who could understand Russian. They seemed to detest him for it, although he couldn't fathom why. Most likely it was because they were hiding something, but what could they be hiding for nearly six years? Misha didn't bother acknowledging them as he walked past. Once he had learned what happened to Russia from them—nothing good—he chose to avoid the crew whenever possible.

Next, he came across Hanna. She was sitting alone and weeping. Misha stopped, not sure what he should do. He knew that she and Alec had a bit of a flirtatious thing going on. Just when he decided to move on, Rifle left his side to go see Hanna, forcing him to go over to her as well.

The dog's snuffling at her arms caused her to raise her head, quickly wiping the tears out of her eyes and off her face.

"Hello, Rifle." She smiled briefly as she pet him.

"Are you okay?" Misha asked, even though she clearly wasn't. Not completely.

"I'm sorry, I'm a mess." Hanna got to her feet, attempting to straighten herself out.

"It's fine. What are you doing out here? Most people prefer to grieve in their rooms."

Hanna gave him a funny look, as if he had caught her doing something wrong. Or maybe he had said something wrong.

"It came over me out here is all," she mumbled, returning to straightening out her clothes which were already straightened.

"It happens. Umm, there's a memorial for those who were killed in the photo display area, if you want to go look at the pictures there."

Hanna suddenly drew in a shuddering breath, a fresh set of tears blazing trails halfway down her face before she thought to brush them away. Misha didn't know what to do. He couldn't even deal well with his own grief, let alone someone else's.

"I think I'll go look. Thank you, Misha." With her head down, Hanna turned and headed for the photo viewing area.

Misha waited a moment, unsure why, and then continued on his own path, Rifle at his side once more.

"Why did you have to draw me into that?" he whispered to the dog.

Rifle looked up at him briefly, acknowledging that he had been spoken to, but obviously having no answer to give.

Finally getting down to the first deck, Misha was once again distracted from his journey to the maintenance office. First, Robin ran past him, completely distraught. She was gone before he could ask what was happening, but it was obviously caused by something going on in the medical centre. Not wanting to get in the way, he stood off to one side, trying to peer through the door. All he could see was a group of people attempting to subdue a scrawny man who Misha didn't recognize. They were tying his wrists behind his back and strapping a mask over his mouth and nose. The man must be infected, as that was the usual procedure. Misha realized the off-shippers must have returned from the foreign cruise ship and brought the man with them, not knowing that he was infected.

Misha's vision was blocked as Mathias stepped out of the medical centre, leading Jon who was bound the same way as the unknown man.

"Christ," Misha muttered, realizing that Jon must be infected as well. Misha liked Jon. He didn't know him very well, but what he did know made him a good guy. It was hard not to like a guy whose actions were almost always driven by a desire to help other people.

"Out of the way, Misha," Mathias ordered, having gone into his cold-soldier personality. It was not a good personality, but it allowed him to detach himself and get things done.

"What option did he choose?" Misha asked Mathias, knowing that Jon couldn't answer, given the way the mask was secured. Everyone who was infected got one of three options: exile to the nearest landmass, death before change by either your own hand or another's, or death after change, which resulted in being locked up.

"Death after change," Mathias told him. "Now give us some distance please."

Misha wasn't really in the way, but infected people were handled very seriously, and no one was supposed to be within reach if they could help it. He stepped further aside and watched as Mathias led Jon toward their holding cell. It was hard to believe. Jon didn't seem like the kind of guy to come back to the Diana if he knew he was infected, but then, maybe he didn't know. Still, to choose option three? Almost no one chose option three. Staying on board like that put a lot of people at risk, not to mention the added grief that came from seeing a loved one turned into a zombie. Misha had always decided he'd take a bullet before changing if he were infected, which was what most people chose. Not only was the idea of being a zombie awful, but having to go through the sickness and fever that came first did not sound ideal. Those who weren't ready to face death, almost always chose exile. It had been a long time since someone had chosen to stay on board in confinement.

The stranger was carried out of the medical centre next. He was unconscious and heavily strapped down to a plastic medical board. Based on what Misha had seen, the man was too frantic to have made a choice. They would put him in the holding cell with Jon until he had calmed down enough to make a decision.

Remembering Robin running past him, Misha went to find her. Even though Misha had so recently proven his inadequacy at handling grief, he wanted to make sure she wasn't going to do something stupid or drastic. Robin was more of a cat person than a dog person, but she treated all animals with love, which immediately put her in Misha's good books. He found her on the fourth deck, outside, leaning on the rail and looking out over the ocean.

"Robin?" He stepped up beside her.

Robin was taking slow, deep breaths. "He was acting so normally. Like nothing was wrong."

"Maybe he didn't know he was infected." Misha quickly picked up the thread of her thoughts.

Robin made a kind of strangled noise that Misha couldn't quite understand.

"What was that?"

"April didn't know either," she managed to get out.

It took Misha a moment, but then he remembered that April was the original owner of Jon's sword. She had gotten infected by zombie saliva during a rainstorm, and it had taken her awhile to realize that she was sick.

"That sword is fucking cursed!" Robin screamed at the sea. "And I gave it to him!"

"Hey now, it's not your fault, and the sword had nothing to do with it. Jon's been carrying that thing around for years, and I'll bet you it has saved his life dozens of times."

Robin ran her hands through her hair, tugging at it slightly, messing up the neat bun she had it in. Her emotions were fighting within her body, making her feel like she was going to be torn apart. Misha knew because he had felt that himself, and he knew there was nothing he could do to help her.

"Hey, I was thinking about working today, but I can't let Rifle wander around on his own. Do you think you could watch him for me?"

Robin looked at Misha, surprised by his request and the sudden change of topic. "Yeah. Sure, I guess."

"He's already pooped, so I don't think you'll need to take him to shit mountain."

"Okay. Yeah. Yeah, I can look after him for you." It seemed the request had calmed her down. Or at least, distracted her temporarily.

"Maybe you could take him to see Splatter." Splatter was Robin's cat, who got along surprisingly well with the big dog.

Robin nodded. Based on her expression, her emotions were slowly building back up again.

"Okay. I'll see you later then. Rifle, stay." Misha slipped away before she started crying. He wasn't sure he had stopped her from doing something stupid—he didn't even know if those kinds of thoughts crossed her mind—but he might have. He couldn't see her shirking her duty to take care of Rifle now that she had agreed to it, no matter what the reason. Even if it had been spur of the moment, Misha thought the idea of leaving Rifle with her was one of his better thoughts. The German Shepherd's silent presence always seemed to have a positive effect on people.

Determined to get to the maintenance office, Misha went back downstairs. Today seemed to be a day of endless grief, and as he walked, Misha sensed that it was far from over.

***

In the water, Misha stared at the section of the Diana's hull in front of him. He wasn't thinking about it at all, just staring at the expanse, his mind lost elsewhere.

"Misha," the voice of Holmes, his dive master, buzzed in his ear.

Misha snapped out of his thoughts and looked around. Holmes was floating nearby with Misha's dive partner, Sarah, but the rest of the group had moved on to the next section. Both sets of eyes had looks of concern in them.

"I don't think you're okay, Misha," Holmes told him, "exit the water."

Only the dive master had a mask that allowed him to speak while underwater, so Misha couldn't argue against him. Even if he could, he wasn't sure he would. He hadn't been paying nearly enough attention to things since he had joined the dive. Not only could he miss an important stress fracture on the Diana's bulkhead, but if a zombie floated up from the deep... He didn't want to think about any more death.

Nodding his agreement, Misha gestured to the pair that he would swim back to the surface on his own. Normally, Sarah would accompany him, but they let him go on his own this time. It just went to show how worried they were about the vessel. A cruise ship like this was normally dry-docked every five years for routine inspection and repair. It had been seven years since the Diana last exited the water. Despite the fact that she was being looked over a lot more often, inspecting things underwater was different. And there were certain mechanical bits they couldn't look at without taking things apart, and certain things couldn't be taken apart in the sea.

As he headed for the surface, Misha heard a peculiar buzzing under the water. It sounded like a tender boat moving, but no one would have started one up without sending word to all the divers.

Stopping his ascent just in case, Misha focused on the sound. It was much higher pitched than the tender boat motors, which had Misha thinking it was a much smaller engine. Looking around, he spotted the hull of a tiny boat cutting through the water toward the Diana. It wasn't any boat that Misha recognized.

His first thought was pirates, except they usually came in swarms, not alone like this. As the boat slowed down and made its way to the docked tender boat that the divers had used to get into the water, Misha swam toward it, breaching the surface far enough away to go unnoticed, but close enough to know what was happening.

The boat was a small aluminium, which was strange to see so far out at sea. In it were two black men and a black woman. The woman was badly beaten and bound, and one of the men was a huge mound of muscle; neither of these things instilled good feelings. On the tender boat, a man on the ship's defence crew blocked their way aboard, while another on the upper level pointed his rifle down at them. Someone else was surely getting one of the five ship leaders, perhaps even all of them.

"Please, let us on board," the small man asked of the guard.

"You have to wait until someone from command arrives," the guard replied. "You can talk to him."

The man looked like he wanted to say more, but stayed quiet, perhaps realizing that the stern-faced guard wouldn't listen to him no matter what he said.

After nearly ten minutes had passed, in which the smaller man became more and more anxious, Lieutenant Boyle, the leader of all civilian classes, arrived with the two submarine captains, Karsten and Bronislav. It was unusual for both of the sub captains to be on board the Diana at the same time, but after the explosion last night, it was essential.

"I'm Lieutenant Boyle, how can I help you?" he asked the people in the small boat.

"We were attacked by pirates," the smaller man told him, gesturing to a fresh injury above his eye. "We caught this one while fleeing," he waved at the woman, "but the rest took over everything. All our people are being held captive."

Boyle looked at the woman, who was shaking her head. The smaller man noticed.

"Liar! She refuses to speak. Maybe she can't because my companion strangled her a little too much while subduing her, but I assure you she was with the pirates."

"What is it you want?" Boyle asked.

The man seemed taken aback, as if he thought Boyle should already know. "Some shelter for now. We've been travelling for a very long time, searching for anyone. We'd also like some help if you could spare it. My friend and I want to drive the pirates out of our home and save our people."

"What are your names?"

"I am Sher. My friend here is Bob, and I do not know the pirate's name."

From where Misha was watching, he knew Lieutenant Boyle had seen him, but the woman also appeared to have noticed him. She was the only one on the little boat completely taking in her surroundings.

"We can take you aboard for some time, but you'd have to be examined and stay in quarantine for a few days. As for helping you with the pirates, there's nothing we can do for you."

The man, Sher, was crestfallen.

"We're a community here, and we take care of our own. We don't go off and fight battles that don't affect us."

Suddenly, the woman shot to her feet and leapt over the side of the small boat, nearly tipping it over.

"Stop her!" Sher shouted, wheeling around.

"Calm down," Boyle told him, "there's no harm she can cause in the water, other than to herself." He looked up at Misha then.

Taking the hint, Misha started swimming toward the woman. She was actually trying to swim to Misha already, but with her arms bound behind her back, she was having a tough time of it.

"It's all right, I got you." Misha grabbed the woman, using his flippers to keep both of them afloat. She struggled for a brief moment, but quickly relaxed, letting Misha do most of the work.

"Why don't you come aboard so we can examine you?" Boyle told the two men.

"Yeah. Okay," Sher replied, but he was looking at Misha and the woman with an unreadable expression on his face.

"We'll have to check you for weapons, you understand?"

A smile creased Sher's face just before he turned back to Boyle. "Of course." Taking Boyle's hand, he stepped up onto the higher tender boat. The man with him, Bob, climbed up on his own. That man looked like he couldn't be disarmed without surgery.

Once they had disappeared into the Diana, Misha swam toward the tender boat. The little aluminium was in the way, and so a guard helped Misha lift the woman up into it. While she sat on one of the bench seats, Misha struggled to pull himself into the boat without flipping it, his underwater gear hindering him. When he finally did get up, he freed himself from the tank, headgear, and flippers.

The two submarine captains had remained behind, and sat with Misha and the woman once they got up into the tender boat.

"What's your name?" Captain Karsten of the German submarine asked her.

The woman remained silent. She was clearly paying attention to them, but was also taking in her surroundings.

"Are you a pirate as they say?" Captain Bronislav asked next.

To this, the woman shook her head.

"Then why won't you tell us your name?" Bronislav continued.

Again, the woman's only response was to look at him. Her eyes were cold.

"Can you not speak because those men choked you?" Karsten realized.

The woman bobbed her head in a way that was neither yes nor no, and made a show of rolling her eyes. She was trying to communicate an answer that was complicated.

"You can't speak but not because those men strangled you." Misha figured it out before anyone else.

Bronislav gave him a look that suggested he should be keeping his mouth shut. If it were up to Captain Bronislav, Misha probably would have been tossed back into the water.

"We'll get you something to write with then," Karsten continued, ignoring the silent interaction between Misha and the other captain. "We'll have to test you for infection though, before we untie you."

The woman nodded.

"I'll go find a doctor who can bring a test kit here," Misha volunteered.

"Thank you," Karsten nodded for him to go and do just that.

Granted Misha was curious about the woman, he was glad nevertheless to leave the area. The air was virtually humming with intensity between her and the two captains, especially Captain Bronislav. Ducking back inside the Diana, he set out to find Robin. She was probably still very emotional and likely still upset, but he thought the opportunity to focus on work—especially when the 'patient' had no connection to her—would help. Besides, the other doctors were probably still busy with everything else that was going on, including the two men who had shown up.

When he didn't find her out on the fourth deck where he had left her, or in the medical centre, Misha headed for the theatre on the off chance that she was visiting Quin. Quincy Beharry had been the lead singer for the famous rock band Gathers Moss before the Day happened. He and Robin had survived the ordeal together, but all his bandmates had been lost in the process. Now, he was listed as Robin's guardian—she had been only sixteen on the Day—and worked with an artist and a b-list actor to organize entertainment aboard the ship. Every two weeks people were borrowed from their usual duties to help put on different bi-weekly shows, which usually consisted of singing, dancing, instrument playing, or acting out a play. So far, Misha had been lucky enough to avoid recruitment.

Entering the large theatre by its ground floor entrance, Misha scanned the seats for Robin. Up on stage, a piece of plywood with a forest painted on it, was being repainted as a brick wall, while their resident actor sat on the far side giving tips to a young teenager. It looked like the next show was going to be a play of some sort.

Robin didn't appear to be in any of the seats, but when a ball came rolling out from behind stage, with Rifle chasing after it,

Misha knew she was there. Climbing up onto the stage, he found her sitting on a box off to one side, just beyond the curtains. She wasn't crying anymore, and didn't look as upset as she had previously. Rifle was about to give her the ball, but upon seeing Misha, he brought the ball to him instead.

"Misha, you're off early," Robin commented as he approached her. As he got closer, he could see more of the area behind the stage where Quin was putting together a cheap car prop, his black fedora pushed up and balancing precariously on the back of his head.

"We had some strangers show up in a small boat. Two men and a woman," Misha filled her in. "The men are claiming the woman is a pirate, but I don't believe them. Out of all the pirates we've seen, only a very small number have been women, and none of them were wearing dresses."

Quin had stopped working and walked over to stand beside Robin.

"We separated the men from the woman, who's clearly been beaten up. She claims she can't speak, although we don't know why. If you're up to it, we need someone to do a blood draw, and maybe look over her injuries."

"You don't have to go if you don't want to," Quin told Robin, placing a protective hand on her shoulder.

"It's okay," Robin smiled up at him, "I should keep working. Besides, it sounds important and I don't want to pull anyone away who could be helping Rose."

"If it overwhelms you, you come back here, okay?" Quin told her, as Robin got to her feet.

"Of course. I expect to see that car done by the time I'm here next."

"She's so demanding," Quin commented to Misha.

Misha just shrugged, which caused Quin to laugh for whatever reason. It was obvious the rocker's faculties weren't all there, probably burned away from drug use, but he was always sober now and did his job with pride.

Robin and Misha headed back up an aisle between the seats, Rifle trailing behind them. The dog still held the ball in his mouth, looking from one to the other, hoping one of them might take the ball and throw it for him.

"What's the play this time?" Misha asked as they made their way through the ship.

"Grease."

"Again? Haven't they done that one already?"

"Not in over four years."

"Wait, weren't you in it the first time?"

"Yeah."

"You're not in it again are you?"

"No. Whole new cast."

"Good. Your singing was atrocious."

Robin smacked his arm but laughed. Her face fell sombre again a short time afterward, probably remembering that Jon had been in the play with her, but Misha hoped that laughing meant she was doing better already. Mourning periods were always extremely heavy since the Day, but they tended to end quickly, as life needed to continue. Those who wallowed in despair too long almost never came back from it.

After a quick stop at the medical centre so that Robin could grab some supplies, they exited onto the tender boat. The woman was still sitting with her arms tied behind her back, the two captains across from her. They had probably asked her more yes or no questions while Misha was gone, but he had no idea the kinds of things they would have asked.

"Captain Karsten, Captain Bronislav," Robin acknowledged the two men with a nod which they returned. She then turned to the woman. "I'm going to take a sample of your blood, all right?"

The woman nodded her consent. Robin rolled up the woman's sleeve and drew a small bit of blood. Being very careful not to have any contact with it, she made a slide and viewed the blood under a little hand-held microscope.

"She's not infected." Robin was trying to be professional, but Misha picked up on the relief in her voice.

"You can untie her then," Karsten told her.

Robin undid the knot, releasing the tight strip of leather that had bound the woman's wrists. The woman winced as she rubbed them, but then held out her hand, wanting the strip of leather. Seeing no harm in it, Robin handed it to her.

"Do you speak sign language?" Robin asked, gesturing with her hands. She had taught herself to sign many years ago, as a way to communicate without her blind father knowing.

The woman shook her head.

"Hmm. Oh, I have just the thing." Robin reached into one of the deep pockets of her cargo pants and pulled out a small notebook and pen. "Here, you can write your answers."

The woman gratefully took the items and made quick use of them. The first thing she wrote for them was that her name was Freya. The second thing she wrote was that they couldn't trust Sher and Bob.

"Why don't you write out your story while Robin checks you over for injury?" Bronislav suggested.

Freya started writing furiously while Robin started her cursory examination. Misha had no idea what she found, but there were a few observations that he made on his own. Like the condition of her feet. On the Day, when Misha had escaped the city, he hadn't had any shoes. By nightfall, his feet felt and looked like hamburger meat. Looking at Freya's feet, at all the old scars there, it was obvious she hadn't worn any shoes for a lot longer than that. She also flinched a lot, not liking to be touched, but dealing with it, and although she kept writing, she would pause regularly to check on everyone's position. Whoever this woman really was, Misha had already formed two thoughts about her: something bad had happened to her, and she was a fighter.

When Robin was done, she walked over to the two captains and gave them her report. She spoke quickly, not letting Freya hear what she said, which meant that Misha also couldn't hear what she said.

Freya tapped the end of her pen on the metal bench seat to draw everyone's attention back to her. She held out her notebook to indicate that she had finished writing. The captains took the book from her, taking turns reading the several pages she had filled. Once finished, the two rose from their seats, and walked to the back of the tender boat where they could speak in private.

"What do you think about her?" Misha whispered, once Robin was standing at his side again.

"I think someone has done something awful to her. Likely those men she came here with. Have you noticed that she eyes the door to the Diana a lot?"

"I have. It could also be that she's interested in the ship."

"I don't think so. I think she's afraid of the men in the medical centre. I'd bet my day's meals on it." She spoke as a woman who would know.

"Rifle, go say hello." Misha patted the dog's side; he had been sitting quietly beside Misha the entire time, understanding that something important was going on. "Be gentle." The interaction between the shepherd and the woman might tell Misha something about her.

Rifle trotted up to Freya and sniffed at her from a few feet away, his nostrils wiggling while the ball was still clamped between his jaws. Freya tucked her feet up onto the bench. She didn't look afraid of Rifle, but she was wary of the dog.

"Come here, Rifle." Misha patted his leg. Rifle responded instantly, returning to his side.

The captains finished their talk and carried the notebook over to Misha. Whatever they were about to say, it must have been important, because Bronislav's dislike for Misha had left his eyes.

"You're to bring this to Lieutenant Boyle," Karsten told him in a low voice. "Get him to read everything that the woman has written. Tell him that we have no reason not to believe her. Everything we've seen so far backs up her story."

Misha nodded and ran off to perform his duty. In spite of the fact that he was curious and wanted to read the notebook, he didn't. He went straight to the medical centre where Boyle was watching over the examinations of the two men. Sher had a pleasant smile on his face and was attempting to make small talk with a disinterested doctor. After Misha passed on the message to Boyle, he waited around to see what would happen. By the time Boyle finished reading the notebook, Robin had joined him again.

"Go wait in the hall, you two," Boyle told them.

They were quick to obey.

Minutes later, several guards entered the medical centre. Not long after that, Sher and Bob were being escorted back out to their little aluminium boat. Misha followed behind the group, and watched from the upper deck, as the woman had already been led elsewhere.

"You'll regret this," Sher was saying as the guards watched him and Bob get back into their boat. "You're making a grave mistake listening to that woman."

"Just go back to where you came from," Boyle told him, shutting the tender boat's door. "We'll deal with her."

"Oh, I'll go. And then I'll come back, and there won't be just the two of us." Sher's threat was cold, while his eyes glinted with malice. "You chose the wrong woman to listen to. That viper will be your end. We'll be back. We won't forget this."

Bob started the little boat's engine. As they drove away, Sher kept his dark eyes on them, and his posture rigid.

A chill ran down Misha's spine. He didn't know why, but he believed Sher. He was afraid of the man.

6
Hope's At School

"Hope, that shirt is too big for you. Why don't you let one of the older kids have it?"

"No!" Hope had found only one pretty shirt in the pile that Ms. Lauren had let her look through. She didn't care if they said it was too big, she wanted it. It was a splotchy pink that her teacher had called tie-dyed.

Ms. Lauren sighed. Hope made sure not to change her angry expression, understanding on some level that the adult would either give up soon, or force her to give the shirt to a bigger kid and make her have a timeout.

"All right," Ms. Lauren threw her hands up, "you win this one, kid. Although if you keep talking to your elders like that, I'll have to put you in timeout for a week."

Hope held the shirt even tighter, not completely trusting Ms. Lauren to let her keep it, until the teacher turned to help the other kids going through the pile.

"It's an okay shirt, I guess," Dakota commented.

Hope looked over at the ten-year-old, with her oversized cowboy hat balanced on the back of her head. She had told Hope that a superhero had given her the hat, but Hope didn't believe her. Superheroes weren't real, or else they would have stopped the monsters the adults talked about. Hope wasn't old enough yet to learn much about the monsters, only that they were dangerous and you had to stay away from them.

"You can't have it either," Hope told Dakota, reaffirming her grip on the shirt.

"I don't need any new clothes," the older girl shrugged, "and I guess you look good in pink. Although if you ask me, purple is more your colour."

"Purple?"

"Yeah. Like that shirt there." Dakota pointed to a shirt sitting on the edge of the pile.

Hope eyed Dakota, wondering if she was trying to trick her. She didn't think she was. Dakota was one of the nicer older kids. Hope liked her, and didn't want her to move to the big-kid class next year.

Walking over to the pile, Hope looked at the purple shirt without touching it. It wasn't a bad shirt, but it just wasn't as pretty as the pink one. The purple shirt had a rainbow on the front, but the image was all cracked and peeling. Hope looked up and saw Becky eyeing the purple shirt. Before Becky could even think about taking it, Hope yanked it free of the pile and held it aloft.

"Ms. Lauren, I'm also taking this shirt!" she cried.

Her teacher looked over from the far side of the pile and nodded. "Indoor voice, please. And okay, that one should fit you better than the pink one."

"I'm still keeping the pink one," Hope told her, but Ms. Lauren wasn't listening anymore as she helped a boy do up the buttons on a new shirt he had put on.

With her two new shirts, Hope walked over to her seat in the corner, where she shared a table with Peter and Adam.

"I got new shirts!" she told them triumphantly, waving one in front of each of them. "And you didn't!"

"I got some before coming to school," Peter spoke quietly, and was ignored by the others.

"That's only because all your stuff got wrecked," Adam responded to Hope and stuck his tongue out at her.

Hope stuck out her own tongue back at him. Adam thought he was so much smarter, but he wasn't even a whole year older than Hope, even though he was six right now while she was still five. Just because he was the first kid born on the Diana, he thought he was special. Hope thought he was just as dumb as all the other boys. Except for Peter. Peter was her best friend, so he wasn't dumb. Well, most of the time he wasn't dumb.

Once the class had settled down, Ms. Lauren handed out the day's lessons. Hope and Adam got math handouts, which didn't please Hope one bit. Adam was better at math than she was. Glancing over at Peter's paper, Hope saw that he had an English lesson. Because Peter was going to be seven next week, he got different lessons.

"Peter," Hope whispered to him.

He looked up from his paper at her.

"If you help me with my math, I'll help you with your English." Hope was good at English lessons.

"Okay."

"That's cheating," Adam hissed at them both.

"Uh un," Hope shook her head, "we're not doing tests, so it's not cheating. Ms. Lauren says we should always ask when we need help."

"She means that we should ask her." Adam was pouting.

"She didn't say that. You're just mad because I asked Peter before you did."

"I'm not mad," Adam said, although the way he balled up his fist suggested otherwise.

They fell silent as Ms. Lauren began talking at the front of the class. She was teaching the eight-year-olds something about countries. Once Ms. Lauren was well into her lesson and unlikely to notice them, Hope and Peter helped each other with their work, which basically consisted of doing it for one another.

Later, during morning recess, Hope saw Ms. Abby enter the room, with Claire behind her. Claire looked really upset, and when Ms. Lauren saw them, she hurried over. Wondering what was going on, Hope drifted closer from where she was playing near the climbing equipment.

The adults were speaking in a hushed whisper that Hope couldn't quite hear, but they were talking very fast. Claire stood silently, her hands clasped tightly together while she watched the kids in the room. She spotted Hope looking at them, so Hope stopped trying to move closer.

Suddenly, Ms. Abby walked farther into the room. She headed straight for Peter, who stopped chasing Becky in their game of dragon once he saw her.

"Peter, we have to go." Ms. Abby held up her hands and helped Peter down off the slide, ending the game of dragon before he could catch anyone.

"Where are we going?" he asked, but she didn't answer.

"Class," Ms. Abby spoke loudly to all the kids, "Ms. Lauren and I have to step away for a little while. Ms. Ellen is going to keep an eye on you all until I get back."

All the kids started whispering to one another, wondering what was going on. Ms. Ellen taught only the big kids class. She soon appeared in the doorway, and Ms. Abby and Ms. Lauren left, taking Peter and Claire with them.

The rest of morning recess was quiet. No one knew what kind of teacher Ms. Ellen was, they were used to only Ms. Lauren and Ms. Abby, who worked between both classes.

"Okay, recess is over. Could you all take your seats, please?" Ms. Ellen announced.

Hope sat down with Adam. Their desk felt empty without Peter there. Ms. Ellen told them all to continue with their morning lessons.

"Where do you think they went?" Hope whispered to Adam.

"I don't know," he shrugged, "but I don't think they went anywhere good."

"Claire looked sad."

"Yeah."

"What if Peter gets sad?"

"What?"

"What if Peter gets sad? We should be there to make him feel better. Like when Becky's dog died, we were all there to make her feel better."

"We're in class."

Ms. Ellen walked past, ending their conversation. Hope tried to do her work, but she kept reading the same math problem over and over, not understanding it. She wished Peter were there to help her. If Ms. Abby or Ms. Lauren were there, she might have put up her hand and asked for help, but she didn't want to ask Ms. Ellen.

When it was close to lunchtime, a big kid from the other class came in.

"Ms. Ellen? Tommy's nose is bleeding again," she said.

Ms. Ellen sighed. "All right. I'll be right there. Children, I want you to continue working until I get back. We'll have lunch when I return." She left the room, closing the door behind her.

As soon as Ms. Ellen was gone, everyone stopped working and started talking. Hope had an idea, and got up from her desk to go share it with Becky. Wondering what she was doing, Adam followed after her.

"We should go see Peter," Hope told Becky.

"Why?" she asked.

"In case he's sad. We should cheer him up."

"But we don't know where he is."

"I'm sure we could find him."

"But we're in class."

"We'll be quick. Ms. Ellen won't notice we're gone, and we'll be back before lunchtime is over."

Becky looked at the door, thinking it over.

"He was there to cheer you up when you were sad about Shoes," Hope told her.

"That's different."

"No it's not."

"I want to go," Adam added. "These lessons are boring."

"Come on, Becky."

"Okay. But if we get in trouble, I'm not talking to you ever again." Becky got up from her seat. The three of them headed toward the door, but they were stopped by Dakota.

"I heard you talking," she said to them. "Ms. Ellen will notice you're gone, and you'll get into trouble."

"Ms. Ellen didn't do a roll call. She doesn't know who's here," Hope told her.

"But what if she does?" Dakota continued to block their way to the exit.

"We'll tell her we really needed to go to the bathroom and couldn't wait." Hope had done that before when she didn't like the lesson. She had told Ms. Abby she needed to go, and then just played with the taps in the bathroom for a while instead of learning.

"Fine, but I'm coming with you. Someone has to look after you little kids." Dakota turned around to open the door.

"We're not little," Adam objected.

Dakota ignored him as she stuck her head outside of the classroom. "The coast is clear," she whispered back at them.

Hope, Adam, and Becky, followed Dakota out of class.

***

"Where are we going?" Adam asked for what must have been the hundredth time.

"To the place where we had Shoes' funeral," Hope told him again. She was going to hit him if he asked again.

"Yeah, but where's that?" he added.

"On the littler boat attached to this one," Becky said.

"Then why are we in here?" Adam asked.

Currently, they were at the very back of the ship, behind the basketball court. The three of them were huddled inside a small building-like structure that was used to store garden supplies and basketballs. Based on the pictures on the walls, it used to be related to some sport that Hope didn't know the name of; something that involved hitting little white balls with metal sticks.

"Because Dakota is figuring out how to get there." Becky rolled her eyes. "We don't know where the littler boat is parked today."

"Oh. How will she figure out where it is?"

"By looking over the sides of the Diana, duh." Hope was annoyed by all his questions.

"But-"

"Shh, here she comes." Becky had been watching out of a little window.

Dakota opened the door to the building and stepped inside, quickly closing it behind her.

"Okay, it's docked at the front of the ship on the port side," she told them.

"What's port?" Adam asked.

"That side of the ship." Dakota pointed to the left.

"Then why didn't you just say it was that side?"

"Because that side is called port," Dakota informed him. "Now, we'll have to stick close together. If anyone asks us what we're doing out of class, you let me do all the talking, okay?"

The three younger kids all nodded. With Dakota in the lead, they exited the little building and climbed down the stairs that were hidden amongst the plants behind it. The next level down stuck out even further, and was filled with even more potted plants taking in the sun.

This started Hope, Becky, and Adam bickering about whether they needed sunscreen or not.

"Stop arguing," Dakota turned on them all. "You won't need sunscreen because you won't be in the sun a lot." She led them to the side of the ship that she had called port once they were silent.

They walked along the side until they came to a doorway just before the pool area. Hope didn't know why the adults always called it the pool area, or the pool deck; there weren't any pools there. It should be called the tree area, or the tree deck, because it was the only place they were growing big trees. The only pool was a small one near the doctor's office, where Hope had been learning how to swim.

"Adults, hide," Dakota hissed.

The group scrunched together and hid behind a pillar. Adam was practically pushing Hope over. She tried to push him back, but that would have knocked him out from behind the pillar, so he held onto her. The two adults that had been walking toward them passed by without noticing the kids.

"Come on." Dakota took Becky's hand and pulled her inside.

Hope stomped on Adam's foot before following after them.

"Ow!"

"Shut up!" Hope whispered at him, placing her hand over his mouth. There were other adults nearby, taking care of the plants.

"You stepped on my foot," Adam complained.

"Don't be a baby." Hope jogged a bit until she caught up to Becky and Dakota. Adam was right behind her.

Avoiding all other adults, they made their way to a staircase and began climbing down. There wasn't anywhere to hide on the stairs if any adults came across them, but they didn't see any until the eighth deck, where three of them were climbing up.

"Hide," Dakota told them again.

Adam, Becky, and Dakota all ran toward the bedrooms, but Hope went the other way. She ran toward the middle of the ship and ended up hiding in the upper section of the library. A woman who was looking at a book pile didn't notice Hope slip past her. Hope went to the back of the space and squeezed between two piles there. From her hiding place, she could see down the opening in the centre of the library to the lower floor. Looking through it, she saw a man standing near the front of the library, but he didn't look very interested in the books. Then she heard the voices.

Inching closer to the railing, Hope tried to see who was speaking. Whoever it was, must have been underneath her, because she couldn't see him or who he was talking to. Hope wanted to listen to what the men were saying, but she couldn't understand them; they were talking in a different language. Hope sometimes heard other languages being spoken, but not very often. Although she didn't know what the men were saying, she knew they were talking about secrets; why else would they be whispering so quickly?

The woman at the front of the library left, and soon afterward, the other three kids came in looking for Hope. Not wanting to be heard by the adults below, Hope crawled out of her hiding space and waved them over.

"They're talking about secrets," Hope whispered to Dakota, cupping her hands around her mouth.

"They aren't talking English," Dakota whispered back.

"I know."

"Then there's no point in listening. Come on, I thought we were looking for Peter?"

Hope nodded, and the group left the library. As they started climbing down the stairs again, Hope kept thinking about the secret-tellers. She thought she should tell her dad about them, but didn't know how to do that without admitting that she had left school.

7
Hanna's Wandering The Ship

Hanna had gone to look at the pictures as Misha had suggested, but she didn't know why. They just made her start crying again as she knew they would. All the pictures did, not just the photos of Alec. A lot of people had been killed by the bomb.

"Hanna?"

Hanna was startled by the voice directly behind her. She spun on her heels, wiping her hands across her eyes in the same instant in an attempt to clear them. Behind her stood Benny, an Englishman who had travelled across the ocean on the German submarine with Hanna. He was a nice man, and had taught her a lot of English on the way over. Many of the people on the sub had learned English from him, as it was a wonderful distraction from the cramped quarters inside, and the cold outside. Just about everyone who made the voyage would be perfectly happy never to see a submarine again.

"Hello, Benny." Hanna looked down at their feet, hiding her red eyes.

"You probably shouldn't be looking at these photos," Benny told her.

"I know. It is just... I knew a lot of these people. I cleaned rooms for them."

"I know." Benny gently took her arm and led her away from the photo area. "Which is why I know it'll just upset you to be here. Why don't you come to the pub with me and we'll get a drink?"

"I am not sure I want a drink."

"Whether you want one or not, you certainly seem like you could use one. Come on." Still holding her arm, Benny brought Hanna up the curving flight of stairs to the fifth deck.

Together they walked along the promenade until they reached the pub. It was much more crowded than usual. After what had happened, several non-essential workers were skipping their duties, and those who were not on shift, either couldn't sleep, or really needed the drink that Benny was recommending.

Benny was popular among the drinking crowd, and easily threaded his way through it to get to the bar, pulling Hanna along behind him. Not a single stool was empty, so Benny stood, with Hanna right behind him, still looking down to hide her red eyes. Much as it was unlikely that she was the only one crying in this crowd, she'd rather it not be known. She had been embarrassed enough when she broke down earlier and Misha had come across her.

The portly bartender spotted Benny quickly and waddled over. The bartender was one of the few overweight people onboard the Diana. There used to be a lot more, but with everyone kept on a carefully balanced diet, which catered to his or her body type and the amount of exercise they got, just about everyone was kept at a healthy weight. It was the opinion of most people that the bartender kept his weight on by frequently sampling his own product.

"What'll it be today, Benny?" the bartender asked, ignoring the next man over, who had been waiting longer.

"Two shots of whatever's your best today, if you please."

"You got it." He disappeared into the back where the stills were kept. Nearly everyone had to trade something for booze, whether it was a physical item or a service. Junk food was often a form of payment, which might also explain the bartender's weight. Benny didn't pay though, because he was too well liked by men like the bartender. He had an air about him that made people listen to him. Hanna often thought he used to be a schoolteacher, but she actually had no idea what his profession was before the zombies came.

The bartender returned with two shot glasses, each filled with a clear liquid and handed them both to Benny, who thanked the man then turned around and gave one of the glasses to Hanna.

"Cheers," he said, holding out his glass.

"*Prost.*" Hanna clinked her glass against his.

"To life." Benny threw back his head and swiftly swallowed the alcohol.

Hanna hesitated a moment before quickly downing her drink. She swallowed it fast, trying to keep the burn in her stomach instead of her mouth and throat, but was only partially successful. For the bartender's best, it was awful.

"Bet you feel better now!" Benny laughed. "Puts a real fire in you!"

Hanna nodded, even though she didn't really feel any better. Still, she could now blame her moist eyes on the strong stuff.

"Let's go mingle." Benny hooked his arm through Hanna's and led her over to a group of people.

While Benny joined in on the conversation quickly, Hanna stood quietly to one side. There were so many discussions going on at once, and she was having trouble following just one of them. Besides, she didn't want to risk saying the wrong thing.

Once Benny stopped trying to include Hanna, she managed to slip away. The booze actually did help her feel better, or at least detached enough not to care for the moment.

Making her way out of the crowd, she wandered aimlessly about the ship. She didn't have a particular direction in mind, and just placed one foot in front of the other. She could be working if she wanted to be, it was her usual shift, but she didn't have the heart for it. The forward rooms on the seventh deck were her duty to clean for anyone who wanted her service. A large number of those rooms were gone now, and a few of their occupants she'd never see again.

Shaking the thoughts out of her head, she walked outside for some fresh air. The German submarine was floating not too far off the side. Hanna hated the submarine. It had saved her life, but she hated it. Back in Germany, she had been starved and terrified during the outbreak. Her hiding place had changed several times, but at one particular instance, she was holed up in the Deutsches Auswanderer Haus—the German Emigration Center—of all places, in Bremerhaven, along the Weser. While investigating the nearby zoo, she had spotted the U-boat cruising up the river toward the sea. Several people were sitting outside on the deck silently, holding up large signs inviting survivors to come join them. Hanna was so distraught and alone at the time that getting to the submarine became her only thought. Attacked while searching for a small boat, she had wound up having to swim for her life, while sailors gunned down the zombies behind her. She had thought that life aboard the submarine would be better, but it wasn't. The U-boat was overloaded and undersupplied. The food wasn't very good and strictly rationed. There wasn't enough space anywhere, and a schedule was issued for those who had to sit outside on the deck and when. The air inside the sub was foul smelling and stale, while the air outside the sub was cold and damp.

Everyone cheered when the Diana's radio transmission was picked up. It was a unanimous decision to cross the Atlantic to reach her. The Russian sub picked up the same transmission and found them the next day. The Russians were strange. They didn't speak much to the German sub survivors, and refused to let anyone aboard. At least they were willing to share their food supplies, but not much else.

In spite of having a new goal in mind, they found that the ocean voyage was no picnic. They couldn't go top speed without risking the people on deck falling overboard, so it was a much longer journey than expected. Twice, they were forced to dive because of rough weather. If you weren't one of the submarine officers, you literally had no space to move once everyone was jammed in below. During those two dives, every space that could hold a human without hindering the U-boat's operation was filled. Hanna had spent the first dive sitting on Benny's lap, hunched over on a bunk, and wedged between two other people, while another man stood directly in front of her. The second time she had to stand in the captain's eating nook, helping the children that were standing on the table and benches keep their balance.

Hanna had learned to hate the sea during that trip. She still did.

While lost in her memories, Hanna's feet continued to carry her about the ship. When she finally paid attention to her surroundings again, she discovered she was just outside the safety barrier that had been erected to keep people from entering the blast site. Looking over the short barrier, Hanna could see the blackened walls, floor, and ceiling, as well as the light streaming in through the hole in the side of the Diana. She could also smell an ashy scent.

Hanna's immediate reaction was a feeling of nausea. The alcohol in her stomach turned foul on her, and it was all she could do to keep it down. Dashing to the nearest public washroom, she vomited into the first toilet she came to. The entirety of her stomach's contents was emptied into the porcelain bowl. Even after her belly was empty, she dry heaved a few more times, creating a dribble of spit.

Flushing her body's discharge away, she then got up and rinsed out her mouth at the sink. Looking up, she stared at herself in the mirror. Hanna didn't have a high opinion of herself, but today it was especially low. Nothing she saw in the mirror, from her hair to her waist, was good in any way. She thought of herself as an ugly creature, although almost everyone else would disagree. But they didn't see inside her, like she could. They didn't know what she had done.

They didn't know that she had planted the bomb.

***

After hiding in the bathroom for over an hour, Hanna knew she had to leave it. There was a meeting she had to attend, and if she didn't, the others would become concerned and ask questions.

Dragging her feet, Hanna made her way to the Lily Lounge. Passing between two large statues of green tinted Foo Dogs, she entered the large square room that had been left alone as a place for recreational purposes. This was not where the meeting was, as the location always changed, but a man here would tell her where to go. Threading her way around the tables and stacked boxes of board games and puzzles, she headed for the small stage at the front of the room. There, an old man was putting together a large, complex puzzle of Van Gogh's, The Starry Night.

Without saying a word, Hanna stood next to him. She knew that the man would recognize her without the code words. She waited patiently while he found the location for the puzzle piece he held in his hand. Unbeknownst to either of them, Hanna was standing in the exact spot that was a mirror image of the other ship where Jon had had to cut off Rose's hand.

"You're on the basketball court today," the old man eventually rasped in a quiet whisper.

Before Hanna turned away, she picked up a piece of the puzzle and placed it where it needed to go. She never knew whether doing that annoyed the man or not, but every time she was there, she couldn't help herself. Maybe that was why she was a maid; she couldn't help putting things where they belonged.

Without another word, Hanna left the Lily Lounge. She travelled to the rear of the ship, and as she headed upstairs, she swore she saw some children near the library. When she looked again, they were gone. Had they even been there in the first place? Maybe it was some sort of school trip. Hanna rarely had any interaction with the kids on board the Diana. She cleaned up the rooms of a few when asked, but she didn't have any reason to talk to them, and didn't know what they did all day. On days she was being honest with herself, she preferred it that way. Thinking about children growing up in the middle of this horrible mess only depressed her.

It hadn't taken her long to reach the basketball court, but she held back before stepping out into the sun and into view. She could just make out a corner of the meshed-in court, and saw some men she knew throwing a ball around. When she had first been drawn into the group—she still wasn't sure how that had happened—she had thought about reporting the secret meetings. However, she couldn't see anything illegal about them, and she agreed with the group's tenets. They probably didn't need to meet in secret, but ever since the issue with the preacher and his followers a few years back, they thought it prudent.

Pulling herself together, Hanna stepped out into the sun. She didn't enter the actual basketball court, but stood next to the side where she could watch the men with the ball. Most of the people gathering at this meeting would stay outside the court, while only a few would appear to be playing. The idea was that if anyone else showed up, it would just look like a friendly game of basketball. Hanna didn't think the cover would hold if it were needed, especially when looking at all the grim faces that were gathered.

As more people arrived, no one spoke to Hanna, but a few shook her hand in greeting. She knew most of these people by name, as she had been attending these meetings for quite some time now. It wouldn't be a surprise if there were new faces today, considering what had happened last night. What Hanna had made happen.

Once everyone had arrived, about two dozen men and women in total, the meeting began.

"I'm sure you all understand why we're having a meeting today," their leader, Lenny, began. He was one of the men throwing a ball around, but spoke just loudly enough, and clearly enough that everyone gathered could hear him. "I'd like us all to take a moment of silence to respect those who passed last night."

The entire group, ball players included, hung their heads and stood silently for exactly one minute. Hanna did everything she could to think about something else. The fact that Benny, smelling of booze, had managed to find his way next to her actually helped. She just focused on the unpleasant smell that clung to his clothes.

"Now," Lenny continued, "we don't know who was responsible for the bombing, but we're all feeling the effects."

What Lenny said was true, about them not knowing, but for some reason, Hanna felt eyes on her.

"We always knew something like this could happen. We will not let anyone place the blame on us. We must stand strong at this time, and try to use it to assist our efforts. Don't let anyone bully you. I know some of you are wondering, and yes, you'll probably be questioned about it by the authorities. I already have been, in fact, and they seemed to believe me when I said I knew nothing about it. Because I was telling the truth. Please follow my example if you are also questioned. Tell the truth. Don't be afraid, even if you were doing something embarrassing at the time." Lenny took the time to look each person in the eye. A few people were unconsciously nodding in agreement. "I know what happened is tragic. There were casualties on board the Diana. I saw several of you doing what you could to help put out the fire last night—thank you. It's good to see the community pulling together. The seas are dangerous, we've been telling people that all along, and the only reason we've been able to keep going like we have, is because of the community. There's something else however, something we only learned about recently. Benny, do you care to tell everyone?"

Benny stood up straight and glanced at the people around him. Due to his likeability, he was their greatest resource for learning about what was actually happening around the ship.

"There are two things that happened this morning, actually. Firstly, I'm sure you're all aware of the foreign ship in our midst."

Nearly everyone glanced over to where the other cruise ship could be seen floating at anchor.

"I spoke to one of the off-shippers who had gone on board with the advance team, and it isn't good. Apparently, the thing is a floating morgue, packed full of zombies. In fact, a bad injury has been sustained by one of the team members who stayed there overnight, while another has tested positive for infection. Already, there are rumours going around that the ship is cursed."

"Do you know if the off-shippers are going back to it?" someone in the group, whom Hanna couldn't see, asked.

"No one knows yet. Everyone is a little too busy dealing with the explosion right now to think about it," Benny told him.

"What's the gas situation like?" Lenny asked him.

"Last I heard, we still have enough to get to the dry docks in Texas, and we have more than enough to get to one of the larger islands."

The dry docks in Texas had been the group's goal for well over a year now. Everyone in the gathering was sick of living on the sea; they hadn't been on dry land since they boarded the Diana. Sure, they could just have a tender boat drop them off on some island somewhere, but that wasn't a solution. The group knew they were a lot less likely to survive without the bulk of people aboard the cruise ship. They needed the farmers, and the soldiers, and the hunters. They also felt that even those people who weren't part of their assemblage needed to step onto dry land. The group believed that even though no one would admit it, a life on the sea wasn't right. There were children on board who had never stepped foot on land and others who couldn't remember it. People like Hanna would never truly go home, but land was a lot more like home than the ocean could ever be. Not to mention they could grow better food, the animals wouldn't get sick so often, and the thought of someone getting the flu wouldn't be as terrifying as a zombie getting on board.

Only recently had the group been really pushing to go back to land. The fact was that the Diana couldn't float forever. A cruise ship like this was normally dry-docked once every five years for inspection and repairs, and it had been at least seven since her last time. Sure, they had people in the water every day, looking over her hull and performing any needed maintenance, but it wasn't the same. That couldn't last indefinitely. Texas had dry docks of a large enough size for the Diana, and the group thought that once people were on land again, they wouldn't want to leave. Most of the zombies should be rotted down so much that they wouldn't be too much of a threat, and they could find a spot where the radiation levels were manageable or non-existent. It was time to rebuild the world.

"So, we don't need the off-shippers to gather fuel from the other boat."

"Not if we convince the captains to dry-dock in Texas, no."

Lenny threw the basketball when it was passed to him, getting a perfect swish. "I'll bring up our concerns with them again. Maybe they'll listen this time, especially now that there's a hole in our side that can't be fixed with simple spot welding and duct tape. What's the second thing that happened this morning?"

"Strangers showed up in a small boat. There were two men with a bound woman between them. From what I heard, they claimed she was a pirate, but no one believed them. We've kept the woman on board, but the men were sent away. From what I could gather, the men swore some sort of vengeance upon us."

"Do we know how serious the threat is?" Lenny sounded mildly concerned. No one liked the idea of fighting off pirates again.

"I don't know," Benny shrugged. "Most of what I heard is grapevine rumours, and they're still checking out the woman."

"Keep your ears to the ground. That goes for everyone here. If you learn anything about these strangers, please find me at once. We may be able to use their presence to assist us in our goal. Is that all, Benny?"

"That's all."

"Right. Does anyone else have any news?"

No one spoke up.

"All right then. I'd like to meet tomorrow if we can; same time, and find out the location in the usual way."

Everyone agreed to meet again, then broke off into smaller groups and pairs to leave the area. Hanna hung around a little longer, hoping to get a chance to speak to Lenny alone. Lenny noticed, and walked with her to the area where the mini-putt used to be, which now held only plants. They went into a little gazebo that was still standing and sat on the benches inside. Once they were sitting, Hanna didn't know what she wanted to talk about. Maybe she just wanted his presence.

"How are you feeling?" Lenny asked her.

"I am not really sure. Scared. Angry. Sick."

"Because of the bombing?"

"Yes."

"That's understandable. I think the whole group is scared, and you knew the victims better than any of us did. What are you angry at?"

"Myself. The group. You. The Russians. The children. The captains. The ocean. Everything it seems."

Lenny nodded, thinking that she was angry about not knowing who the bomber was and not being able to do anything about it.

The pair sat quietly for a moment, listening to the breeze rustling the plants.

"Are you thinking about hurting yourself?" Lenny eventually asked.

"No. Maybe. I am not sure. I am worried about being questioned."

"There's nothing to worry about."

"Were they angry?"

"What do you mean?"

"When they questioned you, were they angry? Did they shout?"

"No. They were very calm about it, very controlled."

"I see. Is there something I can do for the group? Something that will keep me busy? My usual workload has been drastically reduced, and it is not helping."

"I understand. There's nothing I can think of outside of the usual. Soon, they're going to need people to clean up the fire damage. You could volunteer for that, if you think you could handle it."

"I doubt it. I got sick just being near there."

Another moment of silence passed between the two.

"I wish I could just forget what happened," Hanna suddenly blurted out, her voice cracking as fresh tears sprang from her eyes.

Lenny shifted from his bench to hers and placed his arm around her shoulders. "There, there. I understand."

"Do you? Can you?" The anger Hanna had told Lenny about welled up in her chest. "Alec is dead!"

"I know you had feelings for him."

Hanna got to her feet and paced around the gazebo.

"There was nothing you could do. I know this is going to sound harsh, but you'll get over him. We all have to keep moving forward. We wouldn't be here if we weren't capable of that."

Hanna stopped and looked down at him.

"I understand it's hard. Since the zombies came, nothing's really been easy, but we have to face these challenges head on."

"He was not supposed to be there."

"The bomb wasn't supposed to be there."

Hanna sat down on the bench opposite Lenny and stared intently at the floor between their feet. Why had she put it in Alec's room? Why hadn't she put it in some other room? Her own, even? Lenny had said she had feelings for Alec, but did she? Did she care about him the way she told herself she did, or was it just some mind trick to appear normal?

"Look, I should probably go talk to the captains. Will you be okay alone?" Lenny asked as he got to his feet.

"I will be fine." Hanna's voice sounded far off as her mind turned inward to think.

"You'll be fine when they question you, and I think you should consider talking to Brittany, the grief councillor."

"If you say so."

"I do say so. As for the questioning, they might push a little harder on you, since you're one of the few people who could access those rooms other than their owners, but I doubt they'll push hard. Just stick to the truth and you'll be fine."

Hanna didn't bother answering.

"Okay. I'll see you tomorrow then. If anything comes up, please find me."

Lenny continued to stand at the entrance to the gazebo, waiting for a response that never came. When he finally turned and left, Hanna didn't even notice. She had turned completely in on herself, shutting down all external sensory input. One way or another, she was going to make herself better.

***

"Please state your name for our records," the man in the military gear told Hanna after turning on a tape recorder.

"Hanna Kaufmann."

Hanna was sitting in a bedroom near the bridge of the ship. The room had been set up as a private meeting space for all the captains; however, it was now being used as an interrogation room. She sat at a card table on a foldout chair, while a man who introduced himself as Private Winchester sat across from her. Commander Crichton and Captain Sigvard were sitting at the far end of the room behind him.

"And what is your duty aboard the Diana?"

"I clean rooms."

"Which rooms specifically?"

"All forward rooms on the seventh deck."

"This includes the room belonging to Alec McGregor and Misha Jovovich."

"Yes." It wasn't a question but Hanna answered it anyway.

"Can you state where you were when the explosion occurred?"

"I was reading a book in my room, which is on the other side of the ship."

"Can anyone verify that?"

"No, my room is my own. I was alone."

"What were you doing before the explosion went off? Still reading?"

"No," Hanna shook her head, "I was doing some cleaning. We cleaners do not have a set schedule. We clean the rooms when the occupants tell us it is okay."

"Did you clean Alec and Misha's room?"

"No. I saw them on the stairs when they were going to a... funeral, that is the word. I asked if they would like their room cleaned, but they said no."

"So you didn't go into their room at all yesterday?"

"I did not."

"How do you feel about Alec and Misha?"

"I like them. Misha is quiet and I do not know him very well, but he is tidy. He does not leave big messes just because I can clean them up, and he is always polite. Alec is much more... what is the word I want... open? I like to think we were friends."

Private Winchester jotted down a few notes.

Hanna wasn't at all frightened by the interview. She wasn't scared of being caught. In fact, she didn't think there was anything she could be caught for. While sitting in the gazebo, Hanna had managed to perform a sort of self-hypnosis. As far as she was concerned, she hadn't put the bomb in Alec's closet. It was an extreme form of denial, something that had occurred to several others on the ship during the zombie outbreak. People like Hanna that wanted to forget something so badly, managed to convince themselves it never happened.

"Do you have much contact with the Russians?"

"I just told you I like Misha."

"I mean the Russian sailors."

"Not particularly. I clean a room where two of them sleep. Why?"

"What about the men, Leonard Jackson, or Benjamin Willis?"

"You mean Lenny and Benny. Benny came across the ocean with me on the German submarine. We are friends, he taught me

English. We shared a drink earlier today. I do not know Lenny as well, but he seems nice. He cares about people."

"And do you know a man named Bill Castor?"

"It sounds familiar, but I cannot place a face to the name."

"And Sher?"

"I have never heard of someone with that name before."

"Have you ever lost your key card?"

"No."

"Lent it to someone else?"

"I did when I had a cold last year and needed someone to cover for me while I was in quarantine."

"But not recently?"

"No, not recently."

Private Winchester wrote something else in his notebook and handed it back to Commander Crichton. He read the note, but had no external reaction to it.

"That's all the questions we have for now, Ms. Kaufmann. Could you wait outside for a moment while we discuss things?"

"Of course." Hanna rose from her seat and stepped out of the room. Another folding chair was set up in the hallway and she sat down on it. An armed guard stood close by.

Hanna knew the interview had gone poorly. She had said the words that she thought needed to be said, but she couldn't get the emotion behind them. She barely felt any emotions at all. In an attempt to right herself, she crushed all her feelings down into a place where she could ignore them. She bottled them up tightly. Apparently, that was the wrong thing to do.

While waiting for whatever came next, Hanna looked over at the guard. He held an assault rifle in his hand, but she wondered if he would actually shoot her. If she attacked, he no doubt would, but what if she ran? And if he did shoot, did she really care?

Hanna decided that no, she didn't care.

Like a greyhound whose gate had just opened, she suddenly bolted to her feet and down the hallway. The guard began shouting at her, running after her, and threatening to shoot, but he never did. Hanna was used to moving down the narrow hallways while carrying a load of cleaning supplies, and found it easy to dodge around the people and other items that blocked them. She easily outpaced the guard, and began running down the stairs. Without a plan, Hanna was running on instinct. She had no idea where she intended to go.

After running for what seemed like a very long time, Hanna realized she had lost the guard a while ago. She was alone on another deck of the ship, near the rear, but still in an area with living quarters. Ducking into a supplies closet, she crunched herself down between a rack of linens and a mop and bucket.

What had she done? Why had she run away like that? With the disconnection she had set up between herself and her emotions, all she could feel was confusion.

An announcement came over the ship's PA system, which wasn't used often. It was muffled and hard to hear in the closet, but Hanna could guess that it was about her. They would be looking for her. If she had been wrong about the interview and came across as not guilty, she was certainly being branded as guilty now.

Why she ran didn't matter. What she had done didn't matter. All that mattered to Hanna now, was what came next. She accepted that she was branded as a traitor. So, what did traitors do when they were found out? Anything they had to, to survive.

Hanna would do whatever she had to.

II
Current

Private Winchester followed Commander Crichton and Captain Sigvard to the bridge of the ship. It was obvious now that the girl, Hanna Kaufmann, was in some way connected to the bomb that had gone off. Winchester and Crichton had agreed that something was off during the interview, but that it hadn't been enough to accuse her. The fact that she ran, was.

"At least, we have somewhere to start," Crichton muttered as he stood to one side of the bridge, "and I think we can safely cross off an underground following of Bill Castor as the culprits." Bill had been a religious zealot who had tried to take over the ship in the early days. He and his followers had been banished to Ellis Island back when the Diana used to travel around more northern waters.

Captain Sigvard composed a speech quickly, and spoke over the Diana's broadcast system. He didn't say why they were looking for Hanna, just that if anyone knew her whereabouts, would they please inform a ship defender. As soon as he was done speaking, Crichton lifted his walkie-talkie to his lips, and called a meeting for all the heads of the ship defence watches. Winchester could tell that he would like to gather them right away, but knew that several were sleeping, or handling something else of importance. Outside of emergencies, instantly gathering any sized group of people was difficult.

"So, I think we can assume that Hanna planted the bomb." Sigvard walked over to where Crichton and Winchester were standing.

"But why?" Crichton was always coming back to that question. "She doesn't look like the kind of girl who would want to blow us up, and everyone we've talked to about her agrees. Hell, Misha even seems to think that she and Alec had a thing going. Why would she want him dead?"

"Maybe she thought he wasn't there."

"Then why plant it in his room?" Crichton sighed. "We still haven't been able to find out what the bomb was made of. There are so many tools we're lacking to properly investigate this matter. Private Winchester?"

Winchester stood up straighter as he was acknowledged.

"Go inform the other captains and Lieutenant Boyle about what has occurred."

"Yes, sir." Winchester was always one of the go-betweens for the ship's heads. The use of their walkie-talkies to communicate was discouraged because it was far too easy for someone to listen in. Men like Winchester were used to run communications between them all the time.

Just before Winchester opened the door to leave the bridge, there came a knock. He looked back at Crichton and Sigvard; they nodded for him to open it. Winchester placed his hand on his holstered pistol, not taking any chances since the bombing, and then opened the door.

"It's Lenny, sirs." Winchester quickly checked behind the man, making sure he was alone.

"Lenny, we have no time for this again," Crichton barked. "We are well aware of the concerns of you and the people you talk to. Unless you can tell me something I don't already know, leave."

"Sorry, Commander," Lenny shuffled his feet, "it's just that I heard over the PA that you were looking for Hanna."

"Do you know where she is?" Sigvard asked. He was always the nicest of the heads, and the most willing to take people at their word.

"Sorry, but I don't. I saw her earlier today, however. I don't know why you're looking for her, but I'm concerned. She told me that she was very worried, frightened even, but she wasn't very clear about what was causing it. I thought it was because of the explosion, but maybe I'm wrong."

"Are you sure it's nothing you said or did?" Crichton knew that Hanna was part of Lenny's group, which made all of them suspects.

"I don't think so. If it is, she didn't tell me. She seemed lost. I told her to talk to Brittany."

Winchester couldn't tell if Lenny was lying or not. He must have known that they were suspicious of him.

"Thank you for telling us," Sigvard said to him honestly. "We're very busy right now, however."

"Right. Well, just thought you should know." Lenny stepped back from the door. "People are thinking we should go back to land now more than ever. We're worried about this happening again."

"We know, Lenny." Sigvard waved him off as Winchester closed the door again.

"Did he just threaten us?" Crichton's eyes narrowed, thinking about Lenny's final words.

"Maybe, maybe not. Perhaps he's just trying to turn an unfortunate event to his advantage." Sigvard walked over to where they kept a collection of paper maps. "Come. We should consider the option of landing anyway. We still haven't gotten a full report on the Diana's hull integrity, and it might turn out that we don't have a choice."

After waiting a few minutes to make sure Lenny was gone, Winchester left the bridge. He travelled through the ship at a light jog, stopping to ask a few people if they had recently seen either Captain Karsten or Bronislav, or Lieutenant Boyle.

Lieutenant Boyle turned out to be the easiest to find. He was hanging around the medical centre, waiting on word about the injured off-shipper's condition. Winchester delivered the news about Hanna to him in hushed tones. Boyle nodded wearily.

"Thank you, Winchester. After you've found the submarine captains, I have some news for you to deliver back to Crichton and Sigvard."

Boyle then went on to tell Winchester about the infection in Jon and the man they had brought aboard from the other cruise ship. He also gave him an update on the mute woman who had shown up with the two men. She was clean of infection, but under watch. They had also lost track of the boat on which the two men had left. Winchester agreed to deliver the news, and ran off to find the submarine captains.

While searching, Winchester ran into another message runner who was off-duty. Considering all that was going on, Winchester didn't feel guilty pulling him back on duty. Repeating Boyle's news to him, he got the other man to deliver it to the bridge. At least he got that off his plate.

He found Captain Karsten on the fourth deck gazing out at his submarine. The man looked just as tired as Lieutenant Boyle had, and Winchester couldn't blame him. Just having knowledge of all these things was bad enough, but these men actually had to decide what to do with it. Winchester delivered his message as quickly and concisely as possible. Karsten acknowledged that he understood, and then sent Winchester back on his way. The captain clearly wanted a few minutes alone.

The Russian captain took the longest to find. After searching nearly half the ship, Winchester eventually located him near the library. He was panting as he delivered the news to Captain Bronislav. The man's face was almost always set in a stony expression, but after working with him for so long, Winchester noted a subtle change in it. He thought that maybe the man was relieved. Maybe he was. The bombing concerned him just as much as it did everyone else, but unlike everyone else, he and his Russian sailors were suspects. Everyone in command knew there was something the Russians wouldn't talk about, but no matter what they tried, they couldn't drag the information out of them. It was always a concern, but after five and a half years with them, it had grown less important.

Finally done, Winchester thought it was time to take a short break. This thought was quickly abolished when he spotted four young children scurrying down the steps ahead of him. All the kids should still be in class at this time. He would have heard if there was a class trip.

Doubling back to the staircase on the other side, Winchester hurried down the steps until he knew he was ahead of the kids. Hiding around a corner, he then stepped out in front of the children just as they reached the deck.

"What do we have here?" he boomed as the kids squawked and back peddled at his sudden appearance. "Oh, no you don't."

One little girl had tried to get away, but Winchester grabbed her shirt, picked her up, and placed her with the others. Three of them looked shamefully down at their feet, while the fourth, the eldest wearing a cowboy hat, looked him right in the eye.

"Dakota, I should have guessed you'd be the leader of this great escape." Winchester knew Dakota from back before the Diana. They had both been residents at a motel for a few weeks after the Day. The hat had been a permanent fixture on her head ever since they found the RV in which she and the other kids from her day-care had been hiding.

"We're looking for Peter," she told Winchester matter-of-factly.

"Are you now? And where has Peter gone?" Winchester knew Peter as well. He had been a little baby at the motel, and would be in the same class as these kids.

"Not sure. We were going to check where Shoes' funeral was."

"Is Peter alone?"

"No. He's probably with his family."

With the news that Winchester had gotten from Boyle, he put things together. Lauren was a good friend of his, so he knew her family well. If Jon had gotten a positive infection result, the whole family would be going to see him, which included young Peter. This also might explain how the kids escaped, if the school area was understaffed with Abby and Lauren absent.

"If he's with his family, why are you looking for him?"

"We think he's sad, and want to cheer him up."

"A noble thought, but I think if he was sad, his family would know, wouldn't they? Surely they would have brought you along if they thought you could help."

Even Dakota fell silent, not entirely sure what to say.

"Come on. Let's get you all back to class." He turned the kids around and got them climbing the stairs.

"Please don't tell my parents," one of the little girls said.

"Well, you're in luck, since I don't know who your parents are." Although Winchester knew most of the kids from the motel, there were a lot more he didn't know. "I am going to tell Lauren though, about your little escapade."

The little girl suddenly stopped on a landing and looked at Winchester. She stared especially long at his walkie-talkie.

"Are you a ship defender?" she asked out of the blue.

"Not really. I run messages for the ship's leaders. Come on. Keep climbing."

The little girl didn't move but turned to Dakota instead. "Is he a good man?"

"He's the best," Dakota told her.

"Can I tell him a secret?"

"Yeah."

"I have a secret to tell you," the little girl looked at Winchester again.

Wondering what it might be, Winchester knelt down before her.

"I saw a secret meeting," she whispered in his ear.

"You did? What was it about?"

"I don't know. They were talking a funny language. I thought I should tell my dad, but I don't want to get in trouble for being out of class. Can you tell him you heard it?"

"Sure. How do you know the meeting was a secret one?"

"They were hiding in the back of the library and whispering."

"And you don't know what language they were talking? Did you see them?"

"I don't know the language. And I didn't see them. I heard them though, I swear I did." The girl suddenly turned to the other kids. "You heard them, too."

"We did," Dakota confirmed.

"Do any of you know what language they were speaking?"

All the kids shook their heads.

"It was gruff sounding," Dakota added.

"All right. Did it sound like this?" Winchester cleared his throat and spoke a few words in German.

"Maybe," Dakota shrugged.

"How about this." Winchester then said a few things in Russian. Having worked so closely with the captains, he had picked up a few words and recognized the general cadence of the language. He couldn't understand it, but he had learned to mimic the sounds.

"That sounds more like it," the little girl nodded. The other three kids agreed that Russian sounded more like what they had heard than German.

So, it seemed the Russians were having a secret meeting in the library. Winchester sighed. Maybe the Russians were just talking about how they were going to deal with the suspicion placed upon them, but maybe it was something more sinister. There was a possibility that the relief Winchester thought he saw on Captain Bronislav's face was actually due to them looking in the wrong direction.

"Thank you for telling me." Winchester got back up on his feet. "I'll be sure to inform the right people. Right now, we need to get you back to class. Come on, let's go."

They had started to climb the stairs again when a voice came over Winchester's walkie-talkie.

"Private Winchester, please come to the bridge *immediately*."

It sounded very important. Winchester wouldn't have time to drop off the kids at class.

"Change of plans. You're all going to follow me right now." Hopefully, he could get the kids back to class after finding out what was happening. In fact, it might be good to have them with him when he told the leaders about the secret meeting they had overheard. Maybe they would have other questions for the kids.

The children were confused and a little excited as they followed Winchester toward the bridge. They were no longer dragging their feet, and he could hear them whispering excitedly behind him. When they reached the room in which the interrogations were being held, Winchester stuck his head inside to make sure it was empty. Other than a few dogs that probably belonged to the other men who were called up, there was no one in there.

"Okay, you're all going to wait in here until I get back. Understood?"

"Understood." Dakota saluted, which prompted the other kids to salute as well, as if Winchester were some important person.

"All right. Stay put." Once the kids were inside, he shut the door. There was no way to lock it from the outside, so he was just going to have to trust them when they said they wouldn't go anywhere.

Winchester turned and entered the bridge. All the leaders had already gathered there, as well as all the on duty runners, a few off-duty ones, and several high-ranking members of both the ship's defence crew and off-shippers. Several people were out of breath, having clearly run to the bridge.

Winchester didn't need to ask what was happening. Everyone was gathered around the radio listening to a broadcast that was coming over the airwaves. The voice spoke with a heavy Jamaican accent. It was a man, and he was clearly broadcasting to a specific group of people. It took Winchester a moment to figure out what he was saying, but his blood chilled when he did. The man was calling his people to war, and the enemy was the Diana.

"I think that's Sher, the man we refused to let on board," Boyle informed the room.

"Where's the broadcast coming from?" Captain Sigvard asked his crew.

The radio operator didn't bother to answer with words, and simply raised his hand and pointed out the window. He was pointing directly at the other cruise ship.

No one said a word, all of them coming to the same conclusion. Sher and his man must have boarded the ship after being sent away, and managed to get to the bridge. Normally, they would have been tracked after their departure and it would have been known that they had boarded the other ship, but with everything else going on, it had fallen by the wayside.

Winchester didn't know what he should be more concerned by: the enemy summoning troops, the Russians' secret meeting, the missing girl who may have planted the bomb, or the infection being carried by Jon and the strange man. No matter which way he looked at it, they were in for a rough time.

Section 2:
Found

8
Mathias Can't Rest

Mathias had been off-duty at the time, but he heard the call to go to the bridge and obeyed it. He listened to the single-voiced radio broadcast along with all the others. Eventually, a second voice replied; Sher's men had heard him and would be leaving immediately. Then the broadcast stopped. These men sounded more organized than the usual rabble of pirates they had run into previously. Mathias didn't think it would be as easy to repel them, especially considering the fact that they wanted everyone dead, and not just wanting the supplies they had on board. Sher's men could very well have rocket launchers and intend to sink the Diana.

"We have not been having an easy twenty-four hours," Captain Sigvard broke the silence on the bridge.

Mathias looked at the clock on the wall and realized that although it hadn't been twenty-four hours since the bomb had gone off, it had nearly been that long since he last slept. He was exhausted.

"What are our options?" Captain Sigvard asked next.

"The way I see it, there are two real choices: run or fight," Commander Crichton answered him.

"What are our chances if we fight?" Captain Karsten wondered. "Do we have anything that can take down something like the other cruise ship?"

"Remember that cruise ship is already full of zombies," Lieutenant Boyle reminded everyone. "Those men took a risk boarding it. One of them could be dead already, and the other might be dying."

"We can't assume that," Captain Bronislav spoke up. "They may have enough manpower and weaponry to clear out those zombies easily. In fact, we should be considering the zombies as weapons. They could find a way to move them from that ship to ours."

"That would be a raiding party like no other," Boyle sighed.

"Our weapon count has only dropped since our last meeting. I'm not sure we even have enough bullets to fully load every gun." Crichton looked to James for a proper count. Everyone in that room knew not to speak unless one of the heads requested it of them.

"If we arm all shifts of the ship defence crew and the off-shippers with our best weapons, they can have at least two full magazines each. Some of them can even have three," James told them.

"So few?" Karsten looked crestfallen.

Mathias stepped forward and waited for acknowledgement before speaking. "All ship defenders have only been carrying half loaded magazines for some time, sirs. We don't need bullets often, and have been rationing them for the off-shippers. Unfortunately, they haven't been able to scavenge as often as they used to, and it seems that when they do, they end up spending more bullets than they find." He stepped back into the group once more.

"What about the civilians?" Bronislav asked. "Many of them are carrying around guns. Can we not take the bullets from them?"

"I doubt it," Boyle shook his head. "None of them have more than what their gun can carry. We took all their extra ammo when we had that weeklong standoff with the American pirates last year. If we took the last of their ammo, they would feel defenceless, and we'd end up with a whole other set of problems on our hands. No, I think it's for the best that we let the general population continue to be as armed as they always have been."

"Do we at least have enough close combat weapons for everyone?" Karsten asked.

"Yes," Crichton nodded, clearly relieved to have some relatively good news. "We have more than enough for everyone on this ship to carry something. In fact, I think we should start handing out close combat weapons to the civilians who've only been carrying firearms up until this point. As a precaution."

"They're going to wonder why," Bronislav told him. "Are we sure we want to tell the population what's happening? It may cause a panic."

"This is a large enough threat that everyone should be informed. We can ask for volunteers to take on lookout and patrol shifts, and that way, if something happens, no one will be surprised," Boyle suggested.

"For now, this information doesn't leave this room." Crichton looked sternly at everyone present.

"Is there a way we can take out the other cruise ship before this Sher's reinforcements arrive?" Karsten asked.

"If there is, it won't be easy," Boyle shook his head.

"Maybe we could make a bomb like the one that injured us. Get the off-shippers to sneak it over and place it somewhere below the waterline," Bronislav suggested.

"It's risky, but doable," Crichton agreed.

"We wouldn't have this issue if I still had my torpedoes," Karsten muttered.

"Captain Karsten, we all agreed, you included, that everyone would feel safer if you got rid of both the torpedoes and missiles on your submarine. The reactor on it has people nervous enough," Boyle reminded him.

"Why are we even discussing this?" Captain Sigvard suddenly spoke up again after being quiet during the entire talk of war.

"What do you suggest?" Crichton asked him.

"That we take the other option. That we run," Sigvard said to everyone.

"And where would we run to?" Karsten wondered.

"Texas," Sigvard said with a casual shrug. "Look, I know we haven't been to land in years, but maybe it's finally time. I mean, we have to go back eventually, don't we? The Diana won't float forever, and I'd rather bring her in before she starts taking on water. All the zombies on land have probably rotted to dried-out husks that can barely move by now, and we have a few radiation detectors with which we can check out the area before we dock. I'll admit that I don't know much about nuclear radiation, but it's been at least six years since the plants and storage facilities have gone off. I'm sure we could find somewhere safe. Besides, didn't we hear over the radio that the facilities in the south were setting off controlled detonations to bury the nuclear material safely, once they knew they were going to be overrun?"

"What if this band of Jamaicans follows us? We don't have enough fuel to get there if we go at top speed. We'll have to go somewhat slowly, and they may be able to catch up. What then?" Bronislav asked him.

"Well, then we can fight them with our backs to the shore. If the ship goes down, I'd rather it go down in sight of land, and not where I know there are thousands of walking corpses beneath us. I say we vote on it."

The vote was held quickly. Boyle and Sigvard voted for running to Texas, while Karsten and Bronislav voted to stay and fight. Crichton was the holdout.

"You have to vote," Bronislav narrowed his eyes at Crichton.

"I think this is a decision for more than just us five men. We can't put it to a ship-wide vote, that would take too long, but I hereby give my vote to the rest of the men and women in this room. Let them decide." Crichton looked at the group assembled, all of whom suddenly stood a lot more rigidly. It had been a long time since they had to make a choice this important, or one that affected so many people.

Mathias already knew his choice.

"Those for staying and fighting, raise your hands."

While Crichton counted, Mathias refused to look around. He didn't want to know how many were making that choice, or who they were.

"Those who think we should make for land, raise your hands."

Mathias lifted his arm high. He had a little girl to think about. If he could get her away from the fighting, he would.

When Crichton finished counting, he shared a look with the other ship leaders. He then addressed the entire bridge. "It looks like we're heading to Texas."

***

Mathias left the bridge, feeling like a weight had been lifted off him, but if the vote had gone the other way, it probably would have remained there. He went into the room near the bridge to pick up Milly.

"Milly?" Looking around the room, he didn't see the three-legged husky anywhere. "Milly, where are you?"

"Excuse me." Private Winchester stepped around him and began frantically to search the room.

"What's wrong?" Mathias asked as the other dogs were picked up by their owners.

"I ran into some little kids who snuck out of school. I was just about to take them back when I got the call to the bridge. It sounded really important, so I left them in here." The room didn't take long for Winchester to search. He clearly found no sign of the children.

"Looks like they decided they didn't want you to take them back to class, and they let my dog out in the process," Mathias sighed. Milly was usually a good dog, but she had a tendency to wander off if no one was keeping her in check.

"And I just remembered there was something else I was supposed to report to the heads," Winchester smacked his forehead, clearly frustrated.

"Hey, don't worry about it. I'm sure the kids are fine, and they'll turn up somewhere. There are people all over this ship, and many of them will already be searching for Hanna. I'm sure someone else will find the kids. Hell, someone might have already come across them in this room and taken them back to school."

Winchester nodded, but he was obviously still annoyed with himself.

"You better go make that report before you forget again."

"Yeah. Yeah, I'll do that." Winchester left the room.

Glancing around the room one last time, Mathias determined that Milly was indeed missing. Like the children, she'd turn up sooner or later. She was an easy to recognize dog, and someone was bound to find her and return her to Mathias. He might even go look for her himself, but there was something else he wanted to do first.

The journey to Texas was going to be made public knowledge soon enough, but he always preferred to deliver news like that to his group personally. All of the Diana residents could technically be called his group now, but Mathias still thought of it as those he had lived with for roughly two weeks in a cabin in the north. The ship was full of subgroups like that: people who met and joined together to survive the day the zombies spread across their lives. The first person he was going to tell was Riley.

Heading to the medical centre again, Mathias felt a wave of exhaustion sweep over him. It had been a few years since he last needed to stay awake this long, and it seemed he could no longer handle the hours as well as he used to. Leaning into the corner of the stairwell, he took a short break until the nauseous feeling passed. Pulling himself back together, he continued on his way to the medical centre.

When he finally got there, he found that Riley was out of surgery and taking a break in one of the few waiting chairs they had along one wall. Mathias made his way over and plopped down in the seat next to her.

"I tried to radio you," she said to him, sounding as tired as he felt. All emotion had been drained out of her.

"Did you? Sorry. There was a big meeting and nearly everyone had to turn their radios off."

"You're forgiven. What was the meeting about?"

"I want to hear how the surgery went first. Good news or bad news?"

"A bit of both. Rose should survive the amputation, that's the good news. Great news, really. Jon made a very clean cut, and the other off-shippers stabilized her well."

"What's the bad news part of this?"

"You have to understand that when we're in that kind of emergency, we're completely focused on saving the patient's life. Nothing else."

"What's the bad news?" Mathias sat up a little straighter.

"She lost a lot of blood, and we had to use a lot of our reserves on her."

"That's fine, we can just hold another mandatory donation drive."

"You didn't let me finish. Her blood, the blood that was coming out of her, was infected."

Mathias's back became ramrod straight. The mother of his child had been in a room full of contaminated blood. Looking her over, he noticed that Riley was wearing completely different clothes than she had been when he last saw her, and her hair had been washed recently.

"Have you been tested?" Mathias tried to keep as calm as she was being, but he was pretty sure he was failing miserably at it.

"I have been."

"And?"

"And my blood tested positive."

Mathias's brain stalled. Before his eyes, he saw his friend LeBlanc saying that he was infected, and that he wanted Mathias to kill him.

"You don't understand," Riley shook her head, reading him as she always did, "everyone in that room tested positive. And everyone here in the medical centre."

Mathias looked around the room. How could all these people be infected? Some of them were confined to their beds, and shouldn't have had any contact with infected materials.

"Test my blood," Mathias held out his arm.

Riley smiled weakly at him.

"Come on, just test it. I was here when Jon's results came back positive."

Riley did as he asked, first drawing his blood, and then putting it under the microscope.

"You're infected too," she told him.

"How?" Mathias frowned. "This doesn't make any sense. I didn't come into contact with any blood or saliva."

"I know. A lot of people here haven't. I've spent the last half an hour wracking my brain trying to figure out what's going on." Riley sat back down with a huff. "A few doctors are going around the ship collecting random blood draws right now. They're saying it's for a general population health test or something. They should be back soon."

Mathias rested his head on his hands. How could this be? It made no sense! Unless…

"The bomb. Do you think that whoever set it off could have also been insane enough to somehow taint our water supply?"

"I thought about it. I also thought that maybe it's something we ate. Problem is, we test all meat before anyone consumes it, and the water we use comes from the ocean."

"All the zombies below us?"

"Doubt it. If it were an issue of the debris cloud that floats around them rising up to our water intake, then it would have happened long before now. We've had larger groups beneath us. And we've already determined that the virus can't move through, or really even survive in water without being anchored to something."

"So maybe the virus is changing."

"And there's the dilemma."

Mathias suddenly felt so cold that he shivered. They always worried that the virus would change some day.

"How long do we have?"

"Don't know. Don't know how long we've been infected for. Some doctors are still running a bunch of samples and tests."

Mathias leaned back, resting his head on the back of the chair. This explained why Riley sounded so detached. It was her way of dealing with things like this. She broke away from them, and looked at things only from a clinical perspective.

"So why did you come down here?" Riley suddenly asked.

With the information he had just learned, Mathias didn't understand what she had asked him.

"You didn't hear me radio for you, so what made you decide to come down here? Did something happen in the meeting?"

"Oh, we're going to Texas," he told her. It seemed so unimportant now.

"Texas? Really? Why? I thought we decided it wasn't worth the risk to scavenge there."

"We're not going to scavenge. I think we're finally returning to land. Or at least it sounds like we're going to dry dock the Diana and give her a full inspection."

"Wow. Texas. Do we know where in Texas? And why now? Is it because of the bomb?"

"There's a man who got aboard the other cruise ship and is threatening us. We intercepted a radio broadcast and overheard him calling in some people from Jamaica. How many people know about the infection?" Mathias's mind kept coming back to it.

"Only the doctors on duty right now. We knew something was up when everyone in the operating room tested positive. There is no other place we take that many precautions simply due to regular infections, so even one case is worrisome. We decided to wait until we had more information before raising an alarm. Why Texas?"

"I don't know. It probably has to do with the size of the dry dock we need and the amount of gas we have. There are going to be meetings and announcements later, but I wanted to let the group know ahead of time. What happens if it turns out that everyone is infected?"

"Then everyone is infected. We all turn, and that's the end of it."

Mathias stood up, no longer able to sit, and in need of a distraction. "I'm going to go tell the others about Texas."

"Mathias?" Riley stood up as well, taking one of his hands into her own. "Don't tell the others about the infection, okay? Not yet."

"I won't." He kissed the back of her hand, and then slipped his out of it. Just before he left, he stopped in the doorway and turned to face Riley again. "Maybe you should take the rest of the day off. Get Hope out of school early."

"Yeah. Maybe I'll do that."

As Mathias began to climb the stairs, he knew that Riley wouldn't do that. The only thing she could do right now was look for more information. If she couldn't do that, then she would wait for it. There was no way in hell she'd go anywhere near their daughter until she understood the infection. Even then, if there was any chance it would spread to Hope, Riley would make the choice never to see her again.

***

"Where in Texas are we going?"

"I'm sorry, what?" Mathias's mind had drifted off, thinking again about what he had learned from Riley.

"Texas is big. I was wondering what part of it we were going to," Tobias told him again. The two of them were sitting in the media room, the other reporters having vacated the premises in an attempt to learn more about this search for Hanna.

"Oh. I'm not sure. Obviously, a part that connects with the Gulf of Mexico but beyond that, I have no idea."

"Who else have you told?"

"So far, just Riley and now you. I haven't found the others yet."

"I saw Josh not too long ago. He should be around here somewhere. I think he was making rounds to see his mental patients."

"Thanks. I think I know where he is."

"So, I guess I shouldn't tell the other reporters about this?"

"I'd appreciate it. Besides, by the time I finish making the rounds to the others, I'm sure the ship captains will tell everyone else."

Tobias nodded. He could be trusted to keep something like that to himself for a few hours, unlike the other reporters. "By the way, got any information about Hanna? Is it the woman who cleans my room?"

"Yeah."

"She cleaned Alec's room too." Tobias was quickly putting together the connection between the girl and the bombing.

"She did, and that's all you're getting from me." Mathias stood up from the little chair he had been sitting on. "I should be going."

"One last question."

"What?"

"Should I start making an information video? Like, interview the off-shippers and other people who should have a good idea about what the mainland will be like? We can hook up a few of the screens again, and play it at important junctures around the ship."

"That's good thinking. I have no problem with it. In fact, talk to some of the doctors as well. They probably have some thoughts."

"I will."

Mathias thanked him, and then left the media room. He headed up to the promenade next, figuring there was a good chance that Josh was with his patient, Nicky. Josh wasn't a real psychologist, but he had done a rotation in the psychology ward while still a resident at the hospital that taught him. A lot of doctors had been rescued from the hospital, but since the first zombie patients had been deemed insane, the psych ward was lost too quickly to help the doctors there. This meant that Josh was the only one who had any recent psych training, although the counsellor, Brittany, was learning from him.

Walking into the modified jewellery store that served as the ship's armoury, Mathias quickly noticed that there was already a stronger guard presence here. Once news of the Jamaicans was released to the public, there was a danger that they would rush the place in an attempt to arm themselves better. Not only did the leaders want to keep the bullets and guns for those best trained to use them, but they also didn't want the population to learn just how low on ammo they actually were.

The guards recognized Mathias, but he still had to state who he was and what he was doing there. They confirmed that Josh was there—which was unneeded as Mathias could see him across the space—and informed him that they would send him out when he was done talking to Nicky. Normally, Mathias's position let him roam freely around the armoury; they were really taking this guard duty seriously.

Back out on the promenade, Mathias waited, watching through one of the shatter resistant windows that they had reinforced further with a few layers of chicken wire. Through it, he could see Josh and Nicky. He felt sorry for Nicky. Like Mathias, she once worked for Marble Keystone, the overly rich company that was led by at least one insane maniac who thought humanity needed a reset. Keystone had not only created the zombie virus, but also deliberately released it into the public. Originally, Nicky had worked in a different facility from Mathias, but then she had been moved to the same one just before the outbreak, and subsequently from there to a prison where Keystone had been rounding up survivors. Even though Mathias knew her, he didn't speak to her much. He found it awkward, because she couldn't always remember who he was, or mistook him for someone else. Some prisoners had kidnapped her, and during her ordeal, her head had taken a lot of blows, resulting in brain damage. Her nose was a bit crooked from being broken, and she always walked with a bit of a limp. Still, she could disassemble, clean, and reassemble weapons with ease and efficiency.

At last, Josh finished his meeting with her and left the armoury.

"Hey, Mathias. What's up?" He walked over, but Mathias quickly led him to a more private location. Mathias remembered that back when they had first met, they hadn't liked each other much. Josh had had a crush on Riley—who had worked at the hospital with him—but the two men had since gotten past that, and found they actually got along pretty well.

Once they were in a nook where no one could overhear them, Mathias told Josh all about the Jamaicans and Texas. Josh absorbed the information with very few questions.

"Mary's not going to like this," he sighed.

"Mary?"

"One of my patients. Lauren's mentioned her before."

"Oh right, she was at the motel with her and the kids."

"Yeah. She's finally acting human again; however, she still won't tell me a lot of things. Like her real name, for instance. All I've been able to figure out is that something happened to her child. Whatever it was, it scarred her, and she's not going to want to go back to land."

"Maybe you should be with her when the announcement's made."

"Yeah. By the way, have you seen Misha around? After what's happened, I've been meaning to speak with him, but he keeps disappearing on me."

"I was going to ask you the same question. I saw him earlier today, but don't know where he is now."

"Did he seem okay to you? I'd imagine that Alec's death hit him the hardest, what with them sharing a room and all. And how are you doing?"

"When I find him, I'll let him know you're looking. Honestly, I'm not doing too bad. I had some time last night to sort through my feelings, and since then, I've been too busy to think about it much."

"You look exhausted. When did you last sleep?"

"Before Shoes' funeral."

"As a doctor, I'm prescribing that you get immediate rest."

"After I let everyone know about Texas."

"It's not going to kill them to learn about it from the ship's captains."

"I know, but I want to be the one to tell them."

"By the way, where's Milly? I didn't think she'd be allowed in the medical centre with Riley."

"She's wandered off again." That made Mathias think about how Riley hadn't asked about the dog, which showed just how concerned she was. "I wasn't in the medical centre long, but it looked like something was going on down there. Maybe you should go down and make sure they don't need any help."

"Okay. You said there's still about an hour before the announcement, right? That should give me time to check in there, and then go find Mary."

Mathias and Josh said their good-byes and went in separate directions: Josh toward the medical centre, while Mathias headed for the helipad on the nose of the ship. Just because Mathias had promised Riley he wouldn't tell anyone about the infection, didn't mean he couldn't send Josh down there to find out on his own.

Outside on the fourth deck, Mathias climbed the steps that led to the helipad. His younger brother, Danny, could usually be found there if he wasn't running laps or on a training shift with one of the ship defenders. Danny was only fourteen when the Day happened, but had since grown into a twenty-year-old man who was working hard to follow in his big brother's footsteps. He had wanted to be a helicopter pilot most of his life, and although neither of the choppers were regularly taken out, Danny volunteered his time to keep them in working order, and always went up to learn from the pilots the few times they were flown.

On the helipad, sat a Eurocopter AS532 Cougar helicopter. It was constantly maintained and kept ready to go at a moment's notice. The thing nearly dwarfed the helipad, which was meant for smaller, emergency choppers. In the lower section behind the helipad, was their second helicopter. It was a tiny, two-seater bubble chopper, which was almost constantly in pieces so that it could fit in the space. When the Cougar was taken out for its exercise, the little bubble chopper was then quickly assembled on the helipad, and taken out on its own little scouting trip. Mathias found Danny among the smaller helicopter's pieces—of which there were more than usual—checking them over for salt damage.

"Danny!" Mathias called as he moved toward him.

"Hey!" Danny wiped his greasy hands on a rag and got up to go to his brother. "What's up?"

Mathias usually clasped arms with Danny when they got together outside of dinner; however, he refrained from doing so today. He made it appear as though he didn't want Danny's greasy hands touching him, but really, it was because he didn't want to touch his baby brother if it turned out he was infected. He had been avoiding touching everyone since he learned.

Without delaying, Mathias told Danny all about Texas. Danny just nodded his head as if he had been expecting this information. Maybe he always had been in some way. The kid had grown up constantly being moved from place to place. The Diana had been his home longer than any other place.

"How are you handling what happened to Alec?" Mathias then asked.

The side of Danny's face twitched as he held back some expression. His eyes couldn't hide the pain however. Alec had rescued Danny on the Day. If luck hadn't brought Mathias to them, Alec would still be taking care of Danny. Although Danny never said anything, Mathias thought he saw the man as something like the father he never knew.

"I'd rather not talk about it, if you don't mind," Danny said, staring off at some distant point.

"I won't force you, but don't hold it in, okay?"

"I'm not. Brittany's helping me. I heard about Jon. Is he okay?" Danny and Jon had been foster brothers when the Day occurred, surviving by completely different means but still ending up in the same place. They were closer friends now than they had been back then.

"I don't know," Mathias shook his head. "If I hear anything, I'll tell you."

"Thanks." For a moment, Danny stared at that distant point again. "Well, I should get back to work."

"Yeah, I have to go inform the others. You haven't seen Misha around by any chance, have you?"

"Nope. I haven't seen him all day."

"All right. Thanks. See you at dinner?"

"You bet."

Mathias headed from the front of the ship to the back, keeping a constant eye out for Misha. He didn't spot the scrawny Russian anywhere, so he went to the schoolrooms to talk to Abby. Walking up to the door of the older kids' classroom, he peered in through the window. The teenagers were being rowdy and talkative. It didn't look like they were doing any work. Frowning, Mathias opened the door. Upon seeing him, all the teens fell silent, unsure of what to make of his presence. Sticking his head through the door, Mathias looked around but didn't spot Abby anywhere, or the second teacher who helped out with the teenaged kids.

"Where's Abby?" Mathias asked the classroom.

"Ms. Abby was called away by a ship defender like you," a polite girl raised her hand and responded. "Ms. Ellen had to go watch the little kids' class, so I think Ms. Lauren was also called away."

Glancing around the room again, Mathias noted that Claire was also absent. He realized that they would have been told about Jon, and it was likely that they were off to see him.

"Mathias?"

Mathias turned around to find Abby, Lauren, Peter, and Claire entering the area outside the classrooms.

"Hey, I was just looking for you."

Claire walked straight past Mathias, grim faced, and took her seat.

"I take it she's upset."

"Yeah," Lauren nodded. "I guess you know about Jon."

"I do. Lauren, mind if I talk to Abby alone for a second?"

"Sure, I should probably relieve Ellen of duty anyway." Lauren walked into the little kids' classroom, taking Peter along with her.

"What's up?" Abby wondered.

Mathias closed the door to the teenagers' room and lead Abby to an area where they wouldn't be overheard. As much as Lauren was now basically part of the group, Mathias chose to inform just Abby. She'd likely tell Lauren on her own anyway. Once again, he related the news about Texas.

Abby started fidgeting with the small metal cross hanging around her neck. "First the bomb, then Jon, and now this?"

"I know."

"When's it going to stop, Mathias?"

He didn't know what to say to that. He so desperately wanted to tell Abby about the infection, and that maybe there's something wrong with the test, that Jon could be fine. He had promised Riley though, and the news could easily upset Abby further.

"I just wish-" Before Abby could finish speaking her thought aloud, Lauren came out of her class looking as flustered as a finch in a hurricane. "Lauren? What's wrong?"

Lauren looked at Mathias, and then Abby. "Four of the kids are missing."

"What?" Abby walked over to Lauren and took her hands in her own. "What do you mean?"

"I mean, four of them aren't in class like they're supposed to be. Ellen had to leave them a few times, never for more than a minute or two, to check on the teenagers. Some of them must have slipped out while she was gone, and because she never works with the little ones, she didn't notice they were missing." Lauren glanced at Mathias again.

"I'm so, so sorry." Ellen appeared in the doorway, her eyes full of fright.

"They're not hurt," Mathias told the women. "Private Winchester saw them earlier. He meant to bring them back here, but was pulled away due to an emergency, and then they left the room he had placed them in. I'm sure they're fine, and someone else will bring them back shortly."

"Mathias," Lauren stepped around Abby, "Hope is one of the missing kids."

Mathias's mouth dried up. Everything he had told Winchester, and now the teachers about the kids being fine, flew out the window. It was a completely different feeling when it was your own kid who was wandering around without supervision.

"I'm sure they're fine," Mathias said, sounding not nearly as sure as before. "Milly has also gone missing from the room Winchester put them in, so I'm sure she's with the kids. They'll turn up soon."

Abby took his hand. "We'll help you look for them."

Mathias shook his head, and pulled his hand from hers. "No. No, you keep watch on all the other kids. I'll start an organized search party. One's already being set up to find Hanna, we'll just add the kids to the search list. Who are the other children?"

"Becky, Adam, and Dakota."

"I know Becky and Adam, they're Hope's friends. Which one is Dakota again?"

"Cowboy hat."

"Right. Hope's mentioned her a few times, but they've never played outside of school, I don't think."

"Dakota's ten, so she should be watching over the younger ones," Lauren told him in an attempt to make him feel better. It actually did help a little bit, however, not much. He would have felt a lot better knowing his kid was with a trusted adult.

Pulling his walkie-talkie off his belt, Mathias radioed several people to inform them of the missing kids, and to add them to the search list. One of them replied, saying he'd inform Captain Sigvard so that they could make an announcement over the PA about them.

"I better start looking," Mathias said to the teachers as he returned his walkie-talkie to his belt.

"I'm so sorry," Ellen repeated.

"It's okay. It's not your fault. A lot's been happening lately." Mathias wasn't even listening to what he was saying. He was speaking on autopilot. He was trying to think of where the kids might have gone.

It was hard to think, because one thought kept repeating over and over in his mind: Hope was still learning how to swim, and she had never been in the ocean.

9
Jon's In Prison

Jon paced back and forth in front of his bench, the chain connecting his ankle to a dragon statue rattling across the floor with every step. The lights in there were few and dim, but they were still bright enough for Jon to make out the man from the other ship lying on his bench nearby. He hadn't yet woken up from the drugs that the medical centre had given him. Jon blamed the man for what had happened to him. He didn't think he was infected—he didn't know how he could be—but if he was, it was the man's fault.

Not long ago, Jon's family had been down to see him. There were a lot of tears from Abby, which tugged at Jon's heart. He held firm, however. No matter how much it pained them, he continued to insist he wasn't infected. They would see. In a few days, a week even, he won't have turned. They'll see then that the test was mistaken.

Jon had never been in the Dragon's Den before. It used to be a night-club for young folks, and had two levels. Both of the entrances on the lower level had been sealed, so that the only way into the dance floor was from the stairs that led down from the bar above. Up in the bar, there were at least three guards on constant watch.

Down below, Jon and the man from the ship were the only ones chained to a statue, but they weren't the only ones present. Drifting around, or sitting on benches at a distance, were other people who had broken one law or another. The fact that they weren't chained meant their incarcerations were for nothing serious, most likely drunken disorderliness, or not honouring an agreed upon trade. They kept away from Jon, having been told that he and the other man were infected. Jon told them he wasn't, but they had no reason to believe him.

There was one woman there whom Jon didn't recognize. She kept to herself in the most shadowy spots and moved silently. Her attire was strange as well, not something the people on the Diana were likely to wear. Jon had figured out she was not from the Diana even before he asked Lauren and Abby about her. They said they weren't sure where the woman had come from, but that she was new. It wasn't surprising that she was down here. New people were often placed in the Dragon's Den for a trial period in case they were carrying some other form of illness, and to make sure they weren't violent. If they could handle the Den for a few days, then they should be able to handle life with everyone else.

The Den had no windows, and Jon's watch had been taken from him, so he had no idea what time it was. He had been served lunch, but that was a while ago.

"Uhhhh," the man from the other ship groaned. He smacked his lips while groggily sitting up, his limbs trembling with the effort.

"Hey," Jon whispered as he slid down onto the bench next to him.

The man looked around, confused by his surroundings.

"Hey," Jon whispered again, this time shaking his shoulder gently, "how did you infect me?"

"Not bit," the man replied with a shake of his head.

"Yeah, I know that part. It's all you say. I'm not bit, you're not bit, no one is fucking bit."

"Exactly," the man nodded. He had finally said something different. Just then, he noticed his own lunch. With growing eyes, he stood up and shuffled toward it, but was stopped just short by the chain around his ankle. While the man was sleeping, Jon had taken his lunch and put it just out of reach on his side of the statue. The man made a pathetic sound of distress as he reached for it.

"I'll get you the food when you start giving me answers," Jon told him.

The man continued to reach for a moment longer, but eventually realized it was futile and sat down. Jon knew that what he was doing was cruel, but he had to have answers. His life could very well depend upon it.

"What's your name?"

"Yanis."

"Nice to meet you, Yanis. I'm Jon." Jon got up and grabbed the plate of food. Yanis kept his eyes locked on it.

"I'm so hungry," he said.

"I know. Just tell me how you infected me first."

"I don't know."

"What do you mean, you don't know?"

"Just that. I don't know how I got infected. I don't know how anyone on the ship got infected."

Jon paused a moment, then handed him the plate. Yanis went at it with a will.

"Is that what you meant when you kept saying 'not bit'? That no one on the ship had been bitten?"

"Yes," Yanis confirmed between mouthfuls.

"Tell me what happened."

"We had a camp in Florida, a big one," Yanis talked around his food. "Ate a lot of gators. We were attacked by some people. They had a big pack of zombies following behind them. We were driven to the beaches. I think we were near Miami. Ever seen it? Beautiful buildings. There was a ship in the water. Big ship. Cruise ship. Don't know why it had been abandoned, but a bunch of lifeboats were up on the sand. We took them to the cruise ship, all of us. We had to abandon the lifeboats, because we didn't know how to get them back on the ship. The thing was empty. No food, no weapons, there was only what we brought. Maybe whoever had it before us, decided they didn't like life on the seas. We decided to go to South America, although we weren't very good sailors. Over a week passed, and nobody turned. There was no zombie infection on board."

Here, Yanis paused, staring intently at his nearly empty plate.

"What happened then?" Jon prompted him.

"My wife got sick. Very sick."

"Was she infected?"

"With zombie? No. She was starving. There was a little girl. My wife kept giving her own food to her. There wasn't enough for anyone to eat properly, you see. So, my wife starved herself until she got sick. Other people were sick too. Some got the flu, others were terribly seasick. I don't know what they all had, but there were a lot of sick people. Anyway, my wife died."

Yanis started eating again, finishing off the last of his meal. Jon felt a twang of guilt for holding the food back from him, and now wished he had saved some of his for the man.

"What happened after she died?"

"She came back. Lots of people died, and they all came back." Yanis set his now empty plate to one side. "No one was infected, and yet they all came back. Then some people were bitten. Lots were bitten. I hid. Then you came."

"So, people who died without being infected, came back as zombies?"

"Yes."

"How?" Jon had meant it as a rhetorical question, but Yanis answered anyway.

"I don't know. Maybe it was on the ship. Maybe that's why the people before us left it behind. I don't know. Maybe we already had it and brought it with us. Now you have it."

Jon shifted uncomfortably on the bench. "So, you're saying that if I die, no matter how I die, I'm going to become one of those things?"

"You'd probably be safe shooting yourself in the head." Yanis lay down on his bench again. "I'm tired. Wake me if more food comes."

Jon stood back up and began pacing once more. Was it possible? Did he have some new kind of infection? If he did, how did he get it? Did he get if from Yanis? Or from the other ship?

Most importantly, had he passed it on to anyone else?

As tempting as it was to call the guards and tell them everything he had just learned, he kept silent. He knew they wouldn't believe him. All day he had been telling anyone who would listen that he wasn't infected. They would just think he was making up some story.

Movement to his left drew his attention away from his thoughts. It was the strange woman. She was watching him intently from the shadows.

"I won't hurt you," he told her.

She came forward and held an open notebook in the light. Jon had to move closer to read the words, but kept his distance as much as he could. He didn't know if this woman was dangerous.

On the notebook page, were written the words, *Why are you chained?*

"They tested my blood today and found I was infected," Jon told her.

The woman snapped her teeth, then raised her eyebrows as if questioning.

"Yes, that kind of infection," Jon guessed at what she was asking. "Are you mute?"

The woman nodded.

"Do you know sign language? I understand most of it, my girlfriend taught me." Robin wasn't really his girlfriend, not right now, but Jon found himself wishing she was. He wanted to see her.

The woman shook her head.

"Maybe one day I can teach you. Or Robin can, she'd be better at it. What's your name?"

The woman flipped to another page in the notebook and held it out. *Freya* had already been written on it. She then pointed to Yanis and snapped her teeth while raising her eyebrows again.

"Yes, he tested positive for infection as well. Although, I don't think we're infected. At least, not with the usual kind."

Freya gave him a confused look. She didn't know sign language, but she had clearly learned to exaggerate her facial expressions to help get her thoughts across.

"It's a long story," Jon sighed and returned once more to his bench.

Freya followed him and sat down on the bench next to him.

"I just told you I'm infected, and you're not afraid?"

She made a strange wheezing sound that Jon took for laughter. Writing something new in her notebook, she handed it to him to read. *You haven't changed yet, and if you do, I'll just kill you.*

Jon raised his eyebrows. "You certainly have a lot of confidence in yourself."

Freya gave him a quick smile. Several minutes of silence passed between them.

"So why are you sitting here with me?" Jon finally asked.

Freya frowned, then wrote in her book *I do not like the other men down here.*

"Okay. Why do you like me, then?"

Because you are in chains.

Jon didn't ask what that meant. He wasn't entirely sure he wanted to know the answer. As an off-shipper, he had seen more groups of survivors than most other people on the Diana. Some were friendly and willing to trade, but others... Humans could be very cruel to one another, and now that there was no law enforcement, several had given in to their more primal instincts.

Where are you people from?

"Canada, mostly. We've picked up some people here and there, like you, but the majority of us are Canadian." Jon didn't want to say where in Canada. Sure, there were a bunch of folks from Halifax, and Toronto, but the highest percentage were from Leighton. Early on, the people on the Diana learned that other survivors didn't take too kindly to folks from Leighton. Jon couldn't blame them either. It was the city that had caused this to happen, after all.

Is it nice there?

"Sure. Although, right now, it's probably not. Winter can get real cold, especially in February. It's why we're down here, where it's warmer."

Freya didn't ask any more questions. She just looked at a fixed point with a completely neutral expression. Jon wondered what she was thinking about. He could read her writing just fine; the problem was there was a lack of emotion in it. She held no expression while writing, or while handing him the notebook.

The PA crackled, heralding an announcement. It was Captain Sigvard, as it almost always was. This time, he was telling people to keep an eye out for four children who had wandered out of school. Jon recognized the names as Peter's friends, and groaned internally. Sigvard then announced a ship wide meeting that was to take place in thirty minutes. Everyone was to attend, save a special few who had already been informed of the news and would remain on ship defence duty.

"Hey!" one of the other imprisoned men called up to the guards above. "He said everyone. Does that include us?"

One of the guards descended the staircase, using a flashlight to pick out the speaker. "It does. However, you're all to be handcuffed, and will be brought back here after the meeting. Please line up and don't cause a fuss, or else, you'll be kept down here longer."

The other detainees did as they were told, including Freya. Jon noticed that no one was coming over to take the leg irons off him or Yanis.

"Hey, what about us?" he asked.

"You're to remain here," the guard told him. He wouldn't even look at Jon. They treated him as if he had died already.

"Will you at least tell me what the meeting was about when you get back?"

The guard didn't answer him; however, Freya looked him in the eye and nodded. She'd let him know what was going on. As soon as the other detainees were handcuffed and tied together at the waist, the guard led them up the stairs where they were joined by the other guards. The whole procession left the Dragon's Den.

"Hello?" Jon called up. "Is anyone still up there?"

There was no response. Jon and Yanis had been left alone in the Den. Something about that didn't feel right. Surely, they would have left at least one person on duty. Surely, someone would have stayed, especially if they believed that Jon and Yanis were infected. They'd have someone watching them, keeping an eye out for when they turned. Something wasn't right about them being left alone, and Jon couldn't figure out why they would do it.

***

"So, you think you can stay on the Diana while infected, huh?" a man's voice called from above. It had been a few minutes since everyone else had left and Jon realized he was alone.

Jon stood rigidly, unsure exactly where the voice was coming from, or who had spoken.

"You think you can endanger all of us like this?" the voice continued to speak.

Suddenly, Jon understood. The guards had left him and Yanis alone on purpose. They weren't just there to take the two of them out if they turned; they were also supposed to protect them from people who wanted to kill them earlier. Instead, it seemed the guards didn't like keeping Jon and Yanis alive long enough for them to turn. Maybe they didn't like giving food to dead men. It may have even just been a mistake, but whatever the reason, it sounded like someone was using this opportunity.

Jon quickly assessed his situation. He was to one side of the opening above the dance floor, chained to a statue. His would-be assailant was above him somewhere, circling the opening, judging by the sounds of his voice. Jon was exposed where he was, but considering that he couldn't see the man, he didn't think the man could see him. At least not at the moment. Moving slowly so as not to rattle his chain, he slid into the darkness next to the dance floor. There were a few more open areas surrounding the dance floor, including a kind of hall behind the wall he was against. He slipped around the corner into the hall, nearly at the limit of his chain. Peering around the corner, he watched for the man above.

"What are you doing?" Jon asked in a calm voice. "You know you're breaking our laws right now, right?"

"Killing zombies? I don't think there's any law against that." Based on his voice, the man was directly above Jon.

"I'm not a zombie."

"No, but you will be. That bag of bones, too."

"You can't kill me until I turn. *If,* I even turn that is." Jon needed time to think up a plan. He had extremely limited options.

"You'll turn soon enough, and I'm not going to wait until you're dangerous." He was moving clockwise around the opening.

"Do you know what the punishment for murder is? You get chained up down here until we're near land. Then we drop you off there with no food and no water."

"It won't be murder though. Like I said, I'm just killing zombies. There's no one else up here. Who's to say you didn't turn before I shot you?"

The man suddenly appeared at the railing, holding a massive compound bow. He fired off a shot that thumped into the dragon statue's head. The statue was actually made of a heavy duty plastic instead of cement, but it was still secure enough to keep Jon in place. Jon hid back behind the wall quickly. He had only gotten a brief look at his assailant's face, but he didn't recognize the man at all. He probably wouldn't be able to appeal to his human side.

"Waas happenin'?" Yanis had been awakened by the arrow hitting the statue.

"Your execution." The bow was fired again, and Yanis screamed.

Jon peeked around the corner. Yanis had rolled off his bench and now lay on his side, an arrow sticking out of his belly. He made animalistic sounds of pain, as he sucked in huge gulps of air. Yanis wrapped his hands around the arrow's shaft but he didn't try to pull it out. He was bleeding everywhere.

"Whoops, missed the headshot," the man above laughed.

Jon felt the fire of hatred burn in his stomach.

"Well, maybe I'll just wait until bag of bones there is actually a zombie. It shouldn't take long."

Jon was trapped between a rock and a hard place. If he tried to help Yanis, he'd be shot the moment he left cover. If he didn't help Yanis, he'd have a zombie to deal with. Looking around himself again, Jon once more confirmed that there was nothing that could be used as a weapon. He couldn't even dash across to another wall to hide behind because his chain wasn't long enough. This one spot was it. All he could do for the moment was stand still and listen to the sounds of Yanis dying.

It didn't take long.

In the silence between Yanis's death and his resurrection, the man above began to whistle. He whistled an eerily chipper tune that echoed throughout the empty Den. He stopped when the first groan rattled its way out of Yanis's now deceased throat.

"Here we go!" the man called out.

Jon listened as the chain around Yanis's ankle rattled across the floor. Maybe if he didn't move, if he stayed completely silent, Yanis wouldn't find him.

An arrow ripped past his position, crashing into the far wall, only to ricochet off and clatter along the floor. A loud moan came from Yanis, and his chain rattled some more. He was coming toward Jon's hiding spot. Jon looked at the arrow that had gone past him, but it had bounced out of his reach. Maybe that was a good thing. Yanis would head toward it, not necessarily toward Jon. It would give him the advantage of surprise, as much as a zombie could be surprised.

The arrow sticking out of Yanis's belly became visible first. It gave Jon an idea. As soon as Yanis took another step closer, Jon swiftly reached out, grabbed the arrow, and yanked it out of the zombie's stomach. He had no idea if Yanis was a fast or smart zombie, but he had to take the chance. Odds were, he was a slow one, as most zombies were.

Yanis turned, stretching his jaws wide as he fell toward Jon. Jon had already taken the only step back he could, and now lunged forward with the arrow gripped tightly in both hands.

He missed.

The arrow just missed the eye socket, hitting the hard ridge of bone above it. Yanis's jaws snapped a hair's breadth away from the underside of Jon's arm. Jon held tight to the arrow with one hand, while his other grabbed Yanis's thinning hair. He yanked the zombie's head backward, as its jaws snapped rapid fire, trying to rip out his inner arm. Jon was forced to let go when Yanis's hair ripped out. He quickly swung his arm away, Yanis's jaws following after it like a dog following a bone. Screaming, Jon thrust with the arrow again, this time aiming for the muscles in Yanis's neck. His aim was true, but the muscles weren't cut by a single piercing.

Jon lashed out with his leg, kicking Yanis over and pulling the arrow back out in one move. As Yanis started to get back up, raising his head first, Jon flicked his shackled leg, wrapping his chain around the dead man's neck. He then pulled his leg as far as possible, tightening the coils. Yanis flailed on the floor, trying to both get up and grab Jon at the same time, but failing at both. Jon stomped on Yanis's chest with his unchained foot, holding him down. Yanis clawed at his leg, but his nails were short, and Jon's pants were tough. Risking his balance, Jon continued to pull the chain as tightly as possible. He then bent down, arrow in hand, and began stabbing at the exposed throat between the coils. As the flesh gave way, the chain tightened and dug in further. Jon was screaming again, so much so that it hurt his own throat. He didn't stop until the chain ripped all the way down to Yanis's neck bones. With a few more jabs, Jon severed the nerves. Although Yanis continued to snap his jaws, the zombie could no longer move its body.

Exhausted, but knowing his ordeal wasn't over yet, Jon carefully separated the head and neck. Yanis was now what the off-shippers called a bear trap zombie: one that was incapacitated, but could still bite. He might be useful.

Breaking the arrow in half, Jon created a point thin enough to fit into the lock around his ankle. Picking all sorts of locks with limited tools was something that all off-shippers were taught, and something they practised regularly. This one would be tricky, especially with all the blood congealing on Jon's shaking hands. His system was flooded with adrenaline, making finer work difficult.

"Wow, Jon! I'm impressed. You took him down all by yourself. Tell me, did you use your teeth? Did I miss a zombie on zombie fight?" the man spoke from above.

Jon only glanced up from his work, curious as to how the man knew that Yanis had been taken out. The corpse was mostly behind the wall with Jon; however, one of the dead man's arms was sprawled out beyond it. Jon didn't respond, focusing intently on the lock.

"You're going to make me come down there, aren't you?" the man sighed. "Why don't you make this easy for both of us and come on out? You're dead anyway. I'm sure you have even more bites on you now after that ordeal. Just give up. Let me take care of you." His voice was travelling toward the staircase.

Jon was sweating profusely. He had to get this lock open before the man reached him. The slow opening and closing of Yanis's mouth next to him wasn't helping. Still, the zombie wasn't loudly snapping his jaws, and giving away the fact that Jon had it with him.

The man whistled another song as he descended the staircase. A show tune this time, one that sounded familiar to Jon, but that he couldn't quite place.

As the man reached the bottom of the stairs, the lock finally snapped open. Jon slipped silently out of the cuff and backed away into the far corner, carefully holding the head of Yanis by its ears. With a quick glance, Jon saw the man moving toward the corner around which the chains disappeared. The man was silent now, grim-faced, with an arrow set against the string of his bow.

Jon prepared himself. He grabbed Yanis's hair, gripping more securely than he had before, and began swinging his arm in slow, gentle arcs. Blood was still dripping out of the severed neck.

Everything happened fast. The man stepped around the corner, bow ready, but aiming in the wrong location. Just as his confusion started to become understanding, Jon threw the bear trap zombie, which snapped its jaws in the same rapid fire manner it had earlier. The man turned, saw it flying through the air at him, screamed, and fired his arrow. He missed the head, but Jon didn't know what happened with it after that. He had already dashed around the far corner. Originally intending to run straight for the stairs, he had realized the moment the man fired his arrow that he had forgotten to bring the broken one with him. Jon had no weapon, and odds were, he'd need one. Instead of the staircase, Jon ran to the heavy plastic statue and pulled the arrow from its head. With no time for the stairs now, Jon disappeared into the darkness of the Den's other passageways and openings.

"You son of a whore!" the man shouted. "That's disgusting! Who the fuck throws heads? You sick mother fucker!"

Jon stayed quiet, crouched down in an alcove that held a fake stained glass window, the light that used to be behind it having long since been removed.

"You know that thing almost bit me?" the man cried. He sounded genuinely frightened, but also pissed. He had moved back to the central dance floor, and Jon could picture him trying to decide which way to search. "You are so fucking dead now! I was just going to kill you as a service to the Diana, but now, I *want* to kill your ass."

Jon's eyes kept darting from one location to the next, watching for the man while his brain fervently thought up a plan. The man fell silent again as he hunted for Jon.

There, Jon saw the man pass in front of a light. He had the advantage of being in complete darkness, to which the man's eyes had yet to adjust. He was coming toward Jon's hiding spot, silhouetted by a faint light at his back. Jon hunkered down deeper into the alcove, checking his grip on his arrow.

The man got close enough for his light footsteps to be heard. Jon's muscles tensed up as he steeled himself for what he was about to do. It was kill or be killed with this guy.

When the man approached the alcove, he had his bow ready. He stepped in front of it, facing it and as far back as possible, but again, he was aiming at the wrong spot. He was aiming too high, as Jon sprang up from the floor. The arrow zipped over Jon's head, so close that it passed through his hair with the feathers leaving a friction burn along the top of his scalp. It thumped through the plastic window just as Jon drove his own arrow up into the hollow at the base of the man's throat. Hot, fresh blood poured down over Jon's hands, mixing with Yanis's blood. The man's eyes were wide as he pulled away from Jon, dropping his bow to the floor. He reached up and yanked the arrow out of his neck, causing his own blood to flow even freer. Jon watched as the man choked, his lungs filling. There was a strange whistling from the hole as he tried to breathe, much less tuneful than earlier. Bubbles appeared in the blood between his fingers, as the man tried futilely to hold the hole shut. He fell to the floor.

It took longer for the man to die than Jon had thought it would. He stayed where he was and watched him die, not from blood loss like Yanis, but from drowning. He couldn't get enough oxygen into his blood-filled lungs, and eventually expired.

Jon finally moved, heading toward the stairs. He didn't know what to do. He couldn't stay here. Even if he told the guards everything that had happened, there was no way they would believe he wasn't infected, not with all the blood on his hands and clothes. He probably even had a few drops on his face. No, he couldn't stay here.

Robin. Robin would help him. He remembered how his infection had shocked her into running off, but she would have pulled herself together by now. She'd hide Jon if he needed her to.

At the top of the steps, Jon walked around behind the bar. It was empty. There was still a sink back there that worked, and he used it to clean himself up. He scrubbed hard at his skin and was very careful not to get anything in his eyes or mouth. After taking a long drink straight from the tap, Jon turned off the water and walked back around to the front of the bar. Before he headed to the door, he was distracted by a sound that came from below. It didn't sound like something that Yanis's head could be causing if it were still moving.

Looking over the railing, Jon saw the man stumble around the corner onto the dance floor. His first thought was that he had been wrong, and that the man hadn't died, but that was quickly swept from Jon's mind. This man was now a zombie, no doubt about it, but how? Jon didn't think he had gotten any of his own or Yanis's blood on the man. Maybe the bear trap zombie had bitten him? But the man hadn't said anything about being bitten; in fact, he had said it *almost* bit him.

Not bitten. Yanis's words returned to him. The man had not been bitten and he had turned. But why? He hadn't been on the other ship. Why had he turned after he had been killed?

Before Jon could think upon it further, the door to the Dragon's Den began to open. The door wasn't a regular door, but more like a rounded rotating wall. The entrance to the Den was a small circular room with an opening at both ends. When open, people could walk straight through, but it closed via an inner curved wall that rotated and blocked off both ends. This was not a fast process, giving Jon just enough time to dash back behind the bar. He found a large cupboard that used to hold kegs and scrunched himself down inside it, closing the cupboard door behind him.

It didn't take long for the guards to realize something terrible had happened while they were gone.

**

Jon had been sitting in the cramped keg cupboard for what must have been twenty minutes now. As soon as the guards noticed the zombie shuffling around down below, they had taken it out. An investigation was conducted, with several ship defenders coming and going. Jon hadn't been able to hear everything, but he knew they were looking for him. No one checked the cupboard, because they assumed he must be long gone from the Den.

The other prisoners were led to some different location, but Jon couldn't hear where. He found himself hoping that Freya was okay. Although she appeared tough, he wanted her life on the Diana to get better. Dealing with a prison was already a crappy way to be introduced to a new home, but one with zombies must be infinitely worse.

Finally, it sounded like the investigators were gone. Jon continued to stay put for several more minutes, just in case he was wrong, but he continued to hear nothing. At last, he slowly opened the cupboard door and poked his head out. There was no one behind the bar, as he had expected. The searchers had probably glanced behind the bar, but he learned from their conversations that they didn't expect him still to be in the Den. They hadn't searched it thoroughly before moving on to the rest of the ship.

Jon popped up from behind the bar like a prairie dog, taking in everything at a glance before dropping back down. He hadn't seen anyone in the upper section of the Den. Feeling it was safe to do so, Jon stood up fully and walked out from behind the bar. The Den appeared to be deserted. Walking slowly to the door, Jon looked out through the opening. At the far end, was a guard facing outward and barring anyone from entering. He was also keeping Jon from exiting. It was one thing to attack and kill a man who was trying to kill him; it was another entirely when it was some guy doing his job.

Silently searching the upper level, Jon found no other guards, and nothing that could help him. Looking down at the dance floor, he saw that the body of the man who had tried to kill him had been covered by a tarp. He walked around the opening, observing as much of the lower level as possible, and listening intently for any sounds. As far as he could tell, there were no guards remaining downstairs. They must have learned all they could from there, at least for the moment.

Heading back down to the dance floor, Jon lifted the tarp. He had dealt with plenty of dead bodies as an off-shipper, and so had no problem frisking this one. There wasn't much, but a pocketknife he found in the man's boot might be helpful. Walking around the rest of the area, he discovered that the guards had taken away the man's bow and arrows, as well as covered the body and head of Yanis with two different tarps; they had been too far away from one another to be covered by just one. Other than the tarps, the guards hadn't left anything behind.

Jon went to the only place he thought might hold his freedom. At the back of the lower section, there used to be two, mirrored exits that led to the elevator banks on either side. The moment the Dragon's Den was converted into a holding cell, those exits had been locked and sealed. Jon went to investigate them now. Maybe there was a way to open one of them that no one had thought of yet.

Both doors were the exact same, so Jon spent most of his time checking out the one on the right. It was a glass door that used to slide open via a motion sensor. The sensor was obviously gone, and the glass had been reinforced with several layers of chicken wire. Even if Jon broke the glass—which would certainly draw the attention of the man by the upper door—he probably wouldn't be able to get through the wire. By tugging on the door's small handle, he learned there was no way to open it like that either. When he pressed his head tightly against the glass, he could just make out part of the metal plates that had been welded over the edge of the door and its frame. It also looked like something had been jammed into the slot that the door slid into, so that the door would no longer fit in there, were the welding to fail.

Jon started to pace back and forth between the two doors. How was he going to get out? The only tool he had was the pocketknife. Whatever plan he eventually thought up, he'd have to execute it quickly. He knew that the guards would soon return to pick up and dispose of the dead bodies. Now was the only chance he'd get.

But what could he do?

10
Hope's On An Adventure

The room was boring. Hope liked that Milly was there, and that there were a bunch of other doggies, but it was still boring. There was nothing to do in there.

"We should go find Peter," she told her friends, who were sitting around the small table.

"But the mister said we should stay here," Adam reminded her.

"Yeah, and Ms. Lauren and Ms. Abby always say we have to stay in class, but we didn't do that."

"It's not like there's a reason we have to stay here," Becky sided with Hope. "He's just going to take us back to class afterwards anyway. Leaving here wouldn't be much different from leaving class. Right?"

Dakota hopped off her chair and dragged it over to the door. By standing on the seat, she could look out through the spy hole in the door.

"There's no one outside," Dakota informed the other kids.

"I have to go to the bathroom," Adam announced.

"So do I," Hope realized.

"Okay, we'll all take turns in the bathroom before going. Like when leaving on a road trip." Dakota opened the bathroom to let Adam go first.

"What's a road trip?" he asked as he stepped through the door.

"It's when you take a really long ride in a car," Dakota told him.

When Adam was finished in the bathroom, Hope went next, then Becky, and finally, Dakota.

"Okay, now everyone has gone. Can we go?" Dakota asked.

The other three nodded.

Dakota looked out the spy hole again, informing them that the coast was still clear. After moving the chair back to the table, the four kids left the room. As Hope was walking out through the door, Milly squeezed out with her.

"Milly!" Hope whisper-shouted at her dog. "You can't come. Stay inside."

"No, let her come," Dakota stopped Hope from pushing the husky back through the door. "That way, if anyone else finds us, we can say we were just bringing Milly back to your mom, or dad."

Hope decided that Dakota had a good idea, and let Milly follow her.

"Do you know where we are?" Adam asked.

"Yeah. We're on the wrong end of the ship. Come on, we'll go downstairs first." Dakota lead the group to the nearest staircase, and the four of them descended the steps.

They climbed all the way down the stairs to the fourth deck, where Dakota stopped.

"I don't know if we can get to the other end of the ship if we go lower. I've never been down there," she told the others.

"Then we'll cross here," Adam suggested.

"We can't go outside," Hope told them. "We don't have an adult with us, or lifejackets."

"You won't fall in," Dakota told her.

"We might," Hope replied.

"I don't want to go out there without a lifejacket," Becky agreed. Becky was a good swimmer, but she didn't like the water very much. Hope wasn't a very good swimmer.

"We can go through that place full of plants instead of going outside," Hope continued.

"Don't be stupid. There's going to be a bunch of adults in there. We have to go along the outside deck," Dakota told her.

"I don't think we have to. And I'm not stupid." Hope tried to stand taller, but Dakota was still a lot bigger than she was.

Dakota sighed in the same way that Hope's mom did when Hope couldn't decide what to wear. She looked like she was about to say something when they heard footsteps on the stairs above them.

"Hide," Becky hissed.

Just across from the stairs was a public bathroom. They all rushed inside, even Adam, despite the fact that it was a girl's bathroom. Just in case the footsteps was someone coming to use this bathroom, they went into the handicap stall, and shut and locked the door. Milly had followed them in, and started sniffing around the toilet.

"Hello? Anyone in here?" a woman's voice called from the door.

All the kids paled and stood very still.

"Yes?" Dakota answered in the most adult-sounding voice she could manage. It sounded adult to Hope's ears.

"I'm sorry, but I'm supposed to clean this bathroom. Will you be long?"

"Um. Yeah? Can you clean the rest of the bathroom and just do this stall later?"

"I guess I can do that, yeah."

Hope shot a look at Dakota. Why didn't she make the woman go away? Dakota shrugged and shook her head.

They quietly listened as the woman went to the sinks and turned one of them on. It sounded like she was filling a bucket. Hope and Becky stood to either side of Milly, holding her collar and making sure she didn't move.

Eventually, the tap turned off and the woman began mopping the floor. They knew she was mopping because the spaghetti head swept under the edge of the door. Once it left, Adam lay down on the floor and looked out through the narrow space. Sitting back up, he motioned around his ears and mouthed the word 'headphones.' Apparently, the cleaning woman had headphones on.

Once Milly lay down, they knew they were going to be there awhile.

***

Hope was curled up next to her dog, resting her head on Milly's soft fur. It was really boring in the bathroom. Becky was sitting next to them, while Dakota sat on the toilet seat, and Adam lay on his stomach, watching the cleaning lady's feet. All of them sat up straight when they heard the cleaning lady's supplies rattle over to the door.

"I've done everything else," the woman called out. "I'll clean the other bathrooms for now."

"Thank you," Dakota responded in her adult voice again.

The cleaning supplies rattled out the bathroom door. Adam lay back down and looked underneath the edge of the stall again.

"She's gone," he told them.

"We should wait a little bit longer, just in case she's still near the door or forgot something." Dakota stood up and stretched.

Her motions prompted Milly to stand up, nearly knocking Hope to the floor in the process.

"Milly!" she hissed at the husky, while getting to her feet.

While they were stretching and waiting, a voice spoke over the PA system.

"What did he say?" Adam asked. The PA wasn't always easy to understand.

"He's calling people to a meeting," Becky told him, "and they're looking for us."

"We have to wait here longer," Dakota sighed.

"Why?" Hope frowned.

"Because, now a bunch of people are going to be walking past here to get to the meeting. We're not far from the auditorium. Look on the bright side, while everyone is at the meeting, we can move freely around the ship. We won't have to walk along the deck outside." Dakota sat back down on the toilet.

Hope was grumpy about having to wait again, but kept quiet. She was glad that they could walk through the middle of the ship instead of going outside.

This time waiting wasn't as boring. A number of women stopped in the bathroom on their way to the meeting. A few of them even knocked on the door, checking to see if the stall was empty. Dakota answered every time, and they always went away, but it frightened them all the same. Hope was certain that they were going to be caught, but they never were. Eventually, women stopped using the bathroom.

"All clear," Adam told them after looking under the stall door.

"Come on, let's go before the meeting ends and more women come to use the bathroom." Hope unlocked the stall door and stepped out into the bathroom. She moved toward the door, but stopped when Adam went up to the sink.

"What are you doing?" Becky asked him.

"My mom tells me that I should wash my hands every time I'm leaving a bathroom. So I'm washing my hands." Adam was just tall enough to reach the taps to turn on the water.

"Maybe we should all wash our hands," Dakota suggested. "You girls did touch the bathroom floor with your hands while you were sitting there."

Hope looked at her hands. They didn't look dirty, but maybe Dakota had a point. She walked up to the sink next to Adam, and began to wash her hands.

Once they had all washed up, the four kids grouped around the bathroom door with Milly. Dakota slowly opened it and stuck her head out.

"Okay, there's no one out there. Let's go."

As they walked along, Becky took hold of Hope's hand. She was looking at the dragon statues they were nearing. The statues weren't really that scary, but the doorway beyond them was. It was always dark in there, and Hope knew that's where they put the bad people on the ship.

As they passed in front of the doorway, a monstrous sounding scream echoed out of the room beyond it. Becky squealed, turned away, and hid her face with her hands. Hope jumped back against Becky, and then wrapped her arms around the older girl. Adam ran forward, toward the room full of plants, while Dakota became very still, her eyes locked on the darkness. Milly whined, her ears pressed flat to her head, as she placed herself between the kids and the door.

"Let's go." Hope grabbed Becky's hand and pulled her forward. She also grabbed Dakota's hand as they hurried by.

Going into the brightly lit plant room, they found Adam huddling off to one side.

"What was that?" Becky cried.

"I don't know," Dakota shook her head. In fact, her whole body was shaking.

"I don't like it. We should go back to class," Adam suggested.

"No. We said we'd go see Peter, and that's what we're going to do," Hope said to them all.

"I agree with Adam. We should go back." Dakota had taken off her cowboy hat and was fidgeting with it.

"No!" Hope stomped her foot.

"But it sounded like a zombie." Dakota's eyes were watery, as if she were about to cry.

"It's not a zombie." Hope hadn't thought of that, but the idea that it could be a zombie was frightening. She knew that zombie was the adult word for monster.

"What do you know? You've never even seen a zombie except maybe on film," Dakota yelled at her. She had started crying. "You're not even old enough to learn about them yet."

"It's not a zombie!" Hope yelled back. "My daddy wouldn't let a zombie on the ship! I know he wouldn't. It's not a zombie." Hope could feel tears in her eyes.

"We're closer to Peter than we are to school. Let's just go see him, then hurry back," Becky suggested.

None of them spoke for a moment, the silence broken only by the clicking of Milly's toenails on the floor as she circled around the children.

"Okay," Dakota eventually sighed, "let's go find Peter, but we have to be quick." They hurried through the plant room.

At the other end, they reached the spiral staircase and Hope led them down. The smelly room was at the bottom and Hope realized that Milly might need to go.

"What happened to doing this quickly?" Dakota sounded mad when Hope told her.

"It won't take long. I just have to let Milly go into the room," Hope told her.

"Fine," Dakota crossed her arms, "but hurry up."

Hope went through the door with Milly. She pulled her shirt up over her nose, just like she did every time she came in here with either her mommy or daddy. Opening the second door, Hope let Milly go inside the extra gross room by herself. She waited alone until Milly scratched at the door to be let out. Exiting the poop room, Hope couldn't see where her friends had gone.

"Guys?" she called out.

"Over here," Adam replied. They were in the photo place.

Hope walked over to them and looked at what they were looking at.

"Hey, that's Uncle Alec," Hope pointed out a picture of the man. She learned that Alec wasn't her uncle like Danny was her uncle when they studied families at school, but he was always called her uncle. Like Uncle Misha, and Uncle Tobias. Ms. Abby was even called her Aunt Abby sometimes, even though she wasn't related either. Hope thought that maybe they were called that because her parents were best friends with them.

"There's a picture of Shoes here, too." Becky was standing at a different shelf nearby.

"We just stopped here to wait for Hope to come back with Milly, so let's get going." Dakota was walking back and forth along a row of pictures.

Becky took the picture of Shoes and put it in her pocket. The four kids, plus Milly, then left the photo place. As they neared the spiral staircase again, they heard voices coming down from above.

"Hide, hide, hide." Dakota quickly turned them all around, and they ran back into the photo place to hide amongst the shelves.

Peering around a corner, Hope spotted three men walking down the stairs. They all had dark hair and were talking not-English. They sounded the same as the guys in the library, the ones Mr. Winchester was interested in. Still talking, they walked across the little bridge that led between the elevators and towards the food place.

"Shouldn't they be at the meeting?" Adam whispered.

"Yeah," Dakota nodded, "I wonder why they're not?"

"Maybe they're guard people," Hope offered. "My daddy sometimes doesn't go to the meetings because he has to guard the ship."

"I don't think they were guarding stuff," Becky shook her head.

"Aren't those the same guys Private Winchester was interested in? The ones he was asking us about?" Dakota crept forward, checking to see if they were gone.

"I think so." Hope followed closely behind her.

"Do you think we should tell Mr. Winchester?" Adam asked.

"We have to find Peter first," Hope insisted.

"Okay. We'll find Peter, then go find Winchester and tell him," Dakota decided, "and then we'll go back to class. Okay?"

"Okay," the other three agreed.

While crossing the little bridge, they moved slowly, just in case the men were still on the other side. Hope looked over the railing, down to where the elevators disappeared. They were close to the first deck now.

The men they had seen were gone, so the kids hurried past the entrance to the food place, and headed down the stairs. It didn't take long before they were on the lowest deck, just outside the medical centre. Hope could hear voices coming from inside the centre.

"There are doctors here," she whispered to the others. "My mommy might be here." Like her daddy, Hope's mommy sometimes didn't go to the big meetings, but instead, took care of sick people.

"The tender boat is gone," Dakota pointed out, "which means Peter isn't here." She sounded angry. "We should go back upstairs."

"Too late." Becky pushed them all forward. "There are people up there."

"This way." Adam grabbed Becky and Hope's hands and pulled them toward the center of the ship, and the medical centre.

"Where are we going?" Hope wondered, pulling her hand out of Adam's but continuing to follow him. "My mommy will see us."

"My dad works on the engines. He's taken me in here sometimes." Adam led them past the medical centre and opened a door Hope had never gone through before. A sign on the door said 'Crew Only'.

Milly trotted straight into the medical centre, instead of following the kids to the side.

"Milly? What are you doing here?" Hope recognized her mommy's voice.

"She's going to come look," Hope warned the others, quickly going through the door to which Adam had led them.

"We shouldn't be in here," Dakota said as she followed Hope. "We should have gone to the other stairs. We should be looking for Private Winchester. We said that after we found Peter, we'd go find Private Winchester. Well, Peter isn't where we thought he was, because the funeral boat is gone. It's not safe here."

"It's fine. My dad took me down here before. As long as we don't touch anything we're safe." Adam led them down a short, narrow hallway lined with pipes.

"I don't like it here," Dakota continued. "We should go back."

"My mommy will see us if we do," Hope told her.

"She might not even leave the medical centre," Dakota replied.

Adam led them into a room full of giant machines that were making loud whooshing sounds. He walked around the side of one and suddenly stopped, causing Becky to bump into him. Hope came up behind them and also stopped suddenly. Right in front of them were the men they had seen coming down the spiral stairs.

One of the men started yelling in Russian, and pointed at the kids. Fear shocked through Hope, and she turned to run back to the doctor place. Before she got more than five steps, an arm wrapped around her waist, and she was hauled up off the floor. She tried to scream, but a large hand was quickly clamped over her mouth.

"Let me go!" Adam was yelling at another man who had grabbed his arm. The man's other hand was holding the back of Dakota's neck. Becky stood next to Dakota, unmoving, with both her thumbs in her mouth.

The men were all yelling at each other in that language that Hope didn't understand. She didn't know what they were talking about, but they sounded really angry.

The man holding Adam suddenly cried out as the six-year-old kicked him hard in the shin. He let go of Dakota to hold Adam with both hands. Hope continued to struggle against the man who held her, but he was much bigger and stronger than she was.

Dakota ran for it. The third man ran after her, pushing his way through the other two men and knocking over Becky. Becky started to cry really loudly. She had hit her head on a metal bar and blood was running down the side of her face. Hope had never seen so much blood before.

She bit the man's hand. He cried out and pulled his hand away from her mouth. Hope continued to kick her feet until she hit the man between his legs. The man suddenly dropped her.

Once Hope hit the floor, she started running. She didn't run the same way Dakota had, because she could hear Dakota screaming. The third man had grabbed her and was dragging her back. Hope ran farther amongst the machines. There was a small space between two of them, so she squeezed herself into it. The man had been right behind her. His arm reached through the gap after her, but he was too big. Hope had already gotten far enough that he couldn't grab her.

Reaching the end of the gap, Hope turned a corner so that she was behind the machine. She didn't know what the machine did, and didn't care; she just wanted to hide from the man. She could hear him yelling. He was very angry.

Suddenly, the man stopped yelling. Hope couldn't hear anything above the sound of the whooshing machines. She didn't dare look around the side of the machine in case he was still there.

Hope was crying. She wanted her daddy, or her mommy, or even Milly. She wished Milly hadn't run off. Milly would've bitten the men.

"*Rouff, rouff.*"

Hope peered around the corner when she heard a dog barking. Milly was standing at the end of the gap, looking in at Hope.

"Milly!" Hope cried out, delighted to see her dog. She squeezed her way out, getting her hands and clothes even dirtier. She hadn't realized how dirty it was between and behind the machines when she had first entered the space.

"Hope!" Hope's mommy appeared behind Milly, with Becky in her arms.

"Mommy!" Hope ran to Mommy, so happy to see her that she was crying. "Mommy, I'm sorry!"

Mommy knelt down when Hope reached her, and hugged her with one arm while the other continued to hold Becky.

"I'm sorry, Mommy!" Hope cried. "I'm sorry I left school! I just wanted to make Peter not sad! I shouldn't have left! I'm sorry! I'm sorry! We should have listened to Mr. Winchester! I'm sorry! Dakota knew we shouldn't have come in here!"

"Hope, it's okay. Shh, it's okay." Mommy stroked her hair and back. "You're all right now. You're all right. You're okay." With a grunt, she picked Hope up with her free arm. "God, you girls are getting heavy."

Carrying Becky and Hope, Mommy headed back toward the door through which they had come. Adam and Dakota were waiting there with some other doctor people. The three men were also there, standing to one side with grumpy faces.

"Take her," Mommy said to another doctor and handed Becky over. "Looks like a head laceration, but nothing too severe. Get her to the medical centre. Take the other kids with you."

Adam and Dakota followed the doctor carrying Becky out through the door.

"As for you," Mommy turned to the three men. She was very angry. "What the hell were you doing?"

"We are sorry, ma'am," one of the men spoke. His English sounded funny, and he spoke slowly. "We were down here to turn off the washing machines in preparation for the voyage. We had heard the announcement about the missing children, and assumed it must be them. We were only trying to keep them from running away again. We did not mean to hurt any of the little ones."

"Well you did!" Mommy shouted. "You're going to come with me right now, and we're going to have the ship defenders deal with you."

The three men turned to exit the machine room.

Hope wrapped her arms even tighter around Mommy's neck. She was very glad to have her mommy.

11
Hanna's On The Run

Hanna had watched the conflict between the Russians and the children from her own hiding spot amongst the laundry machines. Even though they had explained themselves to the doctors who had shown up, it looked to Hanna like they had overreacted. The Russians always overreacted though. They always seemed to be hiding something, and a lot of people had learned to ignore that. Maybe it was because of the bomb. Surely, there were people blaming them for what Hanna had done.

As soon as Hanna had been sure everyone was at the large meeting, she had made a beeline from the linen closet all the way to the laundry room. She knew the laundry room well, and knew virtually all of its hiding spaces.

For over an hour now, Hanna had been struggling. She felt like she couldn't control her own body. It felt as though she didn't fit in her own skin anymore. The cause was stress, and no matter what she did, it wasn't going away. Most of the time she was struggling to breathe, as her chest was tight and her throat half-closed. Occasionally, she would cry out high pitched whines, low guttural growls, or long, airy gasps. While in her hiding place, she would sometimes flail uncontrollably, her limbs banging off the nearby machines. She would claw at her skin, dig her nails into her flesh, or even punch her legs. The pain helped. The pain made everything go briefly away, it gave her something else to focus on.

Then her mind would wander and the cycle would start all over again.

When the Russians had shown up, Hanna had clamped her hands over her mouth. Her gasping was unlikely to be heard over the machinery, but she wasn't taking any chances. Now that the Russians were gone again, she threw her head into the machine beside her. She hit it hard enough to leave a dent, and daze herself.

What am I doing, she thought.

Lying down flat on her back, Hanna took several deep breaths. She let the tears come, feeling their heat upon her face.

I should turn myself in.

The thought caused her breathing to start hitching.

I'm a monster.

Her heart was beating terribly fast, and she could only breathe in short little gasps. Turning herself in was the last thing she wanted to do, but what were her other options? Hanna tried to think of the future, but saw only sadness, pain, and death. They would execute her for this. They wouldn't care about the remorse she felt. They wouldn't care that Alec had been the best thing in her life, and for reasons she didn't understand, she had blown him up.

Why had she planted the bomb? Why had she set the timer for then? Had she wanted to kill Alec? Had she wanted to hurt people?

Hanna had never been a happy girl. She wasn't terribly smart, good looking, or funny. She wasn't popular in school, but she hadn't been bullied either. She was invisible. No one paid any attention to the girl in the corner.

So why had she put the bomb in the room of the one person who had truly seen her? The one man who actually seemed to notice her?

Maybe Hanna thought that if she set off a bomb, she'd somehow become important. Men like Lenny and Benny would want to talk to her, to learn about her and her thoughts on things. Sure, they were talking to her now, but it was only because they felt that they had to.

Planting the bomb hadn't made her stronger, it had made her weaker.

Taking a deep breath and lightly clamping her tongue between her teeth, Hanna tried to get her thoughts back on track. Basically, it came down to one thing: she thought she *should* turn herself in, but she didn't *want* to turn herself in. So what did she want?

Hanna thought hard on the question. She wanted to turn back time, and never plant the bomb. And never have the zombies show up. And never have followed Allan to that place where extremists had taught her how to make explosives. These were pointless wishes, as they were never going to come true. What did she want that didn't involve changing the past?

Forgiveness? That would be nice, but she couldn't see a way anyone would forgive her. What else did she want? To be left alone, but how could she be left alone on a ship? Especially when everyone on that ship was looking for her?

The answer was so simple it took a moment for Hanna to grasp it; she would leave the ship. She would leave the Diana. There was that other cruise ship nearby, she could go over to it. There were probably still some supplies on board. She could live there for a few days, gathering supplies, and then go to one of the islands. She could run away.

She knew there were zombies aboard the other ship, but she could handle them. At least she thought she could. In Germany, Hanna had survived a lot on her own, surely she could do it again. Finally sitting back up, Hanna began to plan.

***

Moving silently on the balls of her bare feet, Hanna headed toward the exit. Her shoes were tied around her waist, a trick she had picked up back in Germany. She was quieter without shoes on, and she knew the Diana's floor was clear of debris.

Upon reaching the door, she covered one of her ears with her hand, and pressed the other ear to the slab of metal. The laundry machines were still too loud and the door was too thick to hear any quiet sounds, but she figured if the doctors and Russians were just on the other side, there would probably be some shouting. She couldn't hear anything, but that didn't mean much.

Easing the handle down gently, Hanna did what she could to keep it from creaking. Once it was fully depressed, she opened the door one centimetre at a time. With her eye pressed to the gradually widening crack, she spied on the hall outside. So far, she saw no one out there.

Eventually, the door was open far enough for Hanna to stick her head out. She quickly scanned the whole area. It was completely clear. Voices could be heard coming from the medical centre down the way, but its door was almost closed so that no one could be seen. That meant that no one could see Hanna.

She slipped out of the room full of laundry machines, and quietly padded over to the nearest stairwell. When she decided that no one was on the carpeted steps, she ran up them two at a time. It didn't take long for her to reach the fourth deck: her final destination aboard the Diana.

Hanna knew she couldn't take one of the tender boats or a lifeboat. Not only did she not know how to lower them into the water or pilot them, but she didn't want to steal anything so important to the Diana. In fact, she didn't want to steal anything at all if she could avoid it. That wasn't completely feasible; however, there was at least one thing she had to steal.

Walking up to a section of metal framing along the outer railing, Hanna rolled a fairly large, plastic barrel out of the bottom of it. It was heavier than it looked. After reading the instructions on the side of the barrel, she grabbed a handle protruding from it, and hauled the barrel up and over the railing. The handle remained in her hand, a long rope extending from it, as the barrel plummeted to the sea. Just as the barrel reached the water, the rope reached its limit, giving Hanna's arm a sharp tug. She pulled back hard on the handle, following the instructions, and heard the pop and whoosh of the raft automatically expanding itself out of the barrel. Looking over the side, Hanna could easily see the yellow emergency raft bobbing on the waves.

There was one more thing that Hanna needed to take. After tying the rope around the railing, Hanna located one of the large benches along the wall. There weren't as many out here as there used to be—most of them had been replaced by planters or solar panels—but a few remained. Hanna lifted the seat of the wide bench, revealing a storage box and looked inside. Tools had replaced most of the lifejackets, but there were still a few, and Hanna took one. She pulled the lifejacket on over her head and cinched the belts snugly around herself. Hanna didn't think there would be time to head back down to the first deck to board the raft, and she would most definitely be spotted if she opened one of the doors down there. Besides, the raft wasn't that close to any of those doors anyway.

Heading back to the railing, Hanna climbed over the side between a solar panel and a planter. She untied the raft's rope from the railing, and hooked the handle through the straps of her lifejacket.

The fourth deck suddenly appeared much higher than it had a few seconds ago. Hanna had seen cliff divers before, and had known of a good spot to cliff jump in Germany, but she had never made the jump herself. From eavesdropping on those who had, Hanna knew a few things. She knew jumping feet first was the safest, and that keeping her feet together was very important, as was keeping her arms tight against her sides. It was important to be thin when jumping into the water from a high height, lessening the impact on her body.

Looking down at the water made her dizzy. She wanted to jump, but she couldn't do it. She couldn't even let go of the railing behind her. Hanna was trapped between needing to jump, and being unable to do so.

"Hey!" a man suddenly called from farther down the deck, startling her.

Looking away from the water, Hanna saw a ship defender coming toward her. This was it. Jump or be caught. Sink or swim.

Hanna jumped.

She clamped one hand over her mouth and nose, while the other grabbed its wrist. With her elbows tucked in tightly, her legs firmly pressed together, and her hair flying up above her, Hanna plummeted toward the ocean. The drop was quicker than she had anticipated. Suddenly her feet were in the water, which forced them apart. The rest of her soon followed, her momentum dragging her deep underwater despite the lifejacket. Her crotch hurt as she slowed, the lifejacket's buoyancy taking hold and dragging her back toward the surface. She hadn't kept her legs together tightly enough, which caused her crotch to receive a hard smack from the water. She doubted she would ever do such a thing again, but if she did, Hanna would hook her ankles together next time.

Breaking through the surface, Hanna exhaled explosively, the closest thing she got to the scream she had felt in her chest on the way down. Looking at the Diana, she saw it towering above her. The smooth, white side loomed overhead, broken only by a few circular windows until it reached the fourth deck. The ship defender she had seen was up there, looking down at her. He didn't seem to know what to make of Hanna's jump.

Taking hold of the rope that attached Hanna to the life raft, she pulled herself along. She could kick, but it hurt to do so, and she found pulling herself was easier. What wasn't that easy was getting into the life raft. Despite the ropes along the sides, the sides themselves were slippery, and she was oddly tired. Without a counterweight, the spot she was trying to climb up kept distorting. Thankfully, the raft's size kept it on the surface of the water, and it never threatened to tip over.

Once she was finally inside, Hanna lay on her back and looked up at the ship again. The ship defender was gone. He was probably getting backup and checking with his superiors about what to do. They had never had someone willingly jump over the side without it being a blatant suicide attempt.

Hanna located a tiny emergency paddle and set to work.

The going wasn't easy. The paddle wasn't really meant to move the raft on its own, merely stabilize it or be used alongside other paddles. Still, Hanna dug into the ocean waters, sometimes pushing the hexagonal raft from the back, other times dragging it forward from the front. Her arms were already tiring and she hadn't even made it halfway yet. It might have been easier to swim, but Hanna wasn't a great swimmer and knew she'd tire even quicker that way.

Taking a short break, Hanna looked back at the Diana. With the added distance, it was no longer looming. Pain squeezed her heart. She suddenly felt an intense longing to return to the ship.

This was Hanna's first time away from the Diana since boarding. She hadn't even stepped off the ship before, except for the few times she went into a parked tender boat, and during the mandatory swimming test all new arrivals took.

The Diana was her home. This thought, combined with the sight of the black scar that Hanna had given her, caused further pain and fresh tears. She couldn't go back. No matter how badly she wished to return to the Diana, she could not. It wasn't her home anymore.

Hanna turned away from one cruise ship to face the other. With tears still carving tracks down her face, she continued paddling.

***

The second half of Hanna's journey took a lot longer than the first. She got tired quicker, and recovered slower. Sometimes the waves helped, pushing the raft toward its goal, but most of the time they were a hindrance. Still, she pressed on, knowing that forward was the only direction she could go.

After a long time, and a lot of hard work, Hanna reached the other ship. It loomed over her just as the Diana had, but it felt ominous. It didn't have solar panels and planters bristling along the sides as obvious signs of life. Maybe it was just that the sun was considerably lower in the sky, casting longer, darker shadows.

For a moment, Hanna panicked, not knowing how she was going to open one of the doors from the outside, but then she spotted one already open near the stern. She headed for it, using the side of the ship alternately to punt her paddle against, and drag herself forward using the flat of her hands.

The door was fairly high compared to Hanna's raft, but she found that by standing and reaching as high as she could, she could just grab the edge of the door. It would be hard to pull herself up, but she knew she could do it. First, she sat back down to rally her strength again.

That's when she heard it: the sickly moan of the undead.

Hanna instantly shifted to the far side of the raft, her eyes locking onto the opening above her. The ship was full of zombies. So wrapped up in her own problems, Hanna had somehow forgotten that she knew that. Corpses infested the ship.

She couldn't go in there. Hanna couldn't face the undead, not again. She hadn't had to deal with them since Germany, and she had barely survived her encounters over there. What happened to her in Germany bore forgetting, but that moan had set off a flood of memories. Memories of her family's pale, dead eyes, and snapping teeth.

Without realizing it, Hanna had started a high pitched keening. She scrambled back to the other side of the raft, snatched up the paddle she had left over there, and quickly retreated again. Her breath was hitching once more, her throat closing. She couldn't face them again. She just couldn't.

Turning her back on the black opening, she started to paddle with a furious energy she hadn't previously possessed. Keeping her head down, she focused only on the feeling of her paddle cutting into the sea. It didn't matter what the people aboard the Diana did to her, she didn't care. Execution by bullet was infinitely better than facing the dead.

Looking up caused Hanna to stop in her tracks. The Diana was moving. While Hanna had been paddling, the engines had started up. The Diana was moving sluggishly, but she was indeed moving, the wake belching out of her rear giving it away. What was worse, she was turning away from the other ship. The Diana was leaving it, and Hanna, behind.

"Wait!" Hanna screamed. "Wait! Stop!" She started paddling again. "Please wait! Halt! *Sie müssen anhalten*! Come back! Don't leave me! *Verlass mich nicht*! I'm sorry! I'm so sorry! I want to come back! Let me come back! *Es tut mir schrecklich leid*!"

Hanna stopped paddling when a vicious cramp seized her arm. She slumped onto the inflated side of the raft and watched as the Diana continued its slow progress. They wouldn't stop. Even if they saw her, they wouldn't stop. Why would they? Hanna had blown a large hole into the side of their home, and subsequently through her life.

Everything was gone now.

Sitting back up, Hanna considered her two choices. She could stay on this life raft, eventually dying of either dehydration or exposure, or climb aboard the zombie-infested ship. Neither option was even slightly appealing.

Turning back to the strange ship, Hanna stared at the black doorway. Whether she liked it or not, she would have to board it. Most of her wanted to stay in the raft. Part of her mind kept throwing out strange rationalizations that she could find an island if she paddled far enough, or she could disassemble her lifejacket and fish using threads and metal buckles bent into hooks. Surviving on the life raft was slim odds at best. Hanna knew she needed to board the strange ship if she wanted the best chance at living. And she still wanted to live. So many of her decisions had been the wrong ones, but the choice to live was not.

She crawled across the raft and then paddled to be alongside the cruise ship again. There was a small, plastic emergency kit on the life raft, which Hanna clipped to the straps on one side of her lifejacket, while hanging the paddle off the other. There was no sense in leaving anything behind. After listening for any further moans and not hearing any, Hanna stretched up and grabbed the edge of the doorway. Although her arms still hurt, there was no time to rest now. If she stopped, she might never summon up the courage again.

Pulling herself into the ship was hard. Really hard. She had tried to keep up her fitness levels, but Hanna wasn't as strong as she was when she left Germany. Back then, she could have made this climb with ease. Back then, she would have had to.

As she pulled herself higher, she shifted first one hand to a better hold and then the other. Her chest rose over the edge, her lifejacket dragging across it and protecting her from injury. With her arms shaking, and her teeth gritted, Hanna held back the scream of effort building in her throat. Aware that a zombie was in all likelihood nearby, she didn't look around for it. Hanna's eyes were focused on the floor directly beneath her, shifting only to the left and right when she needed to look for a better handhold. At last, she was able to get one of her knees over the edge, taking some of the strain off her arms, and allowing her to wiggle the rest of the way up.

Once stable, Hanna rolled onto her back, her feet still poking out through the doorway. She was exhausted, and her arms hurt worse than ever. When a groan issued from close by, all of that was forgotten. Hanna flipped back onto her stomach, tucking her feet up under her, and springing upright. She could see the zombie, but it couldn't reach her. An aluminium fishing boat had been placed crosswise between them. Hanna didn't know why such a boat was in here, she was just glad it was.

Based on its clothing, the zombie had once been a woman. It kept bumping into the boat, trying unsuccessfully to get around it. The boat wobbled on its unsteady hull, but otherwise stayed put, too big for the single zombie to move on its own.

Realizing she had some time, Hanna untied the paddle and emergency kit from her sides. Although she didn't know what was in the kit, she didn't want to hang around much longer to find out. Right now, she had to take out the zombie before it attracted others.

By stepping closer to the boat, Hanna caused the zombie to get excited. It began to try harder to get her, its arms reaching over the boat. The boat rocked again, knocking into the zombie and throwing it off balance. The dead woman went down, falling flat on her face in the boat. A sharp crack filled the air as her nose was shattered against the metal bottom.

Hanna watched as the zombie slowly struggled to get back up. She held her paddle tightly in both hands, knowing she should smash in the zombie's skull, but for the moment, she was frozen. Too many memories were flooding her mind, keeping her limbs locked.

As the zombie flailed in an attempt to right itself, Hanna pictured her little brother's broken body at the bottom of the refugee centre's steps. As the cut and bony hand grabbed hold of a bench seat, Hanna recalled the grey-skinned arms of her father reaching around the office door. The corpse lifted its face, bringing to Hanna's mind the image of her mother and aunt stumbling around in the parking lot. When it got its rotting legs beneath it, Hanna remembered watching her cousin being run down by an out-of-control car. The sounds the zombie made brought forth memories of her big sister's slow death by blood poisoning, while the smell was reminiscent of the centres for the sick. The centres she had helped burn to the ground before the contagion got out of control.

As the dead woman finally managed to stand again, Hanna's eyes locked on the blackened teeth. Those teeth were everywhere in her nightmares.

Suddenly, she could move once more. Hanna raised the paddle and lashed out with it. The tip of the paddle blade was thrust into the zombie woman's face, driving the remains of her nose even deeper into her flesh. The flat crack was like the refugee centre's reinforced window beginning to give way. The zombie fell back from the blow, hitting the side of the boat and tipping out of it. Just like Hanna's friend falling off the public pool's rooftop. The way the zombie's legs stuck up in the air as it landed on its back was almost comical, save for the fact that it made Hanna think of her old boyfriend, buried in the rubble after a sewer had caved in. Allan may have just been using her sheepish nature for his own purposes, but Hanna had still cried for days over him.

Hanna had tried to forget all of these things, and more, but this one rotting corpse brought it all back. It brought back the horror, and the fear. It brought back the rage.

By stepping into the boat, Hanna was able to get to the other side of it before the zombie woman could get up again. The paddle was light, and blunt. It took a lot of swings before the zombie stayed down permanently.

Standing over the zombie with the freshly caved in head, Hanna was panting from the exertion. Adrenaline was the only thing keeping her arms from falling off. More zombies would be coming; the kill hadn't been quiet.

Crossing the aluminium boat again, Hanna grabbed the emergency kit she had left there and reattached it to her lifejacket. The small paddle she threw out through the open hatch, as it had become bent and practically useless from the bludgeoning. Besides, there was a better paddle nearby. As Hanna crossed the boat one last time, she freed a long, solid oar from the cradle that held it along the fishing boat's side.

Already the sounds of other zombies were reaching Hanna's ears. They were shambling down the nearby staircases. With a quick glance around the area, Hanna was able to ascertain that this new ship wasn't that much different from the Diana. Even if she couldn't trust it to be exactly the same, especially when it came to hidey-holes, she shouldn't have trouble navigating.

Moving away from the stairs, Hanna hurried past the medical centre, not yet bothering to put on the shoes still tied to her waist. They were soaking wet anyway, which would only make them louder.

Just past the medical centre was an entrance to a crew only area. If it was like the Diana, it would lead Hanna into the laundry room. Once she got through the door and closed it behind her, Hanna had no idea where she was. It was pitch black with the door sealed. Pawing at the closest walls, Hanna couldn't find a light switch.

Her breathing quickened as she imagined what might be in the dark ahead of her. Turning back around, she opened the door once more, but the extremely close sounds of the zombies made her swiftly close it again. Hanna sat in front of the door, pressing her back against it, and tried to calm herself down. The zombies out there were unlikely to know she was in here. By sitting against the door, she was making it difficult to open, especially if the zombies were as weak and dumb as the one by the boat. They were unlikely to try the door, but she would know if they did. Also, by sitting down, she had made herself a more difficult target for the zombies that might be on her side of the door. Zombies tended to shuffle around upright, and they couldn't see any better in the dark than she could. If a zombie's legs bumped into her, it wouldn't know she was a living human, provided she stayed quiet.

Suddenly remembering the emergency container, Hanna unhooked it from herself and opened the plastic canister. She had to go through everything by feel. The first thing was definitely a rope, there was no mistaking its coils. Placing the rope gently on her lap, she reached in for the next object. This one took her longer to figure out. It was smaller than her hand, plastic, and hollow. It had an odd shape, kind of like a peeling cylinder, with a key ring on one end, and when she moved it, something rattled around inside. It wasn't until her searching fingers investigated the slot that she realized it was a whistle. It wouldn't be nearly as helpful as the rope would be. Still, she placed it on her lap with the rope and returned to the canister. Pulling everything out one at a time, she dug through a series of foil wrapped packages, which she had no hope of identifying in the dark. Most of them were small, box shaped packages, but a few were larger, and some contained things with irregular shapes. Everything was added to her lap pile, and she'd figure out what each item was later. The next object Hanna's hands found felt like a revolver. There was no reason for a gun to be in the emergency kit though, which had been packed long before the zombies. Feeling along the short barrel, she figured out that the opening was way too big for bullets. It was an *aufflackern gewehr*: a flare gun. Reaching back into the kit, she felt there was only one more object remaining. It didn't feel like flares, so maybe one of the packages contained them. The final object was what she had hoped for. With its hard rubber, cylindrical body capped by glass on one end, Hanna easily identified it as a flashlight. It was small, unlikely to cast a lot of light, but it was better than nothing.

Hanna hesitated before turning it on. What would she see? She could just imagine a dozen corpses standing a short distance down the corridor from her. If she turned on the flashlight, and they were there, the dead would bury her.

While pressing the glass end tightly against her left palm, Hanna pressed the button on the side. There was a soft click and the flashlight turned on. The only way Hanna could tell that it was on, was the thin, red glow of her palm around the edges of the flashlight. She couldn't see anything beyond that, but she listened intently. The flashlight's click hadn't set off any moaning or groaning, and there weren't any shuffling and scuffling sounds. Continuing to use her hand as a hood, Hanna slowly let more and more light filter out. As she continued to see nothing, she finally took the risk and shone the beam down the hallway. There was nothing there.

Letting out the breath she hadn't been aware she was holding, Hanna bent over with relief. She felt a little like throwing up after everything she'd gone through.

As she packed everything back into the orange container, Hanna read the labels on the packages. One of the larger packages was something called a solar still, while another one was a space blanket. These she put in first, not being able to think up uses for them. The irregular packages were flares like she had thought, a few extra batteries for the flashlight, and a piece of tough fishing line with a hook on the end. The rest of the silvery packs had some sort of food rations in them. Hanna put the food in before the irregular packages, followed by the flare gun. Upon trying to put the rope back in, Hanna realized it no longer fit. Apparently, the supplies had been packed to maximize space, and changing the positions of items had used up more space. It didn't matter. Hanna tossed the whistle in on top of the flare gun and closed the lid. She attached the container to her lifejacket once more, and uncoiled the rope. She then wrapped the rope around the entirety of her left forearm, making a kind of armour against bites.

While doing all of this, Hanna had been holding the flashlight between her teeth. Although this worked, she was beginning to realize that the pukey feeling wasn't just from her stomach. Having her teeth clamped around the end of the flashlight seemed to be causing her throat to open. It was uncomfortable, and made her breathing surprisingly unsteady. Removing the flashlight from her mouth, Hanna retied the rope so that the flashlight was held against the top of her arm.

Picking up the oar with both hands, Hanna was now ready to explore the strange ship. She got to her feet, and settled the oar in a way that kept it at the ready, but still allowed the flashlight to point mostly forward. Even though she was ready gear-wise, it still took her a full minute to take that first step, and then another full minute to take the second.

Progress down the short hall was slow, but Hanna eventually made it. It appeared she was in the laundry room, very much like the Diana's. The layout and machines were different, but this was definitely the laundry room. As she walked through the room, she paid more attention to what was ahead, rather than where she was putting her feet. When Hanna stepped on something cold, and wet, a shudder raced up her spine.

Pausing, Hanna looked down, lifting her foot and pointing the flashlight. It was blood. There wasn't a lot of blood, just a trail of drops, but she had stepped on it. Shuddering again, Hanna untied the shoes from her waist. After wiping the blood off her foot onto the canvas side, she hastily put the shoes on. Damn the added noise they made, she didn't want to step on any more blood with her bare feet.

Continuing through the laundry room, Hanna wondered if the blood she had stepped on was from a zombie. She worried about infection, even though she knew she had no open wounds anywhere near her feet. She also worried about finding the thing at the end of the trail. The blood was very red, however. Hanna had seen enough zombie blood to know it wasn't usually that red, or watery. It didn't take long for zombie blood to darken, and thicken. In fact, according to the doctors aboard the Diana, infected blood began changing while the person was still alive and well. Several possibilities raced through Hanna's mind, none of which she would be able to verify.

The trail of blood drops moved all the way through the laundry room and to the door that led into one of the engine rooms. Hanna paused, unsure what she'd find on the other side of the door. Still, she had to go through it. If she went through the engine room, she should be able to reach the other end of the ship, or at least find some service stairs that would lead her upwards.

She pushed through the door. It was as empty as the laundry room, albeit louder. Part of the ship was still running, but Hanna didn't know enough about engines to know what part. The trail of blood continued through the engine room, leading off into the darkness. She ignored it for now, seeing something much better just a short distance away. There was a staircase here, just as she had hoped there might be. Now she had to decide whether it was better to take this staircase, or continue toward the front of the ship. Looking back at the blood trail, her decision was quickly made; the stairs were best.

Climbing up, Hanna came to a small room at the top. It was a storage room, containing a lot of folding chairs and tables. Creeping over to a door at the other end, she poked her head around the frame. It looked like she was in the conference centre, which was perfect. She knew how to get everywhere from there.

A loud noise from behind startled Hanna. She hurried over to the stairs and peered down, although by then, she knew it was pointless. There wasn't anything to see, because the sound she heard was the engines starting up. It was a very loud sound, the kind that would draw zombies.

Hanna ran back out into the conference centre. She didn't know how smart these zombies were or whether they could find the door to the engine room, but she wasn't going to take any chances. Best to get as far away from there as quickly as possible. Locating the stairs, she ran up taking two at a time. The fourth deck brought sunlight and a zombie. Hanna just ran past the zombie and headed straight outside. She kept running along the deck until she hit the stairs at the front that led to the helicopter pad. Up there, toward the interior of the ship, was a gated door leading to a little enclosed area that had been set aside as a sort of outdoor break room for the crew. After closing the gate behind her, Hanna looked out through the bars. If the zombie was able to follow her outside, it was unlikely to follow her all the way here. Even if it did, it would probably take a few minutes.

While looking out through the bars, she saw that the ship she was on was turning. It was turning toward the Diana, in fact. Was it possible that people from the Diana had come over here and were taking this ship so that they could strip it for supplies later?

It was impossible to know. All Hanna knew for now was that she wasn't alone on the ship. Her plans would need to change again.

12
Freya Attends A Meeting

Freya hated having her hands bound together, but there was nothing she could do about that now. If she wanted to stay on this ship, with these people, she had to obey their rules. Right now, that meant walking with the others from that dungeon-like place, called the Dragon's Den, to some sort of meeting. She had a feeling she knew what the meeting was about: Sher. He would not let Freya go so easily. He would fight for her. Freya hoped she wasn't placed in front of all these people and blamed.

The guards led the line of prisoners into an auditorium. It was a very large room that was full of people. The prisoners were led to a section along one side where no one else was sitting. From what Freya could hear, no one there knew what this meeting was about. They were talking and whispering to one another, discussing their thoughts. Most of them seemed to think it was about some sort of explosion that had happened before Freya had arrived. From what Freya could put together, the explosion had been the cause of the smoke she had seen. It also made the people living on this ship extremely nervous. Freya didn't like nervous people.

Once Freya was seated, she took the time to study the area. There was one large entrance at the back of the auditorium, and two smaller ones on either side of the stage. No one was entering the space through the smaller ones, so they were likely service entrances, leading to the ship's less polished pathways. Above her was an upper deck of seating, but she could see only one entry to it on the far side. There was likely another entryway above her, and she noted the staircase leading up near the main doors. From the angle she was on, Freya couldn't see much behind the stage. She guessed there were exits back there leading to the service passageways, but she had no way of knowing for sure. If forced, the door to the side of the stage nearest her was the best escape route. She had no idea what was beyond it, but thought it was better than taking a risk backstage, or trying to get past the many people between her and the main entrance.

With all the exits located, Freya took a moment to take in everything else. She saw that no one here was being treated as a lesser being than anyone else was. These people probably grouped themselves based on their jobs, or who they knew before getting on board the ship, but there was no distinct underclass. Other than the prisoners, everyone got to sit wherever they chose. Despite the general feeling of nervous tension, several people were laughing and smiling, telling jokes here and there. They were comfortable.

Looking up at the stage again, it was obvious some sort of play was being planned. There were large boards with partial backgrounds painted on them, some of them still in the process of being changed from one background into another. These people put on plays. Freya couldn't remember the last time she had seen someone put so much work into something whose only function was entertainment. She was going to keep obeying the rules on this ship. Based on what she had seen so far, she wanted to be like these people.

After about ten minutes, five men walked out on stage. The crowd of people quieted down in a hurry, and those still standing quickly found a place to sit. There were more people than chairs, and so many of them just sat on the floor in the aisles. Freya recognized two of the men on stage as those who had talked to her when she arrived. The other two she didn't know, but it was clear that they were in command. With distaste, Freya noted that none of them was female.

"I know you're all wondering why you've been called down here," one of the men started. It was the man who had talked to

Sher. "There are some things going on that we would like to bring to your attention."

Freya listened with interest to the information that followed. They started off by saying they didn't know who had caused the bombing yet, but they were looking for a person of interest named Hanna. It was emphasized that Hanna may have had nothing to do with the bombing, and that they just wanted to talk to her. If anyone saw her, or had any information about where she might be, they were encouraged to tell someone called a ship defender. Freya figured that a ship defender must be something like a police officer. The people were likewise told to come forward if they could think of anything that might be related to the bombing.

A moment of silence was held for those who had been killed by the bomb. Their names were read, and it was announced that a memorial of sorts had been set up in the picture shop. The names of the injured were also read, and their states of recovery were given. It sounded like they would all pull through. Freya could feel the wave of relief that went through the people upon learning that there were unlikely to be any more casualties from the bombing.

The next point they touched on only briefly. Apparently, some kids had slipped away from school and were running around unsupervised. Freya was amazed that this place had such an arrangement. An actual school for the children. At least that explained why she hadn't seen any kids yet; they were off learning somewhere. It was announced that anyone who saw them should report it, and if possible, return them to class.

With those updates given, they came to the meat of the meeting.

"As some of you have already heard, we have a new member on board." Boyle was speaking again, and he looked directly at Freya. "You'll have a chance to meet her once she's out of quarantine, but I'm certain she'll make an excellent addition to our extremely extended family."

Freya felt uncomfortable as a few people turned to look, but she remained calm on the outside, refusing to squirm or fidget. She wasn't going to show any weakness to these people.

They didn't look for long, as Boyle moved on. He mentioned that accompanying Freya were two men whose admittance they hadn't allowed. The gathering was told about the threats the men had made as they left. They were then told about the intercepted radio communication.

Freya sat up straighter at this. She remembered seeing the other cruise ship when Sher had driven them into the area, but it had an abandoned look. Apparently, Sher had driven over there, instead of trying to make his way home. Freya mentally chastised herself for not thinking about it sooner. Of course, he would have gone to the other ship. The little aluminium boat didn't have enough gas to make it back, not to mention their lack of radio communications. The big ship had both.

A man Freya didn't recognize had taken over the speaking at this point. He explained the threat as he knew it, which caused an uncomfortable ripple through the crowd. It seemed they had dealt with pirates before, but they were smart enough to realize that Sher was no mere pirate. He practically had an army. It wouldn't be long before one of those five men came to Freya to ask questions about how many boats and fighters Sher had.

There was a pause, as the five men seemed unsure who should deliver whatever news was coming next. In the end, it was the other man whom Freya did not know. He was clearly not military like the others appeared to be. He explained that shortly after the meeting they were going to fire up the ship's engines and head for the mainland.

The people were unsure how to react to this. Many of them were confused.

The man on stage went on to explain that they weren't going there to raid coastal cities, like they had apparently done several years back before coming to the islands. They were going to something called a dry dock, which would lift the big ship out of the water or something to that effect, and allow them to make any needed repairs. This meant being on the mainland for some time.

Several people in the crowd began speaking at once. Some were delighted at this idea, some were horrified, and a great many had questions. The men on stage settled the crowd down, and said they'd answer any questions provided they were given in an orderly fashion. This meant one would have to raise his or her hand and wait to be called upon.

Freya found the whole process very interesting. Sher would never allow such an open forum, where people could ask questions and state their concerns. Not only that, but the men in charge were very kind with their answers. They provided as much information as they could, without ever once belittling the person who spoke. No question was a dumb question.

Sometimes a statement was made that caused an argument or debate, but it never lasted. It seemed the men in charge had already discussed most things, and although not everyone was going to be happy, the decision had been made. Freya had no opinion on the decision to go to land, for she had no idea what life upon the sea had been like for these people. However, by listening, it seemed the largest concern was radiation. They hadn't had any solid contact with America in a long time, and couldn't be sure if what they had heard about controlled self-destruction burying the nuclear material had really happened. Based on the questions, radiation was a problem they had encountered before. Sadly, the only way to find out was to go there.

The meeting was long as no question was going unanswered, but eventually they ran out. Freya sat with the other prisoners and their guards, watching as the rest of the gathering slowly departed up the aisles. She watched their faces as they went. Some were happy about the decision, some were angry, some were upset to tears, but most appeared undecided. There were a lot of brows pulled together in thought.

Once the general crowd had departed, Freya and the other prisoners were ordered onto their feet. They made their way to the aisle and headed back out the main entrance. There wasn't a great distance between the auditorium and the dungeon. All they did was climb one set of stairs just outside the large space, and then it was the first door on the right. Still, Freya studied what she could in between. The stairs had an open back, and she could see that the lower section of the dungeon was beyond them. Two blocked off doors were to the left and right of the opening that the stairs passed over. Freya had already investigated those doors from the inside. Directly beneath the steps, she could see a hallway, but not the rooms to which they led. A man was walking a cow down the hallway. The cow was bony, and underfed.

At the top of the steps, across from the dungeon, was a nautical themed area labelled as the Champagne Bar. Freya bet it had been a long time since champagne was served there. Now it was being used as a place to dry certain plants and animal skins.

"Keep them out here!"

Freya was instantly on the alert as a man came rushing out of the dungeon.

"What's going on?" the guard who led the prisoners asked.

The man who came out of the dungeon looked at the line of people. His face was terribly pale, like a man who had seen a ghost. Freya suspected that maybe that wasn't far from the truth.

"It's... Well..." The man clearly didn't want to say. Maybe he didn't want to frighten anyone within hearing distance. "Just take them somewhere else."

"Like where?"

"I don't know!" When he shouted, people within the drying area looked up. The man's ashen skin suddenly flushed a bright red and he lowered his voice. "Take them to the Lily Lounge. Tell everyone in there it's temporarily closed while this problem is resolved."

"They're not going to be happy about it."

"Well, bully for them. Just do it." The man turned on his heel and ran back into the dungeon.

"All right," their guard turned to the prisoners with a sigh. "You heard the man. We're going up to the Lily Lounge. Don't get too comfortable up there, you're still going to serve out the full term of your sentences, and as soon as we can, we're moving you back into the Den. Let's go."

Freya studied the route there, also a short one, just up a few flights of stairs. Back before the zombies, it had been Freya's job to entertain and inform tourists who were visiting Jamaica, many of whom travelled there on cruise ships. Despite this, she had never been on a cruise ship herself. Back then, she probably would have been amazed by the ship's grandeur, but now she just saw everything as tacky and pointless. Like the fake jade Chinese lion statues outside the cutesy named Lily Lounge. The people living on this ship seemed to have modified everything for different purposes, but Freya wished they had removed the junk in the process.

Inside the Lily Lounge, Freya saw several people sitting around tables playing games and chatting. It seemed the lounge was still a lounge. When the prisoners were walked in, a silence fell over the room.

"Hate to break it to you folks, but we need to commandeer this room," the lead guard announced.

He got several loud groans in response.

"Sorry folks, take it up with your superiors if you don't like it, I'm just doing my job. You're welcome to stay, but these are prisoners behind me, and I don't think they'd be much fun."

The room's occupants rose from their seats and began to depart. The lead guard thanked a few of them for understanding, and took verbal abuse from a few who didn't. Once the room was empty, the prisoners were clumped together in a corner, while the rear guard cleared out a lot of games and folding tables and chairs from the middle of the room. The space looked like some sort of dance floor, and Freya couldn't help but wonder why the prisoners were always being kept in places where people used to dance. As the space was cleared, the prisoners were walked to the open area and told to sit down anywhere on the floor. Although the handcuffs remained on, the rope that tied all the prisoners together was removed. The guards then stationed themselves at various points around the prisoners, the lead guard sitting on a chair up on a small stage.

Freya was glad to be freed from the other prisoners. She didn't like them. New to the ship, she had no way of knowing what they had done to become incarcerated. Thankfully, they seemed equally wary of her, and were fine with keeping a distance between them.

Once again, Freya studied where all the exits were in this new room. She told herself that she should stop being so defensive. So far, the people aboard this ship had given her no reason to mistrust them. Still, she felt that something bad was going to happen. Something she needed to be ready for.

***

It took longer than she thought it would, but eventually someone came for Freya.

"Commander Crichton would like to speak to her," the man who showed up spoke to the guards.

The lead guard gestured for Freya to get up and go with this new man.

"You can take the handcuffs off her. I'm sure there won't be a problem that requires them."

The guard nearest to Freya removed her cuffs. She rubbed her wrists a bit, but they didn't hurt. The cuffs hadn't been very tight. She then walked over to the new man, and followed him out of the Lily Lounge.

"I'm Mathias Cole, by the way." He turned around, offering a hand to shake. "And you're Freya? I heard that you can't speak."

Freya nodded while briefly shaking his hand. She had a sudden thought and pulled out her notepad.

Was your child one of the missing? Cole?

Mathias looked at what she had written and nodded. "Yeah, Hope. I still haven't had a chance to talk to her and find out what happened, but she's with her mom now."

While waiting for someone to come get her, Freya had heard the announcement informing everyone that the four missing kids had been found. Having had first-hand experience with wild children, Freya didn't much care for a bunch of them running around free. She figured these kids were better behaved than the ones she knew, but they still made her tense.

While walking, Freya studied the man with her as well as her surroundings. This Mathias was a lot more open than the guards were. Those men had been unreadable, but this one was very different. She could tell that he was exhausted. Maybe it was just because his kid had been missing, but Freya didn't think so. He had the bone weary look of a man who's done more than he should. She suspected he was going to collapse if he didn't get some sleep. Not now, but soon.

Mathias led Freya toward the ship's bridge. They stopped before entering it, however, and went into a room to one side. Two men sat at a table within the room. One was the submarine captain she had met earlier, Captain Bronislav, and the other was one of the men on stage that she didn't know. She suspected that this was Commander Crichton, and he confirmed it by introducing himself and offering her a seat.

"Cole, you look terrible," Crichton commented.

Mathias simply shrugged.

"I heard they found your daughter. Why don't you go see her? In fact, take the whole night off. You look like you could use it."

Mathias frowned. "Are you sure that's wise, sir? What with our departure soon, people are going to want our routines to stay the same. I'm not even sure I could find someone to take my place on such short notice."

"All the off-shippers will be staying on board, so James Brenner can take your place. When's the last time you slept? Over twenty-four hours I'm betting. Go lie down before you fall down. That's an order."

"Yes, sir." Mathias nodded curtly and left the room. Freya had a feeling he wasn't going to go to sleep just yet.

"So, Freya," Crichton turned his attention to her, "do you know why Captain Bronislav and I asked you here?"

Freya nodded.

"Excellent. What can you tell us about Sher?"

Freya wrote in her notebook, *what do you want to know?*

"For starters, how many fighters does he have?"

Freya had to think that over. There were the men around the camp, but she knew that they weren't the only ones. It was hard to keep track of how many people could be in the other camps, but based on their comings and goings, she could guess.

Using her hands, Freya indicated two hundred. She had to do the motion twice, before Bronislav figured it out.

"Two hundred fighters? You're sure?" the submarine captain frowned, deeply crinkling his forehead.

Freya didn't respond to his question. She wasn't positive, but it was the best estimate she could come up with.

"What about boats? What kinds of boats does he have?" Crichton continued.

Freya shrugged.

"You don't know?"

She shook her head. Picking up her notebook, she explained that she was familiar with only one area where Sher kept his boats. It harboured mostly the smaller boats like the one in which she had arrived. Sher didn't keep all of his boats in one place, and the only reason Freya knew there were more was because they occasionally drove past the beach.

Crichton handed her a fresh sheet of paper. "Write down the numbers and types you know about on here."

Freya did.

"What would happen if we killed this man named Sher?" Bronislav asked. "Would it be like cutting the head off a snake? Would we kill the body?"

Freya shrugged again. When it looked like they wanted more information, she began writing once more.

Maybe. Some are loyal dogs and would hunt you down. Others wouldn't care. Depends on who takes over after him.

"So there's no set chain of command." This wasn't a question, but a statement; one spoken with interest. "Tell me, who's in charge while Sher is out here?"

Freya shrugged and wrote, *Lieutenants.*

"Why would Sher leave them in charge to come after you?" Bronislav asked.

Freya gave no answer. She knew of course, but it wasn't something that they needed to know.

"Is there anything you can tell us about the man who is with Sher? I believe his name is Bob?" Crichton moved on.

Freya nodded then wrote one word: *Brute.*

"So he's the muscle. Is he intelligent?"

Freya seesawed her hand. Bob wasn't the brightest bulb in the pack, but he wasn't stupid.

Bronislav suddenly rose from his seat and peered out through the curtains. "We have begun to move," he stated.

Freya shifted in her seat slightly. She hadn't felt anything, which was a touch unnerving if Bronislav was telling the truth. There was no reason to think he wasn't.

"How long do you think it will take Sher's men to reach us?" Crichton asked.

Midnight, for the fast boats. Depends on how fast you're moving. Took me all night and most of the morning.

Crichton nodded. "And ammunition? How much ammo does he and his men have?"

This time Freya shook her head, shrugged, and raised her hands, palms up. She had absolutely no idea how many bullets Sher had access to. Extra guns were kept as far away from people like Freya as possible

"That's all for now. We're not going to return you to the prisoner's holding, if that's all right. We'd like to give you your own room, where we can find you if we have further questions. You'll be confined to the room, but there'll be a bed and running water."

Freya nodded. It sounded good to her. She couldn't remember the last time she had slept in a real bed, or had running water. Just using a toilet sounded fabulous.

As Crichton and Bronislav began to rise from their chairs, Freya held up one finger, asking them to pause a moment. She wrote on a fresh page of her notebook.

Are you going to kill Sher?

"If we have to, we will," Crichton answered.

If you do, I want to be there.

"I'm not sure that would be a good idea."

Freya simply looked him in the eyes, exerting as much of her will through her own as she could.

"I'll consider it," Crichton told her.

Freya got up from her seat, knowing that was the best she was going to get from this man. The two ship leaders walked her outside, where another guard was waiting to take her to her own room.

The room wasn't far, just off a neighbouring hallway, and it had no windows. Upon entering the room, she closed and locked the door, grateful to be alone. Completely alone, where she didn't have to see anyone unless she opened the door for them.

It was a little unsettling having only one entrance to the room, but there was nothing Freya could do about that. She explored the small space, testing the bed, the couch, and the taps, not minding the dim lighting. She actually got excited when she saw there was a bit of soap in the tiny shower. Stripping down to her undergarments, Freya turned on the water and stepped in. She wasn't yet comfortable enough with this place to get completely naked, but there was no way she could resist a shower. A hot shower no less.

Back in Jamaica, she got to bathe only on rare occasions, and always in the falls with a group of other women. It was in those falls that she had found most of her sling stones. Those stones were gone now, taken by Sher and Bob. She still had the leather sling, but no ammo to go with it. Perhaps she'd search the ship for suitable ammo once she was allowed to roam around freely.

Freya lingered in the shower longer than she needed to, but eventually stepped out. The bathroom was full of a misty fog as Freya wrapped one towel around her hair and another around her body. She sat down on the lid of the small toilet and examined her clothes, searching them for tears or spots that were wearing thin. When she and her brother had been growing up, she used to patch all of his clothes for him. He was always getting into scrapes, or clumsily exploring places he shouldn't be, absolutely destroying whatever he was wearing. Remembering that boy with the bright smile hurt Freya's heart.

She quickly drove the memories out of her mind. Memories had never done her any good before, and they wouldn't do her any good now. Hate replaced the nostalgia within her heart. Hate for Sher and what he had done. He had killed her brother, and then used Freya to initiate his new troops, his new boys. She wanted to dig the eyes out of his skull, and peel off his face. There was a time when Freya could have killed him. Early on, there had been moments when they were alone, and a knife was within reach. She hadn't been able to do it then. She couldn't bring herself to do it, even with the seed of hate growing inside her.

Freya could do it now. She could do it with ease. The seed of hate had grown into a powerful tree, consuming all other emotions. And she had learned to control that hatred.

After scrubbing herself down one last time with the towels, Freya then put her clothes back on. There was once a time when putting on dry clothes while her underwear and hair were wet would bother her, but no more. Folding the towels neatly, she replaced them on the rack and then returned to the main room.

At the far end of the room, where a window would normally be, there was a large mirror. Freya walked up to the mirror and stared at herself. She had aged over the last six years, far faster than all the years previous to the outbreak. The lines on her face were deeper, her hair was lank, although surprisingly not at all grey yet, and her skin was sallow. She looked a lot more like her mom.

A soft knock on the door interrupted her thoughts. Using the peephole, Freya was able to check out who it was before showing herself. She wouldn't know most of the people on this ship, but it would give her a chance to judge facial expressions before letting anyone in. Freya was surprised to see the boy who had saved her in the water. He was carrying a tray of food.

Freya opened the door.

"I don't mean to bother you, but I brought you something to eat."

She stood to one side and let him enter. The dog that had been with him earlier trailed after him.

"I'm Misha by the way. I can't remember if I told you that." He placed the tray on the desk.

Freya walked over to the bed and sat upon it, wondering what he wanted.

"How are you doing?" he asked.

She gave him a thumbs up without smiling.

"Everyone's been treating you well?"

She nodded. There hadn't been abuse of any kind yet. Even being around the prisoners hadn't been bad.

"This is Rifle," Misha gestured to the German Shepherd standing beside him. The shepherd was calm and content, yet Misha appeared nervous. He kept looking around, and shuffling his feet.

Out with it, Freya wrote on her pad.

"This Sher guy, should we be worried about him? I know the ship leaders are bringing us to shore, but will they follow us all the way there? And what would they do if they catch us? I was there when Sher made his threats. He didn't seem like the kind of guy who would make them idly."

He's not.

"So we should be worried then."

Freya nodded.

This seemed to calm Misha down. Apparently not knowing bothered him more than confirmation.

"We'll have to fight, won't we?"

I'd say it's likely.

Misha nodded, now focused on a patch of wall to his left. He had trouble with eye contact, at least when it came to Freya.

"That's all I really wanted to ask."

Despite his statement, he continued to stand in the room. Freya wondered what he was thinking. There was something about him that reminded her of herself, only without the tree of hate inside.

"Is there anything else you need?" he finally asked.

Freya shook her head.

"All right. I'm sure the guard outside could get you something if you really needed it." Without saying any sort of goodbye, he turned and left the room, his dog following behind him.

Once the door was closed, Freya walked up to it and threw the deadbolt. Having done that, she turned to the food on the tray. There wasn't much, but it was better than nothing. Vegetables took up most of the space, with a few puny fruits. There were also two hardboiled eggs, and a glass of water. Freya noticed that she had been given a knife along with a fork. When she finished eating, she planned to keep that knife.

It was impossible to tell how late it was. Without a window or a running timepiece, Freya had only her own internal clock to tell the time, and that clock had never been right. She thought that maybe she would sleep. If she was right about when Sher and his men reached them, she wanted to be rested.

Turning off the one light made the room pitch black. After a few seconds of total darkness, Freya realized her eyes would not adjust to it, and so turned the light back on. It was one thing to hide in the shadows, it was another to be entirely blind.

Stripping off the bed's sheet, Freya reset the duvet and lay down on top of it, and then covered herself with only the thin fabric. She lay as if in a coffin, on her back with her hands folded across her belly. Staring up at the ceiling, she thought about Misha and his questions. What would happen when Sher caught up to them? There would be a battle, no doubt, but how would it go? Freya had never seen a battle on the ocean. Their camp had been raided by pirates before, but she had never seen a boat attack another boat.

Closing her eyes, Freya attempted to sleep. She thought of her brother, back when he had been known as Sheraton. Back before Sher had turned him into a monster and killed him. Freya hadn't been able to kill him when he took over the group because she still hoped her brother lived inside the monster. She would see his face and think of Sheraton. But Sheraton was dead now. There was only Sher left.

Freya could kill him now.

13
Where's Misha?

After his visit with Freya, Misha headed for the stairs. It was still too early for his dinner, which he wasn't much looking forward to. He didn't really want to see his friends, not right now. All day he had been worried about Sher and his threats, and he had finally found an opportunity to confirm them. There was a battle coming. Surprisingly, he didn't much care about when it came, just that it was coming. He always had a spear gun strapped to one leg, but now Misha was thinking about going to the armoury and picking up something like a machete. First, he went down to the second deck.

During his down time, Misha had been hanging around the veterinarians. He had no interest in changing jobs, but he wanted to understand Rifle better. If Rifle ever got sick, he wanted to know the early warning signs, and what he could do to help.

Looking down at Rifle, Misha saw that his ears were pricked as much as possible, and his tail was held higher than usual. Rifle always got excited when they came down to Noah's Ark

The two of them walked into one of the examination rooms, but there was no one there. This didn't bother Misha.

"Rifle, up." He patted a metal table, prompting Rifle to climb the little staircase next to it.

Rifle watched his paws as he walked onto the table, and then carefully laid himself down upon it. Misha searched for the dog anatomy book that Cameron had shown him before. He remembered when he first met the basset hound, Shoes, the dog had been fine, but after a few days, he appeared to be sick. It turned out the dog was just in mourning for his lost little girl, and became himself again once Becky was his new owner. With the death of Alec, Misha suspected Rifle might go into mourning. The German Shepherd probably didn't know what had happened, not yet, but over the next few days, he'd realize that Alec was gone. Misha was worried that if something was actually wrong with Rifle during that time, he might mistake it for a dog in mourning, based on his experience with Shoes.

"Misha."

Misha nearly jumped out of his skin, hearing his name whispered in a room he thought was empty.

"Who's there?" Misha wheeled around, searching the room while placing a hand on the butt of his spear gun.

Rifle jumped down off the table and scooted over to a large gurney in the corner, sticking his nose under the sheet that hung from it.

"Ack, go away Rifle, your nose is cold."

Misha walked over to the corner and lifted the sheet up off the gurney. Jon was scrunched up underneath it, with Rifle sniffing him all over.

"Jon? Aren't you supposed to be in prison?"

"I escaped. Can you give me a hand? I'm caught on something." Jon gestured toward his back.

Kneeling on the floor, Misha looked up underneath the gurney. The collar of Jon's shirt had somehow become entangled in part of the structure. Misha carefully freed it, managing not to rip the fabric.

"Thanks, man." Jon crawled out from beneath the gurney, but both he and Misha remained sitting on the floor together. Rifle sat down next to them.

"Why did you escape from prison?" Misha asked him. "And how?"

"It was decided that since I was there for testing positive, I was a dead man and didn't need to know what the meeting was about. A guy showed up and tried to kill me. He *did* kill Yanis, the man I brought back from the other ship." Jon sounded a little shaken by what had happened, but he was dealing with it. "I had to kill the man, or else he would have killed me. You understand that, right?"

"Yeah. I do." On the Day, Misha had killed his best friend for the same reason. His friend had been a zombie, but Misha didn't know that at the time. The world was very much kill or be killed these days.

"I killed him. I don't know who he was, but I got a knife off of him." Jon held up the knife. It wasn't bloody, so it wasn't what he had used to kill his attacker. "You know the fake stained glass window between the sealed-off exits?"

"The one above the hallway just outside, under the stairs," Misha gestured in its general direction.

"Yeah. The plastic was tough, but I was able to cut through it with the knife. Some guards were coming back, so I hid in here after jumping through the opening. Cut my arm a bit on the plastic." He held up his arm to show Misha the scratch. It was an angry red, and looked like it had been bleeding earlier, but had since stopped.

"What do you plan to do now?"

"I need to get to the medical centre. There's something strange about this so-called infection of mine."

"What?" When Misha had heard that Jon was claiming he wasn't infected, he believed Jon. There were a few people outside his group that he trusted to be honest about such things and Jon was one of them.

"I don't know how I could have gotten infected, for one. The man I killed, he turned afterward. I don't think he was infected either."

The hair on the back of Misha's neck bristled. How could someone turn into a zombie without being infected?

"Yanis said that people on his ship were dying due to various illnesses and malnutrition. It had been several weeks since anyone in his group had had contact with a zombie, yet when they died, they turned."

Misha shifted his position on the floor. Rifle, who had lain down while Jon was talking, lifted his head, noticing Misha's discomfort.

"I feel I need to tell this to someone in the medical centre."

"Yeah. Yeah, you should," Misha agreed.

"Can you help me get there? Just scope out the hallways and stairs for me. We're not far."

No, they weren't far. The medical centre was just at the other end of the ship and down a level.

"We'll have to use the hallways up here. We can't travel through the engine rooms. There will be people all over the place down there, now that we're moving."

"We're moving?" Jon paused and cocked his head, feeling the motion of the ship. "So that's what it is. I thought it felt like movement, but just assumed I was dizzy or something because of what happened. Why are we moving?"

"There's an attack coming. The ship leaders are trying to avoid it by taking us to Texas, but I don't think that's going to work. I think the attackers will catch up with us."

"Pirates?"

Misha shook his head. "All the pirates we've come across are in small bands. This won't be a small band."

Jon nodded. "All right. The information I have might be even more important, given the chance of gunfire."

"I'll get you to the medical centre."

Misha and Jon both got up off the floor, which caused Rifle to do likewise. Misha walked over to the door and stuck his head out. The hall was still empty, so he waved Jon forward.

"Too bad we don't have a hoody or something for you," Misha commented as he headed down the hall. If they had something to cover Jon's face with, this would be easier. It didn't help that Jon was a fairly well known guy, and therefore recognizable.

Jon only shrugged in response.

Rifle trotted happily ahead, disappearing around the corner into one of the major hallways they needed to traverse to get to the other end of the ship.

"Hey there, Rifle!" a happy voice cried from around the corner.

Misha and Jon froze.

"What are you doing here? Is Misha with you?"

Gesturing for Jon to prepare to run, Misha went around the corner to see who it was. The voice was very familiar, and as it turned out, it belonged to Riley's twin sister, Cameron.

"There you are," Cameron said, looking up from where she knelt on the carpet rubbing Rifle's shoulders. "Came to do some more studying?"

"Yeah, but something came up and I need to go see your sister."

"Oh? What about?"

"It's kind of personal."

Cameron cocked her head to one side. "You know you fidget when you lie?"

Misha stilled his hands that had been picking at his wet suit. This was going poorly. He should have planned what to say.

"Did you break something in the exam room?" Cameron asked, trying to wheedle the truth out of Misha.

"No. No, I didn't break anything."

With a sigh, Jon stepped around the corner. "Well that was short lived."

"Jon?" Cameron got to her feet. "I thought you were being held in the Dragon's Den?"

"I got out. It's actually me that needs to see Riley. Something came up that'd I rather not discuss in the open."

A deep frown creased Cameron's face, making her completely indistinguishable from her more serious sister. She was clearly thinking about what to do, which meant that telling the ship defenders was an option for her.

"It's a pretty serious matter that affects all of us," Jon continued. "I promise I'll go back into holding after I give my news. It doesn't even have to be Riley, but I need to talk to someone in the medical centre."

Cameron didn't answer as she continued to think things over. Suddenly, Misha had an idea.

"Why don't I go get Riley and bring her here? Jon can stay in one of the animal pens until I get back."

"Works for me," Jon agreed.

Cameron kept thinking. Rifle looked at each of the people, and then chuffed softly, wondering why they weren't moving.

"All right. He can stay in one of the animal pens, and I'm going to keep an eye on him," Cameron finally relented. "Go get my sister."

"Thanks," Jon sighed with relief.

"I expect an explanation when this is all over though," she admonished them. "I'm also going to call the ship defenders if I think you're up to something."

"Understood."

"Come on, Rifle." Misha stepped around Cameron and patted his leg. Rifle turned to follow him down the hall.

"In here," Cameron led Jon into a nearby animal room.

***

When Misha reached the medical centre, he stopped just outside the door. He could hear voices inside and they were speaking in Russian. Although the voices were muffled, he stopped to listen to what he could. Most of the words were indistinct, but there was one word he picked out: *bomba,* bomb. He strained to hear more. They were talking about a bomb they had set off. Suddenly, Rifle pushed his way through the door, forcing Misha to stop listening and follow after him.

The Russians were sitting in the waiting chairs near the entrance. They all looked up and stopped speaking as Misha entered the centre. He chose not to look directly at them, hoping he wouldn't give away the fact he had heard something they didn't want him to. It sounded like the Russians had set off the bomb that killed Alec. A tightness wound up Misha's guts, while his heart was squeezed up into his throat.

Rifle trotted over to a bed that Milly was lying beside. She stood up as the shepherd approached her, and they began their sniffing routine. On the bed sat a sullen looking Hope, and Becky, who had a bandage wrapped around her head. Across from them sat two other kids, one of them an older girl wearing a cowboy hat.

Misha suspected that these were the recently found missing children.

"Misha, what are you doing here?" Riley strode over from where she had been changing a woman's IV bag.

For a second, Misha couldn't remember. All he felt was a red hatred for the men in the corner. When he did remember Jon, he drew Riley to one side, where his whispers wouldn't be overheard.

"Jon escaped from the Den," he told her. "He says there's something weird about his infection, and the man he brought in told him a pretty disturbing story. You should probably hear it from him."

"Where is he?" Riley didn't sound very surprised by what Misha had just told her.

"Noah's Ark. Your sister is keeping an eye on him in one of the pens."

Riley sighed. "I can't go see him just yet. I need to wait here with the kids for their parents to come pick them up."

"I can watch them." Misha wasn't so sure he'd be watching the kids so much as watching the Russians.

"No. I don't want to leave Hope. Besides, the parents are expecting me to be here."

Misha shuffled his feet. "Well, how long is it going to be?"

"Not long. I suspect the parents have been found and told where their kids are by now. They should be coming to get them any minute."

"Has Mathias been here?"

"Not recently. Although he should be here. Why?"

Misha lowered his voice even further, placing his lips right up against Riley's ear as he spoke. "Because I heard the Russians mentioning a bomb they had set off."

Riley's eyes widened. They darted over to the Russians, and then quickly back to Misha. "I knew there was something up with them. The kids were found because they came across those men in the laundry room. They claimed they were just shutting down the machines for departure, but that was before the large meeting was even over, and they were pretty rough with the kids."

"They killed Alec." Misha's hands were clenched so tightly, he was going to have indentations in the palms from his fingernails.

"It's possible, but you could be wrong. You may have misheard." Riley placed a hand on his shoulder, and discovered just how rigidly Misha was standing.

"I didn't mishear."

"Doesn't matter. They could have been talking about something else. A ship defender should be on his way down to talk to them. You can mention it then."

Misha looked over at the three men who were watching their whispered conversation with interest. He wanted to strangle them. Not having had a lot of experience with killing, even when it came to zombies, Misha nevertheless thought he could easily watch the life go out of those men's eyes.

"Fine. I'll wait," he eventually said through gritted teeth. "I'm not sure if your sister will though."

"She'll wait. She knows that if I'm in the middle of something, wild horses couldn't drag me away from it. Besides, how many times have both she and Jon been at our dinner table? She knows him, and will give him the benefit of the doubt. Why don't you sit down?"

"I don't want to sit down." Misha wasn't even sure he *could* sit down. His muscles felt like they had been bound by wire.

"You're going to sit down. I want you to sit down before you do something stupid. Come on, doctor's orders." Riley placed her hand on his shoulder again and led him toward an empty bed just past the children. She pressed down on his shoulder until he sat. "Now, I have a few more patients to check on. You're not to move." Riley then turned away from him.

"Are you in trouble too?" Hope whispered across the gap between their beds.

"No, I'm not in trouble," Misha told her.

"You look like you're in trouble. You look mad."

Misha looked down at his hands and noticed they were still clenched painfully tight. Slowly relaxing them, he realized he was probably going to have small bruises from his fingers as well as indents. At least his nails were brutally short, or else he might have found himself bleeding.

Rifle walked up to Misha and lifted his head as high as he could, just able to place the end of his chin on Misha's knee. Rifle's ears were pricked high, and his tail wasn't wagging. He understood that something was upsetting Misha. Misha scratched his muzzle, prompting a slow tail wag, but those alert ears didn't lower and his eyes didn't leave Misha's face.

"Is your doggy in trouble?" Hope asked next.

"No, he's fine."

"My doggy is in trouble."

"The same trouble you're in." It wasn't a question. Misha knew that Milly would have been with the kids given the chance.

"Yeah."

"Misha?" This time it was Becky.

"What?"

"Do you think Shoes is in a better place?"

The question hit him off guard, slipping past his defences and striking him right in the heart. Suddenly, his heart was in his throat for a completely different reason.

"I'm sure he is," Misha managed to croak.

"So the ocean is a nice place? I don't really like the ocean."

Closing his eyes, Misha took a steadying breath. He had just assumed that Becky had been referring to heaven, but apparently, she hadn't.

"Yeah. The ocean is a nice place," he lied. The ocean wasn't a nice place. It was full of zombies, and pirates, and sickness. He couldn't tell that to a little girl though. Especially not this one, whom he had saved by diving off the wing of a sinking plane. Becky would have drowned before reaching the Diana if it hadn't been for Misha. He couldn't blame her for not being very fond of the ocean.

For reasons Misha didn't understand, the two kids from the other bed hopped off and walked over to his bed. They then sat on either side of him without saying a word. Maybe it was because they were scared. Rifle walked up to both of them and sniffed their feet.

"You kids want to see a trick?" Misha asked them.

All four of the kids nodded their heads.

"Rifle," Misha got his attention. "Rifle, up." He raised his hand up over his head. "Up, Rifle. Dance." He spun his hand in a circle.

Rifle pushed up onto his hind legs and half hopped, half walked in a sort of circle, spinning himself around. He stumbled back onto all fours a few times, but he would pop back up when he saw Misha still signalling for him to do so. The children started giggling.

Misha lowered his arm and let Rifle stop. He slid off his bed and knelt on the floor, giving the dog an affectionate rubdown.

"Good boy. Good boy." Misha glanced briefly at the kids then looked back at Rifle. "You ready for another one, *bratishka*?"

Misha got to his feet facing the dog. Rifle's eyes were locked on him, ready for the next command.

"Up," Misha gestured.

Rifle stood on his hind legs again, but this time Misha caught his front paws. Humming a song he couldn't remember the name of, Misha guided Rifle back and forth between the beds as if they were dancing. Rifle's head kept jerking up and down, looking from Misha to his paws.

The kids were now in a full-blown laughing fit.

Misha let Rifle go so that he could stand on all four legs again.

"Okay, one more trick." Misha couldn't help but smile at the laughing children all around him. Rifle seemed to be enjoying it too, with his tail swishing furiously back and forth, and a grin splitting his face while he panted.

Using his finger and thumb, Misha made a fake gun out of his hand. He pointed it at Rifle, who stopped panting and wagging his tail. The dog stood stiff and still. Had Misha been holding a real gun, Rifle would have attacked, but the finger gun was a signal for a game.

"Bang!" Misha shouted, tilting his hand back as if there was a recoil.

Rifle let out a low howl and lay down, then rolled onto his back so that all his legs were sticking up in the air. Hamming it up, the dog even twitched one of his back legs while he lay there.

As if she had been trained as part of the act, Milly trotted up to Rifle and began sniffing him over, letting out concerned little whines as she did so.

The kids were practically busting a gut, holding their bellies and rolling on the beds.

"Rifle," Misha patted his leg.

Rifle suddenly rolled back onto his feet and stood up, startling Milly and causing even more laughter. He padded up to Misha and sat beside him.

"And, bow." Misha bowed to Rifle, lowering one of his hands in the process so that Rifle bowed back. Using hand signals and bowing himself, Misha got Rifle to turn and bow to each of the beds.

The children applauded.

"How did you teach him how to do that?" the girl with the cowboy hat asked.

"Can Milly do that?" Hope followed up.

"My friend Alec taught him all that when Rifle was still young. I'm sure Milly could do it if she had been trained to." Misha knelt in front of Rifle and gave him a lot of love and attention, as reward for doing his tricks. He didn't have any treats to give Rifle, but later he'd find something special for the dog. Alec had trained him well. A brief pain tugged at Misha's heart, but it was quickly swallowed up by the children's laughter. Technically, Alec hadn't taught Rifle all his tricks. Misha had been the one who taught him how to dance while holding his hands. Because Alec had trained Rifle while being rehabilitated after his injury—something he claimed helped him through that painful process—he hadn't been able to teach the shepherd any tricks that involved standing with him.

"Adam?" a woman's voice called from the medical centre's doorway.

"Mom!" the little boy crowed and bounced off the bed on which he was sitting. Arms outstretched, he ran to the woman, who knelt down and opened her arms in return. Such relief washed over her face as they embraced. A man stood behind her, one Misha had seen around quite a few times since he worked on an interior maintenance crew. He also looked relieved, but he looked angry as well. Riley walked over and they spoke briefly. Misha noticed the man had an Australian accent.

While Riley was explaining what she knew about the boy's disappearance and discovery, Becky's parents showed up. They were an odd pair: the woman was maybe in her late-twenties-early-thirties, and the man was at least sixty. If Misha hadn't known them from his visits to see Shoes, he wouldn't have believed they were together. Behind them stood Becky's brothers, Larson and Bryce, which meant that school had been let out. Misha wasn't surprised it was that late judging by the fact he had delivered an early dinner to Freya, but conversely, he was also surprised that it was still early enough for them to be up. This had been a very long day.

Misha watched as the boy and his parents left, then Becky with her family. Rifle saw that their golden retriever, Maggie, was with them and wanted to follow, but Misha clicked his tongue, which caused the dog to stay. Milly, on the other hand, had to have her collar grabbed by Misha to keep her from following the other dog.

The cowgirl's guardian or parent showed up a few minutes later. She didn't have the same relieved-scared-angry expression as the others. Looking at the cowgirl, the woman just shook her head, her features not quite hiding the disappointment in them. The woman had no interest in hearing what happened from Riley. The cowgirl just walked up to the woman, took her hand, and the two of them left in silence.

Now it was just Hope and Misha remaining. With her friends gone, and Rifle no longer performing tricks, Hope started to sulk. Misha sat down next to her on the bed, not really knowing what to do. He had run out of tricks and he knew no jokes. The Russians hadn't moved, and they hadn't spoken a word since Misha's appearance. He hated the way they watched him.

It took nearly ten minutes before a ship defender showed up. It was Mathias accompanied by another man whose name Misha didn't know. Mathias went straight to Hope and scooped her up into his arms.

"You had me so scared," he told her, sounding both angry and relieved like the other parents. He smothered Hope's cheeks with kisses.

"Daddy! Daddy!" Although Hope had been glad to see him at first, she now pushed him away, trying to get him to stop kissing her.

Riley walked over to her husband and quickly assessed him. "Bed. Now. The both of you."

Mathias frowned at her.

"You're about to drop. Take Hope and Milly, and go to room 6372." She handed Mathias a key card. "I've arranged for us to sleep there tonight."

"Is it all right if we get dinner first?" Based on Riley's tone, Mathias was treading on dangerous ground. And he knew it.

"Yes, but no eating in the dining room. And no dessert." She looked directly at Hope for that part.

Hope's eyes watered up, but she knew better than to talk back to her mom.

"Can I at least hear what happened before we go?" Mathias wondered.

"Nope. Dinner, then bed. Hope can explain everything to you on the way." Riley's voice suddenly softened. "You've done too much today, Mathias. You need to let someone else handle things now. Please, get some sleep. You look awful."

"I feel pretty awful," Mathias admitted.

"Go on now, and take Milly with you."

Mathias shifted Hope to his other arm and patted his leg. Milly trotted over to him, and then followed the pair out.

Riley turned to the other ship defender who had come with Mathias.

"I'm White," he said, holding out his hand.

While Riley shook it, Misha strangled a laugh before it could escape his throat. It had taken him a second to reason that White was the man's name, and not just a statement about his appearance.

"Riley Bishop." She then went into the story again, explaining all she knew about the kids' escape, and how it ended with the Russians. "This is Misha. He said he overheard the

Russians before coming in here, and they were saying something very interesting."

"They mentioned something about a bomb, one which they had set off," Misha told White.

All three Russians suddenly became rigid. They weren't the only ones either. Misha had a flash thought that this was the real reason Riley ushered Mathias out of the room so quickly. She knew that he wouldn't be able to leave this alone, that it was the kind of thing he had to see through, and that he just didn't have the energy for.

White turned to the three Russians.

"Get Captain Bronislav," one of them suddenly said, "he can explain."

"No," White told them, "you're going to explain, and then we'll get the captain."

The three men looked at each other, but didn't say anything.

"We can talk about this in the Dragon's Den if you'd like. You know there was an incident with a zombie in there earlier today?" White informed them.

Riley looked at Misha, no doubt thinking about Jon. Misha twitched his hand, trying to tell her that they would get to that later.

The Russians said nothing. At least not for several minutes.

"I cannot take it anymore," one of them finally spoke. The other two snapped their heads to look at him, their faces full of disapproval. "I hate all the secrecy, and I hate the accusing looks we have been getting since last night. We had nothing to do with the bomb on board the Diana."

"What were you talking about then?"

"*Zatknis'*!" one of the Russians barked at him.

White looked at Misha.

"He told him to shut up," Misha translated.

"No. Not this time. Not anymore. It has been over five years now, six even," the one continued.

"Tell us," White urged him.

"We were not talking about the bomb that blew up on the Diana. We were talking about the bomb that blew up Moscow."

"*Ebar'*," one of the others grumbled.

White again looked at Misha.

"It was an insult. What about Moscow?" Misha had asked the Russian sailors a lot about his homeland when they had first arrived. They hadn't said much, only that it was bad.

"Moscow was the first city to be infected. It was quickly overrun."

The other two Russians stayed silent now, looking down at their feet. Now that the one had started speaking about their secret, they almost seemed glad that he was.

"There was no way to clear the infection out of it. So we were given the command."

"What command?" Misha had all but forgotten about White and Riley standing on either side of him. He focused entirely on this one man.

"We were ordered to fire upon Moscow."

"With missiles?"

The man shook his head. "Just one missile. A nuclear missile."

Misha's legs were suddenly like water, and his vision swam. His immediate family had lived nowhere near Moscow, but he had some cousins and an aunt and uncle there. On top of that, it was his capital. No matter how much he loved Canada, Russia was his first home. A nuclear missile had been unleashed upon it. The big one. A nuke.

The ground rushed up at Misha, but everything went dark before he hit it.

***

Misha woke up with Riley leaning over him, and Rifle whining by his feet.

"How long was I out?" he asked in barely a whisper.

"Just for a second," Riley told him. "Are you okay? How's your head feel?"

"Like it hit the floor." He sat up slowly with Riley's help. Touching the back of his head gingerly, he used his fingers to check for blood but didn't find any. Riley was more thorough, parting his hair and looking directly at the spot that had struck the floor. Misha was dimly aware that White was radioing for some people, including Captain Bronislav.

"Come on, up on your feet." Riley hooked her arms underneath Misha's and helped him stand. He wobbled a bit, feeling as if his blood was rushing to all the wrong places, then steadied.

"I assume I heard right," Misha whispered to Riley.

"Yeah." Her voice was soft. She felt bad for Misha, but he didn't want her to. Riley was the tough one, she wasn't supposed to feel bad for people, especially not Misha.

"Tell me when you're ready to see Jon." He made his way to a bed and sat down on it.

Riley followed closely behind him. "We can go now if you're ready."

"Really?"

"The ship defenders and the captains will deal with this mess now."

"All right then. Let's go." Misha slid back onto his feet.

"You're sure you're good?"

"I'm fine."

"Let me make sure." Riley grabbed a pen light from nearby and checked his eyes. "You seem all right."

"Then I must be. Come on."

Riley explained to White that she and Misha had to be somewhere. White said they were free to go, but they might call on them later if a statement of some kind was needed. Or if they needed Misha to translate something. Misha saw the same pity and concern in White's eyes. He didn't like it.

Leading Riley out of the medical centre, Misha headed for the stairs, with Rifle tailing him. They made their way without speaking to the room where Cameron was keeping Jon.

"Took you long enough," Cameron huffed, rising from the stool she was sitting upon. Jon had clearly been pacing, while a goat in the room lazily chewed on something Misha couldn't identify.

"Sorry, there was a lot I had to do," Riley told her twin.

It was always weird being around both of them at the same time. The length of their hair was the only physical difference. Their voices were the same, even their choices in clothing were very similar.

"So, Jon, tell me what's going on?" Riley asked him.

Jon looked at Cameron.

"I'm only going to tell her later, so you might as well explain it to us all."

Jon nodded and went into the whole story, starting with his boarding of the other ship and ending with his escape from the Dragon's Den.

Cameron's eyebrows looked like they were trying to join her hairline by the time Jon stopped speaking. Riley, on the other hand, didn't look at all surprised. In fact, she looked like she had expected just such a story.

"Thank you for telling me all of this, Jon," she said.

"What do you know?" Cameron asked her, suddenly seeing the same expression that Misha had seen.

"Everyone in the medical centre had their blood tested today after we found out that Rose was infected. Everyone in the centre came back positive, including those who were nowhere near the operating room. I even tested Mathias when he came to see me, and he tested positive too. So did a swab of blood I took from Becky's head injury."

"You're saying everyone is infected?" Misha felt his skin crawl.

"Yes, but this infection is different," Riley quickly told them all. "It's in the blood, but it's dormant. It's not moving. Or at least it's not moving when the sample is fresh."

"What happens if the sample isn't fresh?" Cameron asked the obvious question.

"Once the blood has congealed to a certain point, it seems the hybrid-virus wakes up. It becomes active and looks like what we're used to seeing in zombie blood."

"So once a person has died who's been infected with this new crap, they become a zombie," Jon stated.

"It seems so."

A moment of silence passed between them all, as everyone tried to comprehend what that meant.

"But how did we all get infected?" Misha asked.

"We're still not entirely sure, but based on the spread of the infection, I'm betting it's through the air we're breathing."

"And after that big meeting today, I'm betting everyone has it," Jon figured.

"I should test the animals," Cameron suddenly realized, looking at the goat. "This kind of thing could infect them differently. It could cause them to spontaneously zombify, or result in infected meat."

"Test Rifle," Misha told her, placing a hand on the dog's head. "Test him first."

"All right. Come on," Cameron headed for the door, as there was no equipment she could use in the room. Stopping so suddenly that Misha nearly crashed into her, Cameron turned around, unhitched the goat, and then walked it toward the door, planning to test it also.

"What should I do in the meantime?" Jon wondered.

"Wait here while I talk to the right people," Riley told him.

"I have one last question."

Misha waited at the door to hear what Jon was going to ask.

"What's that?" Riley wondered.

"Why didn't any of the other off-shippers test positive for infection?"

"I'm not sure," Riley shook her head. "Best guess? They weren't near Yanis as much as you were. They weren't around him or the zombies long enough to be infected. Or at least not long enough for the infection to show up in our tests. Everyone that helped Rose that I know of was wearing a mask, which I guess was good enough to protect them from the worst of it."

Jon sat on the stool that Cameron had vacated. "So I just have bad luck."

Riley shrugged, and then she, Misha, and Cameron all left the room. Riley went one way, heading for the stairs, while Cameron and Misha led Rifle and the goat to the animal examination room. Once there, Misha got Rifle to hop back up onto the exam table as he had earlier, but this time the dog remained standing.

After Cameron had tied up the goat, she retrieved a needle, which caused Rifle to start whining.

"It's okay, boy." Misha stroked the German shepherd. "It's okay. It's just a little blood draw."

"I may need you to help me hold him," Cameron told Misha.

Misha climbed onto the table with Rifle. When Cameron neared the dog with her needle, Rifle buried his big head into Misha's chest, nearly knocking him over in the process. Misha wrapped his arms around the dog, and rubbed his fur.

"It's okay, *bratishka*. It's all right."

While Cameron drew his blood, Rifle let out some whiney little yelps, but he didn't move. Cameron was quick, taking the syringe of blood over to a small microscope.

"It's all over, you big baby." Misha rubbed Rifle some more, giving his sides a few hardy pats. "She's all done. You're fine, *bratishka*. You're fine."

Rifle lay down on the table, placing his head and forelegs on Misha's lap and curling his tail tightly around his side.

Misha continued to talk soothingly to him, running his fingers through Rifle's fur while Cameron checked his blood.

Cameron sighed, and Misha's head snapped up. Was it a good sigh, or a bad sigh?

"Looks like dogs can't be infected by it," Cameron turned to Misha with a smile.

Misha heaved a huge sigh of relief. He couldn't take any more bad news today. If Rifle had been infected, he might have snapped, and who knows what he would have done then.

Cameron then tested the goat's blood, and got the same result.

"So far so good," she nearly laughed. "Hopefully, the rest of our menagerie will test just as well."

"Test the pigs next," Misha insisted, remembering a video Tobias had shown him from the time he had been attacked by infected pigs.

"Of course. I'll go around and collect blood samples from all our animal groups and bring them back here for testing."

"Mind if I hang around here? I want to know the results."

"Of course."

Cameron gathered up a bunch of needles and syringes, placing them in a small bag that easily clipped onto her belt.

"Shouldn't take me too long. I'll be back in a couple of minutes."

"Sure."

Cameron left the examination room, leaving Misha alone with Rifle and a goat.

Misha bent over and kissed Rifle between his ears. At least he didn't have to worry about his best friend. But more zombies. Zombies after non-zombie deaths occurred. It would change everything. Especially with gunfire coming.

III
During

Sher watched the radar in front of him, careful not to touch anything. It had taken Bob a few minutes, but he had gotten the cruise ship's engines started up and now they were turning to face the other one; the one with the men who had insulted Sher. Bob was good to have around. He wasn't just a mountain of muscle, he was also smart, especially when it came to ships. There had never yet been a ship or boat that Bob couldn't start up or repair.

"Can we keep pace with them?" Sher asked, looking out through the large windows.

"Easily," Bob grumbled. He was moving from station to station, monitoring all the screens and readouts.

"Good." Those sons of bitches were going to pay. How dare they refuse Sher entrance aboard their ship? Did they not know that he was king of these waters? Not those cesspool pirates who tried to claim the title, but him, Sher. He had a whole kingdom, and he was going to bring it down on those assholes' heads.

"Sir?"

"What is it?"

"They have a submarine."

"What?" Sher walked over to where Bob was pointing out the window. Sure enough, on the other side of the ship, a surfaced submarine was following alongside them. "Do we have to worry about it?"

"Don't know. Impossible to tell from here if it's armed or not."

"We'll assume it is and hit it with the small boats first." Sher wasn't an idiot. Submarines could be dangerous if they still had torpedoes and missiles on board. The small, fast boats could take it though. Once night fell, the small boats could zip up alongside the sub and dispatch boarders. Toss a few grenades down the hatch and goodbye submarine. Provided they weren't seen on approach that was.

A moan at the door derailed Sher's thoughts. He hated the stinking corpses almost as much as he hated that other ship. They were annoying, disgusting, and smelly. But these particular zombies might come in handy. He wasn't completely sure how yet, but an idea was prickling the back of his mind.

"How long until the others get here, do you think?" Sher asked Bob. He had his own estimates, but he wanted to hear what Bob thought. Sher might know the men better, but Bob knew the boats.

"The fastest of them should arrive around one a.m."

Sher nodded. That was what he was thinking. "We should sleep in shifts until they get here. Tell me what I need to know to keep us on their tail."

Bob went over the controls with him.

***

Sher was awakened by the crackle of his personal radio.

"Boss?" a small, tinny voice came through the speaker amidst a storm of static. "Boss, you there?"

Sher pulled his radio off his belt as he got to his feet. "I'm here. Who is this?"

"Ricky."

Outside the window, it was dark save for the lights from the ship ahead of them. An extra black spot on the ocean marked where the submarine was. It would have been better if it was even darker out, but at least the moon wasn't a bright and full disc tonight.

Bob pointed to the radar. Several small shapes were tailing behind them, while a few cruised along the sides. Sher would bet that some were so close they weren't showing up on the radar.

"They have the same technology as us," Bob informed him.

"I'm aware." Sher grinned and brought the radio to his lips. "Ricky?"

"Yeah, Boss?"

"Round up the fastest of you and take out that submarine now."

"You got it." There was a glee in Ricky's voice that Sher liked hearing.

"Are you ready, Bob?"

"Just tell me what to do, sir."

"We're going to get my dear old sister back, kill all these cunts in the process, and reap the spoils." Sher's grin widened. His sister belonged to him. He owned her, and no one else was allowed to touch her without his say so. Freya was his favourite.

"You got it, sir."

Section 3:
Fight

14
Mathias Was Asleep

The fire alarm was like taking an ice pick to the skull. Mathias shocked awake, sitting upright and grabbing Hope to him in the same moment. Hope, who had woken up in the same instant, grabbed on tightly to his shirt. She was so frightened and confused that she didn't make a sound, while fat tears streaked down her face. Mathias looked around the room but didn't see Riley anywhere.

Was it another bomb? Mathias could barely think straight, what with the noise and exhaustion. How long had he slept? It was still dark outside and impossible to tell.

The alarm suddenly cut off, causing a frightened squeak from Hope.

"Attention Diana! Attention Diana!" a voice boomed over the PA system. It was louder than Mathias had ever heard it before. "We are under attack! I repeat, we are under attack! Everyone report to your stations at once! This is not a drill! We are under attack!"

"What's happening, Daddy?" Hope finally found her voice. "Was it another bomb?"

"Hush, Hope." Mathias was trying to think, to remember the day before. His thoughts were completely scrambled.

"Was it another bomb?" Hope persisted, even louder. "Or is it the big wave? Daddy!"

"Hope, be quiet!"

Hope started to wail. She wasn't used to her dad yelling at her. The sound was worse than the alarm because it broke Mathias's heart.

"I'm sorry, honey. I'm sorry. I didn't mean to shout. It's okay." Mathias pulled her close to his chest. "Do you remember the pirates? Do you remember when the pirates came and wanted our stuff?"

"Yes." He felt her nod against him.

"This is just like when the pirates came. I have to go and help get rid of the pirates."

"No, Daddy!" Hope shouted. "I don't want to be alone! Where's Mommy? Did the pirates get Mommy?"

"No, no, no, of course not. The pirates didn't get Mommy. She's just working late. And you won't be alone. I'll find someone you know to take care of you." Mathias slid out of bed, releasing Hope to get his boots on.

"I want to stay with you!" Hope bawled.

"I'd love to stay with you too, pumpkin, believe me I would, but I can't. It's my job to get rid of the pirates. Milly will be with you."

Hope didn't use words this time, just made that half-screaming sound that crying kids make. Mathias did his best to ignore it while he finished getting ready, wrapping his belt around his waist and checking his pistol.

"Milly," Mathias called, bringing the dog out from around the far side of the bed. She looked up at Mathias with her ears flat, disliking Hope's crying as much as Mathias did.

Mathias went to the bed and scooped Hope up with one arm. She quieted some, perhaps thinking that Mathias was taking her with him, but continued to sniffle.

Moving toward the door, Mathias used his free hand to open it and step outside with his child and dog. The hall was a mess. People were running every which way, heading toward their stations, trying to find friends and family from whom they had been separated. Mathias scanned all the faces around him, looking for someone he knew and trusted enough to watch over Hope.

"Mathias!"

Mathias turned and spotted Abby down the hall. He ran toward her, narrowly avoiding a few collisions.

"Can you watch Hope?" Mathias asked pointlessly, as Abby was already taking Hope from him.

Looking into the room that Abby was in—no doubt a donated room, as the bomb would have also destroyed hers—Mathias saw Lauren shifting a mattress to cover part of the glass window. They would leave the door portion of it uncovered in case they needed to escape, but covered half to reduce the risk of injury if the glass broke. Claire and Peter were also in the room, huddled together on the floor.

"I'll take good care of her," Abby told Mathias. "Go do your job."

Mathias kissed Hope on the head, pushed on Milly's behind so that she'd go into the room, and then took off running down the hall. He stopped and briefly turned around.

"I love you, Hope!" he shouted.

He thought he heard Hope's small voice respond, but he couldn't be sure. There was no time to check as he turned back around and ran for the stairs.

Flying down the steps, he nearly went too far. It took him a second to realize that he had been on the fifth deck, not the seventh, and therefore needed to go down only one deck. Bursting outside, he just about crashed into another ship defender on her way to her own position. The two of them ignored one another and continued on to their own locations. Mathias reached the railing adjacent to the steps that led up to the helipad where his little brother would no doubt be. As with Riley and Hope, he had to shove Danny out of his mind and focus on what was before him.

Out at sea, Mathias could make out the shape of the German submarine. It was diving. Men, who had likely just boarded the craft in an attempt to take it, were now scrambling back to their own boats. Most were still close enough to their craft just to jump back in, but a few dove off the sides of the submarine, hoping to swim far enough away to be safe from the sucking pull of water around the sub. The submarine would be safe beneath the surface of the waves.

From a higher deck, someone fired off a flare. The ocean lit up beneath its burning red light. There were dozens of boats in the water, all of them speedsters and carrying armed men. They raced through the water alongside the Diana, assessing her and occasionally firing shots at the defenders near the rails. Mathias fell back as a bullet *whanged* off the metal above him, but he quickly returned to the railing.

"Rifles only!" he shouted at the men and women under his command along this section of the ship. "Only those with rifles should fire, and only if they have a clear shot!" Mathias left the railing to walk behind the line, making sure his orders were heard and followed. "We don't have the ammo for suppressive fire!"

"What are we supposed to do then?" a boy not much older than Danny asked him.

"Keep an eye on them, and keep your head down!" Mathias shouted so that his answer could be heard by all. "There are only two ways to get on the Diana! They either have to go through the doors on the first deck, which are hard enough to open from the outside, and are being reinforced as I speak! Failing that, they're going to raise ladders to this deck here! That's when we can get them!"

Everyone was nervous, but they obeyed his commands. Mathias couldn't tell if everyone else around the ship was being as reserved, but he hoped they were. They were going to need the bullets.

Returning to his position, Mathias went back to watching over the edge. As he tracked the progress of one boat tearing through the water along their side, a shot rang out from a higher deck. The driver's head all but exploded in a shower of blood, brain, and bone, the boat suddenly making a sharp left turn away from the Diana's side and spilling a man with a machine gun out of the back. Mathias's first thought was of Alec, who could have made that shot, but then he remembered that Alec was no longer with them. His rifle hadn't even survived the blast. Maybe it was one of his shooting students. Mathias hoped more people could shoot like that.

The 9MM semi-automatic pistol in his hand felt useless. It wasn't accurate enough to be taking pot shots at the invaders. He gripped the gun tightly, his finger outside the trigger guard. At least he had a second magazine full of ammo for it. After bringing Freya to Commander Crichton and Captain Bronislav, he had gone to the armoury to get it. The armoury had been busy, running with its full staff, as they supplied all the ship defenders and off-shippers with extra ammunition. Some citizens had been there, willingly giving up their firearms to the better shooters, while others had just been picking up melee weapons. Everyone had known that this attack was a possibility, they had just hoped it wouldn't happen, or happen so soon.

Another bullet cracked near Mathias, this time into the solar panel in front of him. He winced more at the panel's loss, than the shot's close proximity.

"That's something we can do," he muttered to himself. "Everyone!" he called to those in his command. "Try to save the plants and solar panels! Unhook them from the railing and then place them against the far wall! Do not put yourself at risk! If you can't save it without putting yourself in danger, don't bother with it!"

Everyone looked relieved to have a specific task to do, and set to work immediately. Mathias started on the solar panel that had been hit. Despite the bullet, the engineers and electricians on board might be able to save parts of it.

Getting the panels and plants off the railing was harder than Mathias had expected. Although construction clamps held on a few of them, most had been screwed or bolted in place. A quick survey of his whole group revealed they had only two screwdrivers and one pair of pliers. Still, they were making it work. Once they got a rhythm down, things picked up. While a few people worked on the screws and bolts, others kept watch on the boats circling the Diana. When it looked clear, Mathias and three others would grab the planter or solar panel, pull it off the railing, and move it against the far wall. The solar panels took extra work, as they had wires hooked up to them that needed to be dealt with.

Everything was going well until Mathias was shot.

***

"One, two, three, lift!" Mathias called out. He and the three others lifted the solar panel as one, quickly pulling it over the side of the railing, and hurrying it to the back wall.

"Take a breather, the next one is giving the guys some trouble," a woman watching the boats told Mathias's group.

Mathias was grateful for the short rest. The panels and planters were heavy, and he hadn't had nearly enough sleep.

"Bet you didn't expect to be spending your night like this, huh?" he said to the man standing next to him, an exhausted smile on his sweaty face. Mathias had been in combat several times, even before the day the zombies came. Although his adrenaline levels were spiked, he almost felt at home.

The man he had spoken to chuckled right before his neck exploded.

Machine gun fire rattled from the water below, and a spray of bullets assaulted their position. Deadly ricochets bounced off nearby metal objects and pipes. One took out the man next to Mathias, but he barely had time to register it before a sharp, hot pain buried itself in his leg. Crying out, Mathias fell to the deck floor, the dying man collapsing next to him.

The team dropped to the deck floor, covering their heads with their hands. None of them fired back, but whether that was from obeying Mathias's orders or from fear, he didn't know. As soon as the gunfire passed, a few ship defenders crawled over to Mathias's position.

His leg was on fire. Mathias had previously taken two shots to a bullet-proof vest, but it had felt nothing like this. Lying on his back, Mathias gritted his teeth, his uninjured limbs squirming on the deck.

"Christian's dead," a woman reported from beside the man who had taken a bullet to the throat.

"Mathias, I need you to hold still while I look at your leg," a man was speaking next to Mathias's head.

Mathias's eyes were squeezed shut, so he had no idea who was talking, but he nodded. A pair of hands touched his calf, near the wound. He cried out as fresh pain shot up his leg. Finally opening his eyes, Mathias propped himself up on his elbows to see the damage. He was surprised to find Josh cutting away a section of his pant leg.

"Josh? What are you doing here?" He was confused, and looked around, verifying that he was still outside on the fourth deck and not in the medical centre.

"Someone up front was shot. I was on the way back to my position when I saw you get hit." He spoke with a cold efficiency that was unlike him. Mathias noticed that Riley had the same tone whenever she was working on somebody.

"Danny?" Danny was up front.

"He's fine," Josh assured him, finally freeing his wound so that he could look at it.

Mathias looked at his team, who were watching the proceedings. "Get back to work!" he barked at them. "Don't wait for another pass before getting the last of those planters and panels off the railing!"

His team flinched and quickly turned around. They were even more scared now than they had been previously, and Mathias couldn't blame them. A man was dead, while their leader lay injured.

"Ahh!" Mathias couldn't help crying out as Josh touched his leg again.

"The bullet went clean through," Josh told him. "Looks like it missed your major arteries. You're lucky."

"Too bad Christian wasn't." Mathias looked past Josh toward the dead man. He was lying in a spreading pool of his own blood, head cocked sideways, one eye open while the other was half closed.

Josh stuck a needle into Mathias's leg, drawing his attention back to his own problem.

"What was in that?"

"Morphine."

"We don't have a lot of that. Why did you waste it on me?"

Josh looked at him like he was crazy and didn't bother answering.

"It's not going to mess with my head too much, is it?"

"No more than the pain would. I didn't give you that much."

"Now what are you doing?" Mathias watched as Josh prepared another needle.

"I have to stitch up this hole, which means numbing the area around it."

"Okay."

Mathias watched as Josh first numbed up his leg, and then began stitching. It was a strange sensation. He felt no pain, but he could feel the needle tugging at his flesh.

I was shot once in the leg. How many times had Alec been shot? he found himself thinking. A lot more than once, that was for sure. Mathias wouldn't have to worry about being trapped in a wheelchair for the rest of his life.

Josh washed the blood away from the wound and then wrapped it up in a bandage.

"Try to stay off it," he told Mathias.

"I can't abandon my post," Mathias frowned at him.

"That's why I said try."

The body behind Josh twitched. Mathias assumed that it was just some post-mortem thing, but then the body moved its arm in a way that was definitely not a post-mortem thing.

"Josh, turn around." It was possible the morphine was messing with him.

Josh did as he was asked. He saw the arm movement, which was followed by an unsteady head movement. Understanding it wasn't right, Josh moved from Mathias's leg, to his head, away from the corpse.

"What's happening?" Josh asked him.

"Riley knows more than I do, but just accept for now that that man has turned into a zombie and others who die without being infected will do the same." Mathias pulled his gun and pointed it at the zombie's head.

"Don't waste the ammo." Josh took a scalpel out of his medical kit.

Just as the zombie was becoming aware, just as it was starting to reach for Mathias, Josh crouched down next to it and drove the scalpel deep into its left eye, jamming it in with the flat of his hand. The zombie's body flailed once, then stopped for good.

"Who knows about this?" Josh turned to Mathias, his cold, clinical attitude saving the less important questions for later. For now, he simply trusted Mathias.

"I don't know. Riley and whoever was on staff with her when the off-shippers came back. Me, I guess, although I wasn't sure this would actually happen."

"People need to be warned."

"It's going to frighten them."

"Better than getting eaten by a zombie!" Josh spoke louder than he meant to. He was angry. What, exactly, he was angry about, Mathias couldn't say. It could be that Riley knew something and hadn't told him, or it could just be the presence of a zombie on board. Josh hadn't had to face a zombie in a long time. He was quick to rein his emotions back in.

"Then tell people. Ask Riley if you want details, and then tell people," Mathias told him.

"I'm going to do just that." Josh suddenly got up and disappeared, leaving his scalpel buried in the former-zombie's eye, only the very end of it shining silver through the blood.

"What's going on, Mathias?" someone from his team asked, eyeing the body that Josh had stabbed.

"There's no time to explain the details, but you need to understand something." His team turned away from the last of their duties to listen. "If anyone dies by something other than a headshot, they're going to come back as a walking corpse."

A man and woman gasped in unison.

"Just accept that fact and get back to work," Mathias said before anyone could ask any questions. "Come on, we have a ship to defend, we can deal with that problem later."

They were slow returning to the task that Mathias had given them, but they did return to it. Mathias dragged himself over to the railing, where he lay on his stomach and watched the waters below. It seemed like there were more boats now.

Shifting himself, Mathias poked his head out briefly to look down the length of the Diana. He could see the other cruise ship trailing behind them with most of its lights off. He also saw a lot of other boats around it. It seemed that Sher had summoned every boat that could make it out here. Some even appeared to have been towed by the faster boats. One boat in particular stood out. Or rather, one *ship* in particular stood out. Mathias didn't know the name for what it was, but it was old, with sails, and made out of wood. The Diana passengers had seen a few ships like it in their travels, but they were always tourist attractions, and almost always anchored or docked. It seemed Sher had brought this one back into service on the high seas. Based on the angle it was coming toward them, it must have been somewhere different from the other boats when Sher had called it. Hopefully they'd be able to outrun it. Had Sher also gotten the cannons functioning? If he had, and the ship was able to reach them, then the Diana was in a lot more trouble than anyone realized.

Mathias helped keep an eye out for other strafing boats while the rest of the solar panels and planters were removed. Once they were gone, the team spread out along their section. The panels and planters had actually been providing cover, so now everyone was lying down on their bellies like Mathias.

"What did the sheep say when he met Michael Jackson?" Mathias found himself saying.

The team members nearest to him looked at him like he was crazy.

"Who's *baaaaaaa*-d?" Much as he had been thinking of Alec a lot lately, Mathias suddenly found himself thinking of LeBlanc, LeBlanc who knew an endless stream of bad jokes, which he trotted out whenever the people around him were stressed. They weren't really good jokes, but people laughed anyway.

No one laughed at Mathias's joke, but at least one person grinned. If he could get that one person to play along, then maybe he could reduce the tension.

"Knock, knock."

No one answered.

"Come on, knock, knock."

"Who's there?"

"Interrupting cow."

"Interrupting co-"

"Moooooo!"

That one got a few chuckles, probably because they had heard it, or even used it, as kids.

"Loserssaywhat." Someone else from down the line spoke quickly, mashing his words together.

"What?" Mathias hadn't caught it.

The speaker laughed. "Guess our leader admits to being a loser."

Thinking back, Mathias realized what had just happened and chuckled. Good, they were getting into it now.

"What has four wheels and flies?" a woman asked.

"A garbage truck," another answered.

"A man walks into a bar. Ouch."

"Second man ducks."

"What did the bartender say to the moose? Why the long face?"

Everyone was in on it now. Once a joke was told, people would chuckle, and then someone would tell another one. A few were real groaners, in fact, most were, but it was easing the tension. It helped people forget that there was a dead man behind them. There was no way to forget the men with guns in front of them, but that was a good thing.

"Ladder boats!" the man on the end suddenly called out, cutting off a woman mid-joke. Everyone was suddenly silent and focused.

A boat was driving up alongside the Diana, close to her hull. From their high vantage point, the defenders could clearly see that there was a long, hook-end ladder on board. A man at the back of the boat was scanning their deck, looking for the best place to raise and attach the ladder.

"Remain calm!" Mathias ordered his team. "Remember your firearms training! This is no different than when we were attacked by pirates!"

"Except for the fact that there's a lot more of them," a man down the line remarked snarkily.

"True enough, but all that means is we're going to be out here longer. Just remember, don't take a shot unless you're sure you can hit your target!"

Mathias peeked over the edge. The man in the back of the boat saw him, and fired wildly in his direction. Quickly pulling his head back into cover, Mathias managed to avoid being hit.

He wondered how other sections of the ship were doing. The front, where Danny was, was probably doing fine. They were higher than Mathias's position and had more room to manoeuvre. These guys didn't seem stupid enough to cut in close to the Diana's nose where they risked getting smashed to bits by her.

The balconies above them had less room, but like the front, they had a higher position. From Mathias's understanding, there were a lot fewer people up there than there were down here, and most of them were holding rifles. A few times, he heard the sharp report of a shot, and every time he hoped the bullet found its mark.

Mostly, he worried about the men and women on the other side of the ship, the ones on the same deck as him. No doubt, there would be ladder boats on that side as well, and the back. The back of the ship had its wake to defend it from invaders getting too close, but there was also that other cruise ship to think about. If Sher had men with rifles, they could easily board the other cruise ship, get up onto the helipad, and open fire on the rear defenders. Maybe there weren't as many ship defenders or off-shippers at the back as there were in other locations. That's what Mathias wanted to think.

A gunshot boomed just a few feet away from him, as a woman on his line fired over the side.

"Did you get him?" the man next to the woman asked as she pulled back into cover.

"Not a kill shot, but I'm pretty sure I winged him in his arm. It's hard to tell in this light."

The woman had a point. The flare was the best light they had for viewing the water since all the ship's lower windows had been covered at the start of the siege, but the flare's light was weird, casting odd shadows and bathing everything in an unnatural colour. They had to make do.

Mathias and his team defended the side of the ship. More and more ladder boats came, and as they did, Mathias's team had to fire more shots. The riflemen on the decks above them were clearly helping, but often it came down to Mathias's team. The curve of the ship's hull made it difficult for those higher up to see the ladder boats, which stuck dangerously close to the Diana's side.

Several times Mathias saw the hook end of a ladder rise up above the floor of the deck he was lying on. Each time that happened, one or two gunshots would rip through the air and the ladder would lower. At least once the ladder fell into the water, eliciting cheers from the team, but they were quickly cut off as they learned the ladders floated. It was short work for another boat, or perhaps even the same boat, to drive by and scoop it up.

Mathias had shot and killed at least three men so far, wounding half a dozen others, and only completely missing twice. He was nearing the end of his first ammo mag when he heard the sound that sent a chill through his bones.

The railing clanged as a ladder hooked onto it.

"Ladder! Ladder! Ladder!"

15
Misha's With The Animals

Misha hadn't bothered going to sleep. He stayed down on the second deck, near his post, keeping out of the way in one of the inner hallways. He had watched Cameron for a while, noting all the animals that came back negative for infection. It seemed that whatever the new version of the hybrid-virus was, it hadn't been passed on to any of the animals on the ship. Misha wondered if that would remain true if a human bit a live animal. It wasn't something anyone would try out, but it was a curiosity.

For now, Misha sat next to one of the storage rooms and waited.

"What do you think I should do when the time comes?" Jon asked him. Jon had nowhere to go while waiting for Riley to explain everything to the ship leaders, so he decided to hang around with Misha.

"I don't know," Misha shrugged. "What's your usual post when pirates come?"

"I go with my team up to the front of the ship and assist the pilots on the helipad."

"Then go there."

"But people don't know about the infection yet. They'll think I'm infected."

"They're your team, right?"

"Yeah."

"Then they're not going to kill you. I don't think they'd care what's supposedly wrong with you, so long as you're doing your job."

"You really think that?"

"Don't you?" Misha wasn't particularly close with his own working team, but he knew they would never think of killing him. And off-shippers? Of all the working teams, Misha had noticed that they were the closest knit groups. Misha's close friends had become his close friends by surviving the zombies together; off-shippers went out and faced zombies all the time, so it stood to reason that the teams would end up very close.

"Would you come with me when I go up there?" Jon asked.

"I have a job to do down here."

"What's that?"

"I help block off all the portholes down here."

"A lot of people do that, so it shouldn't take long. What do you do when you're done?"

Misha shrugged. "Usually I stay down here and help keep the animals calm."

"But that's not a job assigned to you?"

"No."

"So you could come with me?"

"Why do you want me to?" Misha wondered.

"I don't want to go alone," Jon shrugged. "There will be other people between me and my team, and all I have is this knife I found if anyone decides to attack me."

"Yeah, but why me?"

"Because you believed me. You could have easily turned me over to the ship defenders but you didn't."

Misha shrugged. "Lots of people would have believed you."

"Not really," Jon shook his head. "A few, yeah, but not a lot. I'm not sure Lauren and Abby completely believed me when I said I wasn't infected. Claire did. She believed me. Peter probably would have believed me if he fully understood what was going on, but Abby and Lauren? My guardians? I don't think they did, even though they wanted to."

"Well that was before even you had seen someone turn without being bitten," Misha commented. "Are you sure you even believed yourself at that point?"

Jon looked at his hands, squeezing his fingers together in a way that suggested to Misha that he hadn't completely believed himself.

"Just come with me," Jon looked back up at him. "You and Rifle."

The German Shepherd looked up from where he was lying on the floor when he heard his name.

"All right, we'll come with you, but I have to finish my job down here first."

"That's fine. I'll help you with it."

"I'm not going to be of any use up there. Spear guns aren't known for their accuracy."

"That's fine. You and Rifle can hang back in the safest zones, and maybe relay a few messages from one zone to another. The helipad is fairly large for the number of people we send up there, so we section it off. Unfortunately, it makes communicating between us not that easy. What do you say?"

Misha sighed and looked down at Rifle. "What do you think, *bratishka*? Think we should follow Jon into the danger zone?"

Rifle chuffed, an answer that could be either yes or no. Not like he understood what Misha was asking him anyway.

"Thanks for this, Misha," Jon said after a quiet moment, understanding that by asking Rifle, Misha had agreed.

Misha brushed off his thanks with a mumble.

"What do you think Robin is doing right now?" Apparently, Jon wanted to keep talking.

Misha shrugged.

"Probably sleeping," Jon suggested. "I'm glad she's not a field medic in these situations. She doesn't even work in the primary medical centre downstairs, but in the smaller one. They turn it into an emergency centre when we're being attacked."

That was understandable. The smaller medical centre used to be a dentist office and a spa. It was still a dentistry—whenever the one dentist on board was on duty—and was also used for general check-ups and examinations. A lot of stuffy noses went through there.

"Do you have a girlfriend, Misha?" Jon asked, seemingly out of the blue.

Misha just shook his head.

"Any one of interest?"

He continued to shake his head. Since the Day, Misha had found himself not really looking at girls. At least not like that. Sure, he still thought most of them were pleasing to look at, and he had the same kinds of dreams about them as he did in college, but he couldn't see himself in a relationship. Not yet at least. He couldn't imagine having to take care of anyone else, or having to worry about her whenever stuff like this happened. Just watching out for Rifle could be stressful enough, and after what happened to Alec... No, he didn't see a relationship anywhere in his near future.

Jon had run out of things to talk about, at least for the moment. The two of them sat there in companionable silence, each with his own thoughts.

Rifle lifted his head and looked down the hall, his ears pricked. He was very focused on something, but when Misha looked down the hall, he couldn't see anything. Just as he was about to open his mouth and say something, the fire alarm began to blare. Its sound pierced through Misha, startling him up onto his feet. His heart was immediately racing.

When the siren cut off, it was replaced by a voice over the PA. "Attention Diana! Attention Diana! We are under attack! I repeat, we are under attack! Everyone report to your stations at once! This is not a drill! We are under attack!"

Despite his foreknowledge and the fact that he had done this before, all thought was suddenly gone from Misha's mind. He couldn't remember what he was supposed to do, or where he was supposed to go.

"Come on, Misha!" Jon called out as he ripped open the storage closet door.

Shaking his head once, Misha turned to the closet. Inside, it was full of mattresses, heavy blankets, and wood.

"What do we start with?" Jon wondered. He had never done this task before.

"The mattresses. Come on." Misha grabbed the side of one and yanked it off the pile. "Rifle, stay close to me."

Rifle didn't need to be told twice, or even the once. He was as close to Misha's legs as he could be, without actually touching them and getting in the way.

Jon grabbed the other end of the mattress and lifted. He and Misha carried it out to the outer hallways, toward one of the rooms on Misha's list.

"Be careful of the animals," Misha told Jon. "We do the rooms with the small animals first, giving the larger ones a bit of time to calm down before we go in there. They'll be agitated, and can be dangerous."

"What's in the first room?"

"Ducks, so we shouldn't have to worry too much."

They approached the room and Misha let go with one hand to reach over the half-door and undo the latch. Once it was open, Rifle scooted into the room ahead of them, and the boys carried in the mattress.

"Watch your step," Misha warned Jon.

Scattered all over the floor was straw and duck shit. There was also a plastic kiddie pool full of water in the middle of the room, a kind of hutch made out of nightstands and blankets in a corner, and a large slab of wood bolted into the floor. Rifle was keeping the families of ducks inside the hutch and out of the way. Every now and again one of the ducks would quack at him, but Rifle didn't move from his guard position.

"Prop it up." Misha and Jon manoeuvred the mattress so that it sat on the floor and leaned up against the porthole window, which already had a covering of chicken wire bolted into the frame. "Come on, next one."

There were a total of five rooms on Misha's list to take care of. They grabbed a second mattress and headed for the next one. This room contained chickens. It was very similar to the duck room, except it didn't have a kiddie pool, and contained more nightstand-hutches and chicken shit. Rifle had a harder time keeping the chickens in their hutches, as there were more of them to guard, but every time one of them thought about straying, the German Shepherd was there to keep it inside.

The third room they carried a mattress into was full of nervous sheep.

"Easy, Rifle. Be gentle," Misha reminded him. They didn't want to overexcite the sheep.

It was harder to move around in that room, as the sheep were always standing in the way, but the mattress was placed over the window in the end.

The fourth room had goats in it, and went nearly as smoothly. One of the goats butted the back of Jon's legs, but it wasn't a hard head-butt.

"We have to be extra careful with this last room," Misha told Jon as they approached it.

"What's in this one?"

"A bull."

"Sounds dangerous."

"Depending on his mood, it is."

Misha actually hesitated outside the door. This one was a full door, but the peephole had been reversed so Misha could look inside. He could only see the bull's tail swishing back and forth in the main section of the room.

"Rifle's going to go in first, and we're going to give him a second to determine the bull's temperament."

"You're the boss." Jon stepped closer to the wall as a man dragged a mattress past, heading for another room.

"Rifle?"

Rifle looked up at Misha.

"This is a *bull*. I hope you remember that word. Bulls are big, and they can be tough. Try not to get hurt."

Rifle just continued looking up at him, waiting for a command. Heaving a sigh, Misha undid the latches and opened the door. A loud snort came from the room beyond. Rifle didn't pause, he walked straight into the room. Misha lingered at the doorway, watching carefully.

As Rifle approached the bull, he did pause for a moment. The dog then circled wide around the back of the bull. There was another snort, and Misha listened to the clattering of hooves as the bull turned to face Rifle. The tail disappeared as the bull completely hid behind the bathroom. Rifle's whole body was tense as he faced the bull. Misha watched for a few breathless seconds, frightened for his best friend.

Rifle suddenly relaxed and began wagging his tail. Misha relaxed at the same time.

"Seems the bull is fairly calm. Still, I'm going to have to halter him to the wall. Give me a few seconds to start this, and then drag the mattress in."

Jon nodded.

Misha stepped into the room and walked down the short hall. He deliberately made some noise as he walked so that his appearance wouldn't startle the bull. Although Rifle surely knew that Misha was coming, he didn't once look at him. The dog's eyes were completely fixed upon the bull. As Misha reached the end of the hall, the bull turned its head toward him. Misha froze, but the bull just snorted and pretty much ignored him. Misha breathed a sigh of relief.

The bull wasn't terribly large. He was a bit skinny, which was actually good because it meant they could walk him through the halls. Any bigger and the bull would be too large to exercise, and they'd have to put him down and turn him into beef. The bull also had no horns, or at least not very large ones; they had been carefully shaved down into hard nubs by the veterinarians. Despite these deficiencies, people had still been hurt by this bull and others. When they got their ire up, the bulls could still deliver a bone cracking head-butt or sharp kick. It was always best to proceed with caution, even when a fire alarm *hadn't* blared several minutes ago.

Misha stepped slowly past the bull, picking up the end of a rope that was attached to the wall. He proceeded to move just as slowly toward the bull's head.

Jon entered the room, dragging the mattress behind him. Just before Misha could grab the bull's halter, its head swung to the side to look at the newcomer. Misha completely froze, his hand hovering part way toward the bull, open in a grabbing position. Jon also froze, unsure about what to do.

Rifle yipped in a friendly way, drawing the bull's attention back to him. The bull's head swung close enough that Misha was able to attach the rope to his halter. While Jon propped the mattress up on his own, Misha grabbed another rope from the opposite wall and attached it to the other side of the bull's halter. The second rope would be in the way when they had to bring in more equipment, but it was better to have the bull secure.

Gunfire rattled off the hull. The bull startled, dancing in place, shifting as far left and right as the ropes allowed him. Misha quickly dashed out of the way of the beast's bulk.

"Okay. Hardest part is done," Misha sighed. "On to the next job."

Jon was distracted by the gunfire and stared at the outer wall.

"Jon," Misha tapped his arm, "come on."

Jon startled briefly, but then followed Misha carefully past the bull. Rifle came once they had reached the door.

"What's next?" Jon asked.

"Now, we take the wooden panels and brace them against the backs of the mattresses with the beams."

They grabbed a large wood panel and two beams, and brought them to the bull's room. Misha explained that the bull was fairly calm right now, so it was best to board up his room as quickly as possible, before something else happened to agitate him. The wood panel was pressed tightly against the back of the mattress, and then the two beams were angled between it and the board that had been bolted into the floor. In the bull's room, the board in the floor had gouges and chunks taken out of it by the bull's hooves, but it was still strong.

"Once we do this in the last four rooms, we're done."

Both Misha and Jon were sweating. None of this stuff was light, and they were running around with it in one of the hottest areas of the Diana. There were no complaints though. Misha didn't even complain when one of the goats butted him so hard it knocked him to the floor. He just got up and helped Jon wedge the second beam in place, while Rifle bullied the goat into a corner.

"So that's it?" Jon asked as they finished up in the duck room. In there, the mattress had fallen over and they found a fresh bullet hole in it and a matching one in the glass.

"That's it."

"So we're going up to the helipad now?"

"If that's what you still want to do." Misha didn't particularly like the idea of going up there, but he had already agreed to it.

"Yeah. Come on." This time Jon led the way.

As Misha followed behind him with Rifle, nimbly dodging out of the way of other people, he felt the hairs on the back of his neck rise. Something was telling him that the worst was yet to come.

***

Misha thought he saw Mathias outside one of the doors when he and Jon reached the fourth deck, but then Jon led him to the door on the other side of the ship. Outside, the defenders were all huddled down against the floor, keeping out of sight of the boats in the water below.

A bullet whined past, ricocheting off something. Misha flinched, hunching closer to the floor. Rifle pressed himself tighter against Misha's legs. It was impossible to tell how close the shot was, but any sort of close was too close. They were going to be killed out here.

Jon seemed to ignore the bullet. He hunched slightly over and stuck to the wall, leading Misha, and by extension Rifle, toward the front of the ship. The stairs up to the helipad were for the most part enclosed, and Jon sprang up the steps two at a time. Misha moved slower, preferring the partial protection of the staircase as opposed to the open area ahead of them. He wished he had stayed down below with the animals.

The helipad area was large, but only two teams moved about on and around it: half of Jon's off-shipper team, and the flight team. The off-shippers were dashing around the edges, tracking the boats below, while the flight team was doing something with the helicopters. A single bright flood light illuminated the centre where the flight team was working, while an orange flare lit up the side Jon and Misha had come up, and a red flare bathed the far side in a light that was a bit too much like blood for Misha's tastes.

"Jon!" someone Misha couldn't see called out from nearby.

"Brunt!" Jon replied, moving partly across the space to meet up with the man.

Misha followed hesitantly behind Jon. Now that he was here, he didn't know why he was, not really. Jon had begged him to come, afraid that someone might assault him on the way. Given what had happened when he was in the Dragon's Den, this was understandable, but no one had assaulted Jon on the way up here. In fact, no one had even given him a second glance. They either didn't realize he was supposed to be locked up, or they didn't care. Misha didn't know what he was supposed to do now.

"Glad you could make it." The man named Brunt slapped Jon's shoulder.

Jon only grinned in response.

"Who's your friend?" Brunt looked over at Misha. "Sorry, I don't know your name. Seen you around, but never been introduced. I'm Brunt." He held out his hand.

Misha briefly shook it. "Misha, and this is Rifle."

"Rifle." Brunt held his hand out to the German Shepherd to let him sniff it.

Instead, Rifle sat down and placed his paw in Brunt's hand.

"Ha!" Brunt cried out, shaking it as briefly as he had shaken Misha's hand. "He's a smart one."

"He is."

"Come to help?" Brunt directed this question to both Jon and Misha.

"Yup. What can I do?" Jon asked.

"Well, we've only got one rifle up here, not including this furry one, so shooting is pretty much out of the question. Rose was always our best shooter." Brunt shook his head sadly.

"She'll be all right." Jon's voice wavered slightly, unsure of his words.

"Mostly, we're counting boats," Brunt continued. "We're trying to determine just how many there are out there."

"Wouldn't that make more sense from the back of the ship?" Misha couldn't help but comment.

"Yeah, they're doing the most counting as far as I know." Brunt shrugged. "Our more important job has been to warn the flight crew when it looks like one of the boats is about to fire upon us."

"How can I help?" Jon asked.

"Brewster's been covering the left, and Shaidi's been covering the right. If you want, you can go up onto the nose."

"You got it." Jon took off toward the steps that would take him up to the helipad, where the forward-most point of the ship was.

"You here to help?" Brunt asked Misha.

"Not really." Misha looked down at his feet, heat spreading across his face. "I was just accompanying Jon up here in case he ran into trouble on the way."

"That's fine. You should ask the flight crew if they need any help. You're on the maintenance team, right?"

Misha was confused until Brunt pointed at his wetsuit.

"I'm on the underwater team. I don't know much, if anything, about helicopters," Misha admitted.

"That's fine. They might just need an extra set of hands to hold things. Now if you'll excuse me, I better go get the newest counts from Brewster and Shaidi." Brunt jogged off to where a very large man was leaning over a railing.

Misha continued to stand where he was, unsure about what to do. He didn't really want to be up here, but he didn't want to head back down to the fourth deck either. That just seemed like asking for a bullet. When he spotted Danny, he decided he might as well try to be useful.

"Danny!" Misha trotted up to where the younger Cole was bolting some pieces together.

"Misha!" Danny raised a hand in greeting, and then went back to working the wrench.

"What are you doing?" Misha asked as he reached him.

Rifle went straight up to Danny, sniffing his shoulders. Danny gave his head a quick rub with a greasy hand.

"Well, we can't completely build the bubble copter, there's not enough space, but it's in a lot of pieces right now. We're trying to put it back together as much as possible, so that if we need to, the Cougar can take off and we can quickly assemble the smaller one on the platform." Danny spoke in a distracted voice, searching for a certain part or tool. "Could you hand me that piece behind your right foot?"

Misha pointed to what he thought Danny was referring to.

"No, the other one. Next to that.

Misha pointed at another piece.

"That's the one."

"Why's the little helicopter in so many pieces?" Misha asked as he handed Danny the whatever-it-was. He had no idea what any of the parts were for.

"We had taken it apart for a thorough cleaning. Didn't expect to be attacked by... They're not really pirates, are they? What should we call them? An army?"

Misha just shrugged. He didn't know what to call them. They were enough like pirates for him to feel comfortable calling them that, even if they weren't.

"Anything I can help you with?" Misha asked.

"Sure. You can fetch me stuff."

"I won't know the names of things. I barely know the names of most tools."

Danny chuckled despite the sounds of gunfire from the water. "That's okay. I'm still learning most of their proper names myself. I'll point to what I need, or try to describe it in a simple way."

"Okay."

Misha liked helping Danny. It kept him busy, and it kept him out of harm's way. Every now and again Jon or one of the other off-shippers would call out, warning them that a boat looked like it was about to fire. Everyone would lay flat until it passed. Sometimes the boat did fire, and sometimes it didn't. Even when it did, there was nothing above them for bullets to ricochet off, and in the middle of the area, where Misha was with Danny, a ricochet off a railing was unlikely. Most of the shots went way over their heads, as the attackers were aiming at the bridge several decks above them.

Sadly, Misha didn't get to help Danny for very long.

Shaidi's scream caused just about everyone to drop what they were doing, the only exception being two men on the flight team, who were holding up a large panel of glass for which the bubble chopper was named. Rifle had been sniffing around the tools and parts and staying away from the edges, but now he placed himself in front of Misha, his hackles raised and a low growl in his throat as he tried to frighten off the unseen threat.

Jon reached Shaidi first, running on feet of lightning. One of his team members had already been badly injured, so Misha could only imagine the load of fear and adrenaline that coursed through Jon's veins when that scream pierced the air.

Brunt reached her next, but he was closely followed by Misha and Danny, and then Brewster who had the farthest to run but was a lot faster than he looked.

"I'm all right," Shaidi was gasping, her cat-like eyes wide open. "I'm all right."

"No, you're not. Keep quiet," Jon told her while looking over her body. "You've been shot in the hip."

Misha stood to one side as Brewster gently moved her away from the railing, and while Jon accepted a shirt from Danny and held it to the wound. Shaidi sucked in a sharp breath of pain, but didn't complain. Brunt had begun radioing the medical team the moment she screamed and was now describing the injury to whoever was on his or her way.

It was probably only a couple of minutes, but it felt like a lot longer before a doctor finally arrived. The doctor turned out to be Josh.

"Misha, Danny," he nodded to them curtly before dropping down next to Shaidi.

Brunt assisted Josh, mostly by holding a flashlight, while Jon stood behind them like a nervous mother. Brewster, Danny, and Misha all kept out of the way. The rest of the flight team was clearly interested in what was going on, but they kept working. Everyone not assisting Josh probably should have kept on working, but they didn't, and Misha had no right to tell them so.

Next to him, Danny shivered slightly. With the Diana in motion, there was a breeze, which was chilly for someone who no longer had a shirt. A flash of memory went through Misha's mind; he remembered the Day, and how he had been running for his life in nothing but a pair of shorts. He now had nothing but a wetsuit, only a slight improvement.

"All right. I think she'll be fine," Josh finally said. He sat back on his heels. From the way he had been kneeling over Shaidi, it looked like he was rising up from prayer. Perhaps he was, under the circumstances.

"Thanks, doc." Shaidi shifted herself into a more comfortable position, wincing as she did so.

"Don't treat it like it's just some flesh wound," Josh warned her and everyone around her. "You're out of commission. I'm going to send up a stretcher team to bring you to one of the medical centres."

"Oh come on," Shaidi rolled her eyes, "it's not that bad, is it?"

"You should be monitored by someone on the medical staff. It could easily be worse than it looks to me." Josh spoke very firmly about this. "If you're worried about taking up a bed someone else needs, don't be. At this moment, most of the beds are empty, and if someone worse does come along who needs it, we're not afraid to put you on the floor somewhere."

Shaidi grinned, finding something amusing in that.

"Stay put, and wait for the stretcher bearers."

She nodded her consent.

"Good." Josh looked at everyone hovering around. "If she doesn't, and ends up hurt even worse, I'm going to hold you guys responsible."

"We'll make sure she stays out of things," Brunt assured him.

Josh radioed for the stretcher, and to say he was heading back to the medical centre.

"Take care of yourselves, guys. I don't want to have to come back up here," Josh told them all as he got to his feet.

Danny and Misha both said goodbye to him, and then Josh left.

"Sorry about your shirt," Shaidi spoke to Danny. She held his shirt out in one hand. It was soaked in blood.

"It's fine." Danny shrugged. "If I hadn't offered it, someone else would have. I can live without a shirt for a while."

"Come on, back to work." Brunt slapped his hands together for emphasis.

"What about the rifle? I was the one carrying it," Shaidi told Brunt.

"Give it to Misha," Danny said.

"*Me?*" Misha was startled by Danny's words.

"Yeah. You trained under Alec, didn't you? Give it to him."

"I did, but I don't know if I'm any good or not."

"Oh please, you know as well as I do that anyone who got training from Alec is at least good. And remember, I was on that plane when you shot a zombie before boarding it."

"I got lucky."

"Take the rifle." Brunt had picked it up from where it lay next to Shaidi and shoved it into Misha's hands.

As everyone began to disband, Misha had no choice but to accept the weapon. He held it tightly against his chest, unsure what to do.

"I found the best spot to shoot from is near the top of the stairs," Shaidi spoke to him from her prone position, pointing with one slender arm to where she was referring.

Misha walked toward the railing. When he realized that Rifle was following him, he stopped.

"Rifle, stay," he commanded the dog, his voice wavering a little.

Rifle cocked his head sideways, but obediently sat down.

Misha continued on. Just before he reached it, a bullet *whanged* off the railing to the left, causing him to jump back. His heart was racing in his chest and his hands shook. Taking a deep, steadying breath, he shuffled back up to the railing.

Boats cruised past below. A few looped around in front of the Diana, giving her prow a wide berth to reduce their risk of being run over. Misha looked at the men aboard the boats. Here were thinking men, with ideas and fears. They operated machinery and waved guns around.

Misha raised the rifle in his hands, putting one of the boats into his sight line. This was not like killing a zombie. Misha had killed several zombies, but these were not zombies. These were not hollow shelled corpses, but living, breathing people. The closest Misha had ever come to killing someone, was when he had inadvertently led a man into a zombie, but it hadn't been his idea to do that. Now, he was about to fire upon and attempt to kill a man.

Thinking back on his training with Alec, Misha managed to steady his hands. He tried to think of his target not as a person, but just a target. He tried to imagine the stuffed dummies Alec had set up as practice targets for his shooting students, back when they had enough ammo for such things.

He squeezed the trigger.

The head of the driver that Misha was aiming at exploded. Misha cried out a strangled sound, feeling actual pain for what he had just done.

The heads of the others whipped around to look at him, but Misha held up a hand, letting them know he was all right. Somewhere behind him, at a safe distance, Rifle began to whine.

That first shot wasn't the only one to hit its mark, but it was the only one to cause such a reaction in Misha. The rest of the time, he remembered his training. It became easier as he started to think of them as infected. He knew from Jon and Riley that everyone was now carrying the infection, but he put that out of his mind and imagined it was only those men down there who were.

Misha didn't fire often, but he fired enough times that the boats started shooting back fairly frequently. Several times Misha had to drop to the deck and cover his head, as bullets whined past. Still, he continued to do the job he had been assigned.

After one such duck-and-cover, Misha sprang back up, intending to take out the shooter. Just as he was lining up the target in his sights, the whole ship shook.

The entire Diana shuddered violently. Misha was thrown into the railing in front of him, and before he realized what was happening, he was being thrown over it.

Nothing but air surrounded Misha as he went overboard.

16
Hanna's On The Other Ship

Hanna had fallen asleep in the employee's rest area, curled up beneath a table that was bolted to the floor. She didn't know how long she had been there, but it was long enough for the sun to have gone down. During all that time, she couldn't think up a single plan. She had no idea what to do, and so had eventually fallen asleep.

Her dreams were as confused as her thoughts had been while awake. It wasn't a restful sleep, and she woke up several times, but was always able to fall asleep again.

Eventually, she woke up and heard an unusual sound. Along with the hollow whistle of the wind and the shushing of the ocean being cut by the hull, there was a buzzing sound. Hanna continued to lie under the table, unmoving and looking at nothing, trying to identify the sound. It was familiar, but she couldn't place it.

A much closer sound distracted her. A rattling groan became her sole focus. It sounded close. Much too close.

Moving her head so slowly it was barely perceptible, Hanna scanned the area with her eyes. The owner of the rattling groan was standing three tables over. She could see its legs, along with a dangling bit of guts. There was no question about whether it was a zombie or not. The thing wasn't moving, and Hanna could see no way it could have gotten in there with her. She looked toward the gates on either side of the sitting area and noted that they were still closed and locked. Hanna was disheartened when she saw at least two zombies lingering around outside either gate. The bars were too close together for the zombie near her to have squeezed through them, so there must be another way into the seating area that Hanna didn't know about. Probably one that led inside the ship.

Mentally, she took stock of her supplies. Only the oar was a good weapon. There was the flare gun, but that wouldn't be very effective. Even if she hit the zombie and the thing caught fire, it would take far too long for the brain to burn away, and then she'd have a flaming zombie to deal with. Besides, she wasn't even sure being hit by a flare would cause combustion. After several mishaps in Germany that she narrowly survived, she learned to mistrust things she had seen in action movies.

Pushing herself up onto her hands and the balls of her feet, Hanna slowly and quietly eased herself out from beneath the table. Some of the zombies at the gate nearest to her spotted Hanna, and began making a lot of awful noises, including the rattling of the gate. She froze to watch what the legs would do. The zombie shifted, reacting to the ruckus being caused by its undead brethren, but it mostly stayed in place. Hanna was relieved the zombie was too dumb to figure out what the other zombies were complaining about.

Once she was no longer underneath the table, Hanna shifted her legs beneath her and sat up. Every time a buckle or something on her lifejacket made a sound, she paused to watch the zombie legs, but each time all the other sounds drowned it out. The zombie continued to be unaware of her presence, even when she picked up the oar and held it firmly with both hands.

Moving slowly, in an uncomfortable crouch, Hanna headed toward the zombie's back while keeping below the tabletops. She got very close, and positioned herself to come out behind the zombie based on the direction its feet were facing.

Gripping the oar tightly, Hanna sprang upright and out of cover. And then froze. The zombie was looking straight at her.

The thing had the decayed look of all the other zombies, but some extra trauma had befallen this one. Its torso was twisted nearly one hundred eighty degrees, its right side torn, allowing a bit of its guts to hang free. Had this zombie been one of the fast ones, Hanna's pause would have been her end. Mercifully, it was slow and dumb. The twisted torso left it uncoordinated between its upper and lower halves. The thing stumbled, unsure which way was forward and which way was backward. After just a few steps, it figured it out and then moved toward Hanna.

By then, Hanna had gotten over her shock. As the zombie came within range, she swung the oar like a massive baseball bat into the side of the zombie's head. There was a crack as the skull fractured, and an even larger crack as something in the neck broke. The spinal cord must not have been severed, because the zombie continued to have use of its motor skills, except they were even more uncoordinated now that its head was lying on its shoulder. Hanna raised the oar high above her and brought it swiftly down onto the same bit of skull she had struck earlier. A large dent appeared in the side of the zombie's head, and this time it collapsed. Hanna didn't bother to find out if she had destroyed the brain or severed the spinal cord. As soon as the thing was down, she spun around to face the direction from which she believed it might have come. No other zombies were sneaking up on her, lured by the sounds of those at the gates. The space was empty.

After a quick readjustment of her lifejacket and the supplies that hung from it, she moved under a dark overhang. While waiting for her eyes to adjust, she realized there was something wrong with the light. Turning around, Hanna looked up at the night sky. Above was the usual collection of stars, but ahead, two flares were brightly burning. Her ears then picked up the sound of gunfire. Hanna remembered that the ship she was on had turned to follow the Diana. She had assumed this strange ship was being piloted by off-shippers, but now she knew that was the wrong assumption. There must have been people on this ship, ones who weren't friendly with the Diana. They were attacking her.

A sick worm rolled over in Hanna's belly. When she had planted the bomb, she knew this ship was in the area. She knew it was possible that unfriendlies were on board, and she had gone ahead and crippled her home anyway. And why? Because she was seasick. Not the kind of seasick that resulted in spending all day lying down or throwing up in the toilet, but the kind that made her desperate to be on land again. To feel earth against her feet, to see a steady, solid horizon, to feel a large, strong, old tree beneath her fingers, and to walk away from everyone whenever she felt she needed to. Being on the Diana had begun to feel like being a rat in a cage, but she had been wrong to do what she did. She had been so very, very wrong. She should have remained peaceful like the others. She should never have let that old side of her take control again. That side that had somehow been sucked into a terrorist cell so many years ago. That side for which she should probably be taking medication. It was her fault this was happening.

Turning away from the sky and her thoughts, Hanna stepped back under the overhang. She walked through the dark until her eyes adjusted and her hands reached the back wall, which was gently curved, and she found an opening that led behind it. Following the back of the wall, she came across a hallway and was mildly startled. Steady, electric light was coming from an open doorway off to one side. Hanna hadn't expected to see any lights on in this ship. She had assumed that it was like the Diana, and set up to conserve power.

"Assume makes an ass out of u and me," Hanna whispered to herself. "Only in this case, it is just me."

She tiptoed toward the door with long, ballerina-like steps. Once, a lifetime ago, she had wanted to be a ballerina, but hadn't been able to take the criticism from her teacher and had quit. Her teacher was probably dead now, just like everyone else she used to know.

Holding the oar above her head, Hanna stepped around the doorway, prepared for any zombies that might be in there. The small room was clear of the undead. It seemed to be a tiny kitchen and storage area for the cruise ship's staff. After closing the door behind her, Hanna searched the cupboards, fridge, and unlocked lockers for anything useful.

She found some food that hadn't gone bad, mostly stale chips, and made a meal out of them. The food in her emergency kit would last for a longer period of time and was already packed away, so she saved it for later. In the lockers, Hanna found some sweaters, a few jackets, two pairs of men's shoes, a purse, a gym bag, and a handful of personal knick-knacks. She was briefly paused by the photographs lining the inside of one locker. They were full of happy faces from long gone days, when the dead were dead and the living didn't fight over every scrap of food like wild dogs. The people in the pictures were healthy and excited about life. Hanna couldn't leave the photos. She carefully pulled them down, separated the sticky blue stuff from the backs of them, and carefully slipped them down the side of her emergency kit, where they could nestle up next to the fishing line and spare batteries. In the purse and gym bag, she found wallets that had small photos in them, but those she felt fine leaving behind. They were professionally done portraits of families that felt impersonal after the locker's photos.

Once she had gone through everything, Hanna grabbed a thick sweater and put it on under her lifejacket, unwrapping the rope from her arm to do so. Although it was still hot, she could put up with sweating for the added protection. If the sun had still been out, however, it would have been a different story. The sweater had a hood, which she pulled up over her long hair and then used the drawstring to tighten the hood around her face so that it wouldn't affect her peripheral vision. She also took the time to adjust her shoes, which she hadn't properly tied while in the ship's belly, and carefully wound the rope around her arm again. With that done, she went over everything in the room a second time, specifically looking for something to use as a weapon. Even though her oar had served her well, it was large and somewhat cumbersome; not very good for the confined spaces in which she'd find herself. In a drawer beneath the oven, Hanna found a stock of frying pans. She picked out a very solid looking one that wasn't too heavy to wield with one hand. It would do better than the oar.

After placing her ear against the door and hearing nothing, Hanna stepped back out into the hallway. There was a room across from the kitchen-like place, which she investigated. There was nothing dead or helpful inside, only useless cleaning supplies. She had turned the light on when she had checked it out, and now left it on as she made for the end of the hall. It wasn't a long hall, and it ended in a T-junction, both arms appearing to head back outside. Turning to the starboard side door, Hanna peered out the little round window set into it. There were no zombies outside. It looked like the door led out onto a narrow walkway, which was used for boarding the lifeboats. Opening the door, Hanna stepped out into the night air. The lifeboat that would normally be in front of her was gone, giving her a vast view of the ocean.

Hanna watched a handful of boats slowly passing the cruise ship. In the light from the flares, she could make out that they were full of men with guns. Surely, they couldn't all have come from this cruise ship. It couldn't be people from the foreign cruise ship who were attacking the Diana. Then again, these new boats were completely ignoring the ship that Hanna was aboard. There was clearly some piece of information that she was lacking.

Sitting down on the walkway, Hanna stopped to think about what she should do next. Her original plan had to be put on hold. There was no way for her to know which way they were heading, or where the nearest land was. Nor did this seem like a good time to be scavenging the ship.

One idea was just to wait. She could find somewhere on the ship to hole up, and then just wait things out. It wasn't a bad idea, but Hanna didn't like it. There was no telling how long she'd be waiting. Besides, those men with the guns might end up searching the ship from top to bottom, and they might find her.

She could always join the men.

The thought was quickly expunged from Hanna's mind. The idea made her feel sick to her stomach. There was no way she could betray the Diana again. If the men with guns found her, she'd fight them to the death before joining them.

That left just one last option that Hanna could think of: fighting the men. She had no way of attacking the boats slipping past, but it was clear to her that someone on their side was driving this ship. She had made a lot of bad assumptions and even worse decisions in the past, but this one seemed right.

A lot of your other decisions seemed right as well, Hanna thought to herself, and it was true. The bomb hadn't really seemed right, but a lot of what she had done afterward did. How many times had she made the wrong call? Done the wrong thing?

Sitting on the small walkway, Hanna really thought this one over. She tried to come at her predicament from all angles, but they all led to the same place. She should go up to the bridge and fight whoever was there. The plan sounded like suicide, and maybe it was, but Hanna felt she needed to do this. If she could stop this ship, then maybe, just maybe, she could redeem herself for the bomb. Obviously, there was no way anyone could forgive Hanna, she couldn't even forgive herself, but maybe they would allow her back on board. Maybe she could go home and live the rest of her life in confinement, which was more than she thought she deserved.

Hanna got to her feet. She had made her decision. Whether it was the right one or not, she was going to find out, but she had made her choice.

***

From the walkway alongside the remaining lifeboats, Hanna made her way back inside the ship. It was a lot noisier since the last time she was in there. It seemed all the zombies on board had become active. There were a lot of groans and moans echoing about the ship. Hanna noticed there wasn't any screaming, which she found odd. Although a lot of zombies were slow and shambling these days, there were still a few smarter and faster ones, and they occasionally screamed a blood-chilling cry. Based on the sounds alone, this ship contained no fast zombies. That was good. The fast ones were terrifying. The slow ones were scary as well, especially in hordes, still it was the fast ones that Hanna feared most. They were like animals that were unable to feel either pain or fear, just hunger for flesh.

Hanna shuddered despite the warmth of her sweater and the southern night air.

She was currently on the fifth deck, and needed to get up to the tenth deck if she wished to enter the bridge. After making it up only a single flight of stairs, she ran into trouble.

About a dozen zombies lingered on the steps above her. The nearest of them spotted her and stumbled down the stairs, prompting the others to do the same. Hanna turned and ran for the steps on the other side of the ship, only to be confronted by nearly a dozen more of the dead. Hanna had no choice but to dash into the café between the staircases. Unbeknownst to her, she found the same barricade that Jon had, and came to the same conclusion it had been built as some sort of last stand. She ran toward it, intending to scramble over it, and maybe escape through the back. There were a handful of zombies hanging around in the café, all of them slowly turning toward her, but Hanna was sure she could reach the barricade ahead of them.

Just as Hanna was about to climb, the head of a dead one rose up over the edge of the barricade. The thing scrambled up on top of a table, not even pausing for a moment before coming at Hanna.

Hanna backed up two quick steps; all she had time for before the thing was on her. It was a smart one. She had hoped that no screams meant there were no smart ones, but she hadn't been lucky enough for that.

As the zombie grabbed at her, its mouth hanging silently open, Hanna lifted one of her feet and kicked as hard as she could into the thing's stomach. Her foot didn't just press against the flesh, but punctured partly through it, covering her shoe in thick, black goo that had probably once been blood. The zombie's broken fingernails scraped down the sleeves of her sweater as it was knocked back, somehow managing not to find purchase. As it came at her again, Hanna raised her frying pan and smashed it across the face, knocking the grotesque thing down.

The other zombies were closing in now. Soon, Hanna would have to deal with them as well as this fast monstrosity. She backed up several more steps, heading toward a door she could see in a corner near the entrance. Only one zombie was between her and that door.

The fast one was up again, moving toward her before it even got its feet completely under it. Hanna wound up and smashed it again. The blow should have been a skull crusher, but the zombie either ducked or stumbled at the last moment, its shoulder rising up to take the impact instead. Although not taken out, the fast zombie was sent sprawling to the floor again.

Hanna turned, still swinging her frying pan. The slow zombie had gotten close enough for all of its teeth to get smashed in. It fell to the floor in a crumpled heap. Hanna didn't wait to see if it was going to get up. She bolted for the door the moment the path was clear.

Behind her, she could hear the fast zombie running after her. Its dead feet sounded disturbingly alive.

Bursting through the glass door, Hanna quickly turned and tried to slam it shut. The hydraulic hinge worked against her. The zombie smashed into the door, attempting to force it back open.

Hanna was on something similar to the walkway she had been on earlier. The door led out onto a little platform, which had a staircase leading down to the walkway. Hanna had noted the staircase earlier, but had decided to enter the ship through a different doorway. Now, bracing her back against the railing, she tried to hold the door closed with both hands.

The zombie's rotting face was flattened against the glass. Suddenly, it pulled its head back and smashed its forehead into the clear pane. Then it did it again. And again.

Hanna had no idea how strong the glass was. It was possible the thing would kill itself before bursting through, but she couldn't take that chance. Besides, the other zombies in the café were going to build up behind it, and then the zombies from the stairs were going to build up behind them. There was no way to hold them all back. Hanna's only option was to take on the smarter zombie, and outrun the dumb ones.

She waited for the zombie to pull its head back for another smash, and then threw herself toward the stairs and down them. The door burst open, and the zombie's momentum carried it forward into the railing. If it had been on its own, the zombie might have recovered its balance, but as it was, all the zombies behind it crashed into the thing. More of the fast zombie's stomach was split open as it was pushed over the railing. Guts fell out and became tangled in the flailing arms and legs of the stupid zombies behind. The smart zombie fell to the walkway below, its intestines trailing behind it. Hanna wanted to vomit, but she saw an opportunity. The fast one was held in place, tangled up in a leash made of its own organs. As disgusting as that was, it gave Hanna time to run down the walkway.

It wasn't long before those same footfalls as in the café were after her again. The fast zombie must have broken free of its own guts.

She turned and made her stand. The zombie was running full tilt at her, head lowered, mouth open, stomach skin flapping to reveal brief glimpses of a mostly hollowed out gut.

Hanna wound up with the frying pan again.

As the smart and fast zombie got close, she swung. If she wasn't sure it had ducked before, she was sure it did this time. That was okay, she was prepared for it. Hanna wasn't aiming for the head, but swung low, striking the zombie in the ribs when it raised its arms. There was a loud snap as several ribs broke. The force of Hanna's blow knocked the zombie off its feet for a third time. It was slammed into the walkway's railing, and Hanna made sure it went over by swiftly grabbing its leg and heaving the thing over. Other bones broke as it crunched into the solid wood deck beneath the walkway.

Hanna knew there was no quick way up from the fourth deck to that section of the walkway. If the fast zombie was still mobile, it wasn't going to be a problem for a while. Hanna went through the nearest door that led back inside, before the slow zombies falling down the stairs and over each other could assemble themselves to come after her.

Needing to go forward, Hanna instead headed for the rear of the ship. Zombies were still likely to be congregating around the staircase she had first tried, and she thought the stairs at the back were a better idea. She made it up to the seventh deck before zombies blocked her way again. They didn't notice her like the others had. Hanna checked both the port and starboard side stairs, but there was no way to get past them on either side. She didn't like it, but she headed for the front of the ship once more. She was only one deck higher than the last time she had been forward and hoped it was enough.

Sticking to the hallway on the opposite side from where she had attempted to go up before, Hanna moved as quickly as she dared, holding her frying pan at the ready. There was only one zombie in the hall, and it was painfully slow. She dispatched it easily, leaving the corpse behind her with a caved in skull.

As she came upon the staircase, she slowed down considerably. Creeping along the wall, Hanna approached the stairs as cautiously as she could. There was nothing around the landing. She inched closer and closer, more steps becoming visible with every movement. When the landing came into view,

Hanna stopped again. There were feet on the landing. Lots of them.

Crouching down, Hanna brought more of the scene into view. There was a cluster of zombified children, all shuffling in a circle, one following the other. Hanna shuddered. Undead children were the worst to see. She found it easier to pretend they were just little people. Sometimes this was hard to do, especially when some of the kiddies still had braces, or large, childish ribbons in their hair, or were dragging around a tattered stuffed animal.

She couldn't see a way to get past them, or even approach them without being seen. Maybe there was a way to get into the spa? Just as it was on the Diana, the spa was located on this deck. There was a single spiral staircase on the Diana that connected the spa with the workout facilities above, but there was no way of knowing if this ship was like that as well. Besides, the more Hanna looked around, the more she realized there was no way to sneak by the children without being seen.

Moving back, Hanna went to where the bank of elevators was situated. Through the glass sides, she could just make out the staircase on the starboard side of the ship. A few zombies were lingering around it as well. How was she supposed to go up with all the staircases blocked?

Movement drew her attention directly across the opening above the promenade. One of the glass sided, pill-shaped elevators over there was moving upward. While Hanna watched, it stopped at the deck below hers and opened its doors. Nothing went in or out, and then the elevator closed its doors and moved upward to Hanna's deck. A zombie was standing inside the elevator repeatedly pressing all the buttons. When the doors opened, the zombie stopped, looked at them for a moment, and then went back to pressing the buttons. It paused and looked at the doors for the same length of time when they closed again. Hanna wasn't sure the zombie actually knew what it was doing. She bet that if she waited long enough, the elevator would come back down, stopping at every deck, and the zombie would still be inside. Some faint memory, possibly muscle memory depending on what the zombie had done in life, remembered that buttons were to be pressed, but probably didn't know what those buttons did.

Still, it helped Hanna out of her predicament. As she had assumed with the lights, she had thought the elevators would be on lockdown to conserve energy. She was so used to them not working on the Diana that she hadn't considered them an option.

Making an ass of yourself again, she thought.

Hanna pressed the button nearest to her and then went to the end of the elevator nook where a small balcony jutted out over the promenade. Crouching down on the balcony, she was hidden from the elevators. There could easily be another zombie hanging around in one of them on her side.

A soft *ding* filled the air as the elevator cab arrived. The skin on the back of Hanna's neck prickled as she realized the children might be drawn to the noise. It wasn't one of the glass elevators jutting out over the promenade that had arrived, but one of the closed in ones along the opposite wall. Hanna could see the open door, and watched for anything that might come out of it. Nothing did, and the doors eventually slid closed on their own. Hanna waited a little longer. Finally, she crept off the balcony and moved to where she could see the children. As far as she could tell, they hadn't reacted to the elevator at all, and continued to wear a ring into the carpet with their shuffling feet. Hanna went back to the elevators and pressed the call button again.

The same elevator as before opened, as it was still sitting there. Hanna frowned. She didn't want to ride in that elevator; she'd rather be able to see what the floor was like through the glass siding of one of the other elevators before getting off it. She ceased frowning when she thought up a simple solution. Pressing the button for the tenth deck, Hanna slipped out of the elevator cab before the doors closed again. Once it was moving, she pressed the call button for the third time and returned to her hiding place on the balcony. From there, she watched one of the glass elevators rise up to her position. She could see that it was empty, and was grateful for it.

As Hanna entered the glass-sided elevator, she suddenly worried about the one she had already sent up. The children may have ignored the elevator's arrival, but that didn't mean that any zombies up on the tenth would do the same. If that were the case, they'd already be lingering around when her elevator arrived. She thought that maybe she should go up to the eleventh deck, so that she could assess the state of the tenth as she passed it.

The elevator doors slid closed while it waited on Hanna to press a button for the floor she wanted. She shook her head and pressed the number ten. There was no point in going to another deck; there could just as easily be a bunch of zombies up there. The elevator rose swiftly and relatively silently. Hanna watched the other floors as she went up. There were a few zombies here and there, but no real gatherings. Only one of the dead noticed her as she went past the eighth deck, but it didn't know how to reach her. The zombie walked into the railing and reached up, looking like a refugee crying for help. It was almost sad.

The doors slid open with another soft *ding* as Hanna reached the tenth deck. She held her frying pan at the ready even though she saw nothing through the glass doors. No zombies came rushing around any corners, which allowed Hanna to relax a little. Before the doors could close again, she stuck her foot in the gap to keep them open. Hanna noticed a panel inlaid in the floor of the elevator cab when she did this. It had Tuesday written upon it. Hanna couldn't remember what day of the week it was, but she didn't think it was Tuesday. She hoped it wasn't; she had never liked Tuesdays in her old life.

Hanna tiptoed out of the elevator, keeping a sharp eye out for undead. She moved toward the hallways with no problem; it was the hallways themselves that were the difficulty.

Looking toward the bridge, Hanna saw that the narrow passage was packed with zombies. Apparently, they had learned that someone was in there and were trying to get through the door. There was certainly no way around these zombies, not like the others. She needed a distraction, something that could lure them away, but what?

Hanna retreated to the small balcony off the elevator nook where she felt safe enough to go through her supplies again. She found that she was hungry again, and ate a bit of the emergency supplies. They tasted like dust, but nourishment was nourishment. Still, she wished she had a bit of water with which to wash it down. Hanna looked over the supplies while she ate. Most of them couldn't help her at all. The whistle had promise, but she wasn't sure how she could use it. Simply blowing the whistle would draw the zombies straight to her, and she didn't think she'd be able to give them the runaround up here. As Hanna looked at the flare gun, she realized what she had to do.

Tearing open the package of flares, Hanna found three of them inside. Instructions on how to load and use the flare gun were printed on the backside of the package. Reading the instructions carefully, and following the diagrams, Hanna loaded and unloaded the flare gun several times, making sure she had it right. It was very simple, but she really didn't want to screw this up. When she felt she had it right, Hanna repacked everything. The two extra flares she put into the front pocket of the sweater she took, which hung below the edge of her lifejacket. Taking several slow, deep breaths, Hanna steadied herself for what she was about to do. Before indecision could take hold of her, she got to her feet, the frying pan in one hand and the flare gun in the other. The whistle was clamped between her teeth.

Hanna went back to the hallway. She checked only once and then didn't hesitate to follow through with her plan. Hanna blew a short blast through the whistle, then quickly snaked her arm around the corner and fired the flare gun. The flare burst forth, launching itself down the hall and away from Hanna and the zombies. Hanna didn't watch where it went or what the zombies' reactions were. She quickly returned to the elevator nook and hid on the small balcony again.

A chorus of groaning and moaning informed Hanna that they were at least reacting to the whistle. She lay on the floor and waited. From her position, Hanna could see the area between the staircases on a few other decks, as well as her own. On the other decks, zombies were reacting too, but most of them didn't seem to know where to go. The whistle blast had been too short for them to pinpoint its location, and so they shambled back and forth, looking irritated. Some zombies on her own deck either had been able to locate the source of the sound, or were at least reacting to the noises the other zombies were making. She watched as they came out of the far hallway, and crossed from starboard to port.

After several minutes, when the trickle of zombies from the other side of the ship stopped, Hanna knew her plan must have worked to some degree. The zombies must have gone after the flare, or else the elevator nook would have filled, and her hiding spot on the balcony found.

Hanna reloaded the flare gun, just in case, and crept out of her spot. The area was clear, so she moved to the hallway. A bright light was stuttering from where she had shot the flare, but it could barely be seen for all the corpses in the way. They weren't as far down the hall as Hanna would have liked, but it was good enough. She thought she saw the children from the staircase as she turned away from the mob, but couldn't be sure and wasn't going to hang around to find out.

It was only seconds later that Hanna found herself in front of the door to the bridge. With the hand holding the flare gun, she tried the handle. It was locked. Of course it was locked, why did Hanna think it wouldn't be? She began to feel distraught. She had nothing to pick a lock with, and even if she had, she didn't know how to pick a lock. Build a bomb, sure she could do that, but get through a locked door without one? Not a chance. The zombies would become disinterested in the flare at any moment now. What was she going to do?

Hanna tucked the flare gun into the belt of her life jacket and knocked.

"Hello?" she called through the door. There was no turning back now. If this didn't work, she was zombie chow. Her heart raced in her chest, while her stomach fluttered, threatening to eject the food she had so recently eaten.

"Hello in there? Please help me. I have been waiting ever so long for help to come. Please let me in." Hanna's voice sounded false to her own ears, but she had to continue. "Please. I am not bitten, you can check. I am desperate, I will do anything if you will just let me in. Hurry, they are coming back." The fear rising in her voice wasn't false. Hanna didn't dare look over her shoulder, but she knew the zombies were coming. "Let me in. Please, for the love of God, let me in. Open the-"

Hanna cut herself off as she heard the lock snap open, and pulled out the flare gun. The door opened, and Hanna fired.

A man screamed as the flare was propelled directly into his face, ricocheting off it and flying further into the bridge. Hanna threw herself through the door, and then quickly closed it behind her. For a split second, she was able to see just how close the zombies had been to her. Any longer and she'd be dead.

Wheeling around, Hanna held her frying pan aloft. She had time to register two things. The first was that the man she had hit with the flare gun lay on the floor, holding his head and rolling in agony. The second was a massive man's hands reaching for her.

Hanna swung her frying pan, but the big man paid no more attention to the strike on his shoulder than he would a fly. He grabbed Hanna, lifted her off her feet, and threw her deeper into the bridge. Hanna hit the floor hard, the flare gun flying out of her hand and skidding away. She managed to hold onto the frying pan.

Getting up, her head spinning, Hanna saw the man coming toward her. He held up a meaty fist, cocked back and ready to break Hanna's nose. As it came flying toward her, Hanna held up her frying pan. The man's fist struck the edge of it, glancing off the lip, and then following through to smash its middle. Most of the blow's energy had been diffused by the frying pan, but it was still enough for the pan to be knocked back into Hanna's forehead.

This was a dumb idea, Hanna thought as stars exploded behind her eyes. *Why did you think you could kill these men? Why did you want to try?*

At some point, the flare had exploded. Hanna's world was filled with a bright red light that stung her eyes. Before she could locate the flare's position, the big man was throwing her again. This time she made it all the way to the front of the bridge, where she bounced off the reinforced glass. Somewhere along the way, her frying pan had slipped out of her hand, but she didn't know where. Everything was spinning in the red.

The big man came for her again. Hanna's body wasn't reacting properly, she couldn't get ready. The big man's hands came toward her in the shape of claws. He was going to strangle her.

Hanna managed to get control at the last moment. She whipped her head sideways and sank her teeth into his wrist. The man howled with pain. Hanna grabbed his arm and continued to bite down while he tried to shake her off. He shook her as though she were a small dog attacking him.

Eventually, the man grabbed her hood, yanked it down, and then grabbed her hair. Hanna's hair was nearly ripped out by the roots, but still she tried to hang on. She wasn't successful, and ended up being thrown to the floor.

Before she could push herself up, the big man was on her back. He wrapped a massive arm around her throat and pulled up, cutting off her air. Hanna struggled, but she couldn't get any strength to her arms, and her back was painfully arched.

She could see out the window though. As the edges of her vision began to go black, she saw the Diana. She saw the Diana very clearly. Very closely. In fact, she could pick out the defenders back there running away in terror.

The prow of the foreign cruise ship slammed into the stern of the Diana. There was a horrible squall of screeching metal, and suddenly Hanna could breathe again. The man had been thrown forward during the collision, and off Hanna, who gasped, sucking in great lungfuls of air. Her throat was painfully swollen, and the world was spinning even worse now.

Pulling her legs under her, Hanna attempted to get to her feet. She was unsteady, but she got up. Before she could make a run for it, the hands had her again. Hanna screamed hoarsely as she was pulled backward into a tight embrace. A bear hug like no other.

The big man was leaning against the glass, holding Hanna tightly to him. He probably wanted to strangle her again, but Hanna wasn't going to give him the chance. She screamed and kicked wildly, making sure he had to use every ounce of his formidable strength just to hold onto her. Her eyes were squeezed shut, tears streaming down her cheeks.

"No, don't!" the big man behind her suddenly cried out, his arms slackening slightly.

Hanna opened her eyes just in time to see the muzzle flash.

Ich wünschte ich hatte nie das U-Boot gesehen, was the only thought she had time for.

The man she had hit with the flare gun was standing behind the control console with a pistol in his hand pointed at Hanna. He unloaded the clip, every bullet striking Hanna's torso.

Hanna had no way of telling how many times she was shot. After the first bullet struck, everything was pain. All she could feel and think about was pain.

The bullets had passed through Hanna into the man behind her, and then out through the reinforced—although not bullet-proof—glass. The combined weight of Hanna and the big man who held her was no match for the weakened window. It cracked behind them, and they fell.

Hanna was dead before they hit the balcony railing below them, bounced off it, and then slid down a curved support brace all the way to the deck with the helipad.

***

It took at least ten minutes for Hanna to turn. The big man who had held her was broken in every way, but his body had protected her on the way down. Specifically, it had protected her brain.

Hanna rose from where she lay in a pool of quickly congealing blood, getting unsteadily to her feet. Stumbling around, she didn't register much. All her dead brain really picked up on was the stream of other corpses walking past her, and that she should follow them. She joined the horde headed for the helipad, which was imbedded into the Diana. From there, she and the other dead things could get onto that ship of the living.

As Hanna shuffled along with the crowd, she didn't notice the fact that the smart zombie shuffled along beside her with one very badly broken leg, hindering his formerly quick movements. They would find the living together.

17
Jon's Gotta Help

"Misha!"

Jon didn't know who screamed louder, he or Danny. All he knew was that Misha had gone over the railing, and now, he and Danny were running for the spot where it had happened. The ship had shuddered, badly, but there was no time to think about that now. In the back of Jon's mind, he wondered if this was what it was like for the people aboard the Diana when the bomb had gone off.

Rifle reached the railing first, and then Danny a second after that. Jon was next to them in a heartbeat. Together they looked over the side, not expecting to see anything. If Misha had survived the fall, which was possible, he'd already be a quarter of the way along the hull, and most likely trapped underwater. It was a surprise for everyone when that wasn't the case.

"Help!" Misha screamed up at them. "Help!"

He was hanging upside down in mid-air. Whether it was on purpose or not, the spear gun strapped to Misha's leg had gone off. The barbed spear had passed through one of the few links of the anchor chain that weren't hidden within the ship and had somehow become wedged, leaving Misha hanging by the connecting wire. Jon knew the underwater crew had the wires attached as a way of retrieving their spears, but now the practice had saved Misha's life. That, and the once in a lifetime, million-to-one-odds shot.

"That spear won't be able to hold forever." Danny's comment fell only on Rifle's ears, as Jon was already running off to find rope.

It was a miracle that the spear was even holding at all. Most of the time, straight spears were used, and the ones that were barbed didn't have very big spurs. Those little points of metal were probably the only things keeping the spear from slipping out of the chain links. Time was of the essence, as the saying goes.

Jon flew down the steps, jumping over the last six and thumping onto the deck. He didn't register that the gunfire had momentarily ceased, but he did see that all the planters and solar panels had been removed. Those he noticed because a few were stacked on top of the storage box that he needed to get into.

Screaming in frustration, Jon began trying to move the heavy stuff by himself. It wasn't long before others were helping him.

"Jon, what's wrong? Is it Danny?" Mathias asked from somewhere nearby.

"No. Misha," was all he replied. As soon as the box was clear, he ripped open the lid. The rope he needed was blessedly right on top and coiled nicely. He grabbed it and ran off without as much as a thanks.

Leaping up the stairs two at a time, Jon felt certain that he was too late, that he had taken too long, and Misha had fallen. When the sound of Rifle whining reached his ears, he felt even more certain of that fact.

Thumping into the railing alongside Danny, he peered over, assuming the worst, but Misha was still there. He wasn't moving, and Jon's first thought was that he had been shot, but then Jon put himself in Misha's position and realized that he wouldn't move either. Uncoiling the rope, he lowered it over the side.

"Get the others," Jon told Danny.

The task didn't take Danny long. The others were all hovering nearby, wondering what had happened. Jon stayed focused on the rope. As soon as it lowered to where Misha could grab it, the young Russian clutched the rope to his chest like... well, like a man grabbing a lifeline.

"Tie it around your waist!" Jon shouted to him, lowering the rope some more to give him slack.

Misha didn't tie it around his waist but around his chest, just under the armpits. When he was done, he gave Jon a thumbs up.

Jon turned to see everyone standing behind him, including the flight team. Even Mathias was painfully making his way to the top of the steps, something clearly wrong with his leg.

"Everyone take hold of the rope." Jon passed the end along and they all formed a single line. Before everyone had grabbed hold of the rope, it suddenly pulled in the opposite direction. Jon's hands were slightly rope-burned before he and the others could secure a tight hold.

"I'm okay!" Misha's voice drifted up from over the side of the ship. "The spear gave way!"

Those who didn't already have a hand on the rope were quick to find one. Mathias had made it up the stairs and was limping along the railing toward them.

"Pull!" Jon screamed. "Pull!"

Like slaves on a rowing ship, they pulled in rhythm. Rifle danced around next to Jon, alternately looking down at Misha and at what Jon was doing. Once the dog noticed there was slack hanging off the end of the line, he ran to it and picked it up in his teeth. He no doubt intended to help with the pulling.

Mathias reached them, but with his leg injured, he'd be no help pulling. He stood next to the railing and looked over it, watching Misha's ascent for them.

"I got him!" Mathias called out as he clasped hands with Misha. While the others continued to hold the line, Jon let go and leaned over the railing. Misha had one hand firmly gripping Mathias's while the other had a white-knuckle grip on the railing's lower bar. When Jon reached down, that grip quickly switched from the bar to his arm, immediately cutting off his blood flow. Jon and Mathias pulled on Misha's arms while the others continued to haul on the rope. Once he was over the railing, Misha collapsed in a heap on the deck. Rifle ran to him, and at once, began covering his face in wet, doggy kisses. Misha didn't push him off, but instead, wrapped his arms around Rifle's neck.

Mathias eased himself to the deck, tired and sweating profusely. Jon and Danny sat down nearby, while Brunt coiled the rope, and the flight team went back to work. Brewster walked off to check the other side of the ship.

"What happened to your leg?" Danny asked his brother.

"Got shot. What happened to Misha?"

"Fell over the edge," Danny told him.

"You all right, Misha?" Jon asked him. "You are one lucky son of a bitch that spear went where it did."

Rifle finally stopped smothering him in kisses, allowing Misha to prop himself up on his elbows. "Yeah, but my hip hurts like a *suka*."

Jon could only imagine. It would be similar to a short drop with a sudden stop, involving one's leg instead of their neck.

"Let me see." Jon shuffled over next him and felt along the outside of his hipbone and thigh. "I'm no medic, but it feels to me that your leg managed to stay attached to your hip."

"Hooray," Misha sighed with no joy.

"Do you know what happened?" Danny asked Mathias. "What caused the whole ship to shake like that?"

"The other cruise ship, the one Sher's in command of, rammed into the back of us."

"What?" Jon quickly turned his attention from Misha to Mathias.

"Yeah, some guys fleeing from the back end told us. They rammed us hard, and punctured us good."

"Are we sinking?" Misha asked him.

Suddenly, bullets were punching into the hull and pinging off the railings again. Danny and Jon each grabbed one of Mathias's arms and quickly hauled him away from the edge. Misha moved even farther back, holding onto Rifle's harness so that the German Shepherd could assist him.

"I don't know," Mathias said in answer to Misha's question. "We don't know what happened, but I don't think it was intentional."

"Why don't you think it was intentional?" Jon asked.

"Because of the way the other boats disappeared. They were falling back to see what had happened. They're back again though, so I guess Sher ordered them to resume the assault."

"Danny!" the flight crew's captain bellowed. "We need your help!"

Danny got up and ran off to assist.

"I lost the rifle," Misha suddenly said. He sounded very sad about it.

"It's okay." Jon put his hand on his shoulder.

"No, it's not. We don't have that many rifles, and we could have used the ammo in it." Misha shrugged his hand off.

"Hey," Mathias forced Misha to look at him by using a harsh and nearly angry voice. "It's a hundred times better to have you than the rifle."

Misha rolled his eyes. "Not really. I would have been just one more casualty among many."

"Fuck you!" Mathias actually shouted at him, startling Jon. "Quit your whining."

Misha stayed silent, not betraying whether his thoughts on the matter had changed or not. A lot of emotion was flying around, along with the bullets.

Brunt walked up to Jon and handed back the rope. At the same moment, the radio on his belt crackled. Jon watched as Brunt lifted it up and pressed his ear against it. He suddenly turned and walked away from Jon, Misha, and Mathias, as if he didn't want them to hear what was going on. Jon was immediately concerned. Was it bad news about the collision?

When Brunt was done talking, he waved Brewster to him. They held a whispered conversation between the two of them, with Brewster pointing at Jon at one point. Brunt looked at Jon over his shoulder, assessing him. Although he really wanted to know what was going on, Jon waited patiently.

"I should get back to my team," Mathias spoke.

"It's too dangerous to hold onto the railing with those boats going by," Misha told him. "I'll help you get there."

Misha stood up, favouring his leg, and helped Mathias stand, who favoured his own.

"Be careful," Jon said to them both, half-distracted by whatever Brunt and Brewster were discussing.

"Wait." Brunt had seen Misha and Mathias about to leave, and came over to stop them.

"What is it?" Mathias asked him.

By this point, Jon had also gotten onto his feet, and Rifle was sticking close to Misha's side.

"We're going to board the other ship," Brunt told them all.

"Who is?" Misha frowned. His tone of voice suggested that he had no interest in the other ship. "And why?"

"The who hasn't been finalized yet. As for why, the other ship is still ploughing into us. We can't get her off, some or all of our rear engines have been damaged, so we're stuck at this slow speed. Frankly, the fact that we're still going straight is a miracle, but that may not last. We might get turned."

"Wouldn't turning free us?" Mathias wondered.

"It might," Brunt shrugged, "or it might start us capsizing. The fact remains that the captains want to send a team over."

"Just one team?" This time Jon was frowning.

"Men have been watching that cruise ship since it started following us. No one has boarded it," Brunt informed him. "Just Sher and his one man should be on board."

"Plus all the zombies," Jon reminded him.

"Plus all the zombies. But most of them are moving forward, and we plan to board from the back."

"Wait, moving forward?" Misha paled, something Jon wasn't aware he could do, given how white his skin usually was. "The zombies are boarding us, aren't they?"

Brunt's lips pursed into a tight line. "No one said that outright, but yes."

Mathias sighed. "This is all fucked up, but what does this have to do with Misha and me? Why did you stop us?"

"Well, my off-shipper team is the one that has been chosen to board the other ship, and we're down two men."

"I'm going," Jon told him, putting as much steel into his voice as he could.

"I know you are." Brunt gave him a smile for volunteering so quickly. "But that doesn't change the fact that Shaidi is lying in a medical centre somewhere with a hole in her hip, and Rose is in no condition to do anything but lie still."

Mathias waved at his injured leg. "I can't really help you there."

Misha nodded his agreement with Mathias.

"I don't expect you to," Brunt chuckled. "What I'm asking is, do you know anyone who might volunteer for this mission? Nearly all the other off-shippers have been repositioned to the back already to deal with the zombies. The other team we usually pair up with was already stationed back there, and they haven't all been accounted for yet, so I can't call on them."

Both the injured men stood silently for a moment, propping each other up while they thought.

"What about the silent woman?" Misha spoke up.

"Who?" Mathias turned his head to look at him. "Freya? The one who first showed up with these assholes?"

"Yeah. If you ask me, she has a serious rage against these men. You can see it in her eyes. She might go."

"Couldn't hurt to ask," Brunt shrugged.

"I talked to her a bit while in the Dragon's Den. She seemed to like me, or at least like me better than the other people in there. Want me to go ask her?" Jon offered.

"I'll radio to the captains and check with them to see if they approve of it, but yeah, go now. If the guard doesn't let you past, then you know they said no. Come right back here, yes or no. By then, we should have found other volunteers."

After Mathias gave him the room number, Jon was about to run off, but then stopped. "How do we plan to board the other ship? The water's aren't exactly safe."

Brunt hiked a thumb over his shoulder. "What do you think those guys are getting ready for?"

Jon looked past him and saw that the flight team had moved from working on the small chopper to preparing the big one. The back of his neck bristled looking at the large army chopper. Although a few off-shippers had been transported using it, he had never been one of them, and if they were boarding the rear of the other ship, then that would mean rappelling out of it.

"I'll go get Freya now." Jon turned and ran for the stairs, trying his best to hide the butterfly of fear that fluttered in his stomach.

***

Jon trotted down the hall toward Freya's room, where a single guard stood before the door. The woman was nervous, likely never having done this sort of job before. She didn't even have a gun, just a hatchet held in a sweaty hand.

"I'm Jon," he said as he approached her, "did someone tell you I was coming?"

"Yes," the woman sighed with relief. "Tell me, what's going on out there? What was that explosion?"

"Don't worry, it wasn't an explosion. Am I allowed in?"

The woman nodded. "I hope she goes with you. I don't like just standing here."

Jon nodded to her, then walked up to the door and knocked.

Freya cracked open the door and peered out at Jon.

"Remember me?" Jon asked her.

She nodded.

"Can we talk?"

Freya's hand appeared, gesturing that he could talk where he was standing.

"Sher's on the other cruise ship."

Freya didn't react. Maybe she knew that part already.

"That shaking you felt earlier was the other ship ramming into the back of us. We can't shake him off, so a team is being put together to board the other ship. Someone suggested you might like to go."

The door closed suddenly. Jon knew she might not have said yes, but he didn't expect her to slam the door in his face. Just as he was about to walk away, the door was pulled wide open, and Freya was shoving her notebook into his hands. Jon looked down at the page.

Will I get to kill Sher?

"If you can, no one is going to stop you."

Freya smiled, showing all of her teeth. A cold shudder ran down Jon's spine as he realized the smile didn't reach her eyes, giving her the look of either a shark or a crocodile. Too many teeth.

Freya wrote something else. *Do you have smooth stones I can use with my sling?*

After Jon read it and looked up at her, she patted the leather band tied around her waist. He noticed then that she was no longer wearing her jean skirt, just a pair of tight biking shorts.

"Sorry, we don't have stones like that on board. Although..." Jon had an idea. He turned to the guard and borrowed her radio, calling Brunt and sharing his idea with him. Brunt said he'd see what he could do.

"So, I can leave my post?" the woman asked as Jon handed the radio back.

"Yeah, I guess."

The moment she was relieved of duty, the woman ran off. Jon suspected there was someone on board she was worried about.

"Come on," Jon waved for Freya to follow him.

She complied, and as they walked she wrote, *So, they let the infected out during times of war?*

Jon was going to correct her on her use of the word war, but then didn't. It seemed fitting. "It's a long story."

Tell me.

"I'll break it down as quick as I can. Basically, I escaped from the Dragon's Den. Because of what's happening, people seem to have forgotten that I'm supposed to be down there, or don't care for the moment. I shouldn't even have been down there in the first place. The doctors have recently found out that everyone is infected."

Freya didn't stop walking, but she gripped his arm hard, her eyes wide.

"Not in the usual way," Jon held up his free hand, trying to get her to relax. "No one is going to turn all of a sudden. It's some new form, possibly spread through the air. It only turns you once you've died."

Freya released Jon's arm and pointed to herself.

"Yeah, you're probably infected too. So don't go dying on us, all right?"

They reached the door that led outside and stepped through it. Mathias was with his team, defending the sides from the ladder boats that had resumed attacking them since the collision. He didn't notice Jon and Freya go past. Misha and Rifle were nowhere in sight.

Jon led Freya up to the helipad, where Brunt and Brewster were waiting.

"Thank you for coming. I'm Brunt, and I'll be leading this raid." He held out his hand.

Freya shook it briefly.

"This is Brewster. Jon you know. We're just waiting on the last two members of our party before heading out."

"Two?" Jon raised an eyebrow.

"Someone from the medical team is coming with us. After what happened last time we were aboard that ship, they don't want to take chances."

There was no need to remind Jon about what had happened over there. He couldn't help but hope that Rose was sleeping through all of this. If she wasn't, she was probably beating herself up about not being able to help, or arguing with the doctors to let her go, even though there was no way she was healthy enough to be running around right now.

"You flying us, Danny?" Jon noticed his former foster brother was wearing a flight helmet.

Danny just nodded while he continued a pre-flight check with the other pilot.

"Ah, here they are."

Brunt's words caused Jon to turn around to see who would be coming with them. His heart sank into the pit of his stomach. His eyes tracked Robin as she jogged toward them, leaping up the steps to the helipad with ease.

"You're not coming," Jon was saying before he had a chance to think over his words.

"I volunteered, and the medical staff doesn't need me presently. I'm coming whether you like it or not. Here." Robin thrust the katana she was carrying into his hands. "You have more experience with that thing than I do. Also, take this." She then handed Jon a fully loaded pistol. "There's no spare ammunition."

"Robin-"

"No need to explain about your infection. Everyone on the medical staff has been informed, and quite a few people have been figuring it out for themselves with all these bullets flying around."

"Robin-"

"You can't tell me not to go, Jon. I'm going."

"Robin, stop for a second." Jon placed his hands awkwardly on her shoulders, trying not to drop the gun or the sword. Robin fell silent and looked into his eyes. There was no stopping her, it was obvious. What he was going to say became lost, so instead, he pulled her into a tight hug. "I don't like this. You stick right behind at all times, okay? I don't like this."

"I know."

Jon released her. "What do you have in terms of weapons?"

Robin showed him her shotgun, as well as the ice axe hanging off her belt.

"You stick with me."

"You got it."

"Jon, Tobias found what you requested," Brunt interrupted them.

Jon looked up to see that the final member of their group was Tobias. He looked unsure of himself, standing there in a flak jacket, holding a fire axe in one hand with a crossbow slung over his shoulder. He held a cloth sack in his other hand, which he held out to Jon.

"Are these good? They were all I could find on such short notice."

Jon took the bag and looked inside. It was full of marbles and ball bearings. "I don't know, ask her." Jon handed the sack to Freya. "Will these do?"

Freya poked through the items in the sack, checking out the various sizes and testing their weight. She untied the sling from around her waist, picked out a marble, and deposited it into the cup. After a few experimental swings, she shrugged and tied the sack to her belt.

"Here," Jon held out the knife he had taken from the dead man.

"I brought something better for her," Tobias told them. He pulled a machete off the back of his belt and held it out to Freya. "Are you comfortable using this?"

Freya nodded and accepted the blade.

"But are *you* comfortable using *that*?" Brewster asked, pointing to Tobias's crossbow.

"Not really. I've never used one before outside of a few training sessions, but I couldn't find any more pistols."

"I'll trade ya." Brewster offered his own gun while holding out his other hand for the crossbow. "I've used one a couple times when my uncle took me hunting. I'm also pretty sure I can pull the line back and reload quicker and easier than you could."

Tobias agreed with this and traded weapons, handing Brewster both the crossbow and a small quiver of bolts he had.

"All right. We don't have time to prepare our usual kits," Brunt announced to the group. "We're going to have to go with what we have, unless someone can think of something that is an absolute necessity to bring."

No one spoke up. Jon still had the rope they had used to rescue Misha, which he now slung over his shoulder alongside the katana. He threaded the pistol's holster through his belt while everyone piled into the back of the Cougar. Robin was the only one with a pack. It was bright red with a white cross on top so there was no getting confused about what was in it.

"Strap yourselves in!" Brunt ordered while the engines started up.

Jon did just that. Robin was sitting next to him and he soon found their hands entwined. Jon didn't know whether it was he who had grabbed her hand, or she who had grabbed his.

"What's that thing on your shoulder?" Jon shouted to Tobias who sat across from him, while the blades above them began to spin.

"A camera," he patted the small, shiny object attached to his flak jacket. "The media guys insisted I wear it. I feel I should warn you all, I don't have much luck when it comes to heights."

"What do you mean?" Jon's question was either buried under the noise or ignored as the helicopter rose.

They took off fairly quickly, rising straight up over the Diana. Jon looked out of the door they had left open next to him. Things looked bad from up here. Tracer rounds marked where gunfire was taking place, and there was a lot more hitting the Diana than being thrown out by it. A few of those rounds came at the helicopter, but Danny and the other pilot seemed to ignore most of them. Given the height and speed of the copter, the attackers were hard pressed actually to hit them. Things had started to get dark, as the first two flares got farther away, but two more were fired off near the front of the Diana. One was the same red as before, but the other was green. It painted the scene below them in inappropriate Christmas shades.

As they neared the back of the Diana, Jon's grip on Robin's hand tightened. The collision was worse than he imagined. The entire helipad of the foreign cruise ship was buried in the Diana's stern. Most of the scene was obscured by a cloud of black smoke, which the pilots flew them around. Jon could see the zombies gathering toward the coupling, moving from the ship of the dead to the ship of the living.

Then they were past the damaged zone, flying along the length of the other ship. Random lights were on here and there, including a few around the pools. It was strange to see those pools, after becoming used to the fruit trees growing in their own. The water looked stagnant, covered in a green film.

They flew over the highest section of the ship, which would be the chapel if it was the same as the Diana, and then hovered over the sports section. Brunt got up and approached the door next to Jon. He grabbed a large, thick rope that lay curled on the floor and threw it out the door. Brewster did the same with a rope on the other side.

Speaking with a lot of hand gestures, Brunt explained how to rappel down the rope, and in what order they should go. Jon was one of the first.

Robin, perhaps seeing the fear on his face, placed a hand on Jon's shoulder. When he looked at her, she nodded. It told him that he could do this. Jon nodded back and prepared himself.

"Go!" Brunt shouted.

Both Jon and Brewster hopped out of the helicopter, descending down to the ship from hell.

18
Freya Boards The Other Ship

Freya watched Jon and the large man named Brewster descend from the helicopter. She had never rappelled from anything before, and so studied the process closely. Once the two of them were down and had made sure the area was clear, Brunt signalled for Freya and Robin to get ready. Brunt assisted Robin first, and then came to Freya's side. He told her all the things she had heard him tell Brewster, and supervised her as she prepared. Once she was out of the helicopter, she was on her own.

"Go!" Brunt shouted in a voice loud enough to be heard by both Robin and Freya.

Freya hopped backward out of the helicopter, her legs and arms wrapped around the rope the way Brunt had shown her. Fear tried to rise up out of her belly, but she quickly killed it with rage. This was the chance she had been hoping for. Not only could she mentally bring herself to kill Sher, but she was also being given the opportunity to do so. During the helicopter ride, Brunt had introduced her to everyone as well as giving her a quick briefing about what was going on. Freya was especially interested in the part where no one had observed anyone else boarding the ship, meaning it was likely just Sher and Bob were here.

As Freya's feet hit the basketball court and moved her away from the bottom of the rope, she thought of the women back in Jamaica. There were so many of Sher's men here, it seemed as though he had summoned all of them. All of his boats at any rate. And why not? The people aboard the Diana had taken Freya from him, what he probably considered the worst offence. With all of these men here, Freya hoped the women back on the island would rise up against whatever guards had been left behind. They wouldn't be able to leave Jamaica, not if Sher had all the boats, but they could go to high ground and arm themselves for when the men returned. This was all a dream of course. Most of the women were too cowed to do anything. Still, it was a chance for those few who were like Freya and Teal, the girl who had followed her.

On the ship, Freya prepared her sling and watched as the final two men prepared to exit the helicopter. They took longer to prep, probably because Brunt had to assist Tobias, and then get himself ready. Brunt rappelled down quickly, the only one with experience, while Tobias was much slower.

A streak of light and smoke suddenly appeared, heading for the helicopter. Brunt dropped off his rope, only a couple of feet off the court. Tobias was much higher as the helicopter rose and banked sharply to one side, narrowly avoiding the rocket-propelled grenade.

"Tobias!" Robin was screaming.

The man swung with the rope for a moment before letting go. He wasn't nearly as close to the deck as Brunt had been. His lanky body was thrown sideways into the netting that encircled the upper half of the basketball court. The mesh folded around him, as the weak posts groaned and bent with the force.

Robin and Brunt ran to him, while Jon and Brewster continued to watch everybody's backs for threats. Freya looked up at the helicopter and saw it was circling overhead.

"He's okay!" Robin called out.

Freya glanced over and saw Robin and Brunt helping Tobias out of the netting that was tangled around him. Once he was freed and standing on his own two feet, the helicopter left the scene.

"Told you I have bad luck with heights," Tobias grumbled while he worked out the sore spots. He may not have had any major injuries, but Freya would bet he had a lot of bruises, a few over-extended muscles, and probably some friction burns.

"Right, we should get going. We have a whole ship to cross," Brunt took charge.

Freya had a thought and quickly wrote it down, holding it out to Brunt for him to read.

They know we've boarded. Sher's men may board too.

Brunt nodded. "That's a good point, and all the more reason to move quickly. Come on."

They left the basketball court with Brunt in the lead. Jon and Robin followed along behind him, while Brewster and Freya brought up the rear behind Tobias. Freya wasn't too keen on Brewster. So far, he had done nothing against her, but his large frame reminded Freya too much of men like Bob. She was going to keep an eye on him just as much as everything else around her.

From the basketball courts, the group entered the pool area. Lounge chairs were scattered everywhere. A few were piled up along the side of the ship, others looked like they had been in use not long ago, while still more sat crooked or inexplicably on their sides. The only light came from the flares high overhead, and bulbs that were on inside the pools, beneath the water line. The combination lead to strange, moving shadows. The group came to a stop just inside the pool area, watching and waiting for anything that might come out of those shadows. Something did.

A zombie—formerly male by the looks of it, but now, mostly the gender neutral of rot—came shuffling around a pillar. It didn't spot them right away, but the moment it did, the thing changed its course to come straight at them. Freya had heard someone once say that zombies reacted to the living like moths to flames. She didn't see it that way. Moths were erratic, fluttering, and even spastic. There was speed to them that most zombies could never possess. Not only that, but some moths circled the flame for some time, flitting about it before finally getting too close and ending up with singed wings or death. Zombies had no such inhibitions. Freya thought that they were more like magnets. They took a straight route to their target, even when there was something else in the way, and the closer they got, the stronger the attraction became. This zombie was no exception, as it stumbled into the lounge chairs. The racket the thing caused drew more zombies out of hiding, all of them converging on the group.

"Stick to your melee weapons as much as possible," Brunt told everyone, his voice stirring up the zombies even more. "Save your ammo."

Freya hefted the blade in her hand, testing its weight. It had been a long time since she had to kill zombies, but she figured this would be easy. A zombie was a lot easier to kill than a living man was.

Jon drew his long sword. With his free hand, he briefly grasped Robin's, squeezing it firmly. The sight managed to find and hit Freya's heart. She didn't know such relationships could still exist in this world. Once Jon let go, he stepped forward and easily removed the head of the first zombie that came near.

Things happened rapidly after that. All of the zombies in the pool area, which was a surprising number given how many were moving to the front of the ship, came at the group. Everyone naturally clustered together along one wall, moving forward slowly, as the blades flashed in the strange light. Only Brewster wasn't using a blade. He stood in the centre of the group with his crossbow, thinning out the larger collections of zombies before they reached their targets. Freya enjoyed the attack. To every zombie she killed, she mentally attached the face of a man back in Jamaica. This one was Henry, and that one was Simeon. Here was Deshane, and there was Martel. Freya only wished Sher could be here right now.

It didn't take long for them to cross the pool area. Not all the zombies were dead, the slowest and farthest away were still stumbling around in an attempt to get to them, while several had fallen into the pools. Brunt kept the group moving forward, leaving the idiotic dead things behind. Freya and Brewster could easily defend their rear from them if need be.

They had no problems on the stairs, and got down the single flight with ease. Brunt checked out the hallway ahead, then directed everyone into the elevator corridor.

"There's a few zombies in the hallway," he whispered just loud enough for them to hear him over all the other noises. "It looks like the door to the bridge is open, and they're all shuffling through it."

This angered Freya. If the zombies were on the bridge, then where was Sher? There was no way he would have let the zombies get him.

"What's the plan?" Jon asked, his voice equally quiet.

"You'll go in first with your sword. Brewster will follow right behind you, crossbow ready. Next will be Robin and Tobias. You two keep a gap ahead of you in case the guys need to retreat. Freya and I will guard the rear. Jon, you're going to keep your distance from the zombies and follow them in. If you think it's possible to take them out, by all means do it, but if the situation is bad, get us to fall back to this position, got it?"

Jon nodded curtly.

"I smell smoke," Robin whispered to the group.

Brunt nodded. "A bit of the hallway carpet back that way seems to be on fire." He gestured with his thumb in the direction he meant. "It's not bad, but we don't want to hang around long enough for it to become a problem."

No one had any other questions or concerns.

Jon led the way back to the hall. As Freya followed Tobias, she looked back at the fire. Brunt was right when he said it wasn't bad, but it wouldn't take very long before it was. The source of the fire was obvious, as a flare continued to sputter in the middle of the blooming flames. Looking forward again, Freya watched as Jon very slowly and very quietly approached the back of a zombie. He made no move to take it down, but kept his sword in a tight and ready grip. The group kept pace with the zombies making their way into the captain's bridge. Freya frequently checked behind her, as did Brunt, but there was nothing there.

Once the last zombie entered the bridge, Freya felt an urge to rush in behind it. She didn't care if it alerted the zombies to their presence. She wanted to know what had happened to Sher. She refused to believe he was dead until she saw him with her own eyes. In one hand, she bore the machete, and in the other, her sling was weighted down with the largest ball bearing she could find. Slowly, the group inched forward, closer and closer to the bridge.

Jon entered the bridge first, followed by Brewster. When they didn't come back out, the rest of them went in. Freya took in the scene quickly. The zombies were still shuffling forward, toward a broken section of window. They didn't stop upon reaching it, but walked right through and then fell out of sight. On the floor near the window lay a frying pan, while a flare gun lay even closer. An actual flare was burning brightly on the control console. She was aware of the smell of burnt plastic mixing in with all the other odours in this place. There was no one living in the room.

Once the last zombie dropped out, everyone except Freya relaxed. Jon checked that the other door was locked, while Brewster and Tobias walked up to the control console. Freya went straight to the broken window and looked out. A lot of zombies had fallen on the balconies below, but a few managed to hit an arcing support beam and get all the way down to the deck. Those on the balconies got up if they could, then struggled until they managed to get over the railing, only to fall down to the next balcony. At the bottom, several had become trapped within a walled-in area with cage doors. The zombies that still functioned were pressed up against the barred doors, trying to get through them so they could invade the Diana. Freya knew that if enough of them ended up down there, they'd start climbing over each other. None of them was Sher as far as Freya could tell.

Looking up at the Diana, Freya thought that the smoke was even worse than when they had passed by it in the helicopter. It might have just been the new angle at which she was viewing it, but she didn't think so. Something was burning and they were having trouble controlling it.

"Fuck!" Tobias yelled, drawing Freya's attention to him.

"What's wrong?" Brunt asked, from where he was guarding the door they had come in through.

"The controls are fucked," Tobias threw his hands in the air and walked away from them.

"We can't turn off, or reverse the engines," Brewster explained. "This flare has fried everything."

It was hard to look directly at Tobias and Brewster, who were standing close to the bright red light of the flare. Both of them were shading their eyes with their hands. Freya held up her hand to block the source of the light, and that's when she saw it. Behind the men was another door. It was a simple door, clearly not the same as those that led back out into the hallways. She didn't think anyone had bothered to check it, probably already aware there was nothing related to their mission beyond it.

Freya knew—she *knew*—that Sher was behind that door. Whatever that room was, Sher was in there, waiting for them to leave. The grip Freya had on her weapons tensed, but she gave no other sign that would betray her thinking.

"Is there anything else we can do?" Robin asked.

"I can think of two things, but I don't know if either of them would work." Brewster was shaking his head, still looking at the dead controls. "I'd imagine there's an emergency shutdown somewhere around the engines themselves, but I have no idea where such a thing would be located."

Brunt sighed. "I knew we should have found someone on engine maintenance to come with us. What's your other idea?"

"Well, if we can't find an off switch, we could always try dropping the anchors. I don't know if the Diana's engines are still running after that collision, but if they are, they might be strong enough to pull away from this ship if we stop it with the anchors."

Brunt nodded. "We'll go to the engine room first and see what we can there, then check out the anchors."

Before they could do anything further, the crack of an explosion filled the air. Everyone ran to the windows, but Freya knew what it was before she had even turned around.

The ship with sails. Freya had seen it from the helicopter, and again when she looked toward the Diana from where she stood. The collision had slowed them down enough to allow it to catch up. The old wooden thing had lined itself up with the Diana, and fired the one cannon Sher's men had managed to get working. Freya had once heard Sher bragging about it. They had only the one cannon, but his team had worked at it until they had become experts. Every man aboard that ship had been specially trained to sail it, purely for the cannon. Wherever they had aimed, they had probably hit their target. Freya suspected it was one of the doors on the lowest deck that had just been pulverized, especially when a swarm of small boats headed for the area. It looked like the sailing ship was now moving farther forward along the Diana, perhaps to fire at the next door.

Everyone on the bridge stood in silent horror, taking in what had just happened. As they did, Freya looked over her shoulder, watching the door to make sure Sher didn't try to sneak up on them or sneak out.

"They're boarding the Diana." Robin spoke barely loudly enough to be heard.

"Come on!" Brunt clapped his hands together loudly, snapping everyone out of their daze. "The faster we get this done, the faster we can get back to the Diana and help them."

The group moved with a renewed purpose. They gathered behind Brunt and followed him to the door they had come in by. Freya made sure to stay at the back of the group. Once all the others had passed through the door, she closed it and locked them out. It took them only seconds to notice.

"Freya!" Jon screamed through the door. "Freya, open up!"

Freya wasn't going to listen to him.

"Come on, Freya!" This time it was Brunt shouting. "We need you!"

Freya knew they didn't. She stood with her back against the door feeling the thumps of their fists against the other side.

"Freya, what's wrong?" Robin was gentler than the others were. "Why did you lock yourself in there?"

Oh, how she wished she could speak! Freya just wanted to tell them to go on without her, to leave her alone, but she couldn't. Maybe she could write it and toss the note out, but that wouldn't get across the emotion she wished to display. No, let them figure it out on their own.

After a few more attempts at coaxing her out, they stopped trying. Freya waited another minute before leaving the door. She was alone with Sher now. Her blood was pumping hard in her ears, and behind her eyes. Soon, there would be death, and she wasn't entirely sure whose it would be.

***

Freya stood facing the wooden door. She waited with her machete up and her sling swinging a slow pendulum. After several minutes, she decided that Sher wasn't going to come out on his own. Maybe he was waiting for his men outside to radio him when they saw the Diana's group leaving the ship. Or maybe he knew Freya was still on the bridge; it was easily possible that he had heard the others banging on the door. Whatever the reason, Freya would have to go to him.

With long, graceful, and silent steps, Freya walked up to the door and flattened herself against the wall beside it. She closed her eyes for a moment as a memory of Sheraton flashed through her mind. When he was six years old, and she was ten, she had taught him how to ride a bike. One day, when he had gone riding on his own, he had come back with scraped knees and had made Freya promise to always go bike riding with him after that.

At least he never touched me, not the way he let others, Freya thought, burying thoughts of Sheraton under thoughts of Sher. *He never did that.*

Reaching forward, Freya gripped the doorknob with the hand that held her sling. Slowly, she turned it until the latch cleared the jamb, and then threw the door inward. As the door opened, she was quick to withdraw and hide her arm along with the rest of her body up against the wall.

Nothing happened. Sher hadn't been standing behind the door, waiting for it to open as she had thought he might be. Or he was smart enough to realize that no one was within the doorway, and was waiting.

Not once did Freya think that he might not be in there. She knew it like she knew her own name. The only question was what was he doing? There was only one way to find out.

Freya quickly rounded the doorjamb, machete up. Sher *had* been waiting for her. Her eyes flashed, taking in the scene in less than a second. Sher was standing in front of her and something was wrong with his face. It was hard to tell in the weird flare light, but one of his eyes was definitely swollen shut, and not from Freya's earlier rock throw. The other one had a wild, dangerous look in it. Sher was standing with his arms above his head, shaking under the weight of what appeared to be a microwave, or maybe a toaster-oven. Whatever it was, he brought it down hard toward Freya.

She reacted fast, bringing up the machete. The appliance hit the blade instead of her face, careening to one side and twisting the machete out of her hand. Sher reached for her, but Freya danced speedily back onto the bridge, abandoning the bladed weapon. Sher picked it up as he stalked past it, his one eye focused intently on Freya. She spun her sling in fast, tight circles, and then let the ball bearing fly. The metal ball struck his inner arm sharply, like the sting of a massive insect. With an involuntary yelp of pain, he dropped the machete.

Screaming with rage, Sher ran at Freya, his hands held up like talons meant for her neck. There was no time to load the sling again. Just before Sher reached her, Freya lashed out with her leg, her foot connecting with his crotch. Although it looked like Sher forgot all about Freya in a cloud of pain, it didn't stop his momentum. He crashed into her, falling on top of her as they struck the control panel. Sharp pain shot through Freya as she struck the metal instruments, some of them shocking her with the electricity that still ran through their broken parts.

Sher recovered from his pain before Freya could recover from hers. His hands found her neck and he began to squeeze. Freya struggled and lashed out at him, her nails scraping along every piece of flesh they touched, but he kept his head tilted back, his sensitive eyes out of reach. This was just like it had been on the boat. Freya fought for her life, but Sher had the advantage of size, and even more so, of gravity. Spots began to appear before her vision.

Freya had the heinous thought that she wasn't going to make it this time. This time, there was no one to draw him off.

Sher didn't say anything as he looked down at her. Nothing needed to be said. That one eye and those bared teeth said it all. Freya was going to die here.

"Hey, fuck face!"

Sher turned his head, his angry growls suddenly turning into another bellow of pain. He stumbled back from Freya, letting her drop to the ground. Just as before, Freya was immobilized as she lay gasping for breath. A crossbow bolt was sticking out of the meat of Sher's thigh. Sher grabbed the machete off the floor and charged at Freya's saviour, who could only be Brewster.

Freya did everything she could to rise. Last time, her saviour, Teal, had been killed. She wasn't going to let that happen again. She wasn't going to let this play out a second time. As she fought her body to get up, she spotted something under the control console. It was a flare shell, unexpended. Freya grabbed it, then paddled her arms and legs, moving in any way she could to where she had seen the flare gun. Scooping it up, she loaded the flare with trembling, traitorous hands. Her breathing was still rough, but she was beginning to get back control of that. Her head pounded.

The flare gun was loaded, and Freya managed to find her feet. She looked up and saw Sher hacking away at Brewster, while Brewster defended himself from the blows with the side of his crossbow. Brewster was surprised, shocked even, at the ferocity of Sher's attack. Before Freya could raise the flare gun, Sher lunged, driving the end of the machete into Brewster's gut.

Freya's mouth opened wide to scream, an involuntary reaction, but nothing but a harsh rush of air left her lips. She fired the flare just as Sher turned toward her and Brewster collapsed in a heap. Sher yelped, and dove out of the way, as the flare sizzled toward him. It was at that moment that Freya realized it must have been the flare on the console that had damaged his face. She wasn't exactly sure how she knew that, but something about the almost childish way Sher fled from the flare made her believe it was true.

As the flare bounced off the glass and skittered toward the wooden door where it burst open with light, Freya ran and grabbed the frying pan. It was the only other weapon she knew of in the room. She turned, quickly locating Sher. He had the machete, and stood on the other side of the control console, bathed in flare light from both the front and the back. Freya raised the frying pan as she had the machete earlier. The two siblings stood watching each other, studying the minutest moves the other made.

Startling Freya, the shaft of a crossbow bolt appeared in the middle of Sher's chest. Sher looked down at it, confused, and then collapsed. Freya ran around the console, ready to bash his face in, but there was no point. He was already dead. Looking up, Freya saw Brewster sitting slumped against the window, one hand pressed against his stomach while the other still held his crossbow. Somehow, Sher's attack on it hadn't damaged it beyond use. Freya looked back down at Sher and kicked him. He was truly dead. He was dead and it wasn't by Freya's hands. She felt robbed.

"Take this." Brewster slid the crossbow along the floor. He couldn't even put enough energy behind it for the thing to reach halfway.

Freya walked over and picked it up as Brewster tossed her a crossbow bolt.

"Load it."

Freya did as he said, having to brace the device with her feet and use both her arms to pull back the heavy draw.

"I'm dying," the big man told her. "I don't have long, and there's nothing you can do to save me. I want you to shoot me with that the moment I'm gone. Here, in the head. Do you understand? I don't want to come back as one of those things. Can you do that for me?"

Freya held the loaded crossbow, but didn't acknowledge what he had said. The man had killed Sher. He had taken from Freya the thing she had boarded this ship to do. He stole her dream. Why would she want to do anything he asked?

Don't be childish, Freya thought. She raised the crossbow, carefully aiming at Brewster's head.

"There's another bolt if you want to take care of him too." Brewster flapped a hand in Sher's direction.

Freya didn't wait for Brewster to die of his wounds. What was the point? She pulled the trigger, and the twang of the drawstring made a shaft appear out of his eye. It was easier than waiting.

By frisking Brewster's body, she was able to load up with the rest of the crossbow bolts, find an oddly curved knife she attached to her belt, and locate a small leather case containing what looked like lock picks. The lock picks explained how he had gotten into the bridge.

Freya went around the room next. She reloaded her sling and took the machete from Sher's slowly chilling hand. The crossbow she wore on her back with the extra bolts. The flare gun and frying pan she abandoned, as they were useless. Investigating the room Sher had come out of, she found an empty pistol. She took it with her, just in case some ammo could be acquired later. There was also Sher's walkie-talkie that she took. There was no way to prove to his men that Sher was dead, but the device might have some use.

Once she had everything, Freya looked down at Sher's body. *Let him become a zombie.*

She then had to decide what to do next. The only thing she could think of was to join the others. If she wanted to become a part of the community aboard the Diana, first, she would have to help save it. They said they were going to the engine room. Freya thought she wouldn't have too much trouble finding it.

With a single look back, Freya left the bridge.

***

Freya was right when she had thought it wouldn't be difficult to find the engine room. Most of the zombies had moved forward by now, so getting there wasn't terribly hazardous either. Those she did run into were swiftly felled by her machete.

As Freya searched the belly of the ship, she heard the loud pop of gunfire, followed by a woman's startled scream. More than ready to fight again, she ran toward the source of the sound as more gunshots went off. She swung her sling as she ran, but didn't get the chance to use it. By the time Freya reached the scene, the battle was over.

A small team of Sher's men lay peppered with holes among the machinery. Brunt was sitting against a support beam, his shoulder bleeding, while Jon handed him something to press against the wound. Jon was also bleeding. He had a vicious gash along the right side of his head, resulting in a chunk of his scalp hanging down. Robin was standing beside the dead men from Sher's army. She didn't appear injured, but was covered in blood. Her shotgun roared deafeningly in the confined space, as she blasted off the heads of all the men, even if they had already been headshot. Freya searched for the tall man, Tobias, and couldn't see him. She moved slowly into the scene, making sure the others saw her clearly, so that they wouldn't fire. A foot stuck out from around a piece of machinery so she went to look. It belonged to Tobias. He was lying flat on his back, his other leg and one arm bent awkwardly beneath him. One of his eyes was half closed, while the other stared widely into the beyond. Just above his left eyebrow was a sort of third eye, both black and bloody. Whatever had happened here, Freya suspected he had been the first to go down. She never got the chance to know him. She returned to the others.

Robin was now seeing to Brunt's shoulder, while Jon sat against the other side of the support beam, his eyelids flickering. The fact that he had managed to stay conscious with such a nasty looking head wound was very surprising, but then the brain sometimes liked to surprise.

Brunt looked up at Freya and said something, but she couldn't hear him over the ringing in her ears. This battle scene was a lot different from hers with Sher. It was brightly lit by overheard lights, and she could hear nothing but the ringing, and smell nothing but blood and gunfire. This fight had been quick and impersonal.

Brunt spoke louder this time. "Brewster?"

Freya shook her head.

"We have to go get him. We have to bring him and Tobias with us." Tears ran down Robin's face, yet, she didn't once stop her work. She pulled a bullet out of Brunt, pulling out a pained scream at the same time.

"We can't," Jon spoke, not able to see them, but he could see Tobias.

"Of course we can!" Robin shouted at him. She drew more pained cries from Brunt as she patched up the hole. Freya noticed that Brunt wasn't moving his injured arm at all.

"If both Brunt and I were healthy, maybe we could get Tobias up on deck." The emotion in Jon's voice kept fading in and out. "*Maybe*, but as we are? No. I'm sorry, but no. And even healthy, we could never carry Brewster. We're not done here either. We still have to find the anchors."

"Fuck the anchors," Robin replied, although there was no anger in her voice, just sadness.

"No. We have to try. If we don't, then all of this was for fucking nothing. We're checking out the anchors."

Robin finished up with Brunt, feeding him painkillers, antibiotics, or both, and then moved over to Jon.

Freya watched with interest as Robin swapped her latex gloves for fresh ones, and then held up the flap of skin on Jon's head like it was nothing more than a piece of peeling wallpaper. She rinsed the area quickly and carefully while Jon hissed through his teeth, and then jabbed the area around the wound with a needle a few times. Freya wanted to ask what was in the needle, but didn't bother. Maybe later, she could find out. Robin then pulled out a medical stapler, and used it on the side of Jon's head instead of stitching up the wound. Jon appeared to be wincing from the sound and the pressure as opposed to pain, so Freya thought that maybe the needle had contained a numbing agent.

"All right, I've done the best I can for both of you right now." Robin rinsed Jon's wound again and taped a pad of gauze over it. "Are you ready to go check out your stupid anchors now?"

"I'm good." Brunt got to his feet, but wobbled a bit and grabbed the beam for support. He shook his head as if to clear it.

Freya noticed his leg was bleeding. She tapped his uninjured shoulder and pointed to it.

"It's just a flesh wound," he told her.

Robin sighed. "Let me see it."

It was just a flesh wound, didn't even require stitches, but Robin still cleaned and bandaged it. While she was doing that, Jon crawled over to Tobias's body and started to frisk it.

"I'm so sorry, man," he said as he took the tall man's gun. "I'll tell Anne what happened. We'll take care of her, okay? We'll watch out for her. And those media guys will still get this. I'm sure you'd want them to."

Very gently, Jon began to remove the flak jacket that Tobias wore; the one with the camera attached to it. Freya knelt down and helped him. She had never seen someone take such care around a dead man before. At least not in the past three years. She could feel nothing for the dead, but she could see that Jon did. The humanity of it frightened her. Not because she hadn't seen it in so long, but because she realized it was gone from inside of her. It was then that she knew it would take a long time for her to return to normal, if she ever could.

Once the vest was off, Jon wore it himself. He then closed Tobias's eyes, crossed the man's arms over his chest, and stood up. Robin and Brunt had finished and were standing nearby, waiting. Jon handed Freya Tobias's pistol.

"Let's go check on the anchors." He turned away from the body and led them toward the nearest staircase.

"Wait." Brunt stopped him with a hand on his shoulder. He pointed over at Sher's men. "They might have ammo."

Neither Jon nor Robin wanted to touch the bodies, and Brunt's arm was injured, so Freya did most of the searching. She handed the guns she found to Brunt who inspected them for anything that might cause a misfire. Useful pistols he stuck in his large cargo pockets, along with the ammunition, while the one AK-47 was slung across his back. There wasn't much.

This time Jon led them as the group moved through the ship. Robin and Brunt stayed in the middle, while Freya guarded their rear. With the group reduced as it was, Freya was glad to have a gun. She had never used one before, but understood the basics like the safety. It would be a lot more effective than a simple sling, should they run into trouble.

A few zombies came across their path, but were easily taken care of. They didn't run into any more of Sher's men. Hopefully that meant he had called only the one team aboard, and since he was now dead, he couldn't call any others.

As they approached the front of the ship, the hallways began to fill with smoke.

"Something's burning, and it's not just a bit of carpet this time," Robin commented.

They continued to press on, but the smoke just got thicker and darker. Soon, they began coughing.

"Jon, we have to stop." Robin reached forward and grabbed his arm.

He turned to her with red eyes, although whether that was from the smoke or from crying, it was impossible to tell.

"No," he said, "we have to keep going. We have to try. This can't be for nothing. We have to drop the anchors."

"We can't," Robin insisted. "If we do, we'll suffocate, and what happens then?"

"I'll go by myself." Jon turned to leave, but Robin gripped him tighter.

"No! No, I won't let you. Jon, you can't go. I need you, okay? I need you with me."

"I'm pretty sure we're broken up right now, aren't we?"

"That doesn't mean you're not my friend!" Robin shouted in his face. "Stop being stupid. Is that head injury worse than I thought? Did it rattle your fucking brains? Going forward is suicide. You won't even make it to the anchors based on the level of smoke we're already dealing with."

As if to emphasize her point, a thick cloud of roiling smoke belched out over them, causing couching fits all around.

Jon looked forward again, then back at Robin. He nodded, and pushed past the group, intent on leading them back out.

Freya wanted to tell Jon that this mission was not for nothing. Sher was dead. She didn't know how to communicate how important that was. At least, it was important to her, and probably to all the other women back in Jamaica. Eventually, another team would board this ship, wondering why they hadn't heard from Sher in a while. They might find him dead, or zombified, or not at all. A power change would occur even if he wasn't found. There were enough men who wanted the seat of power for themselves that they would seize the opportunity. Chaos would reign without a single defined leader, and Sher was dead. No matter what else happened, the most important thing was that Sher was dead. Freya's brother could rest in peace now that the monster that had taken over his body was gone.

The group returned to the basketball court. It was nice to be out in the air again, where the ocean absorbed most of the smells of gunfire and smoke. Most, but not all. The fire was bad enough that they could still smell it. Looking up, Freya noticed a blot of stars was missing, eaten up by a pillar of black.

Brunt radioed for the helicopter to come get them, explaining that the mission had failed. There were a few minutes when everyone was concerned by the lack of response on Brunt's radio, but eventually, someone came on and informed them the helicopter would be there shortly.

While they waited, Freya wrote down in point form what had happened on the bridge of the ship and showed it to the others. They took turns reading it, then handed the notebook back. Brunt asked her why she didn't let them help her, but she just shook her head. Freya didn't believe they would understand.

It wasn't long before the air filled with the thumping of helicopter blades. It positioned itself above them, and a rope ladder was lowered. Brunt climbed first, while Jon and Robin held the bottom of the ladder as steady as they could. For having an injured arm, Brunt could climb surprisingly fast. Robin went up next, then Freya. Jon climbed last, having no one to help steady the ladder for him. Brunt, Freya, and Robin pulled on the ladder, enabling Jon to reach the helicopter faster. Once everyone was inside, the helicopter banked away from the ship. There was no RPG launched at it this time.

As the chopper flew out over the ocean, Freya looked down at the water. More flares had been launched, bathing the scene with their weird lights. She noticed that the ship with the cannon had blown holes through both of the doors at the front and back ends of the Diana. A large shadow was beneath the wooden ship however. At first, Freya mistook it for a massive whale. As it rose closer and closer to the surface, she realized it was the submarine. The sub rose directly beneath the old ship, its metal tower crunching into the wooden underside. The whole ship shook and tilted, throwing a few men overboard and causing the rest to scramble. The submarine then started to dive once more. Freya suspected the hole it left behind was massive, as the ship started to sink quite fast.

Freya turned to see if anyone else had seen this, but found their eyes completely riveted on something else. She turned back and followed their eyes.

It wasn't just the other ship that was burning. Flames leapt from various locations along the back end of their own cruise ship. The Diana was burning uncontrollably.

19
Hope's In A Room

Hope sat on the floor with her arms wrapped securely around Milly. She was scared. She was scared, she wanted her mommy, and daddy, but she didn't know where they were. The whole ship had shaken earlier, the same as when that bomb had gone off yesterday. Ms. Abby and Ms. Lauren said they didn't know what it was, but Hope thought they were liars. Ms. Abby had her ear pressed to a walkie-talkie all the time, and since the shake, she kept standing away from everyone else, not wanting them to hear what she was hearing.

Peter sat next to Hope, petting Milly's head. His pyjamas were newly donated to him and looked a lot like Hope's. He didn't look scared. Peter was very brave. He was even braver than Claire was. Claire kept singing under her breath. Hope couldn't figure out what the song was, and that annoyed her. She wanted Claire to stop singing. She wanted to yell at her to shut up again, but she got in trouble the first time she had done that.

Ms. Lauren walked back over from where she had been looking out the window. She looked out the window a lot, pulling aside the curtains a little bit to do so. Every time she pulled back the curtains, Hope could see a little bit outside, but she never saw anything interesting. There was something strange about the light outside, but she couldn't tell what it was from the brief glimpses.

A loud crack like thunder caused Hope to shriek, and the following shudder made Claire crawl over to sit with her and Peter and Milly. She stopped singing.

"You kids okay?" Ms. Lauren asked them.

Hope nodded, and so did Peter and Claire.

Ms. Lauren then went back to the window and peeked out. When she did, Hope saw the top of a ship. It was the kind with big wooden posts sticking up that held large white sails. It was the kind she saw in her books, but never saw in real life. It was a ghost ship.

Hope hid her face in Milly's fur. When she looked up again, Ms. Abby had moved and was now talking with Ms. Lauren in quiet voices next to the window. Something was going on.

Ms. Lauren turned to Hope and the others.

"All right, kids. We have to move to another room."

"Why?" Claire instantly asked, jumping up to her feet.

"It's safer," Ms. Abby told her.

"We're not safe here?"

Ms. Lauren rolled her eyes. She waved for Claire to come to her, which she did. Ms. Lauren whispered something in her ear. Whatever it was, she clearly didn't want Hope or Peter to know. Hope hated it when grown-ups did that. They were always keeping things from her and the other kids when stuff like this happened.

"Come on, Peter, gather any toys you want to bring," Ms. Abby told him. "Hope, you can grab a toy or two as well."

Hope didn't feel much like playing. There weren't that many toys here to begin with, and neither she nor Peter had even touched them. She was too scared for pretend. Still, she picked up a plastic doll with a bad haircut just in case. When she wasn't scared anymore, she might want to play with it. Peter picked up a laser gun. Too bad it didn't shoot real lasers, because then, he could use it on the bad people.

"Come on, let's go. Everyone hold hands." Ms. Abby took Claire's hand, who held Peter's, who held Hope's. Hope held onto Milly's collar with her other hand.

"Now, there's going to be a lot of people out there in the hallways, so be careful and don't let go of each other's hands,"

Ms. Lauren told them from where she stood by the door. She held a box of something in her arms. Hope thought it might be food.

Ms. Lauren opened the door and went into the hallway first. Ms. Abby with her handholding line followed after her. Ms. Lauren had been right about the people in the hallway; they were everywhere. The hallway wasn't wide enough for all these grownups. Looking up from the forest of legs, Hope saw that they were all scared.

Although the crocodile of handholding stuck to the wall, people kept bumping into Hope. They bumped into Milly even more. She whined and crowded up close to Hope, which made it even harder to move. A few times, Hope almost lost her grip on Peter's hand.

Suddenly, Peter stopped.

"What's wrong?" Hope asked him.

"I lost Claire." Peter turned around to face her, his other hand empty. "I don't know what happened. She was there, and then she wasn't. I lost my sister."

"Remember what they say to do when we get lost? We're supposed to stay where we are until someone finds us."

Someone then bumped into Hope. She was hit hard enough for her head to strike the wall. It really hurt.

"It's too dangerous to stay here. We have to go back to the room," Peter insisted.

After hitting her head, Hope wasn't going to disagree.

"Milly, go back," Hope told her dog.

Milly cocked her head to one side, not understanding. Hope pushed her until she did.

Going the other way wasn't much easier, but at least Hope could see when people were coming toward her.

"Hope! Hope!"

Hope looked around, thinking that Ms. Lauren or Ms. Abby had found her and Peter. Instead, Dakota pushed her way through the people and stood with them next to the wall.

"Dakota? What are you doing here?" Hope asked her.

"I got separated from my caretaker." Dakota never called the woman who took care of her mom; she always just referred to her as her caretaker. Like Peter and Claire and a lot of other kids, Dakota was adopted.

"So did we. We were with Ms. Lauren and Ms. Abby and Claire, but now, I don't know where they are. We're going back to the room we were in," Hope told her.

"I'll come with you."

Dakota was bigger than both Hope and Peter. People saw her and were less likely to knock her about, although she was still bumped into a lot. Dakota led them until Hope told her they had reached the room. After opening the door, Dakota held it open until Milly, Hope, and Peter were all inside.

***

"It's scary out there," Hope commented on the hallway.

"It's even scarier out *there*," Dakota gestured to the window. "Have you seen?"

Both Hope and Peter shook their head.

"Come on." Dakota walked over to the window and pulled back the curtain.

"We're not supposed to go over there," Hope told her.

"Both my moms said it's not safe," Peter backed her up.

"It's okay. I was watching from my own room until the evacuation order made us leave."

Hope shuffled closer to the window. "What's an evactation?"

"Evacuation. It's when the people in charge want you to go from one place to another place."

"Why?" Hope shuffled a little closer to the window again.

Peter walked past her and went straight up to it, so Hope stopped shuffling and joined him. They couldn't see much other than the top of the creepy red ghost ship. Hope didn't realize that the ship wasn't actually red, and that it was just the lighting from the flares making it look that way.

"I don't know why," Dakota answered Hope's question, "no one told us. They just said they wanted us to go toward the front of the ship, and that someone there would direct us further."

"Do you think the ghosts are going to board us?" Hope wondered.

"Ghosts?"

Hope pointed to the wooden posts gliding past.

Dakota laughed. "That's not a ghost ship. It's a pirate ship."

"Pirates drive around in those little fast boats," Hope told her. She had seen them when they were attacked by pirates before.

"Yeah, but they used to use ships like that one. Back when pirates wore eye patches, and had peg legs, and parrots on their shoulders."

Hope had no idea what Dakota was talking about. Since there wasn't much to look at, she started to get bored with the window. Walking over to the far side of the bed, she looked through the toys there. She was still scared, but she found a deck of Uno cards that didn't take any imagination to use.

"Do either of you want to play Uno?" she asked.

Both Peter and Dakota said they did, and sat down on the floor with her. Milly lay down behind Hope, her head resting on her one front paw, watching the card games. Dakota won almost every time, but sometimes Peter was the winner. Hope never won. She blamed it on the fact that she was scared and not paying enough attention, even though the others didn't seem to be paying that much attention either. At one point, another thunderous crack shook the ship. Hope screamed again and just about jumped on Milly. The three of them stopped playing Uno then, and simply huddled together.

"Maybe we should evacuate," Peter suggested after a little while, saying the new word carefully.

"We don't know where to go," Hope told him.

"Forward. Where else is there to go on the ship? We just go forward," Dakota said.

"But someone might be looking for us right now." Hope didn't want to wander off and get in trouble like last time.

"Wouldn't they have found us if they were?" Dakota asked.

"We should stay put," Hope insisted.

"If we go forward, we'll find someone and they can tell us where everyone else went," Dakota continued to push.

"When you're lost, you're supposed to stay put!" Hope was getting mad.

"We'll stay here a little longer," Peter told them both.

Hope pouted. She was now both scared and grumpy. She played with Milly's collar, undoing the clip and snapping it closed again, sometimes running it in circles around the dog's neck. Hope did this until Milly pulled her head away, annoyed. After that, she just fidgeted with her fingers.

"I'm going to go look outside." Dakota got up and walked over to the window. "Hey, the pirate ship is gone!"

Hope and Peter both scrambled up onto their feet and ran to the window. Looking out, they couldn't see the posts anywhere.

"I told you it was a ghost ship!" Hope cried. "It disappeared!"

"It's not a ghost ship. It probably just went somewhere we can't see. Or maybe it sank." Dakota tried to find an explanation, but she didn't sound as sure of herself as usual.

"It was a ghost ship," Hope insisted, walking away from the window. She seated herself back down beside Milly, who hadn't bothered to follow the kids to the window again.

Peter soon rejoined her, but Dakota walked right past.

"Where are you going?" Hope worried she was going to leave without them.

"I'm just going to go look in the hallway and see if anyone is there."

"Okay." Hope actually hoped there was.

She and Peter listened as first the door was opened, and then as Dakota screamed. Both of them jumped to their feet, Milly as well, and Dakota came running back to them.

"It's on fire!" Dakota screamed.

"What is?" Peter asked.

"Everything! The hallway! It's all on fire!"

"We're trapped," Hope sobbed.

"Come on, I know what to do." Dakota led them to the bathroom and turned on the tap. "Find clothes or sheets or something. A towel, a towel will work." She grabbed a white towel off the towel rack and stuck it under the tap. "Go find more stuff. And buckets, and glasses. Stuff that can hold water."

Peter and Hope dashed out of the bathroom to find what Dakota had asked for. Hope went through the closet and drawers, while Peter looked for a bucket or something. As Hope grabbed shirts, pants, and socks, she wondered who they belonged to. Ms. Abby and Ms. Lauren had been borrowing this room, just the way Hope and Daddy were borrowing the one down the hall. She carried the pile of clothing back to Dakota, who was shoving a soaking wet towel up against the bottom of the door.

"Great," Dakota said when she saw Hope, "give those to me, then find another bucket like Peter has."

Hope handed over the pile of clothes, and saw that Peter didn't have a bucket, but a flowerpot. The dirt and the plant that had been growing inside lay on the floor. Hope was able to find an actual bucket in the bottom of the closet.

"What are you doing?" Hope asked Dakota who was putting the clothes in the sink and the shower.

"We have to get this stuff wet and place it against the door." Dakota turned on the shower. "We should also flood the sink and the shower. That'll help."

Hope didn't understand what Dakota was doing. She thought you were supposed to put water on the fire, not other places. Dakota was older though, and had taken more classes. She probably knew what she was doing. Besides, Peter wasn't arguing either.

As the clothes were soaked, the kids placed them on top of the towel. Dakota then filled up the bucket and the flowerpot, and told Hope and Peter to splash the water on the door. By now, the shower was about to flood out all over the floor because of the towels Dakota had put over the drain, and the sink was very full.

"Keep filling these up and splashing the door. I'm going to open the door to the balcony."

"But there's bad guys out there!" Hope protested.

"Maybe they went away. Better than the fire in here, I say." Dakota ran for the sliding glass door.

Hope and Peter continued to fill the flowerpot and bucket, and then throw the water on the door and the pile of clothes. Eventually, both the shower and the sink overflowed, splashing water all over the floor. Hope squealed as it washed over her bare feet, soaking the bottoms of her new pyjama pants.

During all of this, Milly kept wandering around the room. She was whining, and sometimes even barking. A few times she got in the kids' way, and once Hope shoved her hard enough to knock her over.

"Is the door open yet?" Hope walked into the main part of the room to ask Dakota.

"I can't get it open!" Dakota screamed.

"Is it too heavy? Maybe Peter and I can help." Hope knew that the doors to the balcony were very heavy and hard to open. She had seen some adults have trouble pulling them open.

"I haven't even gotten to that part yet. Whoever owns this room, they locked the door with this string, and I can't untie it!" Dakota was actually crying. Seeing her tears, Hope immediately began to cry as well.

Eventually, Dakota collapsed to the floor in a huff, wrapping her arms around her knees and sobbing into them. Hope went to her and cried alongside her. Once Peter realized he was the only one still using a bucket, he dropped it and walked into the main room to the find the girls. He didn't cry like they did, but sat on the floor in a tight ball. Milly sniffed each kid, whining deep in her throat. The three-legged husky paced in circles, stopping occasionally to bark or growl at nothing. When she started howling, Hope didn't bother to tell her to be quiet.

"Hope, Dakota, look." Peter pointed at the wall, near the ceiling.

Both the girls looked up. Smoke was coming into the room. There was a small hole near the ceiling and smoke was coming through it.

"Oh no!" Dakota quickly got to her feet and ran for the bathroom. She came out a moment later with the flowerpot full of water, and splashed the water at the hole. The hole got a little bit bigger, there was a hissing sound, and the smoke stopped only for a moment.

Peter got up quickly and grabbed the bucket, running for the bathroom. He returned with it full of water and splashed it over the wall. He and Dakota started doing this over and over again, just the way Hope and Peter had done with the door. Hope searched the room again, but couldn't find anything else that would hold water besides a single drinking glass in the bathroom. She used the glass a few times, but compared to how much water Dakota and Peter were throwing, it seemed pointless. Instead, she knelt in the water covering the bathroom floor, no longer worried about wetting her pyjama pants, and used her glass to empty the water from the toilet. She didn't think about how gross toilet water must be, she thought only about adding to the water on the floor. If there was enough, it would spill out into the room. When the toilet was empty, she flushed it to get more water.

Milly was howling a lot now.

After a while, Hope noticed that Peter and Dakota were no longer running into the bathroom. She got up and walked into the main room to find them. Both of them were sitting against the mattress against the window, panting. They were pooped out, as Hope's mom would say. Hope plopped down next to them in her soaking wet clothes. All three kids wrapped their arms around each other and sobbed. There was nothing more they could do.

When the first flame flashed briefly through the hole in the wall, Hope wailed, adding her voice to Milly's.

This was it. With nothing left to do, this had to be it.

A loud thump came from the door. The kids cried out, frightened. Their scared minds didn't even try to figure out what it was. When it happened again, and again, they cried louder.

"Hope!" a rough voice called into the room.

Hope got up and looked down the little hallway just in time to see her daddy pushing his way into the room around the wet stuff. Thick, black smoke billowed into the room over his head. The big hallway behind him was very bright, with an intense yellow light. While Hope watched, her daddy squeezed inside and slammed the door, narrowly avoiding being grabbed by a man who was on fire.

"Hope!" Her daddy made his way over to her and fell to his knees, sweeping Hope into his arms in a tight bear hug.

"Daddy! Daddy!" Hope cried into his chest. He smelled like smoke.

Daddy let go of Hope and quickly looked around the room. Milly was whining, licking his arm, and wagging her tail, but he ignored her. His face was all sooty.

"Let's get you out of here," Daddy spoke to Hope and the other kids. He then started coughing. When he was done, he got up to his feet and went to the balcony door. He was walking really funny.

"Daddy, you're bleeding!" Hope pointed to his leg.

"I know. Don't worry about it. I'm all right." He was no longer paying much attention to Hope; she could tell by the way that he was talking. She didn't care, she was just glad that he was here. Her daddy was here to rescue her.

Pulling out a big knife, Daddy cut the string that was holding the door closed and then yanked it open. He was very strong, and had no trouble with the heavy door. Hope enjoyed the breeze that came through the opening. She hadn't noticed how hot it was in the room.

Another flame flashed in the wall.

"Daddy!"

Daddy looked outside on the balcony. "Shit!" he cried. It was a word he wasn't supposed to use, a bad word. He came back inside. "All right kids. Stay right here by the mattress for a second."

Hope, Dakota, and Peter did as they were told. Daddy walked in his funny way to the closet and looked inside, coughing the whole time. The flames flashed again, and this time they didn't go away. The wall was on fire. Daddy came back with four lifejackets.

"Come here." He knelt down by the open door and Hope saw it was very painful for him.

She and the other kids gathered close to him, fearfully glancing at the burning wall. Milly crowded up close to Daddy as well.

"Peter, Hope, put these on." Daddy handed them lifejackets.

Hope had been taught how to put one on during her swim lessons and was quick to do so now. Next to her, Peter did the same, and then helped Hope adjust her straps.

"Dakota, this one is adult sized, but it's all we've got." Daddy put a lifejacket on Dakota and tightened the straps a lot. "It may slip off of you. Are you a good swimmer?"

"Yes, Mr. Cole," she nodded.

Once the lifejacket was on Dakota, Daddy took the other adult lifejacket and put it on Milly. Milly didn't seem to like it much; Daddy had put it on her crooked because of her legs, but she didn't try to pull it off.

"What about you, Daddy? Where's your lifejacket?" Hope wondered.

"There aren't any more, but don't worry, I don't need one."

"The fire is getting bigger," Peter pointed out.

Smoke was now filling the room, flowing over their heads and out the open door.

"We have to be quick. Remember to hook your ankles together, press your knees together, and clamp your arms to your sides. Cover your mouth with one hand, and plug your nose with the other."

"What are we doing, Mr. Cole?"

"Getting out of here. Come on." Daddy struggled back up onto his feet and led them outside.

Hope looked toward the front of the ship, assuming that's where they were going. Instead of a clear path, she saw two men having a sword fight. It wasn't like the sword fights she had with her friends; their swords looked real.

Toward the back of the ship, glass exploded outward followed by a lot of smoke and fire. Both Dakota and Hope screamed.

"Remember what I told you in the room," Daddy said as he picked up Dakota.

"I remember."

Suddenly, Daddy threw Dakota over the side of the ship. Both Dakota and Hope screamed again, but Dakota's stopped much quicker this time.

"You're next, buddy." Daddy picked up Peter, and then threw him over the side as well.

"Daddy!" Hope didn't understand what was going on.

"Sorry about this, Milly." Daddy picked up the husky and threw her over the side. Milly yelped as she disappeared from sight.

"Daddy, no!" Hope backed into the wall as he turned toward her.

"It's okay, I'm coming with you. I'm not leaving this time."

A scream farther up the ship made them both turn. One of the men had been stabbed by the other and had fallen to the deck. The man who had done the stabbing, turned toward both Hope and her daddy. He raised his sword and ran toward them.

"No time for diplomacy," Daddy said as he grabbed Hope. "Plug your nose, sweet pea, and take a deep breath."

Hope plugged her nose as Daddy climbed onto the railing with her, and then jumped off, pushing them outward with his not-bleeding leg. Together, they fell through the air. Hope held her breath despite wanting to scream, and clung to her daddy who held her in a crushing grip.

They hit the water feet first, and plunged below the surface. Daddy let go of Hope. She tried to grab him, but her lifejacket soon carried her upward. As she reached the air, she gasped, tasting the nasty seawater. Before she could cry out for her daddy, he popped up beside her.

"Hold my shoulders." Daddy turned around backwards so that Hope could do what he said.

Daddy started swimming toward the back of the ship, which was moving but not very fast. They found Milly first, her eyes wide with terror as she struggled to keep upright. She tried to climb onto Daddy, but he wouldn't let her. With one hand, he steadied the dog, and she began to calm down as she realized she wasn't going to sink. They kept swimming until they found both Peter and Dakota. Somehow, Dakota still had her hat. She must not have listened to one of Daddy's instructions about what to do with her hands.

"You kids all right?" Daddy asked them.

They both nodded. Dakota was struggling to keep her lifejacket from floating up over her head.

"Okay, we have to swim away from the Diana now. Can you do that for me? I want you to hold hands. You too, Hope."

They all formed a line. Daddy was on one end, holding Hope's hand, and helping Milly, while Dakota was holding Peter's hand on the other end, so that she could hold her lifejacket down with her free one. Together, they slowly swam away from the Diana.

"Where are we going?" Peter asked.

"The Diana is going to sink. We have to be away from it when it does. Right now, all we're doing is moving away."

"What about the pirates?" Dakota asked next.

Daddy didn't answer that question. Hope could see some boats driving around, but they didn't make any attempts to be seen by them. The boats most likely belonged to the pirates, and they wouldn't help them.

"Daddy?" Hope suddenly thought of something.

"What is it, sweet pea?"

"What if there's sharks?"

Daddy didn't answer that question either.

IV
Evacuation

Abby was close to losing her mind with worry. When Claire had cried out that she had been separated from Peter, she immediately tried to go back for him, but she couldn't. The press of people evacuating the burning, zombie infested rear of the ship to the relatively safer front of the ship had been too much. Even standing still had been difficult to do, and Lauren had already been lost in the throng. When Claire was nearly ripped away from her in the narrow hallway, Abby knew she had to keep going. With her arm tight around Claire's shoulders, they had gone with the flow. Abby prayed that the kids were following the crowd, or that someone would notice them and bring them along. So far, no such luck.

Abby paced back and forth in the Lily Lounge. It was crammed full of displaced people. So far, no one had brought in Peter or Hope, or even Milly. There was a guard at the door who wouldn't let Abby leave. To reduce the confusion and risk of further accidents, those who made it to an evacuation point were forced to remain there.

Claire stood nearby, watching Abby pace, her hands clasped tightly beneath her chin. They didn't know where Lauren was either. She must have been moved to a different location.

"They must be in a different area, like Lauren," Claire insisted.

"Yeah. They probably are. With everything that's happening, they must not have time to get separated families back together." Abby desperately wanted to believe this.

When Mathias showed up, her heart broke. The way he was looking frantically around, he was obviously searching for his daughter.

"Where's Hope?" he asked, hobbling over on a wounded leg the moment he spotted Abby.

Abby had to explain how they got separated, how she tried to go back for them.

Mathias placed his hands on Abby's shoulders, quieting her down. "It's fine, it happens. But tell me, what room were you in?"

"6368," Abby told him.

"I'll find them. Don't you worry about it. I'll find them." Mathias then left as quickly as his wound would allow.

Despite his words, Abby kept worrying. Now she had even more to worry about in fact. Judging by the white bandage, Mathias's leg had been looked at, but the injury must have reopened. Red blood was staining the bandage, and Mathias's running around on it would only make things worse.

She continued to pace.

***

Down in the medical centre, Riley was frantically trying to get the last of the injured moved out. Not only was the place filling with the smoke of the advancing fire, but raiders were boarding through the door that had been blown out. A team of ship defenders was doing a good job of keeping them back, but they were quickly running out of ammunition.

"He's next!" Riley ordered, pointing to a man who had lost his leg when the cannon ball smashed open their defences. The hallway outside the medical centre was a mess, with debris from their barricade scattered everywhere. A few dead lay amid the wreckage.

Assured that everyone was doing their job, Riley crawled over to the final patient. The smoke was so bad that everyone was crawling now. On the floor, wrapped in a sheet, lay Rose. She was awake and watching Riley above the oxygen mask strapped to her lower face. Her skin was pale, and her heartbeat was very rapid when Riley checked it. Rose shouldn't be moved. She was still very weak from blood loss. There was no choice though. Either they move her, or the fire would get her. If not the fire, then one of the burning zombies that kept stumbling out of it. Riley suspected that the blaze was spreading a lot quicker because of them. Although attempts had been made initially to put out the flames, the zombies kept driving the firefighters back. Now the burning corpses were carrying the conflagration past the areas the firefighters had soaked.

"You'll be moved soon," Riley told Rose, her voice muffled by her own mask. Riley's mask was only a damp cloth, but it was helping to prevent smoke inhalation. Still, Riley could feel the tickling in her lungs, the need to cough. She was trying to keep the coughing at bay as long as she could. She knew that once she started, she'd have a hard time stopping.

Rose blinked once, slowly, deliberately, to let Riley know she understood. She was too tired even to nod her head. It was likely that fear was the only thing keeping Rose awake right now, and even then, her mind wanted to drift off. Riley stayed crouched down beside her, waiting for the next group of stretcher-bearers to arrive.

"Are there any more patients?" Dr. Owen asked as he sidled up next to Riley and Rose, arming the sweat off his forehead at the same time. The heat was rising in the medical centre. Already the major staircases just down the hall were burning, and the patients had to be carried through the belly of the ship.

"No," Riley shook her head. "You and the other doctors get out of here. I'll wait with Rose for the last stretcher team."

Owen nodded, and then went off to inform the other remaining doctors. Riley looked around the medical centre. The beds weren't all empty, but no one living occupied them. A lot of people had already died this night, and she suspected a lot more would follow.

A stretcher team arrived and scuttled over to Riley. Under her orders, they gently lifted Rose in her sheet, and rested her on the orange plastic backboard. Rose groaned, but didn't scream or cry out, and she managed to stay awake. Riley carefully placed the small oxygen tank between her remaining arm and her body where it should hopefully stay put, and then told the stretcher team that she was good to go. As they carried her out, crouching as low as they could, Riley took one last look around the medical centre. This was the place where Hope had been born.

She grabbed her bag, which was stuffed with medicine and supplies. All the doctors had carried out similar bags, and so did several stretcher-bearers, but there were still some things they had to leave behind. It was all non-essential stuff, such as vitamins, but Riley was still pissed she had to leave it. The off-shippers had risked their lives scavenging all this stuff. There were also larger pieces of equipment they could do nothing about.

Out in the hallway, she let the ship defenders know that the medical centre had been emptied. She got a good look at the approaching fire in the process. If the main staircases and elevator shafts hadn't been as close to the medical centre as they were, they would have been smoked out long before they could get everyone out, but thankfully, most of the smoke was being drawn upward and away from them.

The ship defenders left their post and headed to the front of the ship with Riley. Let the raiders deal with the fire, and the burning zombies.

***

Lauren sat sideways in her seat, her eyes locked on the doors into the theatre. No one else had come in for a long time, but still she watched. Abby and the kids must have been directed to another place. Lauren cursed herself for being separated from them. She shouldn't have bothered with the box of supplies. Unfortunately, she had no way of knowing how hectic that hallway was going to be. She thought that because they heard about it on the walkie-talkie, they would have gotten out ahead of the crowd. Apparently, a lot of people were listening to walkie-talkies, and whoever had been going around door-to-door to warn everyone must have started before anything was said on them.

The theatre wasn't packed with people, but there were a lot. Most of them sat quietly in groups, while a few like Lauren sat alone. Some of them were smoky, their faces and clothes smudged black from getting too close to the fire. Earlier, Lauren had seen

Mathias come in. She had waved him down and told him that Abby and the kids had to be in a different room. He left immediately to find them. Since then, Lauren hadn't seen anyone she knew enter the theatre.

On stage, a few entertainers were trying to keep the displaced people occupied. The lead singer of what used to be a very popular rock band, Quin Beharry, was currently working his way through a song. He had a ratty guitar at which he was plucking away, his voice doing most of the work. Earlier, an actor had been reciting monologues. Also on stage was Brittany, the grief councillor, with her little wiener dog, Olivia. Abby had had trouble dealing with the emotional stress of the Day and all that followed, even after being reunited with Lauren. Brittany had helped her a lot, and she was continuing to help people now. Whenever someone needed an ear to listen, she hopped off the stage and went over to them. Lauren admired the woman, who had survived both brain and breast cancer—the latter resulting in a double mastectomy—before the Day happened. Even though there was always the lingering threat of the cancer coming back, and the ship not being equipped to help her if it did, she always had a kind word and a comforting shoulder for others.

It was Brittany who was summoned to the back of the theatre when Captain Sigvard eventually arrived. This wasn't long after a ghostly groan had echoed throughout the entire ship. Lauren couldn't hear what they were talking about, but it was clearly a very serious matter. When they were done, Brittany ran back to the stage, ignoring a man who tried to flag her down. It was very serious indeed.

Up on stage, Brittany silenced Quin and his guitar, and faced the crowd. Everyone was literally sitting on the edge of his or her seat, wondering what was going on.

"Attention!" Brittany called out, her voice powerful enough to fill the room. If there had been someone not paying attention to her before, they were now. "I've just received word from the captain that the Diana is slowly sinking."

A ripple of shock and worry rushed through the crowd, while one woman screamed outright.

"I know this is terrible news for you all, it is for me too, but I need you all to evacuate as calmly as you can," Brittany told them. "Do not rush, do not push. Remain calm and everything will be fine. We've rebuilt once before, we'll rebuild again. The only thing that can't be replaced is you, so be smart. There is absolutely no need to panic. Remember the practice drills, we always knew this could happen. Everything will be fine. Let's go."

Brittany stepped away from the edge of the stage, walking to Quin and gesturing for him to leave the stool on which he was sitting. He did, and then went backstage to gather anyone left behind the curtains.

"Let's go, people!" Brittany called out again as she stepped down.

Everyone started to stand up, one by one. Lauren grabbed her box of meagre supplies, suddenly understanding how much more important they were now. With everything burning and sinking, they'd lose it all. They'd lose everything they weren't carrying. Lauren was glad that everyone had been issued a weapon before the raiders showed up, because if they were going to shore, they'd need them. Tucked into the waistband of her pants, Lauren had a small, six shooter revolver, loaded with three bullets.

Joining the crowd headed for the door, Lauren saw that Captain Sigvard was watching the procession. Several people were stopping to ask him questions, most of them about the raiders. Sigvard patiently answered them the best he could, but most of his answers weren't very satisfactory for those asking them.

"What was that loud groaning?" Lauren walked up to him and asked. "Is it why we're sinking now and not earlier?"

Sigvard nodded. "The ship that rammed us created a large hole, but mostly in the upper decks. The longer they were stuck to our back, however, the farther into us they pushed, and the lower the damage got. That wasn't so bad, as the ship also plugged up the hole it made in the Diana. That groan you heard was it slipping. It's slid sideways, ripping the hole bigger and unplugging it. We're no longer ploughing straight through the water, and the longer we sit this way, the more we're going to be turned. Eventually, we'll be turned enough that the ship behind us will break free, leaving a massive hole, and no longer helping to hold us afloat. We have to be off the Diana when that happens. There's time, but please don't dawdle for anything."

Several people had clustered around Lauren, as they too wanted to know the answer to her question. One of them asked about the raiders again, to which Sigvard's only reply was that they would do their best.

Lauren followed the crowd up to the fourth deck. Above her head, the lifeboats hadn't been launched yet, but through the grated catwalk, she could see the injured being loaded aboard them. It was unfortunate that the fire was keeping them from using the tender boats and a few of the lifeboats at the back of the ship.

Rafts were being tossed over the side and deployed, with healthy people then jumping into the water and boarding them. Rope ladders were draped over the side of the ship so that the rest of them could climb down. As Lauren neared a ladder, waiting in a line that had naturally formed behind it, she noticed that a lot of ship defenders were gathered around the evacuees. Several of them had rifles pointed at the ocean, while others flanked the stream of people and kept them organized.

"Leave that box here, Ms. Sanford," a voice spoke to Lauren.

She knew who it was before she even turned to look at his face. Winchester *always* called her Ms. Sanford, ever since they had met at a motel so long ago during the Day.

"You can't climb down the ladder while holding that box." Winchester held out his arms for Lauren to hand it over.

She did. "You'll keep an eye out for Abby and the kids, won't you?"

"Yes, ma'am," he smiled for her, "*all* the kids."

"What'll happen to the supplies?"

"People first, supplies second. We'll load them onto boats and rafts when we can. The lifeboats are loading up as many supplies as they can between the injured. Don't worry about it. Now, go on, you're next."

Lauren turned and saw that she was indeed next. As she carefully climbed over the railing and onto the swaying ladder, she looked along the deck. The last thing she saw before descending was Brittany, with Olivia in her arms, helping a couple tie a rope around their terrier so it could be loaded onto one of the rafts. Lauren thought that, if everyone managed to keep holding together like that, then they might just stand a chance.

***

Hector sat in his powerboat, rocking on the waves. No one had heard from Sher in far too long, even before that helicopter had landed on the back end of the second ship. He had had a grudging respect for Sher ever since the man had freed him from some Mexican slavers and put him to work with a dignified job and food, but this was madness. The two cruise ships were locked together and definitely sinking, while people died all around. All because Sher's sister had finally fought back.

Originally, it sounded like a great plan. Come out here, take both ships for themselves, and return to Jamaica, as conquering heroes with tons of supplies, but that wasn't how things went. They had expected some resistance, but nothing with this level of organization and force. It wasn't worth it.

At his side, his radio chattered with confused calls from the other men. They didn't know what to do. Without Sher's leadership, they were lost.

"They are lowering boats to evacuate the ship," another man in Hector's boat told him, watching through a pair of binoculars. "Should we gun them down?"

"No. There's no point." Hector pulled out his radio, placing it close to his lips. "Retreat," he spoke with authority he didn't really possess. In the chaos, no one would really know who was speaking anyway. "Retreat! Return to Jamaica! There is nothing left for us here! The supplies we came for are going down with the ships! Do not bother with the people, they are not worth the bullets! Retreat! Retreat! Retreat!"

He continued to repeat his message. With his hand holding down the lever, Hector couldn't hear how other boats were responding, but he wasn't going to give up. The other men in his boat fidgeted nervously, not knowing if this was the best course of action and definitely knowing it shouldn't be Hector giving the orders even if it were.

"They are turning away!" the man with the binoculars announced. "Most of them anyway. I think it is mostly Sher's closest men who are ignoring you."

Hector heaved a sigh of relief. He had hoped that most of the men *wanted* to retreat and were just waiting for the okay to do so. It looked like his gamble had paid off.

Continuing his message, Hector modified it with co-ordinates where the fleet should meet up, away from this war zone. They had to gather together and return to Jamaica as a unified force. On their own, who knew what other pirates might show up to pick them off? The flames from the burning cruise ships were likely to act as a beacon.

"Everyone is heading in the direction you suggested," Hector was informed.

"Good." He finally lowered his radio and slumped in his seat. "Now, when we meet up with them, it wasn't me sounding the retreat, yeah?"

The men in the ship nodded. Nobody wanted to be the man who gave commands without Sher's permission, even if their leader was most likely dead.

"Okay, let's go join them."

With a roar, the engines came to life, the boat lurching forward. They made for the dark shapes and the few glowing lights cast by the other retreating boats. Hector didn't even think about helping the Diana residents, but he knew that to gun them down while they helplessly fled their home was beyond his capabilities. This trip had already turned into a terrible waste of life after so many had already been lost to the undead. Why add to it when there was no gain?

***

There were casualties during the ship evacuation.

A few people had refused to leave their rooms at the back of the ship, only to end up suffocating from the smoke. Although Sher's raiders were disorganized, the majority of them fleeing after Hector's broadcast, a few continued to attack. Some shot at the people in the rafts, while others got on board the Diana during the chaos. Ship defenders did all they could to remove them, but a few were cut down by raiders' swords or gunfire. At least one man committed suicide, jumping from a high window that overlooked the promenade, hitting head first so that his neck snapped like a dry twig.

There were further injuries as well; people being knocked down, or into walls. Thankfully, for the most part they managed not to panic, however there were exceptions. One elderly man broke his hip, while a young woman broke her leg when she was pushed down the stairs.

The submarine had surfaced again, and all the life rafts and lifeboats were gathering around it. A woman who had refused to learn how to swim fell off the life raft she was in. If it weren't for another life raft close behind stopping to pick her up, she would have drowned. One injured fellow did drown when a lifeboat hit the wake of a raider boat and his unconscious body came loose from his straps, slipping over the edge. The metal poles being used to keep his back straight made him sink like a stone.

Several lifeboats, upon reaching the submarine, discharged both the injured and their supplies, and then quickly turned around to pick up more people from the Diana. With their small engines, they were much quicker than the rafts being paddled. Many lifeboats were now tying a few rafts behind them, towing them toward the submarine.

When the other ship broke loose, it did so with a horrendous squeal. Everyone turned to the sound of grinding, twisting metal. The submarine had parked on the opposite side of the Diana from where the other cruise ship was heading, so everyone on that side was out of its path. Unfortunately, several lifeboats and life rafts on the far side of the Diana were not. Due to the forward motion of both ships, it was safer for them to go around the back of both ships rather than try to cross their course, resulting in a stream of fleeing boats and rafts to be in the new ship's path. Those in the way were sucked under the ship, along with a few raider boats that had been buzzing them. Other rafts were overturned by the cruise ship's close passage, its wake throwing them all sideways, but the people in them all managed to climb back aboard or were picked up by other life rafts.

The Diana was sinking, aft end first. As it descended lower and lower into the water, people began to scramble more, and even started to panic. The animals on board had been let loose, chickens, cows, and goats fleeing everywhere. It was mostly ship defenders on board at that point, and a few of them tried to save the smaller animals by gathering them into their arms before leaping over the sides. That's what it came down to in the end. There was no more organization to load the rafts and lifeboats. Everyone remaining on board was now jumping and praying they'd be picked up.

One of the two horses came bursting out onto the fourth deck—which was low enough now to be the third or second—and leapt over the side and into the water. It splashed around, eyes wild and breathing hard. One man who was alone in a raft went to the horse, and risked life and limb to help it scramble aboard. The horse couldn't stand on the raft's soft bottom, and it let a lot of water wash over the sides in the process, but it did get aboard.

A few other large animals were rescued, mostly by swimmers tying lifejackets around them and towing them to the submarine, but the majority were lost.

Zombies claimed a few casualties during the mayhem, on both sides. They took down raiders and Diana residents alike. Many were on fire, and those that weren't shot, were dragged down with the ship.

Once the remaining raiders realized that the Diana was done for, they finally ceased their attack. Those who had boarded her were left there to fend for themselves. One teenaged boy, who had been abandoned by his comrades, joined the Diana residents. He acted like he had always lived aboard the cruise ship, and no one questioned his presence.

The other cruise ship sank as well. It plunged nose first as it continued to push forward, its engines still running at full power. No one paid any attention to it.

There was silence surrounding the submarine as the Diana went down. All eyes that weren't busy were on it. A few people gasped when the limited power winked out, but that was all. As the last tip of the ship sank beneath the surface, people began to cry.

Later, when an attendance was taken, no one was able to find Captain Sigvard.

Section 4:
Flight

20
Mathias Is In The Ocean

Mathias saw the Diana go down, but he didn't pay much attention to it. He was too busy keeping the kids swimming. He was also too busy trying to keep an eye out for sharks. For obvious reasons, he didn't want to tell the kids, especially Hope that there were sharks in the water, but he knew they were there. They had probably been there for hours, feasting on the corpses of raiders and Diana residents. Eventually, they'd tire of dead meat, or there would be more sharks than corpses, and Mathias's bleeding leg would become a dinner bell. Earlier, he had felt something brush against him and feared the worst, but it hadn't happened again.

They were aiming for the submarine. The two cruise ships and the sub had continued to move forward after Mathias and the kids had jumped, and now they were playing catch up. Since the second ship had disengaged, there was no more forward movement, and Mathias was glad for that. Up until then, they had just been falling farther behind instead of getting closer. There was still a long way to go.

"I'm tired," Hope said for the millionth time.

"I know you are. I'm tired too," Mathias told her. "We have to keep swimming though. We have to make it to the submarine."

Hope didn't respond. Mathias could tell she was exhausted just by the tone of her voice, her choice of words, and the fact that she didn't even seem to know she was saying them.

His injured leg burned with every kick. Holding Milly with one hand, and Hope with the other, meant he was only using his legs to both keep afloat and move forward. He was strong, but this was wearing him down. He noticed he was swimming lower in the water, and was relying more and more on Hope and Milly's lifejackets to keep him above the surface.

"Hey!" Dakota called out from her end. "Look what I found."

Mathias looked over and saw her holding a piece of rope, her lifejacket pushing up around her head.

"Great. That's a good find, Dakota." Mathias let go of Hope to reach for the rope. "Hold Milly steady for me."

The kids all stabilized Milly while Mathias tied one end of the rope around his waist. When he was done, he held out the other end of the rope to the kids.

"I want you all to grab the rope. Can you do that?"

The kids nodded and did as he asked. Peter was going to thread the rope through his lifejacket, but Mathias stopped him. He didn't want them tethered in a way that would be difficult for them to let go.

"I also need you to keep holding Milly upright for me with your free hands." Although Milly could swim, the lifejacket and her weight imbalance kept trying to roll her sideways. Mathias wished he could take the lifejacket off her and use it himself, but Milly would never make it. If it came down to it, he'd take the dog's lifejacket, but he wasn't ready for that yet.

Once the kids were all holding onto the rope and to Milly, Mathias started swimming for the submarine again. Being able to use his arms was a huge relief, although it felt like the kids weren't kicking at all now. Still, it was better than it had been before.

Something brushed against him again, and this time Mathias knew it wasn't his imagination. There was no way of telling if it was a shark or not. It could have been a body below the surface, a piece of debris, hell it could have been a swimming zombie or even a dolphin, but Mathias suspected it was a shark. There was nothing he could do about it. This was why he had stopped Peter from tying himself to Mathias. If a shark was going to drag him down, the kids could just let go and be safe.

Mathias focused on nothing but swimming and the submarine ahead of him. It was so far away. He wasn't going to give up, but he felt like he was getting nowhere. The idea of sacrificing Milly appalled him, but he'd do it if the time came. With every stroke, it seemed more and more likely that it would be *when* the time came. Better his dog than his kid.

He swam as long as he could, but eventually his arms tired as well. Soon, he would no longer be able to keep himself afloat, let alone pull the children. He stopped.

"Kids, I need Milly." His voice felt hollow in his chest.

Milly was floated over to him, her legs lightly paddling. Mathias held the shoulders of her lifejacket, looking her in the face. Her bright brown eyes looked back, confused and scared. She wagged her tail a few times, swishing it through the seawater, unsure what was about to happen. Mathias reached for a strap along her back.

"Ahoy!"

Mathias startled, sinking up to his nose briefly, and then turned around.

Misha, and three other people whom Mathias didn't know were paddling toward them in a life raft.

"Hey!" Misha was laughing at the forward edge of the raft, dipping his paddle in and dragging the raft forward. "How the hell did you five end up way out here?"

"How did you?" Mathias asked, as they got close enough for him to grab the edge. "Why aren't you with the flotilla?"

"We boarded on the far side of the Diana. Just missed getting squashed by that other ship," Misha told him while he helped lift Hope aboard.

Two other men assisted Peter and Dakota. The third was dealing with something Mathias couldn't see. By the sound of it, he suspected it was a goat, although that confused him having not watched the last of the evacuation. Rifle was also likely on board, or else Misha wouldn't be anywhere near this cheerful.

"We kept going around the back, not realizing that going around the front would have been faster once the Diana had stopped. We were especially detoured by having to paddle away from the sinking ship so that it didn't suck us down with it."

Considering how much Misha was talking, it must have been rather exciting as well as terrifying. Either that, or he was just that happy to have found Mathias, who was certainly happy he found them. Once Hope was on board the raft, Misha reached down for Milly. He began to haul her out of the water but suddenly stopped halfway, his eyes wide and looking at the ocean just behind Mathias.

There was no need for Mathias to ask what was coming. He saw it in that look. Misha's eyes flicked to his face, about to say or maybe do something, but he never got the chance.

Mathias felt the shark bite into the meat of his leg, felt his hand burn as it was ripped free of the rope he had been holding along the side of the raft, and he felt the ocean invade his mouth as he involuntarily screamed.

Hope was safe though, that's all that mattered to him. Misha would take care of her, and would find her mother. She was safe.

As the pressure built up around him—the shark was pulling him deeper and deeper—Mathias actually hoped that his entire body would be eaten. If not, then at least his head, so that he couldn't come back as something torn and dead.

He felt the other sharks close in.

21
Jon's In The Chopper

The helicopter sped over the ocean, headed for Cancun. It was the closest piece of land they knew about, and there was an airport next to the sea. They could get fuel there.

Jon couldn't stop fidgeting. He didn't think what they were doing was right.

The Diana had hailed them, instructing them not to land. They knew by then that there was a good chance the ship would go down, and so they had told the helicopter to fly straight to the nearest airport: the one in Cancun. There, they would gas up, and return to the Diana if possible.

The Diana would probably be gone by then, it would have sunk beneath the waves, and if there was no gas for their chopper, they'd be on their own, trapped in a place the off-shippers had visited only once before, and that was on a short raid. Jon's team hadn't even been on duty that day, and as far as he knew, neither Danny nor their other pilot—a man who told them his name was Oliver—had been the ones to do the fly over. It was more than likely that no one on the helicopter had been to Cancun before.

That wasn't why Jon thought it was the wrong choice. He didn't think they should have left the Diana and its residents. Not in its final moments like that.

But what other choice was there? The leaders refused to let the chopper try to refuel on the Diana; they didn't want to risk losing it when the ship went down. Without the Diana, where else could they land in the Gulf of Mexico? The helicopter couldn't fly forever, and if they didn't get fuel now, they'd crash.

Still, Jon didn't like it. There was no other option, but he didn't like the one that was forced on him. He wanted to be dropped off, so that he could help people, but Oliver refused. They needed Jon to help them at the airport.

Looking around the helicopter, Jon knew they needed him. Their group consisted of Danny and Oliver, the pilots, who would have to take care of the chopper's needs, Brunt, who still had one arm out of commission, Freya, who couldn't speak or shout any warnings, and Robin and Jon. Robin was currently scrutinizing Brunt's injury again, trying to determine if there was anything more that she could do. Earlier, she had cleaned the wound on the side of Jon's head again, and wrapped it in a clean bandage, being careful to keep it away from his eyes. His head had hurt like a bitch, until Robin had given him some pills for it. He could see that this business of sitting still was bothering Robin as well, but at least she had something to distract her.

Jon looked out through the window next to him. As soon as they knew they were going to Cancun, they had slid shut the doors on the sides. Now, it looked like the sun would be rising soon. Though still dark across the waters below, up where they were the sky was beginning to lighten. Jon could see a faint glow on the horizon. This long assed night of terror was finally coming to an end. Too bad, the day that was coming was so full of uncertainty.

While they were flying, Jon tried to sleep a few times. He was exhausted, but his mind just wouldn't shut down. He sat very still, allowing his body to rest as best it could, but he never actually slept.

Three of his off-shipper teammates, who were also close friends, were badly injured, and another lay dead. More of his friends were dead or injured as well: Misha had suffered a fall, Mathias had been shot in the leg, and poor Tobias had taken a bullet to the skull. How many more? How many more of his friends were injured or dead? He didn't even know. What about his family? Lauren and Abby and Claire and Peter? How were they? Were they okay? He had no idea. They wouldn't let him board the Diana to find out.

"Land ahoy," Danny's voice crackled over the headsets that everyone wore. Jon's was askew on his head to keep it off his injury, but he could still hear over it just fine.

The four riding in the back of the helicopter began to shift. Robin sat down in the backward facing seat across from Jon, looking out of the window. She pointed to something, and Jon looked out. The sun was coming up, bathing the east with a fiery-orange glow.

"Red sky at morning, sailors take warning," Jon muttered to himself.

"What was that?" Robin asked, having seen his lips move and probably having partly heard it over the headset.

"Nothing," Jon replied, shaking his head.

It wasn't much longer before they were circling over the Cancun International Airport with its many abandoned planes and terminals. All eyes were focused outside the windows, searching for any signs of either life or undead.

"Anyone see anything?" Oliver asked.

Everyone replied that they didn't, save Freya who gave no reply at all.

"All right then, looks like we're landing. Hold onto your butts." Oliver banked the chopper, heading toward the place he thought was mostly likely to have fuel. He hovered over it for a minute, searching the area again, and then lowered the chopper to the ground. As the rotors whined down, everyone watched the airport for movement. There wasn't any.

"Everyone take a weapon," Brunt broke the newly formed silence, and handed out what they had. Jon stuck to his pistol and his sword.

"So the fuel is actually going to be in one of those hangars over there," Oliver pointed through the windshield.

"So why did we land here?" Brunt asked him.

"I didn't much feel like flying a helicopter into a hangar. That truck there is a fuel truck," he gestured to the side. "If it's got what we need, we're golden, but if not, we'll use it to get fuel from the hangar."

"What if the truck's out of gas?" Jon wondered.

"Well then, I guess we're hoofing it," Oliver shrugged. "Maybe I'll fly us closer to the hangar then. Danny, stay with the bird. Maybe you should also stay put, Brunt, what with your arm and all. The rest of you can come with me."

Everyone agreed to this and climbed out of the helicopter. Jon quickly scanned the area again now that his vision was unimpeded by glass or the helicopter's shell. There was no movement, but something was bothering him. It was still pretty dark on the ground and impossible to see inside the terminals. Were there eyes watching them? A helicopter was not a silent way to get somewhere. The off-shippers who had been here before hadn't reported any survivors in the vicinity, but that had been over a year ago, maybe two. Things changed. People moved.

"Come on, Jon." Robin was following Oliver and Freya toward the gas truck.

Jon turned and tagged after them. He wished the helicopter had landed closer to the truck, but he knew it required a certain amount of clearance, and Oliver seemed to be a better-safe-than-sorry kind of guy. As Oliver checked the tank, Jon kept his eyes on the terminal and the nearby tarmac. What was wrong? What was putting him on edge?

"Fuck, both tanks are empty," Oliver sighed. "Come on, back to the chopper. We'll go straight to the hangar and land outside it. Pray for long hoses or buckets, and a pump we can use."

As they started away from the truck, the air suddenly filled with a heavy pounding. It assaulted their ears, and immediately set off a headache deep within Jon's skull. He looked at the helicopter, but it wasn't moving. Through the windshield, he could see that Danny was covering his ears.

The thumping was rhythmic, and it wasn't until a wailing siren-like sound kicked in that Jon realized what it was: music. Music cranked up to the highest volume possible. That's what was wrong. There was way too much wiring around the tarmac. The speakers themselves were mostly hidden from their vantage point, but now that Jon was looking for them, he could see several stacks of them placed all around the airport.

The pavement near Freya's foot exploded in a small puff, unheard over the music. She saw it though, and dove for the helicopter, which was closer to her than the fuel truck.

Jon grabbed Robin and pulled her into cover, placing the fuel truck between them and the terminal. It was possible that a sniper hiding in the long grass had taken a shot at them, but Jon took the risk that the shooter was in the terminal. With the heavy music, it was impossible to tell where the shot had come from.

Oliver continued standing in place for a moment, still covering his ears against the music and unsure why everyone had suddenly dived for cover. When another chunk of pavement was punctured near his own foot, he got the idea and quickly joined Jon and Robin. Inside the helicopter, Danny had disappeared from view, presumably hiding out of sight in the back with Brunt and Freya.

While Robin and Oliver huddled against the truck, trying in vain to protect their ears from the auditory assault, Jon dropped to his belly. He tried to tune out the sound—something that would have been easier to do if it were a constant noise instead of music turned up to squalling levels—as he slithered his way underneath the truck's belly. Jon wormed his way just far enough to see the terminal.

Looking back at his legs, he called Robin's name, but she couldn't hear him. He kicked at her, but she wasn't within reach. Thankfully, she noticed his flailing shoes and bent down to look at him. Using sign language that he had learned from her, Jon told her his plan. Once she understood, he untwisted himself and looked back at the terminal.

It took longer for Robin to explain the plan to Oliver, but in the end, he got it. He darted from the truck to the helicopter. As he did this, a shot was fired at him. Jon wasn't watching, assuming the shot would miss like the other two had. After all, Oliver was running this time instead of standing still. What Jon watched for was a muzzle flash, and he was rewarded. The shooter was a lot closer than he expected, firing out of the opened rear door of a 747. Jon carefully aimed his pistol and returned a volley of three shots. None of them hit the sniper, but at least one bullet struck the skin of the plane near the doorway. Whoever it was, Jon had just let him know that he was armed and more than willing to fire back. Not waiting to see how the sniper would react, he scooted backward until he was out of sight of that back door.

Looking toward the helicopter, he couldn't see Oliver or any blood. He must be safely inside the chopper then. Jon was relieved. Now he just needed to get himself and Robin over there. They could find fuel elsewhere.

All of a sudden the music stopped. The sudden silence was almost as painful as when the music had first begun.

Robin asked him what they should do, speaking with her hands and expression as opposed to her vocal cords. Jon first shrugged, and then gestured for her to wait.

"Helicopter!" an accented voice called out. "Can we talk?"

Jon peered around the side of the fuel truck. A man was walking toward them, his hands above his head.

"I have no weapons!"

There was no way to tell if that was true or not. Even if it was, there was no way this man could be the sniper. He couldn't have gotten down here that fast even at a full sprint. Besides, there was something unsettling about his shit eating grin.

"Do you speak English?" he called once more.

"Yeah," Jon called back.

Robin and he exchanged a look. What else could they do right now?

"Wonderful, wonderful. I had hoped so." The man was now close enough that he no longer needed to shout.

"You can stop where you are," Jon told him, spying around the truck's edge.

The man stopped, still smiling and still holding his hands up.

"What is it you want?" Jon asked him.

"Your mighty fine helicopter, of course," the man replied.

"Oh yeah? And in exchange for what?"

"Your lives."

A red hatred flared up inside Jon. These goddamn people thought they could just take what they wanted and damn whoever they took it from! Before he knew what he was doing, Jon swung out from behind the fuel truck, his pistol levelled at the grinning man.

"Yeah? And what do I get in exchange for yours?"

"I would not do that if I were you." The man pointed at one of the bullet holes in the tarmac. "My man is watching."

"Fuck your man!" Jon heard Robin make a worried noise, but ignored her. He was tired of these goddamn bullies. "Even if he were to shoot me dead right now, my finger is so far back on this trigger that I'll take you with me."

The man's grin wavered slightly.

"What gives you the right just to take our shit anyway? What makes you think you're allowed to threaten our lives?"

"You've entered our home," the man gestured around the airport.

A sudden clarity washed over Jon. He understood the true purpose of the speakers.

"This isn't your home," Jon told the man.

From the corner of his eye, Jon could see Robin trying to get his attention, but he refused to divert his gaze from the asshole in front of him.

"It's not?" the man cocked his head to one side, still grinning.

"No. You would never set up speakers like that in a place you intend to live. No, this airport isn't your home. It's your decoy. Gas up the generators, crank up the speakers, and blast the tunes. Every zombie within hearing range would come here, leaving wherever you want to be free and clear." Jon started walking toward the man.

It took the man a moment to realize what was about to happen, so he didn't back-pedal quickly enough. He lost his grin just before Jon's fist smashed into his jaw, hard enough to send him sprawling onto the pavement.

"I'm tired of you fucks!" Jon screamed. "You pieces of shit! All we want is one helicopter-sized tank of gas, and you threaten our lives? You shoot at us? This is your fucking decoy! It's not even, as if you're going to live here! One measly tank of gas is all we fucking want!"

Jon kicked the man's arms and legs a few times. Not hard enough to do much damage, but hard enough to get his point across. Robin grabbed him by the shoulder and waist and pulled him back.

"The sniper," she hissed in his ear.

"Fuck the sniper!" Jon still had his ire up, but didn't strike the man anymore.

The man held up his hands, his pale palms spread wide. Peeking through his fingers with startled eyes he saw that Jon wasn't going to hit him again. He carefully got to his feet, keeping one palm opened toward Jon as if calming a wild animal. Jon didn't feel calm.

"I see you've had some trouble in the past," the man said. His grin was back, but both it and his voice were a little nervous.

"The past? Try a few fucking hours ago! Try that our friends, our *families*, are still in the shit right fucking now!" Jon snapped, gesturing to the bandage around his head.

The man took a careful step back. "I'm sorry to hear that. We have had our share of difficulties in the past, as I'm sure you can imagine. Why don't I get you your gas? As a gesture of good faith?" The man spoke more to Jon's steady gun than he did to Jon.

"I'd rather we get it," Jon growled. Shit on his *gesture*.

"Well, we've stockpiled it elsewhere. I can take a few of you to it and you can pick up what you need, but I think my people would prefer if you weren't one of them." The grin was gone now. The man was ready to deal with them on uneasy terms. "One tank is all you need? I'm sure we can spare one."

"Yes. Just one. Your sniper?"

"Of course." The man turned to where Jon knew the sniper was. He waved his arms over his head, making large Xs as they crossed. Then he began gesturing for the sniper to come down.

Jon watched the doorway as the sniper stepped into it and waved back, then gave what appeared to be a thumbs up. The distance made it hard to tell, but Jon swore the sniper was a girl who couldn't be older than fourteen.

Those who were taking cover in the helicopter had been watching and listening. Brunt, Freya, and Oliver all stepped out, while Danny continued to remain inside.

"We weren't really going to kill you, you know?" the man said to Jon. "We had to try, but we couldn't follow through with our threats."

"I could," Jon told him and knew he was being honest. If he had had to kill the man with the grin, he would have.

It was quickly decided that Freya, Brunt, and Oliver would go get the gas, while Danny, Jon, and Robin stayed with the helicopter.

"And I wouldn't think about trying anything if I were you," Jon said just before the gas party was about to depart. "She can be a lot more deadly than me." He pointed to Freya.

The man quickly took in her solid and confident stance with the AK-47 in her hands, and believed him. They turned to walk to the terminal where the gas was presumably kept.

Robin placed a gentle hand on Jon's shoulder and eased him back to the open helicopter door, where Danny was sitting on the floor just inside, his legs dangling out.

"We could have solved that a lot more diplomatically," Robin commented as she sat down next to Danny.

Jon didn't enter the helicopter or sit down. He stood in full view of the terminal, knowing he was being watched.

"When has diplomacy ever helped with these people?" Jon could not think of a time.

"It could have worked here," Robin replied, but she looked at her shoes and spoke quietly.

"What do you think, Danny?" Jon asked his former foster brother.

Danny shrugged. "I'm just glad we're getting the fuel."

Jon paced for a while longer, but eventually stopped and leaned against the side of the helicopter. He even holstered his pistol.

"You really were ready to die, weren't you?" Robin asked as she looked up at him.

"I don't know. I can't remember what I was thinking when I stepped out there. Maybe I knew I wouldn't be shot, because they had plenty of opportunity to do that when we were between the truck and the helicopter."

"You scared me."

Jon looked down and saw tears in Robin's eyes. Before he could react, she got up and disappeared farther inside the helicopter. Jon made as if to follow, but Danny stood up in his way.

"Maybe we should just leave her for a bit," he spoke in a low voice. "Give her a chance to calm down a little."

Jon stepped back, thinking that Danny was probably right.

Both he and Danny stood on the tarmac, watching the terminal and waiting for the others to return. Jon didn't want to admit this, but he had scared *himself* a little.

***

When the others returned, they were escorted by the no-longer-grinning man and a luggage cart holding bright orange gas cans. Jon and Danny watched them approach without moving. Jon kept expecting a muzzle flash from the terminal, but it never came.

The man stood back and supervised as the gas cans were carefully poured into the helicopter, one by one. Jon didn't take his eyes off him, which, he was pretty sure, made the man uncomfortable, but he didn't care. If the man was planning something, he was hiding it well.

"All right. We're ready to go," Oliver announced, placing the last gas can back on the cart. It wasn't completely empty, and there were two other cans they hadn't even touched, but the helicopter was full.

"Forgive me if I say we hope to never see you again," the man commented, taking hold of the cart.

"Even if things don't work out for us, you probably won't," Brunt assured him.

The man walked back with the cart until he was at a safe distance, then turned and watched as they loaded into the helicopter. Jon got in last, never taking his eyes off the man or the terminal beyond him; he didn't even bother shutting the door.

As the rotors started up, creating a wind fierce enough to kick up dirt, the man took another step back, shielding his eyes with his hand. They lifted off the ground and were soon moving away from the airport. As they passed over the perimeter, Jon saw that zombies were already gathering at the fences, lured by both the music and the chopper. He shut the door as they left Cancun behind them.

The sun was up now, glinting off the ocean as they flew over it. Jon wondered what became of the Diana and its residents. He looked around the cabin, hoping that they weren't the only ones left. While Oliver and Danny were flying, Brunt was slumped over and sound asleep, snoring just loud enough for his microphone to pick it up. Freya looked like she was asleep, but Jon suspected that she wasn't, just resting her eyes and all that. Robin was on the other side of the cabin from him, looking out the window. Jon got up as if moving Brunt's microphone farther away from his mouth was his only purpose, but when he sat back down, he took the empty seat next to Robin.

Robin turned her head to look at Jon, and then turned back to the sea. Jon tapped her shoulder to get her to look at him again.

I'm sorry, he signed to her. *I wasn't thinking when I moved around the truck.*

Robin signed back, keeping their conversation private. *It wasn't just then. On the ship, you wanted to keep going into the fire.*

Jon realized that she was right of course. What had happened to him last night? He was taking unnecessary risks he never would have taken before. Seeing that Robin didn't want to talk to him anymore, he got up and returned to his own window. Freya watched him, her eyes no longer resting. Once he sat down, she got up and moved to the seat across from Robin, writing in her notebook. Jon didn't see what she had written when she handed it to Robin.

"Of course I'll teach you sign language, Freya," she said so that everyone on the headsets understood she wasn't talking to herself. "Do you want to start now?"

Freya nodded.

During the ride, Jon alternated between looking out the window and watching Robin teach Freya. He remembered all the times that Robin had taught him, including the times they had lain in bed together, late at night or early in the morning, happy to have each other's company. Jon didn't think that was going to happen again. They had split up and returned to each other many times, yet he didn't think they were going to get back together this time. Not after last night. Not after Jon had frightened her.

The thought hurt his heart, but not terribly. Maybe because he knew it was for the best. They had tried, but they just weren't meant to be.

Jon turned back to the window, listening to Robin teaching Freya letters and numbers to start with, his own hands forming the symbols.

***

The Diana never came into view. When they reached the co-ordinates where she had last been, there was no sign of either cruise ship. Instead, the ocean was littered with bodies. Some were the bodies of Diana residents, some were raiders, some were animals, and some were the bodies of wrecked and ruined boats and life rafts. Jon's heart squeezed as he looked out the window. A short distance from the mess was the German submarine surrounded by a bright yellow island of life rafts and lifeboats. Danny and Oliver were talking to the submarine right now about what to do. They might have enough gas now to continue on to Texas, but where in Texas? Was that where they still wanted to go?

Jon was only half listening until the decision was made. That decision made his head snap around and his back straighten.

"Has that ever been done?" they were supposed to keep quiet during this communication but Jon couldn't hold his tongue.

"Someone here says a helicopter once made an emergency landing on a submarine in 1956," the accented voice of the radioman replied.

"Yeah, but was it this kind of helicopter?" Now it was Brunt asking, having the same reaction to the idea that Jon had. "And this kind of submarine?"

"We made the necessary measurements and we're not moving, it should be fine. We've cleared the deck whenever you're ready," the radioman informed them.

"Keep quiet, guys," Oliver told them, annoyance peppering his voice. "Let's get this over with. Coming in now."

Jon didn't know whether he wanted to buckle up or not. In the end, he decided not to, figuring that any crash would end in the water, and he'd want to be free to escape if need be. He couldn't help picturing all the boats and rafts around the sub. If they did crash, they'd hit those before the water, taking people out with them.

As they descended, Oliver started humming *The Ride of the Valkyries*. Although it seemed to calm him and even Danny, it did nothing for Jon's nerves. He gripped the seat between his knees with one hand and grabbed a strap over his head with the other.

They got closer and closer to the submarine below. All eyes were on them, faces turned up, waiting to see what would happen.

Jon thought of the airplane that had made a water landing so long ago. He hadn't been aboard that plane, but he imagined those who were on it felt similar to how he was feeling right now. Once they got close enough for the rotor wash to start buffeting people, Jon looked away from the window. Brunt wasn't sitting near a window, and like Jon, he was gripping the seat between his knees with his good hand. Robin and Freya were both looking out the window next to them. Freya seemed unbothered by the whole process, whereas Robin's expression was hidden by the angle and a screen of her hair.

There was a hollow thump and a slight squall of metal as they touched down, but otherwise it was a normal landing. Oliver and Danny began shutting the Cougar down.

"That wasn't so bad," Brunt commented with a smile as if he hadn't been deathly pale just a minute ago.

Jon replied with a non-committal grunt. Once the blades had slowed down enough, he opened the door and slipped out. There wasn't a massive amount of clearance between the edge of the submarine and the helicopter, but it wasn't like they were balanced precariously on the edge either. When the blades stopped turning, several sailors, both Russian and German, ran over with heavy ropes. They were going to secure the helicopter to the submarine. Jon went with the others toward the conning tower that stuck up in the middle. He realized at that point that he knew very little about subs.

"Sorry to say, but there's no room inside the submarine," Captain Karsten informed them after complimenting Oliver's landing. "We're very tight as it is trying to fit sailors, injured, and doctors."

"It's all right, we can find a life raft or something that has space," Oliver told him.

"Have someone pass on word when you do. I'd like to know where you are in case we need you to lift off again."

Oliver nodded and tried unsuccessfully to hide his smile. There were several people on the flight team, all of them with a lot of hours in the bird, but Karsten specifically wanted him.

Jon made his way along the submarine until he came across one of the rope ladders that had been draped along its side. Using it to get down, he carefully boarded the lifeboat below it. That boat was already fairly full, so he crossed it to climb into the next one. Besides, he wanted to find Lauren, Abby, Claire, and Peter. He wanted to be with his family.

As he crossed from boat to raft to raft to boat, he stumbled several times. He rarely fell though, as most people were willing to help him. Some of them he knew and would stop briefly to chat, and ask if they had seen anyone from his family. The look of devastation on nearly everyone's face was disheartening. They had lost everything but their lives, and many people had even lost those. Jon tried to keep positive, searching out the good scenes, like those of people who had saved animals and were keeping them calm and safe, or a woman entertaining some kids by telling jokes. There were a few injured out here, but most of them weren't bad. They were bandaged up, but conscious and mostly functional like he was.

At last, Jon came across a raft with Riley sitting in it, her arms wrapped protectively around her daughter who was fast asleep. He could see his own family in the next raft over, their backs currently turned to him, but he thought he'd stop here for a moment.

"Mathias?" Jon knew it couldn't be good, but he had to ask. Riley's face wouldn't look the way it did, and Mathias would be there if things were okay.

Riley just shook her head, her wide and red rimmed eyes staring off at nothing.

Misha and Cameron were also in the raft, along with Rifle and Milly and one of Hope's friends. Jon asked Misha how he was feeling and he said he was fine. After giving each dog a scratch behind the ears, Jon moved on.

The moment Jon was aboard the next raft, Claire gave him a crushing hug. She had heard his voice in the next raft and had waited patiently for him to join them. Lauren and Abby gave him hugs once Claire released him, and Peter, who looked as tired as Hope, shifted so that he was lying down with his head in Jon's lap. Claire sat down on his other side, holding his hand and asking him to tell her everything that had happened. Jon obliged, glossing over the details about his stand-off with the grinning man and his urge to press on toward the anchors despite the fire.

He was just happy to be with his family again, something he never thought would happen while growing up as a foster kid.

22
Hope's Aboard The Flotilla

Hope woke up when they started moving. She stirred in her mommy's arms, the lifejacket shifting uncomfortably around her body.

"Daddy?" she mumbled before blinking open her eyes.

"Shh." Mommy stroked her hair. "Daddy's not here, baby." Her voice sounded funny.

Hope sat up in Mommy's lap, rubbing her eyes. She knew Daddy wasn't here, but she couldn't remember why.

"When's he coming back?" she asked.

Mommy didn't answer. "Go back to sleep, honey. You haven't gotten enough sleep."

Now that Hope had seen the sunshine, however, she wasn't feeling sleepy. She was tired, but not sleepy.

Looking around the life raft, Hope saw they shared it with Uncle Misha, Auntie Cameron, Milly—who wasn't wearing her lifejacket anymore—Rifle, and Dakota. They hadn't been able to find Dakota's fake-mommy yet, so she was staying with them. Next, Hope looked toward the ocean. She tried to find the Diana, but couldn't see it anywhere. It was gone. She had seen it sink, but part of her had been hoping it would rise up again, like the sub did. Right now, the sub was pulling them. Looking all around, Hope saw that all the lifeboats and life rafts were tied together behind the sub, and that it was taking them somewhere.

"Where are we going?" Hope asked as she wiggled out of her mommy's grasp. Some of her clothes were still wet.

"We're going to land," Mommy told her. When Hope looked back at her, she saw that she had been crying. Hope returned to her mommy and gave her a big hug, just like she did when Hope cried.

"But we're not off-hippers," Hope pointed out.

"Off-shippers," her mommy corrected her. "And no, we're not. We have to go to land though, because the Diana sank."

"I saw it sink." Hope tried to get her lifejacket off. Her clothes underneath were especially damp and uncomfortable.

Mommy stopped her from removing her lifejacket. "You have to keep that on."

"But it's wet."

"Doesn't matter. You have to keep it on while we're on the life raft."

"What if we go to a lifeboat, or the sub?"

"You'd have to keep it on there, too."

"When can I take it off?"

"When we reach land."

"When will that be?"

"I don't know."

Hope crossed her arms in a huff. Other than her and her mommy, everyone else on their raft was asleep. In fact, looking at the other rafts and boats, lots of people were asleep.

"Why's everyone sleeping?" she wondered.

"Because they were up all night, like you were. You should be sleeping too."

"But it's sunny."

"I know."

"Are you going to sleep?"

"They're looking for things to protect us from the sun. I'm waiting for someone to come by our raft with something. I'll sleep then."

Hope looked briefly up at the sun. She remembered being told in school that they should never play in the sunshine for more than a few minutes at a time.

"What will the sun do to us?" Hope returned to her mommy's lap because there was more shade there. She had probably been told the answer before, but couldn't remember.

"Well, when you're in the sun too long, you get what's called a sunburn."

"What's a burn?"

"That's an injury you get when you touch something really hot."

"Like when I touched that metal pole?" Hope remembered she had once touched a metal pole in one of the rear gardens, and had to pull her hand away really fast because it hurt.

"Yes. If you had held onto that pole longer, you would have been burned."

"And the sun can burn you."

"Yes."

"Why were we allowed to play in the sun when we wore hats and shirts?"

"Because your skin was covered. The sun only burns your skin, not your clothes. Sunscreen also protects your skin. You know all this."

"There's no shade out here," Hope noticed.

"There will be." Mommy stroked her hair again. "Why don't you try to sleep? I'll wake you up if Dakota wakes up, or when food comes. What do you say?"

"Will you try to sleep?" Hope looked straight up, trying to see her mommy's face above and behind her.

"As soon as the shade comes."

"Okay."

Hope wiggled and scooted until she was lying down in her mommy's lap again, being cradled by her arms. She still wasn't sleepy, but she was tired. Maybe she could sleep if she kept her eyes closed.

"Mommy?" she asked without opening her eyes.

"Yes, Hope?"

"Daddy's not coming back is he?"

"No." Mommy's voice sounded strange again. "Now go to sleep, sweet pea."

Surprisingly, Hope did.

***

The next time Hope woke up, she was no longer in her mommy's lap. She was lying on the rubbery surface of the life raft, with her head on Milly's side.

"Mommy!" she called out as her eyes opened.

"I'm right here, baby."

Mommy's voice had come from behind her. Hope turned around and saw that she was in a different raft tied right next to hers.

"Why are you over there?" Hope wondered.

"Because we couldn't make shade for all the rafts, so we moved all the nearby kids to one, which includes you." Mommy made a gesture for her to look around.

Hope looked up first to see what was causing the shade. Several pieces of cloth had been tied and strapped together, and then held up on the ends of paddles that were now tied to the raft's sides. The middle part was the lowest, where nothing held it up, but even that part was almost high enough for Hope to walk under without touching it. It was like that time Ms. Lauren had set up tents and they got to play camping. Looking around the raft, she saw her friends. Dakota and Peter were still sleeping, huddled together next to Rifle. Becky was sitting on Milly's other side, petting her dog Maggie's head who was next to her, while Adam sat next to Thomas, an older boy from their class.

"What about your shade?" Hope turned back to her mommy. Her raft didn't have a tent.

"We'll be all right. We have some hats and a few towels and blankets. We can keep ourselves shaded." While she spoke, Mommy pulled a towel up over her head so that her face was in the shade. "See?"

Hope looked at the others in the raft and saw that they were wearing similar hood-like things, or in Uncle Misha's case, a hat with a brim all the way around.

"Dakota has a hat," Hope pointed out.

Her mommy just smiled at her.

Hope looked around at all the rafts tied to theirs. They were full of adults, mostly people Hope knew. Along with her own family were the families of the kids in the raft with her. Except for Dakota's fake-mommy. They must not have found her yet.

"How did you get off the ship?" Hope asked Becky. She was wearing a lifejacket like Hope's. All the kids were.

"I had to climb down a ladder with a rope tied to me in case I fell," Becky told her.

"My daddy and I jumped off the side. He threw Dakota and Peter and Milly first."

"Why'd he do that?"

"We couldn't get down to the boats. There was a fire, and a man with a sword."

"You're a liar," Adam frowned at her.

"Am not," Hope snapped at him. "My lifejacket is still wet from when we had to swim. Come feel it."

Adam did just that, crawling across the rubbery floor to reach her. Hope made him touch the bottom of the lifejacket, which was the wettest part.

"Just because your lifejacket is wet, doesn't mean you're not a liar."

"Wait until Peter and Dakota wake up. They'll tell you. They were thrown off the ship, and then my daddy jumped in with me before the sword man could get us."

Adam looked over at the two kids still sleeping, wondering if Hope was right.

Hope's eyes widened and she quickly spun around to face her mommy to tell her something. Then, remembering that Adam was next to her, quickly shut her mouth.

"Hope? What is it?" Her mommy had seen her turn.

Hope looked at Adam, not wanting him to hear. Her mommy saw the look and got up to lean over to her. Cupping her hands around her mommy's ear, Hope whispered to her.

"I have to pee."

"Okay, come here." Mommy wrapped her arms around Hope and lifted her over to her raft. Mommy was sharing her raft with Uncle Danny and Uncle Josh now, as well as Uncle Misha and Auntie Cameron.

"There's no bathroom," Hope whispered to her mommy.

"You'll have to go in the ocean," Mommy told her.

"With people watching?" Hope squawked.

"No one's going to watch."

"They're going to see, and I'm going to get all wet."

"No one's going to see." Mommy walked her over to the side. Her raft didn't have another one tied to this side of it; it was just ocean that way. "Besides, since you're going to get soaked anyway, there's no point in taking off your underwear. I'm going to dunk you in, and you're going to go. You don't have to poo do you?"

"No." Hope felt her face get warm, and not because of the sun. Her mommy hadn't spoken in a whisper.

"Then you'll be fine."

"Is this how other people have to go to the bathroom too?"

"Yes. Everyone has to go this way."

That made Hope feel a little better.

"Are you ready?" Mommy asked, now that they were at the raft's side.

"Make them turn around," Hope whispered to her mommy, pointing to her uncles.

Mommy turned and looked at everyone in her raft. "Could you all face the other way please?"

They did as she asked.

"Now are you ready?" Mommy asked her again.

"What if there are sharks?" Hope looked over the side of the raft at the water.

Mommy paused before answering. "There are no sharks. We're moving too fast for them and they have no reason to come around here." She had that funny sounding voice again.

"You're sure?"

"I'm sure."

"Okay. I'm ready then."

Mommy lifted Hope by her lifejacket, and dunked her into the water up to her waist. It was uncomfortable, but Hope really had to go. Still, she looked up and down the line of rafts and boats to make sure no one was watching. When she was sure no one was, she peed through her pyjamas.

"I'm done," she told her mommy when she stopped peeing.

Mommy lifted her back into the raft.

"Now my pyjamas are all wet again," Hope frowned down at them.

"That's okay. They'll help keep you cool. If you get too cold though, we'll do something about it."

"I'm hungry."

"So am I. There should be food coming."

"It's a few rafts away," Uncle Danny told them. "I've been watching them. Based on how long it's taken the people with the food to get that far, it'll probably be another fifteen minutes."

"All right. You have to wait fifteen minutes, Hope."

"But I'm hungry now," Hope pouted.

"So are a lot of people, but you have to wait for the food to come to us."

"Why can't we go to it?"

"Because they already took a survey, figuring out how many people are in each boat and raft."

"What's a survey?"

"It's when someone asks the same questions to a lot of people and then writes down the answers. Now come on, you should be getting back to your own raft." Mommy started to guide her back to the tent raft.

"But I don't see what that has to do with food."

"It's easier for them to put together a team to hand out the food, than have everyone scrambling around on the rafts and boats to go get it. They need to know how many people there are, so that they bring enough food to each raft. Come on, upsy-daisy."

Mommy lifted Hope again, and helped her scramble over into the tent raft.

"I'll let you know as soon as your food is here," Mommy told her.

"Okay."

Hope plopped down beside Milly again. Across from her, Peter had woken up and Dakota was beginning to stir. Adam had crawled back over to sit next to the other boy.

When Dakota woke up, she blinked and rubbed her eyes, then looked all around. She looked at the tent only briefly, before looking at all the rafts that surrounded them. She even stood up to look, but then sat down and began to cry. Hope quickly crawled over to her.

"What's wrong, Dakota?" she asked.

"My mom's not here." She had buried her face in her hands and her voice was all muffled.

"Maybe they just haven't found her yet," Hope suggested, rubbing the older girl's back the way her mommy rubbed hers.

"No. She's gone. She wouldn't leave her room during the evacuation. I couldn't get her to come with me. I tried to get other people to go get her, but no one listened to me. After I found you, I thought someone would check all the rooms, but no one did. She's dead."

Hope had never seen Dakota cry before. "It's not like she was your real mom."

"What do you know about it?" Dakota suddenly screamed in Hope's face. She pushed Hope, hard, knocking her over.

Hope was startled and frightened. Dakota had never been mean to her before. She started crying and kicked Dakota. Rifle, who was next to them, started whining, and Milly began barking from where she lay. Dakota grabbed Hope's leg so hard that it hurt.

"You're mean!" Hope screamed at her. "You're mean. It's good that your mommy is gone!"

Dakota stood up and dragged Hope a short distance over the rubbery floor.

"Yeah, well your dad is dead!" Dakota screamed back. "He was eaten by a shark!"

"Girls! Girls!" Uncle Danny had quickly moved from his raft to theirs, and then crossed over to them. Grabbing each girl's lifejacket, he pulled them apart, and then kept them that way. "This is not the time for fighting!"

"She started it!" Hope pointed a finger at Dakota, tears trailing down her cheeks.

"You did!" Dakota shouted back.

"Calm down!" Danny yelled at them both. "It doesn't matter who started it. This is being finished, now."

Both girls continued crying but they kept their mouths shut.

"Everyone is really emotional right now, and really scared. We don't need anyone screaming at each other and fighting one another. We gotta work together. Now, can you apologize to one another? I mean, you two are friends, right? Don't you want to stay friends?"

"I'm sorry, Hope," Dakota mumbled.

"I'm sorry too, Dakota," Hope mumbled back.

Danny let go of their lifejackets. "Now can you apologize to all the people you scared?"

Hope looked around and saw that nearly all the people in the surrounding rafts were watching them. Those in their raft, Becky especially, looked scared.

"I'm sorry, everyone," both girls said at the same time.

"Now, Hope, come sit back over here beside Milly." Uncle Danny helped her back across the raft. He had to walk on his knees and hunch over to keep from brushing the cloth over their heads. Once Hope was seated, Danny climbed back over to his own raft.

"Thank you," Hope heard her mommy say to Uncle Danny.

Not wanting to look at Dakota, Hope turned so that she was facing Becky over Milly's back.

"Is it true what Dakota said about your dad?" Becky asked in a whisper.

Hope nodded as she buried her fingers in Milly's fur, new tears escaping her eyes.

"I'm sorry."

Hope just went on rubbing her hands through Milly's fur. She knew what happened to her daddy, but she didn't like to think about it. It was too scary. Instead, she pretended that he had swum off to save someone else after getting her into the raft with Uncle Misha. Her daddy was a hero.

When the food finally came, all the kids went to the sides of their raft that were abutted to the raft holding their family. Hope's mommy lay on her belly across the two rafts and handed Hope a bun and a carrot.

"This is it?" Hope frowned at the food.

"If you finish it, I managed to get a very special dessert for you."

"What is it?"

"You have to finish your food first."

"You're not trying to trick me, are you?" Hope narrowed her eyes and looked at her mommy's face.

"Never." Mommy leaned even farther forward and kissed Hope's forehead.

While Hope ate the bun, which was kind of hard, and the carrot, her mommy stayed nearby. She had water with her and gave Hope a drink whenever Hope asked for one.

"Do I have to eat this yucky green part?" Hope held up the very end of the carrot.

"No. Hand that to me."

"I can throw it out," Hope told her.

"But we're not going to throw it out."

"But it's the yucky green part. What are you going to do with it?"

"We'll probably feed it to one of the animals."

"Like a goat?"

"Maybe."

"Can I feed the yucky carrot part to a goat?"

"We'll see."

Hope handed over the remaining portion of carrot.

"Here's your special dessert."

Mommy handed Hope a chocolate pudding cup, causing Hope to gasp. She only ever got pudding cups on her birthday. They didn't have a lot of them, and so they were what her mommy and daddy called 'rationed'. Hope wondered where they were going to make pudding cups now that the Diana was gone.

"It's not my birthday yet," Hope said as she took the pudding cup.

"I know. There's no spoon, are you okay eating it with your fingers?"

Hope had no problem with that. She pulled off the container top and dug right in.

"When you're done, don't throw out the trash," her mommy told her.

" 'Kay." Hope was barely listening as she covered her tongue in sweet chocolately goodness. It was so good! Especially after the carrot.

Hope ate every last bit of the pudding cup, sucking it all off her fingers, which were starting to get pruny.

"All done?" her mommy asked.

Sadly, Hope was. She handed the empty cup to Mommy.

"Here, have another drink of water."

Hope did.

"I'm going to sit back down in my own raft now. You'll tell me if you need anything, right?"

"Yeah."

Mommy gave her forehead another kiss, and then returned to her own raft. Hope turned and sat down, still licking the last bits of chocolate that were sticking to her teeth and the insides of her cheeks.

"I got a pudding cup!" Becky told her.

"So did I!" Hope told her right back. "Mine was chocolate."

"I got a vanilla one," Adam added.

Soon all the kids were talking about the pudding cups. Apparently, they had all gotten one.

"I wonder when they're going to feed our dogs?" Becky asked, looking down at Maggie. "They're probably hungry."

Hope shrugged. "Milly is usually only fed at dinner, so maybe they're waiting for dinner."

"Maybe," Becky agreed.

"We should play a game," Hope suggested.

"Like what?" Adam asked.

"We can play I Spy."

"That's a baby game," Thomas told her.

"Well, what do you want to play?" Hope asked him.

Thomas didn't have a suggestion.

"Can I start?" Dakota asked.

"Okay."

"I spy with my little eye, something that is green."

"Hope's pyjamas?" Becky asked first.

"Nope."

"Peter's pyjamas!" Hope guessed next.

"Still nope."

"Umm, Ms. Abby's hat?" Adam was looking around at the other rafts.

Dakota shook her head.

Their game went on for quite a while, all the kids taking turns spotting something and having the others guess what it was. Eventually though, they tired of the game, and sat around in silence.

When dinner finally came around, Hope was starving and whiny. She was very glad finally to get dinner, but there wasn't much more than what she had for lunch. In the orange glow of sunset, she ate with her mommy and complained. Mommy explained they didn't have as much food as they used to on the Diana, but that didn't make Hope feel any better.

"Where are we going?" Hope asked.

"I told you, land. Specifically, we're going to the main land and a place that was once called Texas."

"Its not called Tex-us anymore?"

"We don't know. It's been a long time since anyone has been there. If people still live there, they might have changed its name."

"You can change the name of a place?"

"If everyone agrees to it, then yes."

"Can people change their names?"

"As long as everyone is willing to call them by that name, then I don't see why not."

"Can we change Milly's name?"

"You want to change her name?"

Hope shrugged.

"We could, but it's best we keep calling her Milly. Dogs learn their names, and it's not as easy for them to learn new ones," Mommy explained.

"How long is it going to take us to get to Tex-us?"

"I'm not sure. I don't know where we are right now or how fast we're moving."

"But the sub knows where we are, right?"

"Yes. The sub knows."

When Uncle Misha eventually climbed into their raft with food for the doggies, Hope helped him feed Milly.

"Don't eat so fast, Milly," Hope told her dog, but did nothing to try to slow her down. Her daddy once told her that dogs could be protective of their food and might snap at you if you tried to take their food away. Hope didn't think Milly would ever bite her, but she was always careful feeding her after being told that.

When the dogs had finished eating, and Uncle Misha went back to his own raft, there was nothing else to do. The sun was gone now, but she didn't feel tired enough to sleep.

"Let's have a sing-a-long," Becky suggested.

At first, Hope didn't feel like singing, but when Becky started and then Dakota and Peter joined in, she did as well. Everyone on their raft was singing, and soon, Claire joined in from her raft. Then Jon and Uncle Danny and Ms. Lauren—who's supposed to be Auntie Lauren outside of school, but Hope always called her Ms. Lauren—and Adam's mommy. Everyone started singing. Even Hope's mommy started singing, and Hope almost never heard her sing anything other than a few lullabies when she was little. It wasn't just the rafts next to them either; all the other rafts joined in too. Hope couldn't tell, but she thought that everybody being towed by the sub was singing the same song.

When the song ended, Becky started another one. Just before she did, Hope heard someone start singing a different song from somewhere else. They weren't all going to sing the same song this time.

Several people didn't join in on the second song, including Hope's mommy. Even fewer on the third. On the fourth song, Hope didn't join in, but a bunch of other people did.

Laying her head down on Milly's side, Hope tried to sleep. With the gentle waves rolling beneath her, and the singing of people around her, she managed to do just that.

***

Hope woke up from a crash. The raft was no longer gently rocking, but bucking over larger waves.

"Mommy!"

"Here, sweet pea! I'm here!"

Mommy reached over the sides of the raft and pulled Hope into hers. It was very dark. There were no stars or moon in the sky. A flash of light made everything visible for a split second, and then another crash shook the air.

Hope screamed with fright.

"It's okay, baby. It's okay." Mommy held her on her lap, stroking her hair. "It's a thunderstorm. We're not going to get hit by it though. It's just passing by us."

"You're sure?" Hope screamed her question.

"We're sure."

Another flash was followed by another crash. Hope buried her face against her mommy.

"Excuse me; I'm going to take down the kids' covering just in case."

Hope looked up to watch Uncle Danny climb past them. He was carrying a 'lectric lantern. The raft Hope had been in now had only the doggies in it. While Uncle Danny untied their sun cover and folded it up, Uncle Misha climbed past them as well to help. Although Uncle Danny came back, the sun cover folded up under his arm, Uncle Misha stayed with the dogs, especially Rifle who put his head on Misha's lap.

Every flash of lightning made Hope jump, and the booming that followed made her shake. She covered her ears with her hands but it wasn't any good. She kept her face hidden against her mommy.

"Oh wow," her mommy said so quietly that Hope almost didn't hear her. "Hope. Hope, you should look at this."

Mommy shook Hope slightly, trying to get her to look. Hope only pressed harder into her.

"Hope, it's beautiful. You really should see."

Hope looked up at Mommy's face.

"Look over there, sweet pea. Look at the lightning."

She turned her head to look at where Mommy was pointing, and she saw what she was supposed to see. It was kind of pretty, but its strangeness was also frightening. Still, Hope couldn't take her eyes off it.

23
Freya's On A Raft

Pink lightning. Freya had heard of the phenomenon before, but she had never seen it herself. Every bolt that struck the water had a pink tint to it instead of being pure white. It was beautiful but also terrifying, considering that she was on a flotilla of rafts and boats being pulled by a submarine. Those on the sub had sent word along the flotilla that the storm should pass them by, but that didn't ease Freya's mind. It could turn at any moment. Lightning was even less predictable. There were clouds above the refugees; who's to say a bolt wouldn't strike from them? One wouldn't even have to come from above, it could just curve its way over. Although the submarine was the highest point around, it wouldn't necessarily draw the lightning to it. The tail of the flotilla, the point farthest from the submarine, was in the most danger of a strike.

"Kind of creepy, don't you think?" Robin asked from beside her.

Freya nodded.

When they had to leave the helicopter to join the flotilla, Robin had allowed Freya to follow her. Freya didn't know the rest of these people and was glad that one of the few people she did know was willing to share her raft. There were others in the raft, including a man named Quin who, whenever she looked at him, called on some old memory of Freya's that she couldn't quite grasp. Elizabeth and Harry were a couple who had a child in one of the other rafts to which they were lashed; up until the pink lightning, that was, when they took him into their own raft. There was also a man named Doyle who had a large, stitched up wound along the right side of his face, and a stern looking woman named Cynthia. And of course there was the cat that Robin called Splatter. The cat was an angry thing, not liking their situation one bit. Freya had yet to see its ears not plastered to the top of its head, and it refused to let anyone other than Robin touch it. Even though it sat on Robin's lap, she didn't pet it very frequently for fear of bites and scratches.

"I'm worried about these waves," Harry commented in his Australian accent. It had surprised Freya the first time he had spoken. She had quickly become used to the mostly Canadian accents of the Diana residents, as well as the occasional German and Russian. As far as Freya could tell, Harry was alone as an Aussie.

The waves Harry spoke of *were* cause for concern. The day had been gentle, rolling the flotilla along on smooth, mostly even waves. Now, with the storm right next door, they had become more violent. No longer did the flotilla roll as one, but rose in uneven patches. The hexagon shape of the life rafts meant that they were easily lashed together into a tight block; even those along the edges had four other rafts tied to them. The trailing line was roughly five interlocking hexagons across, with barely a space between them. Despite this, water still splashed up through every crack and gap it found.

Wind gusted across the line toward the storm, hopefully, blowing it away from them, but it licked white caps off the wave tops, spraying those along the far side. For this reason, Freya was actually glad to be on the side of the lightning.

When the wind had picked up, Freya saw the helicopter pilot, Danny, scramble into the kids' raft to take down their sun shield. As he returned to his own raft, which was next to Freya's along the outer edge, she hoped that everyone else who had set up such a thing was doing the same. The last thing they needed was an impromptu sail trying to flip them.

The raft bucked beneath them as a large surface wave rolled by. Freya grabbed the rope that ran along the upper edge of the raft. That rope had been useful when they had to use the ocean as their toilet. All day, people had hung off the sides when they needed to go, or held the children in the water. Sadly, there was nothing they could do for the animals except clean up after them.

Another fierce waved bucked the life rafts. A short scream came from another raft nearby as someone was knocked over from the force. Soon, everyone was holding onto the ropes along the upper edges of their rafts. In the case of the boy, Adam, his parents held onto the rope with one hand each, and held his lifejacket with the other.

"Ow, Splatter! Claws!" Robin chastised her frightened cat who was clinging to her lap.

"Wrap him up in a sweater or something," Quin suggested.

Robin let go of the rope quickly to remove her thin shirt, revealing the camisole she wore beneath. She wrapped up Splatter tightly in the shirt, his claws away from her, then tied it around her own neck using a bandage from her bag so that he hung in a kind of pouch with his head poking out the top. The cat's eyes were massive black orbs in the lightning flashes. The only constant source of light was the solar lantern they had in Danny's raft. Some other rafts had them as well, but they were few and far between. During another flash, Freya saw the cat try to hide its face in the pouch.

On the rough seas, there wasn't anything they could do besides hold on.

Freya felt a drop of wet strike her cheek. She hoped it was just a splash of seawater and not rain. If it started raining, she had no idea what they would do. They had no buckets to bail out the rafts if they started taking on water. Earlier, someone had gathered up the orange emergency pails to add to their supply pile so that the food could be evenly distributed. The pails hadn't been returned and the rough waves made it too dangerous to do so now. Their only option was to get away from here as fast as they could, but they were already going as fast as was reasonably safe. Freya wondered if the submarine would cut them free and dive if the storm changed course and got too bad. Based on her experience under Sher's control, she thought they might, but prayed they wouldn't. Several lifeboats were tied up at the front of the flotilla, taking most of the strain of the tug, while at the back, all the rest were tied like rows of hotdogs, their rudders able to keep the line from fishtailing. If the submarine dove, they could start up the lifeboats' engines, but they would barely be able to move them, if at all. Maybe if the lifeboats were repositioned along the sides of the flotilla they could move them, but how long would the gas last?

A shriek as a particularly rough wave bucked under them drew Freya away from her emergency planning.

"Man overboard! Man overboard!" someone farther up the line was shouting.

Freya looked over the edge of her raft into the water, and saw a young man spluttering in the ocean, trying to grab one of the rafts as they slid past. Without thinking, she whipped out her arm and grabbed the young man's hand, her grip like iron.

"Thank you," he wheezed as Freya continued to hold him while Doyle positioned himself to help her pull him aboard. Together, the two of them got the young man out of the ocean. He quickly scrambled to an open space along the side opposite the sea, and grabbed the rope with soaking, yet strong, hands. He was coughing and shaken, but otherwise seemed fine.

Freya had surprised herself by reacting so quickly, especially after she had been thinking about survival plans. Reaching out to grab the young man had put her at risk, something she would never have done while living in Jamaica. Apparently, these Diana residents were already affecting her, or maybe it was knowing that Sher was dead. Either way, she wasn't entirely sure if it was a good thing or not, not with them returning to the mainland like they were.

The waves gradually grew in size until they were no longer bucking the flotilla. They had become true swells, which the rafts first rode up, and then slid down the backside. Freya noticed they were in line with the swells, whereas before they had been hitting the waves broadside. Either the submarine had turned them, knowing it was easier on the boats and rafts this way, or the storm had shifted. Whatever the reason, Freya had no control over it.

"I think I might be sick," Quin groaned as they headed up another wave.

"Trade places with me," Doyle told him in an odd, wincing voice. The wound on his face clearly made it painful to speak. "If you puke, you can puke in the sea."

"No," Cynthia shook her head. "No one should move right now if it involves letting go of the rope."

"She's right," Harry agreed. "If he's going to blow chunks, we'll just have to deal with it later."

The little boy with them looked very frightened. Wedged between his parents with both of them gripping his lifejacket, he stared out at nothing, his arms wrapped hard around Harry's waist.

Wondering what he might be staring at, Freya looked out over the ocean. As far as she could tell, from his lower position and the angle of his head and eyes, he truly wasn't seeing anything, just the thick, black cloud cover. Freya saw the lightning, however. It was hard to say for sure, but she thought it was farther away than when she last checked.

It seemed that they were riding the swells for hours, and maybe they were. Quin was managing to keep everything down, but he looked as green as leaves and was drooling on himself. Based on what Freya had heard, and at one point smelled, not everyone was so lucky.

Eventually, things began to calm down. The sea was still rough, but it wasn't necessary to maintain a death grip on the rope anymore. The young man whom Freya had saved thanked her again, and then began making a slow journey back to his own raft, making sure to stay away from the water's edge. Freya released the rope and stretched her arms, but then held it again with a looser grip using only one hand. Once Quin saw that it was okay to move, he dragged himself next to Freya and hung limply over the side. He didn't puke, at least not yet, but he was ready if he had to. Not wanting to be next to him if he did, Freya decided to stretch her legs a little as well.

Sticking to the sides of the raft, Freya made her way around to an inner side, checking out the rafts next to hers in the process. Most of them were similar to her own: anxious people relieved that the worst seemed to be over, and sick people either making their way to the edges on their own, or being assisted there. What clean-up had to be done had started. On their own raft, Robin had a ragged piece of cloth for taking care of Splatter's messes. Similar cloths and towels were being used by other rafts, then carried to the ocean to be rinsed.

Sitting down near the children's raft, Freya noticed it was occupied. The man who had pulled her from the water when she had first reached the Diana was sitting in it. Three dogs were clustered around him, and he was stroking them all, one hand alternating between two of them. Freya could just hear the sound of his whispers over all of the other noises. It sounded like he was talking to the dogs in Russian.

Freya settled herself next to Elizabeth. The mother was trying to convince her child that everything was all right now, and that he should try to get some sleep. Freya thought it was sound advice. Still sitting upright, and with her right hand resting on the rope, she closed her eyes. Although she didn't go very deeply into sleep, she slept.

***

Several times throughout the night, Freya awoke. Each time, she opened her eyes and assessed her surroundings. Most of the time, everyone remained asleep around her. Quin had even curled up on the bottom of the raft, although Freya suspected he wasn't asleep; he was still having a rough time with these waves.

One of the times Freya awoke, she saw one of the women in the next raft over get up as if to leave. Freya heard her mummer to her twin something about making rounds to check on all the animals. Her twin, the one with the little girl, asked if she could inquire about a certain patient who was aboard the submarine while she was over at that end: someone named Rose. The one leaving said she would, then slipped silently into Freya's raft, starting her rounds with Splatter. Robin took him out of his pouch to be examined, and then put him back in when the woman was done. Freya suspected she was a veterinarian, as the woman then climbed into the raft with the three dogs.

At another time, the man with the dogs—Misha was his name—passed through the raft next to Freya's to rinse a towel that smelled like dog pee. Freya's nose wasn't looking forward to the time when one of those dogs took a shit, especially since they weren't being fed regular dog food.

When it looked like the sun was going to rise soon, Freya decided to stay awake. Hoisting herself up to sit on the raft's edge, she stretched her body as best she could. Looking across the dog raft, she saw that Jon was awake, and sitting on the edge of his own raft like she was. Freya raised a hand in good morning, and he raised one back. She liked Jon, even when he got angry at the airport in Cancun. He had gotten pissed for the right reasons, which was a lot better than Sher and his men. As long as he didn't start getting angry for the wrong reasons, Freya could get along with him.

It was going to be another long day. Freya had heard they were going to Texas, but she didn't expect them to reach it any time soon. She sat and waited for the rising sun to wake everyone else. Most of the cloud cover from the previous night was gone, but a few puffy white blobs remained. Freya always preferred the heavy cloud cover to the scorching sun, but she could deal with the sun, just the same as she always had on the beach.

The same young girl who had delivered their food yesterday, came back around today to give them their morning meal. This time it was a nutritious paste in a silver package. Freya suspected it had come from one of the emergency kits.

When breakfast was over, and Misha confirmed that the raft was clean, the kids were moved back into it. Danny then unfolded the blanket covering to set it back up. Freya helped by tying a section to the paddle she was closest to. The kids were subdued this morning, most of them curling up to go back to sleep.

"Want to continue your sign language lessons?" Robin asked Freya before cracking her jaw with a large yawn.

Freya took out her notebook and replied with it, *I'd like to take a walk first.*

"All right. Just let me know when you're ready."

If Freya was going to spend another day with these people on the raft, she wanted some time without them first. She wrapped the same scarf she had used yesterday into a kind of hood that would shade her face and shoulders from the sun. Getting up on top of the raft's edge, she found she could balance and walk along it if she was careful. It reminded her of her gymnastics days as a little girl. She had loved gymnastics, and was good at them. Her instructor thought she might be able to go pro if she dedicated herself, maybe even become an Olympian. Then her dad got sick, and they had to spend her gymnastics money on his health care. He had always been Freya's biggest supporter, and when he died, she lost interest.

As she walked from raft to raft, Freya looked around, getting to know the faces of the Diana residents. A few of them said hi as she made her way past, and she was always sure to smile and wave at those people. The smile felt extremely false, and she thought they'd be able to tell, but it was a start.

She headed forward first, toward the submarine. On the way, she passed by the young man she had pulled from the water. He stopped her to thank her yet again, and Freya told him it was nothing, writing in her notebook to do so. When asked about the notebook, she wrote down a quick explanation of why she couldn't speak.

"Oh. You should talk to the off-shippers then. They know some sign language that could be useful to you," the young man told her.

Robin is teaching me, Freya wrote, unsure if the young man even knew who Robin was.

"That's great!" he smiled, probably not knowing.

After he thanked her again, Freya moved on.

The next time she stopped, it was because she spotted someone she knew. One of Sher's men was sitting in a raft. He spotted Freya as well, and quickly turned his head away, hoping he hadn't been seen. From what Freya could tell, he was playing cards with the Diana residents who were in the raft with him. They had no idea who he was. Freya was sorely tempted to rat him out. If the man—*boy* actually—had been older or if he had been one of Sher's favourites, Freya probably would have. As it stood, he seemed small and afraid, presumably just as grateful to be with the Diana residents as Freya was. She said—or rather wrote—nothing.

As she neared the forward lifeboats, she saw that very few people were on them. The boats were occupied mostly by animals.

A few sheep stood in a boat at one end, while a few pigs occupied the boat at the other end. Next to the pig boat were two young cows, calves really, and between them and the sheep was a single horse. The vet who had left in the night was standing next to the horse, brushing its coat and mane and talking to it. Freya didn't know much about horses, but she knew the ocean was no place for one, especially in such a small lifeboat. The thing looked terrified and its coat had an unhealthy sheen that Freya suspected was sweat. At the top of its rear, right leg, a muscle kept twitching and jittering. If they didn't get to land soon, that poor horse probably wasn't going to make it.

Past the lifeboats, Freya could see the submarine. A few men wandered about on deck. One of them looked like a doctor, with a stethoscope hanging around his neck. Some of the doctors were on the rafts, like Robin and Cynthia, however more of them were on the submarine taking care of those patients who were badly wounded and needed a lot of attention. Freya suspected that the night wasn't very kind to them, and that they were like the horse: no land, no life.

Having checked out the front of the flotilla, Freya turned around and headed for the back. As she travelled, she didn't just study the faces she passed, but also the emotions on them. There was a lot of grieving for everything they had lost, but she saw a lot of love too. People were together, talking, laughing, and sharing stories. They played cards if they had a deck, or found other things to play if they didn't. A few men had some fishing line and hooks, and were fishing over the side. They weren't likely to catch anything, Freya couldn't see any bait, but they didn't seem to care. Some people were singing. Yesterday, Freya couldn't join in when the entire flotilla had begun to sing, but she had revelled in the music. It had been so long since she had heard people singing just because they wanted to. That's probably why she had saved that young man last night. Hearing all the Diana residents singing really struck her heart. She thought she might die for them now.

"Freya, wait."

Freya turned around, and nearly fell from her perch. The boy from Sher's army was standing in the raft next to her, looking up at her. By thinking of the singing, she managed to restrain the urge to kick his face in.

"I wanted to say thank you," he spoke quietly so that only Freya could hear him. "I know you could have told them who I am and you didn't. At least I assume you didn't, or else I'd be in the ocean by now. I don't think we ever personally interacted. If we did, I'm so sorry that I don't remember. Either way, I wanted to apologize on behalf of my friends. You... were the initiation for some of them. I think most of them are dead now. I don't know. They left me behind. But still, I'm sorry for what was done to you."

Freya was glad she hadn't ratted out this boy. She saw why Sher hadn't picked him as a favourite, as he had with most of the other young men and boys. This one still felt emotions. He was weaker than the others were.

Taking out her notebook, Freya responded.

I will never forgive your friends.

The boy hung his head. Freya gave his lowered face a hard flick to get his attention again because she wasn't finished.

With time, I may be able to forgive you for doing nothing.

The boy nodded, not exactly relieved by her words, but it was a start. Freya could easily forgive the boy for doing nothing. If he had tried something, he would have been killed. Freya herself did nothing to help anyone else. She knew, however, that the boy was angry with himself for his lack of action. He wasn't ready for forgiveness. Freya would give it to him when the time was right.

Continuing on, she eventually made it to the back of the flotilla where the majority of the lifeboats were tied. Most of the lifeboats in the forward section of this group were occupied by people who were injured. They weren't badly wounded enough to need constant care, but unlike Doyle and Jon, they couldn't function at one hundred percent either. Brunt was there, his arm still hanging in a sling. Freya wondered what was wrong with it. It seemed likely that there was nerve or muscle damage, but she didn't know enough about medicine even to hazard a guess. Since she knew Brunt, she decided to climb into the lifeboat and sit with him awhile. On the next bench over from him, sat a woman with cat-like features, who had some sort of hip injury. The two seemed to know each other.

"Ah, Freya, good morning," Brunt smiled up at her as she slid down onto the bench seat beside him. The lifeboats were a lot more comfortable and stable than the rafts were. "I was just telling Shaidi here about our adventures in Cancun."

Freya smiled and nodded politely at the woman named Shaidi to acknowledge her. She felt Brunt was probably lying about what they had been talking about, as those stories had probably been relayed yesterday, but she said nothing about it.

"What brings you to the lifeboats?" Shaidi asked her.

Needed to stretch my legs.

"Ugh, I wish I could do that," she gestured to her legs, which were lying lengthways along her bench. "I was told I have to keep my weight off. Getting shot in the hip sucks."

"At least you can move your legs," Brunt commented. His voice sounded light-hearted, but his eyes told Freya that he was worried about his own injury.

Is your name really Brunt? Freya wrote.

Brunt chuckled. "No, but everyone calls me that. My real name is Andrew Pike."

"Don't let him lie to you, his name is Brunt, nothing else," Shaidi laughed.

"Well, I was born Andrew Pike."

"Did anyone ever call you Andy? Or Drew?" Shaidi wondered.

"Not that I recall. It was always Andrew growing up. Until I got called Brunt that is."

Shaidi and Brunt continued talking, making sure that Freya was included in their conversation. They didn't seem at all put off when they had to stop so she could write down what she wanted to say. Freya felt included with these people. It probably helped that they were all damaged in some way, at least for the moment.

"So did you see the goats?" Brunt pointed toward the back of the lifeboats.

Freya shook her head.

"Yup. They decided the lifeboats are good enough for injured, and goats."

I saw pigs and sheep up in the boats at the front. I think they're worried that hooves would slice open the bottom of the rafts. While wandering, Freya had seen a few bundled up chickens and ducks, along with more dogs and cats.

"Hmm, never thought of that. Good point though."

"I like the goats," Shaidi told them. "They're entertaining. Every now and then one will escape and start hopping from boat to boat. I mean, it's dangerous and they could easily hurt someone, but it's hilarious as hell to watch their minders chasing after them."

"Remember the one that jumped into the ocean before we started moving, and the minder had to tie a rope around his waist and jump in after it?"

"Yeah, and that other minder had no idea what to do with the other end of the rope, he just kept looking at everyone with his mouth hanging open."

Freya couldn't see the humour in it that they did, but their laughing and smiling was fairly contagious.

I should get going, Freya eventually wrote. *Robin is teaching me sign language.*

"That'll be helpful," Brunt nodded. "I've been meaning to ask her to teach me a few more things other than just what the off-shippers use. You know, if she wasn't turning out to be such a good doctor, I'd say she should spend her time teaching a sign language course to everybody."

"It was very nice meeting you, Freya," Shaidi held out her hand.

Freya shook it briefly and nodded to her again, trying to convey that the feeling was mutual. She then turned and headed back toward her shared raft.

"Looks like you've started a trend," Robin commented when Freya returned.

Gazing out over the rafts, she noticed a lot more people were moving about than there were yesterday, despite the rougher waters. Many of them were trying to walk along the raft edges like Freya had, but most of them weren't very good at it. There were a lot of slips, and a few falls. Watching the expression of surprise as one girl tumbled sideways, and how she and those in the raft she fell into laughed about it, Freya thought that she understood the goat stories now.

She turned back to Robin and let her know that she was ready to continue her sign language lessons. They spent most of the day on the lessons, and Freya felt another stone move from her heart. That pile of rocks had felt like they'd always be there, however, now she thought she was actually becoming human again, one small gesture at a time.

* * *

The sun was considerably closer to the horizon again when the call of land rippled through the flotilla. Just about everybody stopped what they were doing to watch it grow ahead of them.

I have never been to America, Freya wrote and showed Robin.

"Actually, neither have I," she replied. "The Diana once made a stop off Ellis Island for several days, and some non-off-shippers were able to go ashore for a bit, but I didn't go with them."

The land loomed closer and closer, until it filled the horizon. Freya thought she could see where they might be headed, as a few tall ships became visible inside a channel. They didn't go as far up the channel as she expected, but far enough that the back of the flotilla was in it. The submarine slowed to a stop, until they were just floating there.

What now? was no doubt what everyone was thinking.

Looking ahead, Freya assumed the channel wasn't a long one, and that they had to make a decision about where to go. She was proven right when they started moving again, and headed out into a massive bay.

They passed by a large, narrow jut of land that served no purpose that Freya could discern, other than to be the looping end of a long road. A surprising number of cars were clustered and parked around the loop. Freya was on the wrong side of the flotilla for a good look, but she thought she saw the long dead remains of a camp amongst the cars. She bet if they followed the road, they'd find a bunch more cars blocking it off. There was no way of telling if the camp was abandoned willingly, or forcibly.

The bay they sailed into seemed to stretch forever. There were hundreds of places the submarine could be taking them; however, they seemed to be following the shore along the left side.

At one point, they motored past a sharp point of land, which was completely covered with houses and scraggly palm trees. A few large mansions dominated the shore, while smaller, more modest homes could be seen beyond them. It had probably looked attractive before everything went to shit. Now the grass and weeds were running riot, nothing was nicely pruned anymore, a few windows were broken, and several boats were half-sunk while still tied to their moorings. Then they were past the point, and continuing across the bay.

After a while, a large island crept by on the right, but they were too far away to see any details concerning it. A short time after that, another one appeared, or maybe it was a peninsula. This one they were headed toward; apparently, the submarine was going to follow its shore now, as they were much closer to it than the shore on the left. The land was flat, and undeveloped as far as Freya could see. The way this place looked, it probably hadn't changed at all once the people were gone. They followed the rocky shore, gliding by a few remains of metal skeletal structures Freya didn't understand. Eventually, the rocky shore became a sandy one, but the quality of the land didn't improve.

By the time the sun touched the horizon and turned the sky orange, the submarine turned and towed them back toward the left-hand shore. Looking that way, Freya thought she could see where they were going. A jut of land on that side housed a shipping container yard. They didn't cruise all the way to the yard however, where big cranes were once used to move the containers, but stopped at a large concrete dock just before it. At least the submarine stopped there; the flotilla was left trailing out behind it, near some circular structure that stuck out of the water. Everyone was quiet while they waited to see what was going to happen. Freya kept shifting in her raft, trying to get a better view, but there wasn't one to be had.

After what seemed like forever, with the flotilla beginning to distort its nice lines as the current pulled at it, they began to move. The ropes had been disconnected from the submarine, and they were being pulled toward the large dock via a winch.

It was a long process getting everyone to shore. The dock was two long stretches of concrete, with a thicker section connecting them at their far ends. The submarine was docked at the end, while the lifeboats were untied from the flotilla, and powered around to the far leg of the dock. The rafts were pulled into the closer leg, where everyone had to climb from raft to raft to get ashore. The height of the dock also required the climbing of a rope ladder to get onto it, the animals and the weak being hoisted up with ropes. Once up there, everyone started to spread out, most people heading toward the submarine, where it was safer. Freya went the opposite way, toward shore. There was a smaller, lower dock there attached alongside the bigger one, but a boat had plowed into it, destroying a large portion and making it appear quite unsafe. Where the dock connected to the shore, several sailors from the submarine stood guard with guns and close combat weaponry.

"I've been here before," a voice spoke from nearby.

Freya turned to find an Asian woman standing next to her. She sounded like she was talking to herself more than to anyone else in the area.

"Yeah, I have," she nodded. "The Black Box is just over that way." She turned and pointed at what could be a channel or a bay. If they had continued to follow the scruffy land, they would have gone right past it.

Freya placed a hand on the woman's shoulder and held up her notebook. She had written *what's the black box?*

"Oh, it's a Marble Keystone facility I worked at a long time ago. I liked living in Texas."

The name Marble Keystone sent a cold shudder running down Freya's spine. Everyone knew it was the company that had released the zombie virus, and hadn't this woman just said she had worked for them? It was possible. The Diana residents were mostly Canadian after all, and that's where the virus originated. Freya looked around at all the people gathering on the dock. She hadn't thought of it before, but could someone here be the source of all this pain? Probably not. Not everyone here could have worked for the company, not people like Jon or Robin, and they would surely have thrown overboard anyone who had created this thing. Still, having a facility so close was unsettling.

Freya grabbed the Asian woman's hand and began to pull her through the crowds.

"Hey!" the woman startled. "Where are we going?"

Freya didn't have time to write down an answer.

With a speed and skill that was surprising for someone who seemed so distant, the woman pulled her wrist free, grabbed Freya's arm and twisted it painfully behind her back. Freya gasped at the pain caused by the manoeuvre, one of the only sounds she could make.

"I don't like people dragging me places I don't want to go," the woman hissed into Freya's ear, no longer sounding distant. She then released Freya.

Rubbing her arm, Freya glared at the woman who glared back. She was small, but there was power in her eyes. Freya wrote in her notebook and handed it to her.

You should tell the leaders about this black box.

The woman read what she wrote and nodded.

"You're probably right. It would be useful knowledge." The woman began making her own way through the crowd, heading for the submarine where the remaining leaders were conferring with each other on its deck. Freya followed after her, wanting to make sure the woman really told them. There was something off about her that worried Freya.

At the submarine, they were briefly stopped from boarding by a sailor, but the woman explained she had information about the area and was allowed on. Freya followed closely behind her, indicating to the guard that she was clearly with this other woman. Although Freya had nothing to add, she wanted to hear.

"Sirs?" The woman walked up to the remaining leaders and snapped off a salute.

"Nicky? What is it?" Commander Crichton turned to her.

"We're not far from the Black Box," the woman named Nicky told them.

"What use have we for a plane recorder right now?" Bronislav brushed her off.

"No, I'm talking about a place," Nicky's sharp eyes glowered at him.

"I know of it. You say it's nearby?" Crichton prompted her to continue.

"Yes. See that channel there?" She pointed to the same spot she had indicated to Freya earlier. "Through there, and not terribly far inland there's an industrial park. The entrance to the Black Box was built near it, the thing itself expanding underneath some wooded areas."

"Did they do any biological research there?" Lieutenant Boyle asked, perhaps worried about the same thing Freya was.

"No, the Black Box was for developing computer parts and programs. I've never seen anything medical or chemical being worked on."

"And you're sure it's there?" Crichton asked. "You know better than anyone how your mind doesn't always have things straight."

"I know, sir." Nicky looked briefly down at her feet, embarrassed, but then looked Crichton in the eye again. "But I know it's there. I lived there for years."

"Good. We'll take it under advisement as we decide what to do. Would you like to help check the nearby buildings? We're trying to determine if they're safe enough to spend the night."

"If you want me to, sir. But there's something else you should know."

The leaders all looked up at her, and the next thing she said made Freya's jaw drop.

"Sir, they probably still have power down in the Black Box."

24
Misha's On The Mainland

Misha walked around the warehouse with Rifle. Once the area had been deemed safe, all the Diana residents had been moved inside for the night, save for a few guards who were patrolling. Misha wished he was inside now, where it was warmer, but Rifle needed some exercise and a chance to do his business. Pulling the fishing hat lower down on his head, Misha tried to protect his ears from the wind. Texas was colder than where the Diana spent most of its time. At least his wetsuit was doing a decent job of keeping him warm, but he wished he had shoes. Having no footwear seemed to be the standard for him whenever he changed locations. After this, he promised himself he'd never take his shoes off unless it was absolutely necessary.

Once Rifle seemed content, Misha led him back inside. The warehouse was crowded with shelves and boxes, the aisles filled with people. It was also dark, as the only light came from a few solar lanterns and flashlights. Stepping carefully over and around everyone, Misha made his way to where his group was clustered together next to boxes that were longer than he was tall. He suspected the boxes contained refrigerators, but the labels were written in a language he didn't understand. The only one who wasn't there was Cameron; she was too busy with the animals being kept in the other warehouse. Apparently, the horse required a lot of attention.

"I still feel like the ground is rolling beneath me," Claire commented to Jon.

"That'll go away," Jon reassured her. He was the only one of their group who had really been on land since boarding the Diana.

Misha sat himself down between Jon and Danny. Rifle circled the space in front of him, and then laid down, his ears still alert and his eyes looking around. Misha wondered if he felt the rolling sensation too.

"So where do you think we'll go?" Josh asked the group. He must have returned from making medical rounds while Misha was outside.

"I wonder if we should just stay here. You know, in the container yard," Abby pointed to where hundreds of containers were still piled up in forgotten stacks. "Clear some out and we might be able to make a nice living space out of them."

"I'm not sure that's a good idea," Lauren told her as she tucked the blankets more firmly around Peter. Both Peter and Hope were already sound asleep in little nests of blankets and towels next to their respective parents. Dakota was the only child still awake, but she seemed to be drifting off. Misha felt sorry for her. She was currently in limbo, in terms of who would take care of her.

"Why isn't it a good idea?" Josh asked her.

"You weren't at the motel or the prison," Lauren told him. "I remember what it's like seeing the bodies pressing up against the barricades. We had a method to draw them off, but it was dangerous and sometimes the people who went out didn't come back. The people who were at the prison say it was worse over there, because the zombies just kept piling up, and piling up. And the prison had large stone walls. Here we just have a couple of chain link fences."

"But we've all heard the reports from the off-shippers. They say the number of bodies is decreasing. If we keep clearing them out, we might not have a problem. Isn't that right, Jon?" Claire turned to him.

Jon shrugged. "Yeah, but that was before this mutation spread. We'll have to set up a lot of new rules to accommodate it."

There was silence after Jon's words. The mutation had people worried. For now, it only seemed to affect people once they were killed, but there was concern it would mutate again, or affect certain people differently.

Misha leaned forward and stroked Rifle's head. According to Cameron, he was fine, but Misha still worried.

"You should all try to get some sleep instead of talking about things you don't need to worry about," Riley suddenly spoke. "The leaders will decide what we end up doing. They're gathering information and have access to maps and things on the submarine."

Misha suspected Riley just wanted everyone to shut up so that her kid wouldn't wake up. The conversation changed to a lighter, pointless subject, and dropped to a whisper. No one was tired yet, except for maybe Dakota. The little girl with the cowboy hat was losing that fight. She'd be asleep soon.

After at least another hour floated by, Cameron returned. She looked exhausted as she sat down next to Dakota, who was now asleep. The vet adjusted the girl's blankets for her, making sure she was covered. Watching that, Misha speculated that Dakota would be just fine. Cameron had been looking out for her a lot on the rafts, and would probably continue to do so now.

Eventually, the conversation died down, and Misha started to feel weary. He stretched out on the cold floor, and Rifle shuffled around to lay lengthwise next to him. Misha may not have had a blanket, but at least he had a fluffy space heater. Wrapping his arm around the big dog's side, Misha buried his face in Rifle's fur. It smelled like ocean and dog.

Misha drifted off to sleep, and dreamed of being alone on a raft with Rifle, surrounded by sharks.

***

A firm hand on Misha's shoulder drew him awake. Blinking groggily, the remains of his nightmare still clouding his mind, he looked up to see who was shaking him. In the darkness that was broken only by a weakening solar lamp, it took Misha a moment to realize it was Lieutenant Boyle. He dragged his mind into a more alert state, rubbing his eyes with the palms of his hands.

"Sir?" he whispered, not because he realized people were still asleep around him, but because his mouth, lungs, and vocal cords were still waking up.

"Can you come with me?" Boyle whispered back. "Bring the dog."

Misha didn't like the sounds of that, but he did as he was told. Getting to his feet, he patted his leg so that Rifle stood up. Apparently, Rifle had already been awake, or at least had woken up a lot quicker than Misha did. The two of them followed Boyle across sleeping bodies, being as careful as possible not to step on anyone. Boyle led them all the way to a door and outside. The sun was rising, and the morning air was brisk. Misha shuddered slightly as it washed over him. The warehouse had warmed up with the press of the bodies filling it.

"We're putting together a mission," Boyle turned to him.

"What kind of mission?" Misha stifled a yawn.

"There's this place called the Black Box not far from here."

Misha stiffened. "Is that like the White Box?" He had learned all about the mega laboratory underneath the city of Leighton from Mathias. It's where the hybrid virus had come from thanks to some power hungry assholes. Except assholes wasn't nearly a strong enough word for them.

"It is a Keystone facility, yes," Boyle confirmed.

"Why would you want to go there? To blow it up? 'Cause that doesn't sound like a good idea to me if there are possible contagions down there."

"Calm down," Boyle smiled briefly and held up his hands. "From what we know, the Black Box is a lot smaller than the White Box. A *lot* smaller. It also wasn't used to research anything chemical or biological. Nothing medical, no diseases. Apparently, it was all computer software and hardware development."

"So why go there?"

"Apparently, the place has its own power source, one that's likely still running."

That surprised Misha a little. Most places had been shut down before they were abandoned, so long as there had been time. To the far north, there had been nuclear meltdowns, and the last time they had picked up radio transmissions from the mainland, most of the places in the south and west had agreed to a controlled demolition when they knew they were going to fail. Basically, they permanently shut down the power early to save the land from radiation. The Diana survivors had no way of telling which places had actually followed through with that plan, but some must have, because their radiation detectors weren't going off.

"I doubt it's a power source we can just lug around," Misha commented.

"We don't plan to move it. We plan to move *us* into the Black Box."

It took Misha a moment to compute what he had just heard. Move everyone into the Black Box? Why? That sounded like a terrible idea, and it's what Misha told Boyle.

"All the leaders have agreed it's a good idea. We've spoken to everyone we could find who knows anything about the Black Box. A few of our residents used to live and work there. The place is completely secured against zombies, and, with power, we could set up a farm using UV lights."

"I don't like it, but my opinion doesn't count, does it." Misha didn't make it a question, knowing it was the truth. "Why tell me all of this?"

"Like I said, we're putting together a mission. We need a team to go in there and check out the place. Although it's secure against zombies when locked down, we don't know if someone left a door open somewhere. We also don't know if any people are living in there. From what we've learned, there probably are. If there aren't, then the power wouldn't have stayed on, and we can quickly write the place off."

"You want me to go on this mission?"

"Actually, we want Rifle," Boyle looked at the German Shepherd who was sitting next to Misha.

Misha looked down at him too. Rifle was confused by the sudden attention, but slowly wagged his tail a few times, looking back and forth from one man to the other.

"We assumed you'd want to accompany your dog," Boyle continued, looking back up at Misha.

"What if I say he's not going?" Misha continued to look down at Rifle and placed a hand on the big dog's head. Rifle wagged his tail harder.

Boyle heaved a sigh. "Honestly, there's nothing we can do about it. If you say neither you nor the dog goes, then neither you nor the dog goes. We won't force you, but I want you to think about it. Think of all the people in that warehouse. Many of them don't know how to survive in the open, or on the move. I've heard part of your story, how you escaped the city half naked and on your own."

"I wasn't alone. Rifle was with me." Misha crouched down in front of Rifle and massaged his jowls.

"Right. The point is, you survived in the open. A lot of these people haven't, they've just been moved around like cattle, sad to say. They were scooped up from their homes and brought to the prison, and then from there they were taken to the Diana. They need secure walls. They need electricity and people to tell them what to do. It'll be tight in the Black Box, especially if there are people already living there, but it's a place for them. We just have to make sure it's truly safe and secure first, and Rifle would be a huge asset. Personally, I'd like you on this mission as well. Quite a few of our off-shippers and ship defenders have been injured or killed, and we need able-bodied volunteers to go. Rifle is important though. You ask anyone what dog they'd want with them in a crisis, and they'd tell you Rifle. He's smart, and obedient. We want his nose in the Box as an early warning system."

"Stop talking," Misha told Boyle without looking away from his dog. Rifle was *his* dog now. With Alec gone, Misha was his sole owner, although he rarely thought of it in those terms. Rifle was his brother. "Give me a moment to think and talk to Rifle."

Boyle did as he was asked. He even took several steps away to give them some privacy.

"What do you think *bratishka*?" Misha asked Rifle, looking him in the eyes. "Do you think we should go check out this Black Box?"

Rifle blinked, an answer that could mean anything. His ears were alert, focused intently on Misha, waiting for a command or some word that meant it was playtime.

Misha smoothed all the fur on Rifle's face, and then moved down to his shoulders. The dog's muscles were tense, as he waited for what would happen next. Misha sighed. He knew that if Rifle could speak and understand what was going on, he'd want to check out the Black Box, even if he didn't like it. That's just the kind of dog he was; the kind who helped people in need.

"Fine," Misha spoke loudly enough for Lieutenant Boyle to hear him. "We'll go. When do we leave?"

***

It wasn't until nearly noon that the team headed out. It took a while to put together enough volunteers, and then to make sure they were all adequately armed. Misha spent the morning tracking down a pair of shoes he could borrow. It wasn't hard to find a few people willing to lend him their shoes, but it took a while to find a pair that fit.

Now, he was sitting on the deck of the submarine, between Jon and Danny, with Rifle sitting between his knees. The helicopter had just returned from a quick scouting mission, informing them that the way looked clear as they pulled away from the dock. Misha would rather have not had the helicopter do a fly over. Even though it flew at a fairly high altitude, with the flight team inside using binoculars to check out the ground, the sound of the rotors risked drawing out zombies and warning unfriendly humans that they were coming.

"Anxious?" Jon asked him, noting Misha's posture and tapping foot.

"Yes."

"You'll be fine."

"Like Tobias?"

Jon shut his mouth. The words had been uncalled for. Misha felt the sick rolling of his stomach intensify.

"Sorry," he told Jon, "I just don't really want to be here."

"Then why did you volunteer?" Danny asked him.

"They wanted Rifle to go, and I wasn't letting him go without me. It's what Alec and Mathias would have wanted."

Danny nodded, a small wince of pain crossing his face. The guy had lost his brother, Mathias, the last remaining member of his family. His blood family, anyway. Well, there was his niece, Hope, now, and Riley was his sister-in-law and she also brought along her twin, Cameron, into the family. And of course, he always had his survivors family, of which Misha was a member.

Misha should just keep his mouth shut during this trip, as he had managed to wound both of his friends in one conversation. At least Rifle still liked him. The German shepherd sat with him, his big head resting on top of one of Misha's knees.

The submarine rumbled along through the water, with a few lifeboats following behind. They had put together a rather large team for this operation.

"Hello, boys." James Brenner suddenly appeared, finding an empty space to sit next to them. The inside of the submarine was claustrophobic, so quite a few people had chosen to sit up on the deck, now that the helicopter was landing back near the warehouses.

"What's up?" Jon asked.

"I'm here to tell you the plan, specifically your part in it."

Jon gestured for him to go on.

"Well, the important thing for you to know is that you're going to be part of the vanguard."

Misha frowned. "I don't think I know that word." It had been awhile since he had come across an English word he didn't understand. It annoyed him.

"Means we're going to be at the front," Danny filled him in.

"Right. It's going to be you three, myself, and Commander Crichton, along with Nicky."

Misha's eyebrows headed for his hairline. He hadn't realized that Crichton himself was coming on this mission.

"Nicky? Why is she coming?" Jon asked.

"Out of everyone we've talked to, she actually remembers the most about the Black Box. Strange I know, but no one else has lived there as long as she has."

"Can we rely on her memory to stay put? I mean, I don't know her very well, but I know she's got head problems."

Misha suddenly remembered who Nicky was. He remembered seeing her in what the doctors thought was a coma, sitting across the aisle from him on the plane that had to make an emergency water landing six years ago. She had previously been hit in the head a lot. It didn't surprise him to hear she had memory problems.

"We just need her to get us into the building," James explained. "Crichton's actually been to the Black Box before. He doesn't remember it clearly, all these damn facilities start to blend together after a while, but he should be able to navigate it all right. If Nicky's memory stays, great, then she stays with us, but Dr. Owen will be tagging along just behind us in case something happens."

"So we're at the front, following Crichton's direct orders," Danny clarified their role in the mission.

"Correct. Everyone else is receiving their orders now. We're going to be passing between two islands first. In fact, we're pretty much there already." James looked up, ahead of the sub.

Sure enough, two pieces of land were approaching, one on either side.

"The lifeboats are going to detach from us and drop a few men off on each island. Based on the maps, there's nothing really on either of them, but we want them checked out. They could be useful in the future if we can make them secure. Once we're through here, we're making another crossing to the mouth of a river. Following the river, we're going to come to a barge dock. From there, it should be straight up the road to the Black Box. A few men are going to stay behind at the docks, and more will take up positions along the road. We don't want anything sneaking up on us. A few teams will do a thorough sweep of the barge docks, and then any other buildings between them and the Box. Once we're inside the Box, men will be taking up positions behind us at hallway intersections, as well as investigating the smaller rooms we won't be bothering with."

"What sort of rooms will we be looking into?" Jon wondered.

"Large spaces. The hardware research lab, the manufacturing floor, the testing facility, a few open concept work spaces, conference rooms, maybe a few offices, the cafeteria, the exercise room, the pool, and anywhere else like that that I'm forgetting."

"That's a lot of ground to cover," Misha commented.

"The closer to the entrance we are, the more men we will have with us. They'll take up posts in the large spaces once we've done a sweep just in case we missed anything."

"I'm guessing we're not all going to have walkie-talkies," Jon observed.

James shook his head. "There are too many of us, and we lost a bunch with the Diana. One of the reasons we want so many people down there guarding posts, is so that we can verbally relay messages back and forth. Not the best way to communicate, but it's the best we could come up with. That's our reason for dropping men off on the islands. They'll have walkie-talkies, and will be able to relay communications with those still at the container yard if need be. The walkie-talkies don't have the range to reach from the Black Box to the container yard. Any more questions?"

Misha shifted uncomfortably, but he couldn't think of any.

"Right. I have a few more people to see before we get to the barge dock, so if you don't have any more questions I'll be off." James stood up and paused a moment. When still no one said anything, he walked off to another part of the submarine's deck.

Misha shifted himself so that he could see the water. He sat and watched the scenery roll by for the rest of the ride. It took longer to get to the river than James had made it sound, and the river was a lot wider than he expected. At the mouth, they passed by a dock that led up to some large white silo-like containers. Misha wondered what was in them. As they continued along the river, which was wide enough to be a lake, he wondered what would have happened if he had never gone to Canada for schooling. His father had pushed him into it, Misha hadn't had a choice, but if he had, and if he had stayed in Russia, where would he be right now? He thought there was a good chance that he'd be dead. He certainly never would have found Rifle, or rather, Rifle wouldn't have found him. Wrapping his arms around Rifle, Misha leaned forward and planted a big kiss on the side of the dog's face.

When he pulled back, Rifle turned his head and looked at him, as if asking what that was for.

"You're a good boy," Misha told him, the well-known words getting a tail wag in response. *"Ja ljublju tebja."*

Danny looked at Misha. "What was that?"

"Nothing important."

The submarine followed a series of snaking turns, the river becoming narrower the farther they went. There was nothing on the banks now, except trees, rocks, and mud. For those who didn't see much of the land while on the Diana, it was strange to see so much green in February.

"That must be the barge dock," Jon pointed ahead.

They were rounding a corner, and an empty barge gave the place away. It wasn't so much a dock as it was a short wall of cement. The place was a lot smaller than Misha had envisioned. He had a feeling it was a lot smaller than everyone expected it to be. Other than a few shed-like structures near the water, he couldn't even see a building. It wasn't going to take long for that other team to investigate the place.

"Come on you guys," James called to them as he moved toward one side of the submarine.

The three of them stood up and made their way to James. As Misha stood near the edge, watching their careful docking job, he thought about Shoes' funeral. That had been less than forty-eight hours ago, but as it had with the Day, it felt a whole lot longer.

Once the submarine was close enough to the shore, a wooden ramp was heaved across the gap to make a bridge. The first people off had ropes with them to secure the submarine, while Misha and his group of *vanguards* went next.

"I'll lead with Nicky," Crichton ordered them. "Misha, I want you and your dog behind us with Jon. Danny and James, you take up the rear. Let's go."

Crichton started them moving at a brisk jog. Misha was very glad to have found a pair of shoes that fit. He probably looked silly, wearing a wetsuit, running shoes, and a belt holding a pistol on one side and a machete on the other, but he had dealt with worse. He would rather have had a hunting rifle instead of a pistol, but it had been decided that everyone on the lead team would have pistols. They would be more useful inside the Box than rifles would be. Thinking of Rifle, Misha glanced down to check on him. He was keeping up with ease, and seemed to be enjoying the quick pace.

"Think one of those cars or trucks still work?" Nicky asked as they jogged past a small grouping of them. The things looked like they hadn't worked even before the Day.

"Doubt it. It's probably been years since they've been started up," James called up in response. "Besides, we wouldn't want to leave the others too far behind."

By the time they reached the road and were passing another small structure, Crichton slowed them to a brisk walk. Misha was relieved. Although he ran laps every day on the Diana, like many people did, his hip had started hurting again. A fast walk he could manage much easier than a jog.

Like the sub ride, the road was not as short as James had made it seem. It was straight though. Along the left side of the road, there was some sort of white piping. It made Misha nervous about going to the Keystone place, even though they would never have pipes of anything like that out in the open. At one point, they passed a road going to the left, the piping rising up and over it. Trees blocked Misha's view of what was down there. Another team would probably check it out. On their right appeared to be an empty lot with a crane. Investigating it wouldn't take very long. Misha kind of wished he was on that investigation team instead of this one.

Farther up the road, the pipes veered left. They headed to some large, black cylindrical containers. A train was stopped on a set of tracks alongside the place.

"Should we be wearing some sort of masks?" Misha worried.

"It's okay," Jon assured him, "all the chemical leaks have long since stopped and dissipated. At least from the air."

"Don't you guys normally wear masks when you're out here?"

"I don't think a bandanna would do much against poisoned air. We wear them to protect ourselves from zombie blood."

Misha realized they didn't have anything with which to protect their faces against that either. It wasn't as if he could just pull his shirt over his mouth and nose like the others could if they had to.

Beyond the creepy black containers was an empty section of road. The land was pretty much empty there as well.

"Zombie," Danny said, pointing to their left.

Across the somewhat barren expanse, what appeared to be a zombie was stumbling about in some low bushes.

"Ignore it," Crichton ordered them. "If it's not a threat, the others can deal with it."

"This place looks like it was deserted early on," Jon observed. "A lot of stuff around here is intact."

"That's because there's no homes," James pointed out, "and they had advance warning. Tell me, if you heard a zombie plague was coming, would you go to work?" He had a point.

Up ahead loomed a large white building. It wasn't far from the road and most definitely would have to be inspected. Still, their team moved on, not concerning themselves with such things. Misha thought he saw movement somewhere behind the building, but he hadn't been able to tell if it was a zombie or something else.

The main road hooked to the left, but a smaller, gravel road continued forward. Here, weeds were trying to swallow the road, growing up through the rocks wherever they could. Eventually all roads would look like this one, with no one to care for them.

On their right, the scruffy land of trees and bushes continued and on their left, the empty land did as well.

"These fields would be good for farming if we could make them safe," Crichton commented.

Misha had to agree, but how would they make them safe?

After they passed a line of trees that had been obscuring it, another large building appeared across the empty land. The distance and the chain link fencing around it made it impossible to tell what it was, or if anything interesting or dangerous might be there.

At last, they reached the end of the gravel where a gate barred their way. The gate was locked, but it wasn't at all difficult to go to one side and hop over the bars. Nicky and Crichton didn't even bother hopping over the bars; they just walked further to the side.

The fence was only meant to stop cars, and ended not far from the road. It was easy just to walk around.

The road they had been following ended here, with a paved road heading to the left and right. Ahead of them was a gravel lot.

"There it is," Nicky pointed.

A large building was situated past the gravel lot and at first Misha assumed that that must be what she was pointing at. Then he realized she was pointing at the much closer shed, which was nestled in the trees on the lot's left side.

"Doesn't look like much," Jon commented.

"That's the point," James told him.

"Zombie," Danny once again said.

A zombie stumbled out of the trees on the right side of the lot. It spotted them and began its slow shamble in their direction. Crichton looked behind him to check on the progress of their following teams. At least one was already at the fence and waiting for him to continue.

"Come on." Crichton moved them on. They would easily reach the shed before the zombie could reach them. The other teams would take it out.

At the shed, Crichton tried the door's handle.

"Locked."

"You need the passcode." Nicky went up to something that looked kind of like a fuse panel and opened it up. Inside was a small screen and as many buttons as there were on a keyboard. Nicky stared at it.

"Don't tell me you can't remember," James sighed.

"Shut up," Nicky told him. "You know these passcodes are complicated, and the last one I had to remember was for the White Box. Tell me, can you remember the second last passcode you had to learn?"

James kept quiet.

After a minute, Nicky reached up and typed in a complex series of letters and numbers.

"Let's hope they didn't bother changing the passcode," she muttered as she pressed a large green button.

A loud, unexpected thunk came from the shed door. Nicky then pulled it open with ease. The inside of the shed looked nothing like the outside. Whereas the outside was mostly wood and appeared as though a stiff breeze could push it over, the inside was solid metal and looked bomb proof.

Crichton picked up a nearby rock and placed it in the doorway so that the door couldn't close behind them.

"An elevator," Danny noted it at the back of the shed.

"I thought we'd be taking stairs?" Crichton turned to Nicky.

"I guess the stairs were a different entrance," Nicky shrugged.

"The keypad worked, so this place must have power, right?" Jon asked.

"The keypad has its own battery backup that'll practically last forever. It doesn't draw any power until its cover is opened," Nicky told him.

"Well, there's a quick way to find out." Danny pushed the elevator's call button.

They all watched as it lit up, and then a moment later, the elevator's doors whooshed open.

No one stepped inside.

"I guess this means the facility has power," Crichton commented. "It probably also means that at least one person is living down there."

"Are you sure the power can't run without supervision?" James questioned. "I thought most facilities were set up to run completely on their own."

"While that's true, they're also set up to shut down if they detect no signs of life over a certain period of time," Crichton told him.

"Is movement something it uses to determine that?" Danny asked. "Because then what's down there may not necessarily be alive."

Crichton nodded. "The thought had crossed my mind."

Misha looked out the door behind them. Several other mission teams were gathered out there, waiting for them to proceed.

"Are you sure we have to check this place out?" he asked. He really didn't want to go down there. Even if it was just a single living person down there, he didn't care. He wanted to go back to the container yard.

Unfortunately for Misha, Crichton nodded again. "The fact is, the facility will have a fully equipped medical centre. Most of the supplies we brought with us are from our own medical centre, and will go to restocking this one if it's been emptied, but the equipment itself can be used to help a lot of injured people."

Commander Crichton stepped into the elevator first. He was soon followed by Nicky and James. Jon and Danny hesitated a moment, but then went in as well. Misha hesitated the longest. He was afraid of what they'd find down there.

Next to him, Rifle whined. Misha looked down at the dog and saw he was concerned for Misha. He was wondering if something was wrong with him. Misha sighed and stepped into the elevator, Rifle following in after him.

The elevator was fairly large, like the elevator in a hospital. There was enough room for all of them, and there would be enough room to fit the injured *if* they decided to bring them here. Nicky pressed the button for the highest floor other than their own, and the doors slid closed with barely a rattle. The elevator moved like one in a hospital as well. It was very quick and made Misha's stomach lurch.

"Get ready," Crichton told them all as he unholstered his pistol.

Misha did the same. He realized that by being the last person to enter the elevator, he was now the closest person to the door. Jon placed a hand briefly on his shoulder in an attempt to calm him, although he also appeared very tense. Misha noticed his own hand was trembling slightly as it held the pistol. The elevator slowed to a stop, and the doors opened before Misha was ready for them.

"Welcome," a man said from the hall they had opened onto.

Misha just about shot the man in the face. If Crichton hadn't reacted as quickly as he had, he would have. Knocking Misha's arm down and somehow disarming him as he stepped past, he prevented Misha from pulling the trigger.

"Hello. I'm Commander Jonas Crichton." He held his hand out to the man in the hallway. Behind him, about a dozen other people were clustered, at least half of them looking frightened and sheepish.

"Nice to meet you Commander Crichton. I'm William Farnsworth, but everyone here just calls me Will." Will shook hands with Crichton. "We saw you coming on the monitors, and thought we ought to come meet you."

Misha looked up and saw a camera in the corner of the elevator. There had also been, in all likelihood, one up top he hadn't noticed. Bending down, Misha quickly picked up his pistol. The others were still holding theirs, and no one but Crichton had left the elevator so far. Even Rifle stood at attention, his nose wiggling at the new people.

"We've also seen there are more of you up top. We have cameras all over that field."

Crichton motioned for Nicky to come forward without ever turning his back on Will. His firm stance and smooth motion reminded Misha that he had had military training, making Misha feel woefully out of place here. Nicky and James had also had that training, while Jon was an experienced off-shipper, and Danny had wanted to join the military since he was a kid. Misha stepped back into the empty space left by Crichton as Nicky stepped around him. James also stepped forward, taking up Misha's position at the front of the elevator. With one hand, he held the button that kept the doors open.

"Nicky, do you recognize anyone here?" Crichton asked her once she joined him.

Nicky looked at Will and all the faces gathered behind him. She nodded. "Can't say I knew any of them personally, or at least remember knowing them. I don't see any mercenaries here, only a few members of the science team. The rest I don't know."

Will also nodded. "All the mercs are gone. Most of them were transferred out of here before this crap happened. Those that remained... Well, I don't know what happened to them. The facility was supposed to be abandoned. Those in charge told us not to return to it. The passcodes were even changed remotely so that no one could get in. We," Will gestured to his group, "came back here anyway, hoping to find safety. There used to be more of us, but some gave up before we could get in. Morgan there, he was able to hack one of the doors and got us all inside. We reset the passcode in case anyone else showed up, but no one did. Not until you folks, that is."

"So you've been living down here, alone, since the Day?" Crichton asked him.

"What's the day?"

"Since the outbreak became known."

"Not quite that long, but pretty close I guess. We had hoped for a quarantine at first, like most people did, but it was already too late for that. Where have you lot been?"

"On the ocean."

"What brings you here? You're not..." Will didn't finish his sentence, perhaps thinking better of voicing his thought aloud.

"If you mean raiders or thieves, no, we're not."

"We've seen some things on the monitors."

"We were attacked. Our ship sank and now we're searching for somewhere to go."

"You were hoping to live here, weren't you?"

Crichton didn't respond.

"How many of you are there?"

"A lot," Crichton told him, not wanting to give this man their true numbers; not that he even really knew what they were after the attack.

"Depending on how many is a lot, it would be a tight fit."

"We're used to close quarters."

"Well, we're not. You have to understand, we haven't seen anyone outside of each other for years."

Next to Misha, Jon tensed up again. Danny placed his hand on his shoulder, but it looked more like a restraining hand than a calming one.

"We have people with us who are badly injured. They need proper medical attention," Crichton told Will and his collective.

"There are no doctors here."

"But there's a medical facility. We have plenty of doctors."

"Will," a woman at the back of the group hissed, her eyes bright as they looked over the shoulders of the people in front of her.

Will held up a hand and turned slightly. She had apparently been trying to pass on some thought or message, which he already understood.

"Our food supply down here has been sustaining us fine. I'm not sure how it'll handle more people."

"We have some plants and animals rescued from our ship, and people more than willing to scavenge for everything else."

"Give us a minute." Will turned and walked to his clustered group of people. They held a whispered conversation while Crichton waited.

"I don't like it," Jon muttered.

"They're scared, that's all," Danny whispered to him, "they don't know us."

"We'd take them in without really knowing them," Jon countered.

"You mean like the way we took in Sher?" Misha mentioned. "Oh wait, we didn't, and he brought an army down on our heads."

"There are a lot more of us than there are of them," Danny continued. "It's different. They know that if they take us in, they'll be outnumbered. Whatever rules or systems they have set up will be completely changed."

With a heavy sigh, Will separated from his group and returned to talk to Crichton.

"We want you to answer a few questions first."

Crichton nodded.

"Who's your leader? Is it you?"

"There's myself, Lieutenant Boyle, Captain Karsten, and Captain Bronislav. There was a fifth, but he went down with our ship."

"Are there children with you?"

"Yes."

"Have you ever stolen from another group of survivors?"

"Not that we've been made aware of. Our scavengers were careful not to take from anyone living. We usually tried to make contact with those groups, and offer them a home on our ship."

"Did you come from the White Box?"

"Yes," Crichton didn't hesitate, making Misha wince. "At least some of us have indirectly. We still have several Marble

Keystone mercenaries among our ranks, myself, Nicky, and Brenner included, and a few scientists and medical personnel, but no one who worked on the virus and no one from any real position of authority. All the key players in bringing this about were in the White Box while we were stationed outside when the Day came, given various tasks by those in command. If you didn't know already, the White Box is gone. It's been completely overrun by zombies."

Will nodded. "I appreciate your honesty."

"Most of us are civilians, however. A large group comes from Leighton, but we've picked up various people along the way, most notably two submarines, one from Russia and one from Germany."

Will's eyebrows rose briefly.

"I must tell you, your whole group that things have already changed for you, just by having contact with us."

"What do you mean?"

Misha wasn't sure Crichton should tell him this part, but held his tongue.

"The virus has changed. We don't know how, or why, but it's now airborne."

Several gasps came from the group.

"By now, you've all been infected by us. You won't turn, at least not yet. We haven't been able to research it, but it looks like this new version infects your system, and lies dormant. Once you die, no matter the cause, you'll turn. I'm sorry we brought this to you, but I thought you should know in case you do decide to turn us away."

Will turned and looked at his group. A woman near the front nodded, and Will turned back to Crichton.

"I guess it's too late for us to do anything about that. We'll let you stay here. We need your doctors."

The small crowd shifted so that the woman in the back became visible. She was pregnant and fairly far along.

"This new virus won't hurt the baby, will it?" she asked.

"Not as far as we know. If you'll let us, we'd like to use some of your equipment to analyse it further. We won't experiment with it, that's something we refuse to do even with the good intentions of searching for a cure, but we need a closer look to understand it."

"Our equipment is your equipment."

Crichton nodded, finally turning his back on Will. "Nicky, Brenner, you two stay down here with me. Danny, Jon, and Misha, head up top. Let everyone know what's going on, and send a few more people down here. I'm sure they're worried since the elevator hasn't returned and I have my radio off. Start the migration process. Some of those injured need to get here quickly."

Jon nodded while James Brenner stepped out of the elevator, finally letting the doors close.

"I guess we weren't needed, *bratishka*," Misha rubbed Rifle's side.

"Thank Jesus for that," Danny sighed. "Crichton's a much better representative than you, Jon."

Jon's face flushed a bright red. "Shut up," he mumbled.

"I'm glad Brunt can have his arm properly looked at," Danny continued. "I'm worried that he hasn't been able to move it."

The elevators opened again, and this time Misha was presented with a gun in his face. He stood completely still as his own men pointed weapons at the inside of the elevator.

"It's all right, we're not dead," Jon told the nervous men.

***

It took the rest of the day and a large portion of the evening to get everyone over to the Black Box and situated. They weren't kidding when they said space would be tight. The rooms were like suites, with a living room attached to a kitchen, a bathroom, and three bedrooms. Riley, Cameron, Hope, and Dakota were taking up residence in one bedroom, Abby, Lauren, Claire, and Peter, were in another, while a boy named Adam lived with his mom Elizabeth, his dad Harry, and a woman named Cynthia in the third. This left Jon, Danny, Josh, and Misha with sleeping bags and blankets in the living room.

"I suggest we rotate who gets the couch each night," Josh offered.

The others agreed while setting up their spaces on the floor. Rifle continued to sniff all around the place, following Milly wherever she went.

"So how long do you think we'll last in this place?" Jon wondered aloud.

"I don't know about everyone else, but I don't think I'll last long," Misha remarked.

The rest of the guys stopped what they were doing to look at him, wondering what he meant.

"There aren't any windows in this place. I don't like it here, underground. And living in a Keystone facility? These are the guys who caused all this shit in the first place. I don't care if it didn't come from here exactly, I don't like it, and it's not good for the animals. I don't know how long I'll be here, but I have a feeling I'm eventually not going to be able to stand it anymore, and I'm going to have to leave, and find somewhere else."

Danny nodded, understanding him perfectly. "When you do, I doubt you'll be the only one."

"Let's just hope that's not for a while," Josh returned to making up the couch, having managed to claim it first. "The way we're so tightly packed down here, I'm sure they'll be setting up some outposts up top. Besides, they want to set up a farm and keep most of the large animals outside as soon as they can. Once it's safe, you can take a position topside."

"Well, I'm going to go see how the rest of my team is doing," Jon got to his feet. "They've got a space just across the hall."

"Robin's over there too, isn't she?" Danny wondered.

"Yeah, and so are a bunch of other people. You know Misha, my off-shipper team, or whatever the hell we're called now, is permanently down one man and may be down others depending on how well they heal. You should join. It'll get you and Rifle outside often."

"Maybe," Misha shrugged.

"Just a thought." Jon disappeared out into the hallway.

"I wonder why they call it the Black Box? I mean, most of this place is decorated with every colour *but* black," Danny commented.

Misha had noticed that too. Every level of the place had a differently coloured floor, and various coloured lines were painted on the neutral yellow walls to help everyone find their way around.

"Probably has something to do with computers. I don't know," Josh shrugged.

"I'm going to go get something to eat. Maybe explore a little. Either of you want to come?"

"I will," Josh offered.

"Misha?"

"I think I'm going to sit here a little while."

"Suit yourself."

The two of them left, leaving Misha alone in the living room. He could hear the families in the bedrooms around him setting up their own living spaces. Someone in Abby's room was laughing. It sounded like Claire.

Rifle came over and flopped down next to Misha, resting his head in his lap. Misha began absently to pet him. Since the Day, they had kept moving. Every time they had stayed still too long, something awful had happened. The Diana had been perfect because it was a home that moved with them. This place was as stationary as it got. That was the real reason Misha didn't think he could stay here very long. It didn't matter how he felt about the place, or whether they could make it work, the fact was, sooner or later, something would make them move.

As Misha bent over to kiss Rifle's head, he intended to be ready for it when it came.

CHECK OUT OTHER GREAT ZOMBIE NOVELS

Z BURBIA
by Jake Bible

Whispering Pines is a classic, quiet, private American subdivision on the edge of Asheville, NC, set in the pristine Blue Ridge Mountains. Which is good since the zombie apocalypse has come to Western North Carolina and really put suburban living to the test!

Surrounded by a sea of the undead, the residents of Whispering Pines have adapted their bucolic life of block parties to scavenging parties, common area groundskeeping to immediate area warfare, neighborhood beautification to neighborhood fortification.

But, even in the best of times, suburban living has its ups and downs what with nosy neighbors, a strict Home Owners' Association, and a property management company that believes the words "strict interpretation" are holy words when applied to the HOA covenants. Now with the zombie apocalypse upon them even those innocuous, daily irritations quickly become dramatic struggles for personal identity, family security, and straight up survival.

ZOMBIE RULES
by David Achord

Zach Gunderson's life sucked and then the zombie apocalypse began.

Rick, an aging Vietnam veteran, alcoholic, and prepper, convinces Zach that the apocalypse is on the horizon. The two of them take refuge at a remote farm. As the zombie plague rages, they face a terrifying fight for survival.

They soon learn however that the walking dead are not the only monsters.

CHECK OUT OTHER GREAT ZOMBIE NOVELS

900 MILES
by S. Johnathan Davis

John is a killer, but that wasn't his day job before the Apocalypse.

In a harrowing 900 mile race against time to get to his wife just as the dead begin to rise, John, a business man trapped in New York, soon learns that the zombies are the least of his worries, as he sees first-hand the horror of what man is capable of with no rules, no consequences and death at every turn.

Teaming up with an ex-army pilot named Kyle, they escape New York only to stumble across a man who says that he has the key to a rumored underground stronghold called Avalon..... Will they find safety? Will they make it to Johns wife before it's too late?

Get ready to follow John and Kyle in this fast paced thriller that mixes zombie horror with gladiator style arena action!

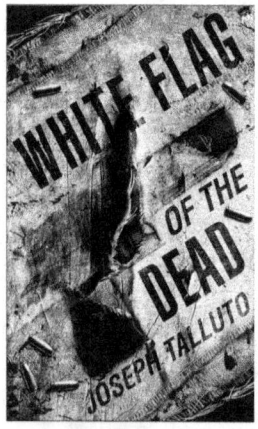

WHITE FLAG OF THE DEAD
by Joseph Talluto

Millions died when the Enillo Virus swept the earth. Millions more were lost when the victims of the plague refused to stay dead, instead rising to slaughter and feed on those left alive. For survivors like John Talon and his son Jake, they are faced with a choice: Do they submit to the dead, raising the white flag of surrender? Or do they find the will to fight, to try and hang on to the last shreds or humanity?

CHECK OUT OTHER GREAT ZOMBIE NOVELS

VACCINATION
by Phillip Tomasso

What if the H7N9 vaccination wasn't just a preventative measure against swine flu?

It seemed like the flu came out of nowhere and yet, in no time at all the government manufactured a vaccination. Were lab workers diligent, or could the virus itself have been man-made? Chase McKinney works as a dispatcher at 9-1-1. Taking emergency calls, it becomes immediately obvious that the entire city is infected with the walking dead. His first goal is to reach and save his two children.

Could the walls built by the U.S.A. to keep out illegal aliens, and the fact the Mexican government could not afford to vaccinate their citizens against the flu, make the southern border the only plausible destination for safety?

ZOMBIE, INC
by Chris Dougherty

"WELCOME! To Zombie, Inc. The United Five State Republic's leading manufacturer of zombie defense systems! In business since 2027, Zombie, Inc. puts YOU first. YOUR safety is our MAIN GOAL! Our many home defense options - from Ze Fence® to Ze Popper® to Ze Shed® - fit every need and every budget. Use Scan Code "TELL ME MORE!" for your FREE, in-home*, no obligation consultation! *Schedule your appointment with the confidence that you will NEVER HAVE TO LEAVE YOUR HOME! It isn't safe out there and we know it better than most! Our sales staff is FULLY TRAINED to handle any and all adversarial encounters with the living and the undead". Twenty-five years after the deadly plague, the United Five State Republic's most successful company, Zombie, Inc., is in trouble. Will a simple case of dwindling supply and lessening demand be the end of them or will Zombie, Inc. find a way, however unpalatable, to survive?

www.ingramcontent.com/pod-product-compliance
Lightning Source LLC
Chambersburg PA
CBHW072109250626
47159CB00007B/2374